MW00334877

ISBN 978-0-692-12676-9

ACKNOWLEDGEMENTS

The author wishes to acknowledge the invaluable assistance of the following people: John Caher for his candid review of the manuscript and his generous endorsement, Maxine Kaplan for correcting the mistakes in the first draft, Arthur Nordlie for his support and assistance in the production of this work, Rolfe Nordlie for using his artistic talent in the creation of the front cover, Geoff King for his contribution of priceless resource materials, and Steve King for his photographic skill. The aforementioned merit my utmost gratitude – thank you.

To Chris,

From the Case Files of

Conrad Blake

The Sleeping God

A novel by A.J. George

This work is dedicated to my wife Cindy, who encouraged me to use my imagination.

And he opened the bottomless pit;
and there arose a smoke out of the pit,
as the smoke of a great furnace…

Revelations 9:2

That is not dead which can eternal lie,
and with strange aeons death may die.

Necronomicon

PREFACE

One afternoon, on a whim, my wife and I attended an auction. Among other things, an antique floor safe came up for sale. The combination had long since been lost or forgotten, and the contents, if any, were unknown. My wife impulsively urged me to bid on the safe, and to our surprise, we won the bidding. We took our prize home in the back of our pickup truck, and even with the help of a neighbor, we had a difficult time getting it into the basement. Neither of us could sleep that night, our curiosity piqued by the mysterious contents. First thing the next morning, we called a locksmith to drill the safe. After the locksmith left, we could wait no longer. Our hearts beat fast with anticipation, and my wife crossed her fingers, as I turned the lever and opened the solid heavy door. We were elated to discover that the safe was not empty, but held a variety of contents.

We first removed a fat envelope, and upon opening it, discovered five hundred dollars in silver certificates of various denominations, dated in the 1920's. Other contents of the safe included: an antique luger pistol tucked in a brown leather shoulder holster, old newspaper clippings, a dented whiskey flask, a small thin metal case, a monogrammed handkerchief with a lipstick stain, and an old black and white photograph. The photograph pictured two men standing in front of an antique automobile. The first had a chiseled face and rugged features, and he was wearing a leather trench coat with the collar turned up and a fedora. The well-dressed man standing next to him had flaxen hair, high square cheekbones, and a cleft chin; a dark kashmir overcoat draped his shoulders, and he was holding a homburg in his hand. My wife remarked that the flaxen-haired man was quite handsome and distinguished looking. Of all the contents, the most notable were the thick files stored in the safe. They had the oddest titles, and curious, we opened one. As we began to read papers browned with age, we found ourselves in Boston, late 1926.

CHAPTER 1

Killing time, I spent the evening at Mahoney's working on a few manhattans. Joe, a lanky and affable bartender, poured me several on the house. The regular patrons were there and jazz music filled the establishment with a festive atmosphere. I was feeling rather good when I left to walk the few blocks back to my office, where my Stutz was parked on the street. The air was electric, sharp, sparkling, and the life of the city pulsed with restless and impetuous energy. I wanted to catch up on the latest news and decided to go up to my office for a while before driving to my flat. Arriving at the door, I slipped the key in the lock. The signage on the smoked glass read: Conrad Blake, Private Investigations. Cindy, my secretary, had long since gone home for the day. All was quiet, and I settled into the leather chair behind my desk to read the late edition of the Boston Globe, the date: Tuesday, December 7, 1926. Eventually my eyelids refused to stay open, and reclining back, I drifted into slumber.

The clock read quarter past midnight when the ringing telephone on my desk rousted me to full consciousness. Initially, I hesitated to answer, but the late caller was persistent, for the phone continued to ring, and ring, and ring, until I was compelled to pick up the receiver, and the familiar voice of JB Hawkins came over the line. JB was a physician working for the Office of the Medical Examiner. He was a good man to know in my line of business and a close acquaintance. I would even consider him a friend. He spoke in hushed tones and hurried jumbles, and based on the frantic tremor in his voice, he was obviously shaken and upset. Amidst the incoherent rush of words, all I could make out was something about a face in the window and someone doing a disappearing act. I finally got him to calm down and asked where he was. He said he was at some seedy flophouse down on the waterfront named the 'Anchorage,' and he gave me a room number, 21. He implored me to come right away; and I told him to sit tight, assuring him I would be right there. His last words before he hung up were "please hurry."

That part of town was not the best; and heeding precaution, I removed my P08 Luger from the top desk drawer and slipped it into my shoulder holster. Donning my hat and heavy leather trench coat, I headed out the door. The coat was tailor made with deep pockets, and those pockets came in handy at times.

As I stepped off the curb, a derelict newspaper page blew past in a chilling gust and tumbled down the sidewalk. I hopped into my Stutz, put the speedster in gear, and started for the waterfront. I kept thinking about the telephone conversation with JB – his jumbled speech and urgent tone. And what was a man like JB doing in that part of town?

In the heart of a neighborhood that harbored the haunts of seamen, where illicit contraband flowed and bootleggers flourished, stood the Anchorage Hotel, a three story ramshackle building, which bore in every feature the marks of prolonged negligence and sordidness. JB's Cadillac was parked across the street, and I pulled in behind. A drunken merchant seaman lay passed out on the front stoop, his hand still clutching the neck of an unlabeled corked bottle. Inside was no better. On a wall hung the telephone from which JB must have placed his call; and behind the counter, an unshaven little man in sullied clothes sat asleep in a chair. A two-bit whore rose from a stained couch, wrapped me in her sleazy embrace, and solicited me. Spurning her advances, I brushed her aside. Number 21 was the first door on the right at the top of the stairs.

Before the second knock, the door opened slightly ajar, and half a face appeared in the open slit. The door flew wide, and JB quickly pulled me inside. He then shut the door and pressed his back against it. Wide eyes full of panic underscored a troubled expression, and his pallor was white as a sheet. A lamp on a bureau dimly lighted the dismal lodging; the drapes were drawn closed, a suitcase lay on the bed, a wrinkled suit jacket draped the chair, and JB's medical bag sat on a yellowed doily atop the bureau. Almost immediately, I discovered the source of his distress. Something violent had occurred, something terrible, something gruesome. Blood mottled one wall, and lines of trickling crimson streams coursed down to where a gory trail led across the floor to the chair. Except for his shaken condition, he appeared unharmed, and no trace of blood stained his clothes or hands. He plopped down on the edge of the bed; and with his head bent low, he combed his long slender fingers through his blond bangs.

"I couldn't call the police. They would never believe me," he said in a faltering voice. "They would think I was crazy. Frankly, I find it hard to believe myself. I didn't know whom else to call. You must help me, Conrad. Please help me," he desperately pleaded.

"Tell me what happened," I inquired.

"My friend – my friend is gone – just gone – vanished," he babbled in broken phrases.

"What do you mean by gone?"

"Gone – just gone," he emphatically replied.

"People just don't vanish into thin air," I asserted.

He lifted his head, looked me square in the eyes, and retorted, "Drafe did!"

I produced a flask and poured him a shot to settle his nerves. With a trembling hand, he put the whiskey to his lips and gulped it down.

I placed a reassuring hand on his shoulder. "Relax and give it to me straight - from the beginning."

He steadied himself, and I listened intently as he recounted the earlier events of that night. As he spoke, he fidgeted with his signet ring, turning it and sliding it up and down his finger.

"I was reading a medical journal when I got a ring from an old college friend. His name is Harold Drayfus, but his close friends call him 'Drafe'. We were roommates during our undergraduate years. After graduation, I entered medical school and he went into anthropology. We kept in touch over the years and saw each other on occasion. In his last correspondence, he was excited about going to Africa to perform fieldwork. That was some eighteen months ago, and I had not heard from him again until tonight. He said he urgently needed to see me; that he had something important he needed to impart to me, and entreated me to come without delay. He seemed quite agitated and begged me to bring a strong stimulant – 'anything to keep me awake,' he said. After hanging up, I removed a couple of vials from the apothecary cabinet, grabbed my medical bag, and drove down here."

His voice grew more emphatic as he then gave me a wild and absurd account of what had occurred after he arrived, which included a three-eyed Negro peering in the window and Drafe being attacked by what he termed as a 'baleful spectre'; and according to the final portion of JB's narrative, just before vanishing, his friend cried out, "Don't let them get you!"

"It all happened so fast, before he had a chance to tell me what he so desperately wanted to say," JB forlornly concluded.

JB was a rational man and not prone to flights of fancy, yet the whole thing seemed so incredible that I did not know what to believe, and his story left me with more questions than answers. Even so, there had to be some logical explanation, some underlying truth hidden amidst the improbable.

"Were you unconscious at any time? Maybe you fainted, and when you came to the body had been moved," I suggested, but JB adamantly professed to be in full control of his faculties the entire time.

Investigation of the scene was imperative, and I started with the door, which displayed no signs of forced entry, and then turned my attention to the window. When I opened it and poked my head out, I saw nothing that would enable someone to gain the second-story height: no fire escape, no ladder, no piled crates; but my eyes did discern the partial outline of a figure lurking in the shadow of a doorway. At that point, a sense of grave concern gripped me. Saying nothing, I casually shut the window and closed the drapes.

Closely examining the blood evidence, I deduced from the pattern of wet stains that the assailant had most likely used a knife or bladed weapon. However, something puzzled me, something that made me second-guess. Intermingled amongst the spattered gore were droppings and traces of a sickly green ooze with an oily texture and a foul scent.

In the pockets of the suit jacket draping the chair, I found a number of items: a U.S. passport, a small key, three calling cards, and a matchbox. The matchbox cover was black with a gold print advertisement.

Regal Diamond Club
'London's finest in music and dancing'
Grosvenor Square
London
Tel: Mayfair-3477

The small collection of cards read like an address book.

Professor J. Chadwick Hanson, Ph.D.
Peabody Museum of Archaeology and Ethnology
Harvard University
Cambridge, Massachusetts

Antonio Barsucci
Proprietor

Quintanos
Rare-Fine Books and Antiquities
Cannaregio 4266
Strada Nova
Venice, Italy

Tel: 3636

Dr. Jacob Greenberg
Hebrew University
Jerusalem, Palestine

The passport was issued to Harold Drayfus, a man of thirty-three, whose occupation was listed as 'anthropologist'. It seems he was quite the traveler, for the pages had a myriad of stamps from all over the globe, the most recent being England. Tucked inside was a folded piece of notepaper with a handwritten name and address: Jake "Brandy" Brandon, Hotel L'Afrique, Douala, Cameroon.

Continuing the search, I rummaged through the suitcase on the bed. A recently published book lay concealed beneath a layer of haphazardly deposited articles of clothing. The leather volume was entitled: "Forgotten Living Cultures, a Study of the Indigenous Tribes of French Equatorial Africa", by Sir Gunston Mallory. Inside the front cover were two folded newspaper clippings from The London Times. The first, dated June of last year, was headlined "Bradford Expedition Departs for Darkest Africa", and the second, dated last March, was headlined "Miraculous Return of Sir Gunston Mallory". The author's card marked a lengthy chapter.

Sir Gunston Mallory
Royal Society
Burlington House
Piccadilly, London

I opened empty bureau drawers and sifted through the pockets of an overcoat hanging on a hook by the door. The coat pockets yielded a money clip holding a meager sum and a cancelled passage from Liverpool to Boston on the 'Lisbon Star'. Nothing remained but the space under the bed, and taking a look, I discovered a large two-handled suitcase tucked away out of sight. It required extra effort to drag the cumbersome thing from its hiding place, only to be confronted with a locking latch. The small key in the suit jacket worked with rewarding success, and the lid opened to reveal a rectangular object wrapped in quilted cloth. Strong curiosity impelled me to unveil the object, but prudence and urgency dictated otherwise; and I shut the lid, locking the latch and pocketing the key.

JB's eyes reflected a maelstrom of anxiety. "Are you going to call the police?" he fearfully asked.

"No, I think that would be unwise. Don't you?" I replied, and his eyes followed my movements as I stuffed the suit jacket in the open suitcase on the bed and shut the lid. "Do you know the way to my flat from here?"

"Yes," he affirmed.

"Good. Then we're going there to sort things out," I resolutely stated. "Grab the smaller suitcase on the bed. I'll take the larger one."

JB complied without hesitation, and we slipped into the empty hallway, quietly closing the door behind us. Downstairs, the whore was absent, but luck took a bad turn when the man behind the counter awoke. He questioningly peered at us through narrow slits that widened to bloodshot eyes and rose to his feet.

"Ere now – wat's dis? I never seen yuse mugs befur. Is dem ya bags? Y'not steelin' nuttin' are ya?" he accusingly inquired.

I set down the case, took out my money clip and peeled off a five. "No, and honest Abe here says the cops don't find out you're running a whorehouse and peddling cheap bootleg," I said, placing the bill on the counter.

He snatched up the bill faster than a frog's tongue could catch a fly. "Whateva ya sey misteh."

When I opened my coat to pocket the clip, he caught sight of the concealed pistol I carried.

His eyes grew wide. "Look misteh – I don't want no troubl' – no toubl' t'all. Forget I sed anyteng," he stammered.

"In that case, we never had this quaint little conversation," I said, buttoning my coat.

Outside, a mist rolled in, cloaking everything in a gray sullen fog. As we crossed the street, the claps of our footfalls on the pavement resounded in the gathering gloom; and all the while, unsettling tension kept my right hand close to my Luger. We placed the suitcases in the backseat of JB's Cadillac, and he settled into the driver's seat.

"I'll follow you. Proceed when you see my headlights," I directed.

He started the engine and its chattering rumble transcended the nocturnal stillness. Approaching my Stutz, I gazed in the direction of the doorway where I had seen the unwelcome watcher, but the murky shadows were empty. Apprehension filled the moments until I switched on my headlights. Wisps of vapor swirled in the delineated beams that kept his half-enveloped motorcar in sight as I followed close behind.

We had driven but a short distance when a pair of headlights reflected in my mirror. With each turn, the vehicle stayed with us, constantly keeping pace and distance, and the conspicuous tenacity of our shadow left no room for doubt as we drew closer to my address. JB parked in front of the boardinghouse I call home, and I pulled in behind him. After stopping, I looked over my shoulder to see our pursuer pull over to the same side of the street about a block behind us and then the headlights extinguish.

I met JB by his Cadillac, and we toted the suitcases to the front door. As usual, my landlady, Mrs. Coggins, had left it unlocked, allowing easy entry. Darkness shrouded the entranceway and staircase, and I closed the door without turning on the lights. Parting the curtains, I peered out to see the illumination of headlights growing brighter as a sedan slowly rolled up the street. As the sedan crept past, another motorcar approached from the opposite direction. Lights from the oncoming motorcar briefly illuminated the interior of the sedan, silhouetting the driver. From the attire, the person behind the wheel appeared to be a woman. She wore a netted veil that masked her face, and a mostly hidden passenger reclined in the backseat. Once past my rooming house, the sedan accelerated. It turned the corner at the end of the block and disappeared from view.

CHAPTER 2

Upstairs, inside my two-room flat, I looked out the window into the street. All seemed peaceful in the still of the night. The only nocturnal patron evident in the pale glow of the lamplight was the beat cop, twirling his baton as he rambled down the sidewalk.

I turned on the lamp. "It's not much, but it's home," I said, locking the door securely and hanging my coat on the rack.

JB plopped down on the sofa and loosened his tie and collar. I offered him a drink, to which he accepted; and after drinking a few sips of the bourbon and water mixture, he reclined back, reached into his pocket, and took out his pipe and a pouch of tobacco. He casually filled the pipe and lit it as if the act was an unconscious reflex. Puffing away, he stared at nothing in particular, and the drifting smoke perfumed the air with an aromatic scent.

"JB, I need you to tell me what happened, just one more time," I requested.

He took a draw from his pipe, and in a nervous voice, once again recounted the events of that night. I listened intently, trying to detect any inconsistencies, but his implausible story was the same; and I found parts of it, if not most of it, extremely hard to swallow.

It was late and any further inquiries could wait until the morning. I strongly suggested that he stay the night, offering him the bedroom. He thanked me and took the last few swallows from his glass.

"Get some rest. I'll sleep on the sofa," I said as he got up to retire. "I'm going to stay up for a while longer and try to sort things out."

I started with the smaller suitcase and removed the pertinent items I had discovered earlier: the passport, the calling cards, the matchbox, and the book. After arranging them on the coffee table, I rifled through the suitcase, but it revealed nothing further. I took the author's card from the book, marked the page, and placed the card with the others. Fishing for answers, I sifted through the remnants and pieces left behind by a man who obviously met with foul play. The prevailing questions that haunted me were who and why? As to how, JB really threw me a curve ball with his story, and it could not have happened the way he said it did. Of one thing I was fairly certain; JB was in the wrong place at the wrong time, and no doubt in danger of ending up like his friend.

Working on a presumption, I figured that at least one of the individuals on the four cards had been in recent contact with Harold Drayfus. According to Drayfus' passport and the canceled passage, his last whereabouts were in England, making the author of the book, Sir Gunston Mallory, the most likely candidate, but he was on the other side of the Atlantic. In fact, only one card had a domestic address, the card for Professor J. Chadwick Hanson, and Harvard University was just across the Charles River in Cambridge.

I removed the newspaper clippings from the book and read the articles in chronological order.

BRADFORD EXPEDITION DEPARTS FOR DARKEST AFRICA

An expedition sponsored by the Royal Society is making final preparations for departure to the Dark Continent. The expedition is to be led by Sir George Bradford of the Royal Society. The primary purpose of the expedition is to search for the whereabouts of Sir Jonathon Mallory, his younger brother Gunston, and his son Master Edward. Sir Jonathon and Gunston are both noted Fellows of the Royal Society, as well as generous benefactors. The Mallorys ventured to French Equatorial Africa to study the indigenous cultures that lie within the uncharted interior of the Dark Continent. No correspondence or word has been heard from Sir Jonathon or his brother since they arrived at Douala, Cameroon on the west coast of Africa over a year ago. Their last correspondence stated that they had acquired a suitable guide, and were heading for the hinterland beyond the eastern arc of the Cameroon Mountains. To this date, the fate of that expedition is unknown. Sir George was quoted as confidently stating, "We will find them, even if we have to turn that blasted continent upside down." In addition to the search for the Mallorys, the expedition will be observing and studying the native cultures and animal life, as well as obtaining specimens of rare native botanical flora. Other members of the expedition include: Sir Charles Franklin Kettering, Dr. Cedric Gibbons of Oxford University, renowned hunter and explorer Lord Robert Huntley and an American, Harold Drayfus of Harvard University. Our prayers are with you gentlemen, Godspeed and safe return.

By all indications, the headline of the second article heralded a successful venture.

MIRACULOUS RETURN OF SIR GUNSTON MALLORY

The Royal Society is celebrating the miraculous return of Sir Gunston Mallory. Sir Gunston has returned to us from the darkest reaches of the African interior. His whereabouts have been unknown for the past two years. Now we discover that he has been cohabitating with the savage natives that inhabit the vast unexplored jungles. During his habitation, he lived as they did, while observing and studying their primitive way of life. He arrived in the company of a young African man who spoke English surprisingly well. Sir Gunston plans to further educate him in the ways of our civilized culture.

Sir Gunston Mallory assumed the family title upon his return. He survives his older brother Jonathon and his nephew Edward. Tragically, his brother and nephew succumbed to fever according to Sir Gunston. Without the aid of civilized medicine, they died. A memorial service was held in their honor last Tuesday.

An expedition sponsored by the Royal Society and led by Sir George Bradford departed some nine months ago to search for the Mallorys. When questioned about the Bradford expedition, Sir Gunston stated that he had never encountered any members of the expedition, nor did he have any knowledge of their whereabouts. Said Sir Gunston in reference to that expedition, "I did, however, hear rumors of white captives taken by the Newandi, a tribe of fierce and savage headhunters. There are countless dangers in the jungles of that region. I am afraid for their safety."

No further inquiries could be made concerning his adventures or his protégé, as Sir Gunston has sequestered himself at his estate in Kent to write a book based on his observations. The book, soon to be published by Oxford Press, is highly anticipated by those in the scientific community.

Obviously, Drayfus survived his trek with the expedition, because he was in Boston this very night. But what of the other members?

Turning my focus to the large locked suitcase, I retrieved the key from my coat pocket, and as the key turned in the lock and the lid opened, both reason and gut feeling alike conjectured that the mysterious package within was the underlying key to everything. Wrapped in quilted cloth, it rested amidst a padding of wadded up cloths and towels. With curious expectation tweaking every nerve, I gently removed the bulky rectangular object, and peeled away the cloth wrapping to unveil a most peculiar and remarkable tablet fashioned from deep ebony stone. A series of drawings were inscribed on the horizontal surface and a succession of strange symbols ran along the vertical sides; the polished surface was smooth as glass, and the markings reflected the light in a way that made them quite distinguishable. So flawless was the craftsmanship that every perfect curve and line appeared to be pressed in, not carved or chiseled. On the other side, random dots and tiny circles speckled the surface, and one circle, larger than the others, was hollowed into a shallow socket.

The tablet was an enigma to me; and with no empirical reference to draw upon, I needed to consult someone who might be able to make sense of the thing. The answer lay with Professor Hanson; after all, he was a scholar and associated with the Peabody Museum. I could kill two birds with one stone, interview Hanson concerning Drayfus, and possibly gain some insight on the meaning or value of this tablet. If not, he may know someone who can. I decided to ring the university in the morning to arrange a meeting.

With that resolved, I turned my attention to the book. I jokingly told myself that it was time for a little light reading and opened the book to the marked page. I figured Drayfus must have had a reason for marking that particular page, so that became my stating point. The title of the chapter read, "The Matoomba Tribe". The reading was tedious, and the terminology and vocabulary were a little above my head, but I did my best to maintain concentration on the subject matter, and I took notes while reading the text. After considerable time had passed, I closed the book and reviewed my notes.

My notes:

- The tribe is secluded from others due to its isolation within the 'Valley of the Matoomba'. They are extremely territorial and outsiders are dealt with in a most violent manner.
- They indulge in the inhuman practice of cannibalism, believing that the consumption of human flesh, especially the heart, will transfer to the eater the soul matter of the viand, and contribute to fertility. The eyes are considered a delicacy.
- Strange rituals are performed, in which masks are used; the participants dance in a delirious frenzy, and the arts of juju and black magic are practiced. One ritual describes a human

sacrifice, after which the sacrificial victim is cooked and devoured in a feast.

- They worship a deity, whose name best translates to English as "the god under the mountain". The god currently sleeps in a mountain the natives call "The Three Sisters", waiting for his time of awakening. Their valley rests in the shadow of this mountain.
- Every so many generations a special child is born that the tribal priests (more commonly referred to as witchdoctors) call a Shamba. The Shamba is destined to become the spiritual leader of the tribe. He is able to communicate with the god under the mountain via dreams, through which, he receives divine revelation and is thus capable of prophesying. He also has the unique ability to control and manipulate the dreams of others.
- Mallory notes that he was made an honorary member of their society after rescuing and saving the life of a Shamba boy.

Knowing that sleep would soon overcome me, I took stock of everything and jotted down in my notebook the information from each card, as well as the handwritten note and matchbox. Hoping to get at least a few hours of sleep, I patted the pillow at the end of the sofa and stretched out. During the night, I had the strangest dream; a face concealed in shadow watched me through the second-story window of my flat as I slumbered.

CHAPTER 3

Sunlight streamed through the window, and someone softly rapped at the door. It was a familiar knock, and collecting myself, I arose to answer. Standing on the threshold was Mrs. Coggins, an apron around her waist and her gray hair up in a bun.

"Good morning, Mrs. Coggins," I welcomingly addressed.

"You missed breakfast this morning, Mr. Blake," she said with a touch of concern. "Would you like me to fix you something?"

"Yes, thank you. A friend stayed the night. Could I impose upon you to…?"

"Say no more," she interjected.

"Mrs. Coggins, you spoil me."

"Somebody has to," she said, her lips curling up in a smile before she turned to go.

I had no sooner closed the door than the telephone rang. On the line was my secretary, Cindy, keeping tabs on me as usual.

"I was wondering when you were coming in. Mrs. Ferguson is already here."

"In my top desk drawer is an envelope with her name on it. Give it to her, and if she has any questions, she can ring me tomorrow," I instructed. "And I probably won't be in today. I'm working on a new case."

"Where can I reach you?"

"Ring Mrs. Coggins, she'll take a message. Stick around in case anybody calls or comes in. Take some money from petty cash and have a long lunch on me."

"Thanks for lunch, and be careful."

"Don't you worry about me," I reassured her. "I'll be in touch."

I jiggled the phone cradle and asked the operator to connect me with the main switchboard at Harvard University. While I waited for the connection to go through, JB walked in looking somewhat refreshed and sat down in the lounge chair. Upon reaching the main switchboard, I asked the girl to connect me with the Peabody Museum and heard a ringing on the line.

A female voice answered. "Peabody Museum, Mrs. Chandler speaking."

I gave her my name and politely inquired if I could speak with Professor J. Chadwick Hanson. She told me that he was giving a lecture this morning, but that he would be in the museum this afternoon doing research. I tried to pin her down to a more specific time frame, and she said that he would be in sometime between one and two o'clock.

"May I tell the Professor the nature of your inquiry, Mr. Blake?" she asked.

"I have an object of antiquity that I believe would most certainly be of interest to him," I replied.

"Shall I have the Professor telephone you?"

"No, that won't do. I need to see him in person." I thought for just a moment. "I will be in Cambridge this afternoon. Would it be possible to see him today?"

"The Professor does not like to be disturbed while he is engaged in research. Please give me the number where you can be reached, and I will have him telephone you to arrange a convenient time for a meeting."

It was like trying to break down the walls of Jericho. I relented and gave her my number.

"In any case, I will be in Cambridge this afternoon around three o'clock and will drop by the museum," I said insistently. "I think it would be in his best interest if he were to consider seeing me. So if you would please let him know that I will be dropping in on him this afternoon, I would greatly appreciate it."

"Very well, Mr. Blake, I will inform the Professor that you will be calling on him this afternoon, but I cannot guarantee that he will receive you."

"Well, that's all I can ask, Mrs. Chandler. Any consideration on my behalf is appreciated. Thank you for your time."

"You're welcome, Mr. Blake. Just see me upon your arrival."

I sat the telephone down and addressed JB. "You graduated from Harvard, right?"

"Yes I did," he confidently replied.

"Do you know Professor Hanson?"

"I know of him. Drafe spoke of him on several occasions. I believe he's the assistant curator for the museum."

"Oh – really," I remarked upon discovering a positive correlation. "Do you know where the Peabody Museum is?"

"Oh yes, I know the university grounds very well."

"In that case JB, I'll need you to accompany me to Cambridge today. And since you know the way, why don't you drive. We'll take your motorcar."

"I think I can manage that," he agreeably said.

JB rang the Office of the Medical Examiner to say that he would not be available today. Then he asked if we might stop by his house on the way.

"Sure, I think we'll have time."

Downstairs, during breakfast, I took the opportunity to ask JB a few questions.

"Did your friend have any enemies?"

"None that I know of. Drafe was a nice fellow. I couldn't imagine anyone disliking him."

"Was he married?"

"No."

"Did he have any close relatives, friends or a girlfriend? Someone who might be able to shed some light on his recent whereabouts or situation."

"His parents and sister reside in Albany. He had many casual friends, but very few close ones, and he didn't have a steady girl that I know of. The last time I spoke with any of our mutual friends, they had not heard from him in quite some time."

"What address did you send your correspondence to?"

"Drafe had a post office box in Cambridge, but I usually sent my letters care of the university. They were always good with forwarding his mail."

With an inquisitive expression, he looked aside for a moment and then looked back with a question in his eyes. "The object of antiquity you spoke of on the phone, is that what's in the large suitcase?"

I leaned forward. "Yes, it is," I replied in a suppressed volume, not wanting Mrs. Coggins to overhear through the open kitchen door. "That's one reason why we're going to see Professor Hanson – that, and he knew your friend. In fact, I found his professional calling card amongst your friend's few belongings. Do you think they were well acquainted?"

"Drafe always placed him in high regard," he answered.

Mrs. Coggins came in to take our plates away, and I thanked her for her generosity. She was a marvelous cook, and her delicious fares were only surpassed by her kindheartedness.

"I can't thank you enough," JB said when she had left the room. "Especially since you compromised yourself on my behalf. The terrible event still has me very much confused. Maybe I should have called the police."

"If you had called the police, you'd be at the stationhouse right now being grilled as their primary suspect. Don't worry, I'll find out who perpetrated your friend's demise," I confidently stated.

"And what then?"

"Let's take it one step at a time," I advised. "I'm going out to get a paper. I'll be right back."

Leaving him to finish his coffee, I walked down to the corner where the newsboy always stood.

"Paper, Mr. Blake?" asked the newsboy.

"Yes, I'll take one," I said and paid him. "By the way, Billy, you didn't happen to see any strangers on the street this morning, did you? Somebody you haven't seen around here before."

"Yea, Mr. Blake. A colored man was gaddin' about on the street, and he was hangin' around across the street from your place for the longest time. He was wearin' a real nice set of threads, if you know what I mean. Oh, and a limey bought a paper from me earlier this mornin'."

"What did the limey look like?"

"Well, he had a big fat moustache."

"Anything else?"

"Umm – no," Billy said, shaking his head.

"Thanks Billy," I said, handing him two bits.

The boy looked at the coin as if I had given him a million bucks. "Gee Mr. Blake, thanks a lot. You're tops."

I tucked the paper under my arm and winked. "Keep your eyes peeled kid, and if you see that colored man or the limey again, let me know and you'll get the same. You take care of yourself now, ok."

Walking back, I scanned the street, but nothing appeared out of the ordinary, just the typical pedestrian and street traffic. However, I descried an empty sedan, similar to the one that tailed us last night, parked halfway down the next block. Back at the rooming house, JB and I went upstairs to my flat. I gave him the key to the suitcase, inviting him to have a look for himself. While he pondered over the tablet, I looked through the paper for any news of what had occurred the night before, but the morning edition held no reference to it.

"This is something quite extraordinary," he remarked, replacing the tablet.

"Would you mind driving your motorcar around to the alley in back, and I'll meet you there in a few minutes," I requested.

He obliged, and watching from the window, I observed him as he pulled out into the street and turned the corner. I waited for the inevitable tail, but none ensued. After pocketing the evidential items, the passport, calling cards and such, I placed the small suitcase in a closet; and taking the larger one with me, I locked up and descended the stairs where I encountered Mrs. Coggins sweeping the foyer.

"My, you're looking lovely today," I complimented with a smile.

"Oh Mr. Blake, always the charmer," she said, blushing and straightening her hair. "Where are you off to? Going on a trip?" she inquired, noticing the large suitcase.

"I'm going to Cambridge, and I may spend the night," I said, continuing on my way.

"Good day, Mr. Blake," she called after as I headed out the back door.

Opening the back gate, I stepped into the alley where JB waited in his motorcar, the engine running. I secured the case with the tablet in the trunk and climbed into the passenger seat.

"Drive up to the street and make a left turn," I directed.

Once on the street, I asked him to drive to my office, telling him I had something to take care of and that it would only require a few minutes. Much to my relief, the sedan never appeared, and after a few blocks it became an ordinary drive. The office was empty when I arrived, and as soon as the evidential items were locked away in the floor safe, I was out the door.

JB headed uptown and drove along Park Street in the direction of Beacon Hill. In that long-standing section of Boston, we parked and I retrieved the case from the trunk. We strolled down a narrow street lined with well-established, stately row houses to stop in front of a red brick residence with tall windows trimmed by black shudders. An oval window of etched glass adorned the black painted door, and a polished brass plaque on the wall by the door read "J.B. Hawkins, M.D.".

Inside, an expansive hall extended beyond the foyer, and an open archway granted access to an elegantly furnished drawing room with a grand piano.

"Please make yourself at home," he invitingly said.

"Do you live here alone?" I asked, setting the case down in a suitable corner by the door.

"Yes," he said lamentingly. "My parents have passed on. My brother practices law in Springfield and my sister lives with her husband in Montpellier."

While he changed, I waited in the drawing room, jotting down questions for the Professor and contemplating future options. Time passed quicker than expected, and he discovered me lost in thought when he returned wearing his coat and hat, ready to go.

I again secured the case in the trunk of his motorcar, and soon we had left Beacon Hill behind on the road to Cambridge. Outside the window, New England displayed her picturesque charm. It was late autumn. Only a few stubborn remnants of foliage clung to the exposed gnarled branches of the trees, and a scattering of fallen leaves draped the landscape. The sun was shining brightly, and the trees cast an artwork of shadows across the road.

We had traveled most of the way when JB's expression suddenly went blank and then exploded into wide-eyed apprehension. "Oh no!" he dreadfully exclaimed.

"What is it?" I asked.

"I left my medical bag in Drafe's room. In our haste to leave, I was distracted and forgot it."

"Can it be replaced?"

"Yes, it can be replaced. I have another. That's not why I'm concerned. I'm concerned because the bag has my name on it in gold lettering and several of my calling cards are inside. What if the wrong people should find it?"

A sinking feeling of anxiety churned in my gut, but I did not want to reveal any indication of my present disquietude. "Well there's nothing we can do about it right now," I said. "All we can do is hope for the best. Who knows, maybe it's made its way to a pawnshop by now. In any case, I'll stop by the Anchorage tonight and check it out."

At Harvard, JB navigated the university grounds with the ease of familiarity, and upon arriving at our destination, he pulled into a lot by the museum and stopped.

Inside the front entrance, a small group was gathering for the next guided tour. I asked the guide where we might find Mrs. Chandler, and following his directions, we made our way to the museum offices. A conservatively dressed, middle-aged woman sat behind a desk. She cordially introduced herself as Mrs. Chandler and asked us if we needed any assistance. Handing her my card, I politely introduced JB and myself. I had two sets of calling cards, one with only my name on it and the other with my profession, office address and telephone number. Not wanting to tip my hand, I handed her the card with only my name.

"You're the gentleman who was so insistent upon seeing Professor Hanson," she said, looking at the card. "You're fortunate, Mr. Blake, the Professor was not objectionable to receiving you. In fact, he seemed quite intrigued in regards to the item of antiquity you mentioned."

"If you would please follow me gentlemen," she directed, rising up from her desk.

She conducted us down a darkened flight of stairs to a lower level and along a hallway to a door. After gently knocking, she opened it, and we followed her into a room in which rays of afternoon sunlight streamed through a small rectangular basement window. A cup of tea and a plate with a half eaten sandwich rested on a roll top desk below the window. By the desk stood a freestanding chalkboard upon which were written lines of Latin script accompanied by scribbled notations. A spacious table, illuminated by a bright lamp and surrounded by several chairs, stretched to an extensive length. Objects of the past were either displayed or tucked away here and there, and volumes of various size and age lined the shelves and lie in stacks upon the table. At the table sat a short rotund man of mature years absorbed in a thick tome. He peered through spectacles that rested halfway down his nose; his silver hair was neatly combed, a well-trimmed beard dressed his face, and a fashionable bow tie decorated his collar. He lifted his head and looked up over his spectacles at Mrs. Chandler, then riveted his discerning gaze upon us. She politely introduced us to the scholarly man, handed him my card, and departed the room.

He briefly looked at the card, gingerly closed the large volume in front of him, and rose up to greet us. "I am Professor Hanson, the assistant curator for the museum," he said, cordially shaking our hands.

When he shook my hand, I could not help but notice the Masonic ring that adorned the third finger of his right hand. JB casually informed him that he was an alumnus of the university, which sparked a smile on the Professor's face, and he invited us to be seated. Topping a stack of books on the table was a leather volume entitled *Primitive Culture: Researches into the Development of Mythology, Philosophy, Religion, Language, Art and Custom* by Sir Burnett Tylor, 1871. Stacked beneath was a volume on Egyptology. The whole room exuded a sage and scholarly air, giving me the distinct impression that we had come to the right place.

"I understand you have an object of antiquity for me to examine. Shall we have a look at it?" he said, glancing at the case.

I removed the tablet from the case and placed it on the table. Once unveiled, its lustrous surface shimmered in the light, and its enigmatic markings immediately captured the Professor's interest. His eyes glistened with amazement and wonder as he examined the mysterious object. He withdrew his attention only to retrieve a magnifying glass, which he used to painstakingly scrutinize every detail while we waited expectantly.

"Exceptional, absolutely remarkable," he uttered after a period of intensive study. "The craftsmanship is unique in every aspect. However, it is this very uniqueness that makes it difficult to determine the origin or age of this tablet, and I am confounded as to its geological composition. It is indicative of basalt, but does not possess all the congruous characteristics.

"These pictographs are fascinating. They seem to depict a spiritual journey of some kind. But it is these runes that I find most intriguing. They are unlike any I have ever seen. They are not Norse, Sanskrit, Hieroglyphics, Aramaic, nor can I attribute them to Mesopotamia or any other known culture, past or present, including the newest of discoveries. Recent excavations in British Honduras are just now beginning to elucidate the mysteries of the lost Mayan civilization, and although nothing is yet known of the Mayan language, the runes do not resemble the symbols on Mayan ruins and artifacts discovered thus far."

Continuing his examination, he gently turned the tablet over, and his curious intellect seemed baffled as he sought to discern the meaning behind the speckled surface. After a brief period, his eyes lit up with understanding, and his lips slowly spread into a smile.

"Yes – fascinating," he uttered aloud to himself. "This, gentlemen, is an astronomical chart, and an extremely accurate one at that. It is none other than a precise depiction of the heavens at the time of the summer solstice, as viewed from an equatorial region. For here is Ursa Minor – 'The Little Bear'," he said, connecting the dots with his finger. "This cluster of stars delineates Ophiuchus 'The Serpent Bearer', and these constitute 'The Serpent', which is divided into two separate constellations, Serpens Caput and Serpens Cauda to the east and west of Ophiuchus."

Then, as his eyes fastened upon the hollowed circle, which was located amidst the stars that comprised 'The Serpent', his edifying discourse ceased, and a shadow of perplexity fell over him. "Based on my knowledge of astronomy, there should not be a star in this position," he said, stroking his beard.

He took a tome from the shelf, placed it on the desk, and began flipping through the pages.

"Ah yes, here it is," he remarked, coming to a particular page. "But according to this astronomical chart, no star is positioned in that location."

He replaced the tome on the shelf and returned his attention to the tablet.

"The existence of this particular celestial body, as portrayed here, cannot be verified. Perhaps it has yet to be discovered, possibly due to an occultation," he conveyed, pointing to the phantom star. An insightful expression lit up his face. "Look here gentlemen!" he emphatically said. Starting with the unknown heavenly body, he pointed to three consecutive stars aligned in a row. "The occurrence of an alignment is evident, one that would create the effect of seeing one great bright star instead of three."

"Something like the star of Bethlehem?" JB asked.

"It would surely produce a similar phenomena," the Professor affirmed. "I would safely assume that this phenomena is represented by the bright star displayed in one of the pictographs. In my opinion, the civilization that fashioned this tablet had a superior knowledge of the universe. Unfortunately, to unlock the secrets of this tablet, one must know the meaning of the runes, and I am at a loss in that respect. Nonetheless, the significance of this find cannot be overstated. Where ever did you obtain this artifact?"

"An anthropologist named Harold Drayfus left it in the care of Dr. Hawkins," I disclosed. "I understand you know of him."

"I most certainly do," he stated. "He is an honorable colleague, who was once my student and protégé. He has done notable fieldwork for the university and the museum and has faced many dangers in the pursuit of Ethnological research. In fact, he was bestowed an honorary doctorate by the university for his invaluable contributions. If you have seen him, this is a truly glad tiding, for I have received no word of him since he departed a year and a half ago to take part in an expedition sponsored by the British Royal Society. Woefully, he was deemed missing with the other members of the expedition when they failed to return. When and where did you see him, Doctor?"

"Last night in Boston," JB responded, albeit reluctantly.

"Harold Drayfus in Boston? I'm curious as to why he made no effort to contact me."

"He only just arrived," JB further informed.

"Where is he staying? How can I reach him?" the Professor earnestly inquired.

"Unfortunately, he has disappeared under mysterious circumstances," I communicated. "And I have every reason to presume him dead. Allow me to be frank. Dr. Hawkins consulted me as a friend. I am a private investigator, and I believe that another interested party orchestrated your colleague's disappearance in an attempt to acquire this tablet. If that's the case, my concern is that the doctor here might be subject to the same fate."

"Then this should be a matter for the police, don't you think," the Professor asserted.

"No," I returned. "The police would only bungle things and confiscate this tablet. Imagine this artifact rotting in the basement of the local precinct, not knowing who could have access to it. If you involve the police, you may as well kiss this tablet goodbye."

"I see your point," the Professor relented. "It would be a considerable tragedy if it were to fall into nefarious hands, especially if your disconcerting speculation is correct. Interested parties, as you put it, do pose a grave hazard in the fields of archaeology and anthropology, both of which are two sides of the same coin. Foremost are treasure hunters, men blinded by greed, and then there are the mercenaries employed by private collectors. Then again, this tablet may constitute a great discovery, and if so, there may be a rival for credit. This concerns me greatly, for Harold Drayfus was more than a colleague. If I can assist you in any respect, please do not hesitate to ask, and I pray that you will find him alive and well."

"There is something you can help me with," I said. "Are you familiar with a British anthropologist by the name of Sir Gunston Mallory?"

"Yes I am. He is an extremely learned man, who has done much to advance the field of anthropology, and his new book is the talk of the Royal Society in London and other scientific circles."

"Do you think he could enlighten us as to the meaning of these runes?" I inquired.

"There is the likelihood that he or one of his esteemed colleagues might be able to interpret them." His eyes suddenly flashed from the rush of a scintillating thought. "I am attending an academic conference at Oxford University in three weeks time. While in London, I could have this artifact scrutinized by the most noted minds within the Royal Society, including Sir Gunston."

"That's a suggestion that merits doing," I responded. "However, I would prefer to accompany you, if you have no objections."

"I hadn't considered it, but I have no objections. Actually, I'm a bit averse to traveling alone, so your company would be welcome. You, of course, will need to make the necessary travel arrangements. I have booked passage to Southampton on the liner America. The ship sails from New York City in three days, and I will be catching the train for New York Friday morning."

"Don't worry, I'll take care of the arrangements," I assured him. "Just meet me on the platform before boarding the train."

Recalling other names from my notes, I asked the Professor about Dr. Jacob Greenberg. He told me that Jacob Greenberg was a Professor at the Hebrew University in Jerusalem, and that he and Dr. Drayfus had participated in an archaeological dig in Palestine some three years ago. I also threw out the name "Jake Brandon", but the Professor had no recollection of anybody by that name.

Having answered my final questions, the Professor returned to the subject of the tablet. "I would be most grateful if you would entrust this artifact to the care of the museum, for I would like more time to study it further. I will ensure that it is placed in the museum vault. Only the curator and myself have access, and I can personally vouch for the integrity of our curator."

"As far as I'm concerned, you may keep it as long as you like," I favorably answered, realizing that a safe place was needed to store the tablet. "In fact, all things considered, it is my firm opinion that it is the rightful property of the museum in due course."

The Professor looked at JB, seeking concurrence.

"Yes, I think that would be best," JB said, nodding agreeably.

"Just one thing remains," I added. "I must insist that you keep this thing secret for now."

"You have my word," the Professor pledged.

"Until Friday then," I amicably said, and with the amenity of parting handshakes our promising meeting was brought to a close.

Once outside the museum, JB stopped me on the front steps to ask two reasonable questions. "Is this trip to London really necessary? Shouldn't we be focusing our efforts in Boston?"

"I'm now convinced that if we solve the mystery of that tablet, we will also solve the mystery of your friend's demise," I replied. "Whoever the perpetrators are, it is my firm notion that they pursued him to Boston, and I don't think we'll discover any more there than we already have. We'd just be dipping into a dry well. His papers gave all indication that he was most recently in England prior to Boston, and there I believe is where the answers lie. Also, your friend had an affiliation with the Royal Society, and that's where I may be able to pick up the trail."

"If you're resolved to make this trip, I'm coming with you," he determinedly stated. "I'm too involved, and besides you're going to need money," he reasoned; and although he presented an unfaltering stature, an undercurrent of foreboding fear shown in his worried eyes.

"Then it looks like we'll both be going to London with the Professor. I'll have Cindy make the arrangements," I said, raising no argument, and we began walking again. "You know, I have the distinct feeling that this trip will turn out to be quite telling."

Back in Boston, JB insisted on stopping at St. Mary's church, and amidst the unfamiliar solemness of a Catholic sanctuary, I sat patiently in a back pew while JB conferred with his parish priest, Father Higgins. The two disappeared through a side door, and sometime later JB reemerged alone. In his hands he had a prayer book, a vial, and a crucifix dangling from a string of rosary beads.

"What's in the vial," I curiously asked as we departed.

"Holy water. I want to be prepared for anything."

"There's no substitute for good preparation," I said, humoring him.

"Conrad, do you believe in God?" he inquired out of the blue.

"Only a fool doesn't believe in God," I answered assuredly.

Taking another detour, we revisited my office, and while JB waited with the motor running, I ran upstairs and deposited my notebook in the floor safe. On the return home, I had him drop me off two blocks from my flat. Betting on the likely chance that my place was under surveillance, I chose to walk the remaining distance.

"Lock all your doors and windows, and sit tight until you hear from me," I instructed, and then I watched him drive away into the night.

Rain clouds unleashed a chilling torrent that beat heavily upon everything, and the wet surface of the lonely sidewalk glistened in the lamplight. The sedan remained parked in the same spot, a signal that some watcher lurked close by; and when the knob on my door turned with ease, every nerve was poised to shout alarm. Before entering the darkened room, I reached into the deep pocket of my trench coat and slipped my fingers into the brass knuckles there. I turned on the light, unready for the surprise I received. Seated on the sofa was a woman adorned in the trappings of refinement. An elegant fur coat wrapped her slender figure, black velvet gloves dressed her hands, and a black netted veil masked her facial features. Barely had the first word left my lips when I felt a sudden excruciating pain on my cranium. The floor came up to meet me and everything went black.

CHAPTER 4

In the early morning, JB responded to determined knocks at his front door. Plainly visible through the frosted etched glass were the silhouettes of three men. At first, he hesitated to answer, but then opened the door to be confronted by a hard-faced man wearing an overcoat and fedora in the company of two uniformed policemen.

He immediately recognized the plainclothesman. "Detective Briggs – good morning," he greeted, unable to subdue the nervous tremor in his voice. "This is most unexpected. Would you gentlemen care to step inside?"

The three men stood firm. "Dr. Hawkins, you will come with me forthwith, sir," the plainclothesman gruffly stated.

"What is this about, detective?" JB questioned.

"All will be revealed when we reach the stationhouse. Now you will come with me, sir," Briggs sternly repeated. "Do not force me to exercise an option that will be unpleasant for the both of us."

"Will you allow me just a minute? I need to make a telephone call."

"Any calls can be made from the stationhouse," Briggs coldly returned.

Perturbed, JB donned his coat and accompanied the police officers as they escorted him to a waiting motorcar. Detective Briggs climbed in the back seat with him, and the motorcar took them away.

* * *

Regaining consciousness, I opened my eyes to see the face of Mrs. Coggins come into focus. She was a kindly widow, who had lost her only son in the Great War and had developed a maternal affection for me. It was a welcome sight, considering what I was expecting. She was holding a cold compress to my aching head, and Mr. Baines, one of the other tenants, was standing over me.

"Oh good, looks like he's coming around," Mr. Baines said.

"Are you all right Mr. Blake?" Mrs. Coggins asked, expressing grave concern. "I was so worried. You've got a nasty bump on your head. An awful ruckus was going on in here last night," she continued emphatically. "I knocked on the door, but no one answered. So I got my passkey, and when I opened the door you were lying on the floor in a heap."

I sat up in a daze, my head throbbing. The place was in a shambles, and whoever did it, did a first rate job. The contents of the drawers and closet were strewn about all over the floor. The upholstery was cut to ribbons and the mattress was overturned. Even one of my few luxuries, a radio, had been gutted.

"Shall I get a doctor? Shall I have Mr. Baines fetch the beat cop?"

"No – no, I'm all right," I stammered out, making an effort to stand up, but the room began to sway, and the two of them helped me into a chair.

I tried my best to assure them that I would be fine, promising Mrs. Coggins that I would indeed ring for a doctor, and finally persuaded them to leave me seated alone amidst the carnage wrought by the malicious interlopers. All of Drafus' remaining belongings had been removed, and as to the identity of the wrecking crew, not a single clue was left behind. Still in a whirl, I reached for the telephone to ring JB. My heart raced furiously as I waited for the operator to connect me, and after endless unanswered rings, a myriad of distressing thoughts filled my mind. With time working against me, I grabbed my coat and hat and rushed out the door.

Scanning the street, I descried a Franklin boattail coupe with a man in the driver's seat, and when I pulled out into the street, the coupe followed. Attempting to be inconspicuous, the driver kept a discreet distance, but I had a good notion as to who was behind the wheel. Evasive maneuvers failed to shake the dogged pursuer and caused delays. Seeing an opportunity, I turned sharply and detoured down a narrow alley with the intention of doubling back around the block. The coupe made the turn into the alley, and then it recklessly accelerated, narrowing the gap. I too accelerated the pace, clipping a trash can that toppled and rolled in front of the coupe, which barreled over the can with a crunch. At the other end, I veered and careened onto the street, screeching the tires and barely missing a truck turning into the alley. The truck and the coupe clashed head to head at the entrance to the alley, and in my mirror I saw the driver of the truck cursing and gesticulating. By the time the jam-up was cleared, I was long gone, and making haste to JB's.

Repeated knocks on JB's front door roused no response.

"He's not at home," said a maid from the doorway of the next house. "I was sweeping the front step earlier, and saw him leave with three men."

"Who were these men? Can you describe them?" I asked.

She described the three men, and said that they and the Doctor had exchanged greetings and conversed for a short while on the threshold before leaving in a motorcar.

"How long ago was that?" I asked.

Thinking, she rolled up her eyes for a brief moment. "A quarter of an hour ago I suppose."

"Did you happen to catch any of their names?"

"The Doctor addressed the plainclothesman as Detective Briggs."

"Did any of them mention where they were going?"

"The detective said something about the stationhouse."

Cursing myself for not arriving sooner, I dashed to the Stutz and raced down to the stationhouse. Lt. Briggs and I went way back, and I was well acquainted with his tenacity to solve a case. Had he been summoned to 'The Anchorage', and thus discovered the medical bag? Then one troublesome thought plagued me. If JB sticks to that story he told me at the flophouse, they will certify him for sure and railroad him straight to the sanitarium.

Arriving at the stationhouse, I approached the desk sergeant to inquire about Briggs. Sgt. Mullins, an indolent simpleton who sat on his brains, was on duty behind the desk, sipping coffee and stuffing his mouth.

"Top of the mornin' Blake. What brings you around?" Mullins mumbled with his mouth full.

"I'm here to see Briggs," I said.

"He brought in a suspect a few minutes ago – the slab stabber from the morgue. Don't' know what it's about, but you can bank on it being a while. Do you want to wait?"

"No, I need to see him now. I don't care if he's busy, just fetch him and get him out here!" I adamantly said.

"I'm not doing that without good reason," Mullins said in an effort to cover his hindquarters. "What do you want me to tell him?"

"I don't care what you tell Briggs, just get him out here!" I barked.

"Ok Blake, simmer down, I'll get him," he said, and then he ordered an underling to fetch Briggs on my behalf. "You're asking for it Blake," he warned me.

I did not have to wait long before Briggs emerged from the inner sanctuary of the stationhouse. We exchanged greetings and shook hands.

"I have fish to fry," Briggs said. "Now what's this about?"

"I know for a fact that you have Dr. Hawkins on ice," I said.

"Yea, what's it to you?"

"He's my friend. What's the charge?"

"I haven't decided. I was just about to question the Doctor concerning his whereabouts and actions on the night before last."

"Why?"

"That's police business."

"Listen Briggs, remember the Carter kidnapping case? You were biting your nails, while I broke it wide open and then closed it for you. And let's not forget the Anderson murder. You got your indictment and a clear-cut conviction on that one."

"All right Blake, since he's your friend I'll give you the scoop."

"And give it to me straight, no double-talk."

"Something happened at this flophouse down on the waterfront named 'The Anchorage', and I believe the Doctor may have been involved."

"Continue," I said, pressing the issue.

"When the proprietor's wife entered a tenant's room to do her cleaning, she discovered bloodstains everywhere and telephoned the police. I checked it out myself and found every indication of foul play. The Doctor's medical bag was on a bureau and all of the tenant's belongings were missing. I questioned the proprietor, and he said two men left in a hurry in the middle of the night, both carrying suitcases, and one was packing heat. On top of that, the proprietor just fingered the Doctor as one of them."

"This is Dr. Hawkins you're talking about," I contended. "The man who does your dirty work for you at the Medical Examiner's office. How many times has his contribution helped you to solve a case? And we both know the man's character is impeccable. It won't be necessary for you to humiliate the Doctor by interrogating him. I can answer all your questions, because I was with the Doctor that night – all night. In fact, he spent the night at my flat."

"Malarkey," Briggs blurted out.

"That's right – me, I'm your second man. I was with the Doctor at that flophouse, and I can attest that he's not involved in any foul play."

"So what's your story?"

"Harold Drayfus, a friend of Dr. Hawkins, was staying in room 21. He gave Dr. Hawkins a ring and said it was urgent he see him. The Doctor didn't want to go to that part of town alone and asked me if I would accompany him. The proprietor was asleep, or more likely passed out, behind the counter when we arrived. No one answered the door to the room; it was unlocked and his friend wasn't there, so we made ourselves at home and waited. When he didn't show up, we left. The Doctor was preoccupied with concern for his friend and forgot his medical bag. As for the belongings, a suitcase was on the bed, but it was there when we left."

"That's good to know Blake, but the name on the register wasn't Harold Drayfus," he said. "Now I'm going to find out what the Doctor has to say. Wait here."

"Why waste your time? He'll just tell you the same. And as for the name on the register, I'm sure half the patrons of that deplorable dump don't use their real names."

"That remains to be seen," he said, stolid and poker-faced.

"Have you got a body?"

"No."

"Have you got a weapon?"

"No."

"Then you've got nothing but the worthless word of a mealy-mouthed, four-flushin' scoundrel. That won't hold up in a light breeze against the word of Dr. Hawkins and myself. Your proprietor deals in cheap bootleg and prostitution. I invite you to go down there and check it out for yourself. You're barking up the wrong tree Briggs, he's your suspect. Maybe he knows something he's not telling you. Maybe he was involved in the nefarious deed and pawned or disposed of the belongings. Can you afford not to check it out? Think about it for a minute. Maybe this thing goes deeper than you think."

His head began to spin with speculation.

"Where's JB?" I subtly asked.

"Inside" he simply said, still chewing on my words.

At that moment I decided to take matters into my own hands, and with brazen determination and fortitude, I brushed past Briggs and burst through the door into the inner sanctuary of the stationhouse. Heads turned as I stormed past a series of desks. Briggs was hot on my heels shouting curses and threats along with "this is highly unorthodox" and "of all the unmitigated gall." I reached Briggs' office only to find JB's coat and hat on a rack by the door. I had a good notion as to his whereabouts, and I acted on it.

The flophouse proprietor was sitting in a chair just outside the door to the office. "Daz 'im, daz de udder mug," he declared, pointing accusingly at me.

I glowered at him, and disregarding Briggs, I continued on to an all too familiar door. Beyond it was a lifeless room where suspects were interrogated and grilled; and opening it, I entered a confining chamber with four blank walls furnished only by a table and two chairs, and a single light hung from the ceiling. JB was sitting in the chair on the far side of the table. His expression changed from despondency to relief.

"Conrad, thank God you're here!" he exclaimed.

Briggs entered close behind me, and I wheeled around to face him.

"For crying out loud Briggs! What were you going to do?! Give him the rubber hose treatment!" I verbally bashed him, pointing to JB.

Briggs stood silent with a blank expression on his face.

"Dr. Hawkins and I will answer no further questions without an attorney present," I stated.

"You know darn well that I can detain you both for twenty-four hours," he returned.

"Do that and you hoodwink yourself," I said. "If you're going to hold us, then you better see the magistrate and obtain a warrant for our arrest. And you better darn well make it stick or there'll be the devil to pay."

Briggs stood indecisively in the doorway. "Ok Blake, you just saved yourself from a night in stir," he said. "But don't play me for a fool. You know something. I'm giving you forty-eight hours. After that, I want you and the Doctor in my office with the truth."

Before Briggs could reconsider, JB got his coat and hat, and we left the stationhouse post-haste. As we departed, I heard Briggs say to the flophouse proprietor, "Sit tight, I've got some questions for you."

JB expelled a heavy sigh as we drove away. "Thanks for getting me out of there. I wasn't sure what I was going to tell Briggs," he said. "I suppose this means we'll have to cancel our trip."

"Nonsense."

"What about Briggs?"

"Don't worry, I can handle Briggs. We'll settle the matter when we get back."

Many things needed to be accomplished before the day was out, and the first order of business was to check in at my office. Old Cyrus Jones ran a shoeshine stand on the sidewalk by the entrance to my building. He was buffing the shoe of a patron when we arrived, and as we passed, he looked up with his dark-skinned, timeworn face to say good morning and then directed my attention to a boattail coupe with a crumpled fender parked halfway down the block. A man occupied the driver's seat, his identity concealed by an open newspaper. Thanking Cyrus, I handed him a bill, which he stuffed into a cigar box that contained his hard earnings. JB tipped his hat, and we proceeded to my office on the second floor.

Cindy was seated at her desk in the front office. She looked up with a twinkle in those green eyes like the emerald isle itself, and a welcoming smile lit up her face. She was a fetching kitten, with fair complexion, delicate features, silky strawberry blonde hair and a cheerful girlish charm to match. She was a real sensible girl, one of those people with great organizational and administrative skills. She kept the files, fielded my telephone calls and screened my visitors; but what was most special about her was her inner beauty and warm disposition, qualities that made her that rare type of person the world can ill afford to do without. She was already acquainted with the Doctor and extended him a friendly greeting. A pot of coffee was brewing on the hot plate, and she asked if we would like a cup.

"I hadn't seen nor heard from you since yesterday morning Conrad, and I was getting concerned," she said, pouring the coffee. "It's good to know you're all right."

I began to swoon, and JB clutched my arm to keep me from falling.

"You're not all right, are you?" Cindy said, suddenly stricken with concern.

"I took a hard blow to the head last night," I disclosed.

Together they assisted me into the leather chair behind my desk, and Cindy fetched a well-used first aid kit.

"You have a nasty cut here," JB said, examining my injury. "But it looks as though somebody cleaned it up already."

"Must have been Mrs. Coggins. It seems I have a guardian angel after all," I said.

"You're probably suffering from a mild concussion, but you should be fine in a few days."

Taking a look out the window, I surveyed the street below. The driver of the coupe got out and stood on the sidewalk in full view, the newspaper tucked under his arm. Trying to look nonchalant, he walked over and leaned against a lamppost directly across the street. All my suspicions were confirmed as to the identity of my recent shadow. No doubt about it, it was Horace Snavely – a name synonymous with shifty weasel, the most unscrupulous and unethical private investigator in all of Boston, and not a competent one at that. No job was beneath him. He would sell out his own mother if it would put a nickel in his pocket. That was all I needed.

Cindy came in with our coffee. I informed her of our travel plans, and asked if she would make the necessary arrangements. She said it was short notice, but that she would do her best to take care of everything, and I had full confidence in her ability to do so.

"Oh, and you're going to need a passport if you're traveling to England," she reminded me. "You better get on it."

I opened the floor safe and removed a sum of cash from the reward money I received for cracking the Carter kidnapping case in which I returned two boys safely to the arms of their wealthy parents. Giving the majority of it to Cindy, I advanced her three months' salary and enough to pay the bills for a good while, with plenty to spare.

"I'm not sure how long I'll be gone," I said. "I'll cable you now and then with developments."

Before closing the safe, I retrieved a nickel-plated 1911A1 Colt .45 automatic, which I placed in JB's hand.

"What do you want me to do with this?" he asked.

"For your own protection," I advised, almost insistently. "The people your friend was entangled with are no amateurs – they mean business. They put my lights out last night, and when I came to, my place had been ransacked. And you and I both know what they were after."

For a moment he wrestled with the implication of my words and then reluctantly put the weapon in his coat pocket.

Prior to departing, I rang the museum and spoke with Mrs. Chandler. I informed her that I would meet the Professor on the station platform tomorrow morning as planned and gave her my office number should anything unexpected arise.

"I'll leave you a note if you don't return before closing," Cindy said as JB and I were going out the door. "Shall I come see you off?"

"As much as I would welcome that, I think it best you didn't," I replied with a reassuring smile.

When we emerged onto the street, Snavely lowered the brim of his hat and slunk back to his coupe. He shadowed us all the way to city hall, and when we arrived, he pulled into a slot just down the street but remained in his motorcar as we made our way to the State Department field office. As usual, the wheels of bureaucracy were slow, which threatened to derail our travel plans, but where there is a will, there is a way, and with a bit of finagling, I expedited the process.

JB needed to see his banker before the bank closed for the day. Fortunately, the Bank of Boston was two blocks away; and walking at a hurried pace, we arrived with time to spare. We had no more than entered, when Mr. Gene Arthur, a pleasant-mannered banker in a crisp suit, rose from his desk on the partitioned platform and cordially greeted JB. Keeping an eye out the window, I waited nearby in the lobby while JB conducted his financial transactions. In addition to making a cash withdrawal, he had the banker issue him two letters of credit, and by the expression on the banker's face, they must have been for a considerable sum.

Once outside the bank, I hailed a taxi and advised JB to go straight home and wait until he heard from me. Hopefully, his place of residence would remain a mystery to Snavely, at least for now. The ploy had worked, for Snavely was still seated in his parked coupe when I returned to city hall. He then had no other choice but to follow me, and follow me he did, as I led him on a wild goose chase through town that ended at my flat. Surprisingly, when I pulled over to park, he did not stop, but drove on past and turned the corner out of sight.

When I got upstairs to my rooms, the door was open and there was Mrs. Coggins. She had cleaned up the mess, and with the help of Mr. Baines, had replaced the damaged furnishings with some furniture she had stored in the attic. I thanked her and gave her a kiss on the cheek, which made her blush. I told her I was leaving on a long trip and asked if she would keep an eye on the place, then shelled out three months advanced rent and stuffed the bills in her apron pocket. She was a bit perturbed that I would be gone so long; but said she would be happy to take care of things, and asked if I was doing any better. I told her I had been to see Dr. Hawkins and that I was fine. She insisted that I have some of her mulligan stew, and without waiting for a response, she excused herself to heat up a 'hefty portion'.

I had not eaten all day, and the prospect of a bowl of Mrs. Coggins' stew was simply irresistible. After packing, I retired downstairs to the kitchen and the inviting smell of the stew. Before long, I had consumed two bowls and a sizable portion of buttered bread. Mrs. Coggins was quite proud and pleased as punch when I requested my second helping.

It was necessary to make one last trip to the office to pick up a few items. Distracted by the day's events, I had failed to give Cindy a ring, and by now she would have closed up and gone home. Chances are, she had succeeded in making the arrangements, and all would go as planned. Evening had cast its darkening shades, and as I drove along familiar streets and avenues, the sparkle of street lamps lit the corners, and people clad against the cold moved like passing shadows down the sidewalk.

Darkness filled the office interior when I arrived, and the door was slightly ajar. My pulse quickened, and the fresh memory of last night flashed in my mind. Cautiously, I nudged the door open enough to furtively slip inside. Cloaking myself in the shadows, I listened intently to hear only the sounds of the outside traffic. The faint illumination from the street projected an askew image of the window on the wall, and the lights of passing motorcars cast nebulous shadows. I waited – nothing stirred. The door to the back office stood wide open; and moving stealthily, I tread a path toward it, my hand reaching for the Luger inside my coat. Pistol at the ready, I stood at the threshold, my eyes keenly scanning every inch of the darkened room. The ticking clock resounded in a heavy stillness that seemed to last forever. Believing that the bird had flown the coop, I discounted a lurking threat and turned on the light to discover an empty office.

Evidence of a recent intruder was clearly visible. The outer door had been jimmied, and someone had rummaged through the drawers and file cabinet.

Atop my desk, amongst the out of place articles, was a note from Cindy with detailed travel instructions.

> *Two first class train tickets for the New York, New Haven & Hartford line to New York on the 9:15 are waiting for you and Dr. Hawkins at the station. I booked two adjoining suites at the Barbizon Plaza Hotel in Manhattan. You can pick up two first class passages on the liner America at the front desk. The hotel was kind enough to make the arrangements, but it's going to cost you. Sorry, after that you're on your own.*
>
> *Stay safe and keep in touch.*

I pocketed the note.

From the untouched safe, I removed my notebook and a thin metal case containing precision locksmith tools, instruments which had been put to practical application on more than one occasion.

I then gave JB a ring. He answered, said all was quiet and that he had made arrangements for his absence, and was preparing for the journey. I told him we had two tickets on the 9:15 bound for New York and to meet me at the station.

In the act of leaving, I caught an anomaly out of the corner of my eye, something that had gone unnoticed – a cigarette butt in an ashtray. Cindy did not smoke. I picked it up and checked the brand. Only one person I knew smoked that brand – Horace Snavely.

CHAPTER 5

Daylight ended a restless sleep. Outside the window, an overcast sky masked the sun, and a dreary haze draped the city in dull colors. I rang for a taxi, and while I waited for a ride to the station, Mrs. Coggins packed a lunch for me. I told her that the train had a dining car, but she insisted I take it anyway.

"There's nothing like home cookin'," she said, handing me the basket. "Besides, you might get hungry after the kitchen is closed."

I thanked her, and she waved goodbye as the taxi drove away.

At the station, I weaved my way through the crowd in search of JB and the Professor. A thick heavy fog had settled in, shrouding the station in a cold, sullen mist, and steam dispensing from the locomotive flowed over the platform. All around me, indiscernible figures were veiled in a cloak of obscurity. I passed by anonymous faces and loved ones bidding goodbye. A porter nearly ran me down with a baggage trolley, followed closely behind by Professor Hanson, who was laboriously lugging the large leather-bound case that contained the tablet. I pleasantly greeted him and relieved him of the heavy burden.

"Dr. Hawkins has decided to join us," I informed him. "He agreed to meet me here. Have you seen him?"

"No, I haven't seen the Doctor," he said. "It would be rather difficult to find anyone in this pea soup. It's fortunate that I happened to bump into you."

Then, I distinctly heard a raised voice calling my name over the hustle and bustle, and turned to see the vague image of JB through the fog. He was standing on the bottom step at the far end of the next Pullman passenger car, holding on to the railing and leaning out over the platform, waving to us from above the crowd. He was shouting loud enough to wake the dead, and by now I was sure everyone on the platform knew my name. Having captured our attention, he stepped onto the platform and eagerly came to greet us.

"Frightful weather," he commented, making small talk.

Upon my gentle urging, we boarded the coach and settled into a sumptuous private compartment with the case safely stored on the rack above my seat. A blast from the steam whistle signaled departure, and shortly the train lurched forward. We had no more left the station than I began to lament my departure from Boston. Soon I would be out of my element, and my gut feeling told me that I would need every ounce of fortitude I could muster before this matter was resolved. I opened a newspaper I had purchased at the station and began reading it in an effort to distract my thoughts. As we rode along in silence, the gentle rhythmic clattering of the wheels rolling over the rails had a soothing effect. I began to feel more at ease and realized I was in good company.

The Professor was absorbed in an esoteric journal, and the atmosphere was quiet and taciturn. JB lit his pipe, filling the compartment with the aromatic scent of his tobacco. The fog had lifted, and as he puffed, he gazed out the window.

The conductor came in to verify our tickets and told us the dining car would begin serving lunch at eleven. When the time came, we decided to take our midday meal in shifts. That way, at least one of us would remain behind to keep an eye on our precious cargo. The Professor took the first shift; and after his return, JB and I made our way to the first class dining car, where we sat at a decorous table while an inspiring vista passed by. Since the Professor was not present, we discussed in hushed tones the events of the past three days. As we ate and talked, I occasionally scanned the coach, scrutinizing the patrons, but not one stood out from the ordinary. I did not want to leave the Professor alone too long; and after finishing our coffee, we decided to return to the compartment.

We had entered our coach, and began navigating our way down the corridor, when the door to our compartment opened. A dark-skinned steward emerged, carrying the leather-bound case.

JB vehemently stretched out his arm and pointed at the steward. "That's him! The face in the window at the flophouse! That's him Conrad! That's him!" he excitedly cried.

Surprised, the steward turned his head and looked at us with a startled expression. I bolted down the corridor, and he turned to run. Unnoticed by the counterfeit steward, the conductor had entered the corridor at the far end of the coach, making his way in our direction. The steward moved swiftly in an effort to escape and slammed into the conductor, dropping the case. It crashed to the deck, teetered over and landed flat on its side. I was closing fast. The steward did not bother to pick up the case; instead, he grabbed the surprised conductor by the upper sleeves, swung him around and thrust him in my path with considerable strength. The conductor and I collided, stopping me dead in my tracks. Maneuvering to get past the conductor in the narrow corridor, I watched the imposter make good his escape, disappearing through the door at the end of the coach. I resumed pursuit, traversing the length of the train in a frantic chase, but the steward was nowhere to be found. Somehow, he had eluded me.

On the way back to our compartment, I met up with the conductor. He said he did not appreciate being manhandled and asked what all the trouble was about. I told him that a thief in the guise of a steward had attempted to make off with some valuable property.

"Did you catch him?" he asked.

"No, unfortunately," I replied.

"Well, he couldn't have vanished into thin air. He's got to be on the train somewhere."

His words brought JB's fantastic account to mind.

"We'll be stopping in Norwich soon," continued the conductor. "You had better return to your compartment. I'll check the private compartments and tell the attendants and other conductors to be on the lookout for your thief. When we reach the next station, I'll inform the authorities."

I thanked the conductor for his assistance, and hastened back to our compartment to find the Professor collapsed in his seat, and JB tending to him. The case lay safely on the opposite seat.

"Is he all right?" I asked.

"He's had a bit of a shock," JB said. "Help me get his feet up and put him in a more comfortable position."

I lifted up his legs and laid them out on the seat, while JB put a pillow under his head. The Professor was quite disoriented, his lurid pallor matched his silver beard and his glazed open eyes stared into oblivion.

He mumbled something.

"I have yet to get anything coherent out of him," JB said.

"Is he hurt?"

"No evidence of physical trauma."

"Can you bring him around?"

"I'll try."

JB made several attempts to rouse him to a more lucid state. Finally, in desperation, he grabbed the Professor by the shoulders and jostled him, then gently slapped his cheeks. The Professor closed his eyes, opened them again, and reacted as if he had been abruptly awakened from a deep sleep.

"Oh my," he remarked.

"Are you all right?" JB asked sincerely.

"I think so, but I had the most unnerving dream," he said, rubbing his forehead. "The case, is it still here?"

"Yes, it's there on the seat," JB said, pointing to the case.

"Oh good, it was just a bad dream, but it was so vivid and so real."

"Professor, what happened after we left?" I asked.

He stroked his beard in contemplation. "Well, let me see. Some time after you left for the dining car, a steward came in and served me a cup of tea. Mind you, it was not to my liking. After that, I must have dozed off, because I don't remember anything but the dream until you awakened me.

"I've got news for you," I said. "A thief in the guise of a steward tried to make off with the case. He must have slipped you a mickey. Where's the tea cup?"

"It was upside down on the carpet. I handed it to the conductor," JB answered.

I crouched down, pressed my fingers into the soaked stain on the carpet, and put them to my nostrils. The residue on my fingertips had an unfamiliar acrid odor. Then turning my attention to the case, I opened it to find the tablet undamaged.

The Professor sat up, rubbed his eyes and forehead, and his expression changed to one of revelation.

"The steward! He was in my dream," he remarked.

"What do you remember about the dream?" JB asked.

While the Professor collected his thoughts, I returned the case to its previous place on the rack.

The Professor donned his spectacles. "Ah, now that's better," he said, easing back in his seat. "After I had consumed some of the tea, I started to feel light-headed, then sank into a somnolent daze. My surroundings were fluid and surreal, and the steward was standing over me. He had changed, and what a stunning sight he was at that. His powerful physique was clad in a leopard skin loincloth, and the hide of a leopard nobly draped his shoulders. Ringlets with dangling strands of lion's mane adorned his wrists and ankles. He wore an ornate headdress and an amulet hung around his neck. Upon the amulet was the symbol of an eye encircled by runes much the same as those on the tablet. In his right hand he held a scepter crowned with a leopard's paw.

"Amidst an ethereal landscape, we stood on a lofty mountaintop, a lush green tropical valley below. He removed his headdress, revealing a third preternatural eye in the center of his forehead – a ghastly sight. Our eyes met, and his mesmerizing gaze transfixed me. His potent telepathic powers held me spellbound, and he intrusively probed deep into my innermost being, exposing my darkest fears to me and threatening to unleash them upon me. I was terror-stricken by the horrid images he conjured in my mind – pictures that grew and lived, portraying themselves so vividly to my inner vision with a degree of reality I was compelled to acknowledge. Then, tacitly he made his demands known to me. I pointed to the case containing the tablet, and he took possession of it. He waved his scepter, and I found myself teetering on the edge of a precipice that plummeted to abysmal depths. I tarried there for some time, petrified and wondering if the slightest force of the wind would cause me to fall. Disembodied voices whispered to me, compelling me to jump. That's when you awoke me, saving me from some inexplicable demise."

Again, a piece of JB's implausible story came to mind.

The Professor looked me straight in the eye. "Mr. Blake, I have come to a realization," he said, raising an eyebrow. "There's something more here than meets the eye. You never gave me any details connected with Harold's disappearance. Is there something more I should know?"

"I can't tell you anything more than what I told you during our first meeting," I said.

"I see." He turned to JB. "Is there anything you wish to tell me Doctor?"

JB paused to carefully consider his words. He looked at me as if seeking my advice or approval.

"I may as well tell him," he said. "He deserves to know."

Relenting, I reluctantly nodded.

JB pulled out his pipe and held it in his hand, but did not fill it. "Professor, I have known you but a short while," he said. "However, I believe you to be a man not prone to postulation or presumptuous misjudgment. Therefore, I trust that you will not think me mad by what I am about to tell you."

The Professor leaned forward in his seat. "I have been researching the field of metaphysics for years, and nothing you could tell me would cause me to question your sanity. On the contrary, I will probably find it most interesting. Now tell me everything. Emit no detail."

JB fiddled with his pipe as he gathered his thoughts, and then he began to recount the events that transpired that night at the flophouse before I arrived.

"Drafe rang me from some flophouse down on the waterfront called 'The Anchorage'. He was rather distressed, and said it was imperative that he see me right away. He said he had something important he needed to tell me, and requested I bring my medical bag and a strong stimulant. When I arrived at Drafe's room, he opened the door and yanked me inside. Before closing the door, he stuck his head out and looked into the hall, then shut the door, and turned the key in the lock. His behavior was erratic and peculiar to say the least. He went to the window, made sure the drapes were drawn closed, and then plopped down into a chair, melting into it. His disheveled hair needed combing, his wrinkled clothes appeared as if he had slept in them, and red halos encircled sunken eyes. It was obvious that he was suffering from anxiety and lack of sleep. He rolled his head from side to side. 'I need to tell you something JB,' he said. 'I've got to tell someone. I know I could always confide in you. You've got to help me! You – you've got to help me! Ple – Please! Don't' – don't let them find me! Don't let them get me! Don't let them win! Somebody – somebody must stop him! They get you JB! They – they get you in your dreams! Awful dreams – Awful! Nightmares – nightmares too horrible to imagine! The dreams! Oh the dreams.'

"He grabbed me by the collar and pulled me closer. 'Don't let me go to sleep! Don't let me go to sleep! Do you understand? They'll get me! They'll get me! Look what they did to me! Look! Look what they did!' He released his grip and unbuttoned his shirt to reveal a gruesome scar on his chest. 'Put your hand on it. Go ahead, put your hand on it,' he insisted. I placed my hand on his chest, and to my utter astonishment, felt no heartbeat. 'Do you feel anything? No – no you don't, do you? No heartbeat.' I took the stethoscope from my medical bag, and put it to his chest to hear only the sounds of his rapid breathing. I felt for a pulse, but couldn't find one. His face was pale, his skin cold and clammy to the touch. He had all the indications and signs of a dead man, yet he was alive and conversing with me. Professor, nothing in all my medical education and experience could explain his condition. 'They took it JB! They took it in my dreams – my heart – my life essence – my soul – whatever you want to call it!' he raved. 'They took it! It's in a doll! Bad Ju-Ju I tell you! You know – black magic – voodoo! Did you bring the stimulant? Please – please give it to me. I need it. I've got to stay awake,' he beseeched.

"I removed a vial from my bag and drew up a dose of the solution into a syringe. He eagerly rolled up his sleeve, and I administered the hypodermic injection. 'Thanks JB, I knew I could count on you,' he said. I told him that everything was going to be fine, and instructed him to relax. I was more concerned with his mental and physical health, and whatever he had to tell me could wait. In fact, Professor, I had not given him a stimulant at all, but a sedative. That's what I thought he needed.

"The sedative began to take effect, and I went to the window to open it. He lethargically begged me not to, but I thought a bit of fresh air would do him good. Upon parting the drapes, I was startled to see the face of a Negro peering through the window, especially since we were on the second floor. He had a bizarre anatomical anomaly – a third eye – yes, a third eye located in the center of his forehead, just the same as in your description Professor. His piercing gaze transfixed me as if he could see right through me. Mesmerized, I reeled back, staring in disbelief. Then, reflected in the window, I first saw it – the thing that took Drafe. Initially, it appeared as a shapeless black cloud of miasma manifesting itself in a dark corner of the room, rising out of nothing as it were. I wheeled around, and before my very eyes, the black mass took corporeal shape and form. Aghast, I watched in a petrified state of indecision as the baleful spectre materialized into some hideous encroaching monster or demon. Its misshapen head had a ring of five horns like a crown and three eyes, the irises of which were as pitch-black bottomless pits; the corneas were crimson red and burned like coals of fire. It had three gaping orifices or mouths bristling with sharp yellow teeth and fangs dripping with a viscous salivation. Oozing pustules and lesions covered its unctuous hide, and its long sinewy appendages culminated in elongated razor sharp talons. Its demeanor was wrought with murderous malignant intent. It seized him and snatched him up out of the chair. Drafe struggled to free himself from its grappling embrace, but in his weakened state his feeble efforts were to no avail. The monstrous thing's talons ripped his clothes and lacerated his flesh, and one of the mouths bit off and chewed his ear. Taking notice of me, the fiendish thing locked its deathly gaze upon me. I turned my face and covered my eyes too terrified to move, gripped by an extreme fear that can neither fight nor flee. I listened to Drafe's nightmarish screams and cries for help, but they seemed muffled and distant somehow. More out of curiosity than courage, I splayed my fingers and looked back. With Drafe in its inescapable embrace, the demon slunk back into the dark corner of the room, and I watched in astonishing amazement as it started to dematerialize. Both began to vanish. Drafe cried out, 'Under the bed!' And then, 'Don't let them get you JB! Don't let them! They get you in your dreams!' His voice faded away, and then they both congealed into a black vaporous cloud; the cloud diminished to nothing and all that remained was shadow. They were gone – just gone! Complete silence shrouded the room and I was alone. I turned toward the window, to find the face no longer there. Mustering my courage, I opened it, and peered out to see the Negro floating like a feather to the ground as if by magic. I called out to him, but he ignored me, and disappeared into the harbor mist. I tried to collect my thoughts and piece together what had just happened, but I didn't know what to think, I didn't know what to do. I thought about calling the police, but then wondered what I would say. I searched my mind for someone in town who might help me, someone I could trust to be discreet, and so I called Conrad. Professor, everything I just told you is true. That's just the way it happened. I wouldn't believe it myself if I had not the testimony of my own senses."

The Professor reclined back in his seat. "That was quite an eldritch experience," he said. He paused for a moment, stroking his beard. "Obviously Doctor, you are man of sober mind and not one with a proclivity to paranoid delusion. Based on my knowledge, and after my experience today, I am inclined to believe every word. I have extensively researched and studied such phenomena, but until today, I have never had first hand empirical experience. And after what you just told me, I am convinced that we are dealing with nothing less than some dark power – a power of illusion with real consequences. The tablet has some grave mystical purpose, and that, Mr. Blake, is why some nefarious party is so desperately eager to get their hands on it. The sooner we interpret the meaning of the runes, the sooner we will know that purpose. From your account Doctor, I would surmise that Harold was under the influence of a powerful imprecation or curse. I cannot account for his scar or absence of cardiovascular function, but I am knowledgeable of the style of curse that held him captive. It is a dark ritual in which the subject's life essence is transferred to a host object. In this case a doll, which would need to be fashioned of specific materials. Once the ritual is successfully completed, the bearer or holder of the host object can command significant influence, and in some cases, complete control over the subject. The black art associated with this particular enchantment has its roots in West African cultures. The practice of the West African black arts was proliferated to the West Indies by means of the slave trade, and has since been consolidated under the title of voodoo. It has religious significance and is widely practiced in Haiti today." The Professor leaned forward again, looked squarely at JB, and in all earnest said, "As for your baleful spectre, Dr. Hawkins, what preyed upon your friend and my colleague was a protean being, most likely summoned, and perhaps even the servant of a greater power."

"A what?" JB asked with a perplexed expression.

"An ethereal being with the polymorphous ability to change form, shape and appearance at will, and able to transcend space, dimension and even time, a malignant spectral creature of demoniacal origin with powers greater than our own. What you witnessed was an avatar, or physical manifestation of that being. I think we should consign ourselves to the disconcerting supposition that Harold Drayfus is no longer of this world, and we may even be exposing ourselves to the same fate."

I could see that JB was hanging on every word the Professor said.

"That's it. I've heard enough," I strongly interjected.

It seemed to me that the Professor had been stricken by some form of temporary madness, and was now infecting JB.

"With all due respect," I said. "I'm sorry, but this is preposterous. Let's not get carried away. There has to be a rational and logical explanation for all this. People just don't get bagged and butchered by monsters in the night. It just doesn't happen. I stopped believing in monsters under my bed when I was a child."

"On the contrary," the Professor said. "I assure you, such forces do exist. The Bible speaks of God and his angels. Although unseen, we have faith and believe in their existence. I, myself, believe strongly in the omnipresence of the Almighty. Yet there are other tomes, some also of ancient origin, that speak of other gods and hosts of unseen intelligent forces working their machinations. Should we so easily dismiss their existence? Mankind has discovered the x-ray, although invisible to the naked eye, it exists just the same. Let us keep an open and objective mind. Just because you can't understand or explain something, is no reason to deny its reality."

"I don't know about you, but I graduated from the school of hard knocks, and I'll believe it when I see it."

"You're a skeptic, so be it," he said.

The train whistle blew, interrupting, as well as ending our conversation. Our speed declined, and we slowly rolled into Norwich depot.

I stepped out onto the platform for some air, peeling my eyes down the length of the train, scrutinizing every face, but failed to capture even a glimpse of the man I had pursued earlier. As the crowd began to thin out, the whistle sounded again, signaling the train's imminent departure. I felt a hand on my shoulder and turned to see JB.

"Is everything all right?" he asked with that soothing manner attributed to his profession.

"I'm fine," I replied.

"How's your head?"

"I'll live."

"The train is leaving. We had better get on board."

When we returned to our compartment, the Professor was staring out the window deep in thought. We settled in, and JB draped his coat over his lap.

At first, the conversation was light, but eventually it gravitated back to the subject of the tablet. Curious, JB made further inquires of the Professor as to the enigmatic mystery surrounding it. As the Professor began to speak, I realized there was a lot of truth in what he had said earlier, especially about keeping an open and objective mind. In my line of business, objectivity was an axiom one strived to adhere to. I could not discount his reasoning, too many uncanny things were happening. Hoping to gain insight, I listened intently to what he had to say, whether I agreed with it or not.

He had attempted to elucidate its meaning the day before, but could only provide speculations. The discussion only served to peak JB's interest in the subject matter, and the conversation took a slight turn. Responding to JB's fascination, the Professor told us at length of his research in the field of Metaphysics. He told us legends, folklore, and of strange and aberrant ancient beliefs and customs. He spoke of an invisible realm all around us, inhabited by incorporeal forces, both benevolent and malevolent. He quoted from the writings of Cotton Mather and a text he called *The Goetia* and made reference to Kabalistic and Apocryphal writings. He said we have only five senses as means of receiving impressions, yet we fancy to comprehend the boundlessly complex cosmos. JB was captivated by the Professor's words, and even I was quite impressed with the extent of his knowledge on the subject.

We stopped again in New London and then traveled west along the Connecticut coast. By the time we reached New Haven the sun was ebbing below the horizon. Suppertime approached, but a trip to the dining car was out of the question, and I insisted we stay put until we arrived in Manhattan.

"I have the answer to our problem," I said and retrieved Mrs. Coggins basket from the rack.

"What's in the basket?" JB asked.

"Mrs. Coggins packed a meal," I replied. "Help yourselves."

"Very resourceful," the Professor remarked.

The basket held the pieces of an entire baked chicken, a half dozen biscuits and two generous slices of apple pie. She had even packed utensils, plates, and napkins. Inside was a folded note, which read, 'Hope this comes in handy. Enjoy your trip and don't worry about a thing. Bring me a souvenir if you get a chance. You can return the basket upon your homecoming.'

The Professor had started on the first piece of pie, and I was gnawing on a piece of chicken, when the latch turned on the compartment door and it flew open. In a flash, a man slipped inside, shut the door behind him, and stood with his back against it, barring any exit. He wore an overcoat with the collar turned up, and the brim of his hat hung low over his face. He withdrew his right hand from the pocket of his trench coat and brandished a .38 cal revolver. His reckless and brazen action caught me completely by surprise.

He lifted his head slightly, exposing his face, and I looked up into the eyes of Horace Snavely. "I know you're packin' heat Blake, so cough it up slowly and no funny business," he said determinedly.

He kept the .38 pointed squarely at me as I withdrew my Luger from its shoulder holster and handed it to him butt first.

"That's Mister Blake to you," I said stoically as I handed him the Luger.

He took my pistol and slipped it in his coat pocket. Shifting his eyes, he looked at JB, then at the Professor, and back at me.

"The tablet, where is it?!" he demanded. "Five'll get you ten it's right up there," he said, glancing up at the case.

"What tablet?" I replied rather evasively.

"Don't play coy with me, Blake," he shot back. "You have a valuable stone tablet in your possession. My client, who claims to be the rightful owner, has instructed me to obtain it by whatever means necessary, and that's exactly what I intend to do. The bonus is worth a pretty penny to me. Let's just say I'll be retiring to the gentry class." Flailing the revolver, he pistol-whipped me. "I'm not foolin' around!" he belligerently barked.

He then waved the revolver back and forth, pointing it at each of us in turn. He trained the barrel on the Professor, who looked quite shocked. "You're a sentimental guy Blake," Snavely said. "How would you like it if I put a slug in your pudgy friend here? One of you hand it over – now!"

Unbeknownst to us, JB had slipped his hand into the pocket of his overcoat, which was still draped across his lap. He pulled out the nickel-plated .45 automatic I had given him and pointed it straight at Snavely.

" If you shoot the Professor, by God you have my word I'll shoot you," he earnestly avowed with his finger firmly wrapped around the trigger.

His hand was trembling, and I wondered if he had the guts to do it. Even if he did, the safety was on. Snavely was surprised and dismayed by the sudden turn of events. As he looked down the cold barrel of the Colt, his bold confident demeanor melted away and his expression changed to nonplussed consternation.

That slight moment of distraction was all I needed, and I immediately took decisive action. I leapt up from the seat, pouncing upon Snavely, one hand reaching for the wrist of his gun hand and the other balled into a fist. I grabbed Snavely's wrist and dealt him a right cross squarely on the jaw. He reeled from the blow and the revolver discharged, propelling a lead slug into the wall of the compartment, narrowly missing the Professor. A simultaneous blow of the train whistle masked the crack of the revolver. We grappled, tumbling into the seat beside the Professor. Locked in a pitched struggle, we wrestled for control of the revolver. Back and forth we tussled, until with sheer brute strength, I wrestled him down, pinning his gun hand. I punched him in the face and then grasped him by the throat. I had his scrawny neck in a vice grip and started to squeeze the very life out of him. He grabbed my wrist, twisting and wrenching it, and making every determined effort to wrest loose my constricting grasp. His face turned red and his eyes began to bulge from their sockets. He released my wrist, reached down into the pocket of his trench coat, and gripped the handle of my Luger. He drew out the pistol, and pressing the barrel into my gut, started to squeeze the trigger.

With not a fraction of an instant to spare, the Professor smashed his plate over Snavely's head. Snavely went limp, releasing his grip on the Luger, and it dropped to the floor. JB reached into his medical bag, pulled out a bottle of chloroform, and poured some of the liquid onto his handkerchief. Only stunned and dazed, Snavely began to recover, and I pinned his arms while JB smothered his mouth and nostrils with the handkerchief. Snavely had no choice but to inhale the anesthetizing fumes, and after a brief but futile struggle, he sank into unconsciousness.

We propped him up in the seat, with his cocked head leaning on the wall. I unloaded and pocketed his .38, then conducted a thorough search of his pockets, relieving him of a stiletto, but not a shred of information as to the identity of his client could be found on his person.

"How long will he stay like that?" I asked.

"He'll remain in that pacified state for at least a couple of hours," JB replied.

"Who is this despicable hooligan?" the Professor asked.

"Professor, let me introduce you to a lowdown rapscallion named Horace Snavely," I said, extending my hand toward Snavely.

Now that the present danger had been subdued, I became aware of a throbbing pain on my cheek; and much to my discomfort, JB tended to the wound Snavely had inflicted with his pistol whipping. Meanwhile, the Professor picked up the scattered shards of plate and spilled remnants of our meal.

"Thanks Professor, it was a good thing you intervened when you did. For a brief moment there, things looked terribly bleak. All things considered, no one will blame you if you want to back out. Seems the fat's in the fire, and it's only going to get hotter."

"Mr. Blake, you underestimate me," he said, adjusting his bowtie and gathering his composure. "Harold Drayfus was my colleague and a most promising anthropologist and archaeologist. His fieldwork would have accomplished great feats in learning. I am more resolved now than ever to unravel the mystery of the runes and ascertain the purpose of the tablet, and my determination to discover the reason for Harold's premature demise only strengthens that resolve."

I had to respect a man who would stick it out after today's events.

"All right then," I said. "The sooner we get that God awful thing to the Royal Society, the better we'll sleep at night."

A brief quiet ensued while I pondered what to do about Snavely.

JB broke the silence. "Wasn't it Machiavelli who said 'Keep your friends close and your enemies even closer'?"

"You're absolutely correct," the Professor affirmed. "And from where I'm sitting, I can't say as I've seen a more poignant demonstration of that principle."

We had a good chuckle at Snavely's expense, which helped to ease the tension.

The train wheeled to a stop just outside of Bridgeport, and we were looking at each other with questioning expressions, when the door opened and the conductor poked his head inside.

"Another train is in the depot. We'll be stopped here for a few minutes. Sorry for the delay gentlemen," he said and closed the door.

He hadn't taken notice of Snavely, and we breathed a sigh of relief.

"We still need to decide what to do concerning the disposition of this man," the Professor said, looking at Snavely.

A northbound freight train sat motionless on a parallel track, and eyeing a boxcar, I suddenly had a notion.

"Help me get him up," I directed JB.

Looking out the window, he quickly deduced my intentions. "You're not going to…?"

"Oh yes I am, and you're going to help me."

Together, we got Snavley up from the seat and braced him between us. Luckily, we were able to slip outside unnoticed, and concealed by the cloak of evening darkness, we half-carried, half-dragged him to the opposite side of the boxcar and out of sight.

His floppy bulk rested on the cold ground while I removed the pin from the hasp and opened the door to an empty car.

"Take him by the ankles," I whispered, and at the count of three, we heaved him up into the opening, and he landed on the dirty floor of the boxcar with a thud.

"I think someone's coming," JB warned.

The distinctive crunch of footfalls on the gravel came nearer, and with the threat of detection looming, I slid the door closed and replaced the pin in the hasp.

Get your pipe out and fill it," I said.

A watchman carrying a club checked the door to the next car and then proceeded in our direction.

"Light your pipe and act natural," I whispered. "I'll do the talking."

JB lit a match and put it to his pipe, illuminating our faces. The watchman took immediate notice. He opened the shutter on the lantern he carried and directed the beam at us.

"Nothing like crisp night air, wouldn't you say Doctor," I said aloud.

The watchman approached. "You there, what are you doing here?" he demanded.

"My companion and I are passengers on the other train," I said, producing my ticket. "Our train is stalled due to congestion on the tracks ahead. We've been cooped up in a compartment most of the day, so we came out to stretch our legs and get some air."

JB puffed his pipe.

"By the way, I'm Conrad Blake and this is Dr. Hawkins," I said, smiling.

JB nodded.

"Les Driscoll," the watchman replied.

"Pleased to meet you Les. Going about your rounds?" I said amicably.

"Yep."

"It's a pleasant evening, isn't it?"

"It would be, if I didn't have to continually roust out the riffraff. Why just several cars back aways, I chased off a couple of freeloadin' hobos. Had to give one of 'em a little persuasion with Annie here," he said, tapping the club on his thigh.

"I'm sure you have enough to do without having to deal with the riffraff," I said.

"You bet, mister," he said, checking the door to the boxcar. "You fellows really should get back to your coach. It was dangerous to cross the tracks, especially at night. Be careful going back."

"We'll do that," I said.

A sharp blow of the train whistle permeated the late evening air.

"You had better be on your way," the watchman said.

I bid him a cordial good evening, JB knocked out his pipe on the rail, and we started across the tracks.

"Go on ahead, I'll be right along," I said. "I've got to go back and remove the pin. I didn't want anyone to get wise, so I secured the door. We can't leave Snavely to rot and perish in a locked boxcar. That's a fate too cruel even for him."

JB jogged back to our coach, while I peered out from between the cars and waited for the watchman to go out of sight. When he was out of earshot, I quickly strode back to the boxcar door, removed the pin from the hasp, and slid the door open a foot. Hastening back to our coach, I had just rounded the corner of the boxcar, and was starting to cross the tracks, when our train lurched forward and began to roll. I jumped the coupler and raced toward the coach. JB stood on the steps with a handhold on the railing, gesturing with the other hand for me to move along.

"Come on Conrad! Come on!" he shouted over the rattle of the train.

I sprinted in an effort to race the accelerating train and catch up to the steps just a few feet away. With a last-ditch burst of speed, I reached the steps, and at a running pace, I clutched the railing and hoisted myself up. JB grabbed hold of my leather trench coat to keep me from falling backwards.

"Whew, that was a close one," I said.

As the train rolled onward, we stood on the steps, watching the boxcar wane out of sight, assured that Horace Snavely would be out of our hair, at least for a while.

We arrived at Grand Central Station in the heart of Manhattan without further mishap. I convinced the Professor that it was best to change his accommodations and stay at the Barbizon Plaza with JB and I. I didn't want to take any chance of him being harmed or ransomed for the tablet. I hailed a taxi just outside the station on 42nd and Park Avenue. We loaded our belongings and climbed in. As the cabby pulled out and we headed west on 42nd Street, I noticed another taxi following close behind. After a couple of blocks, our cabby turned north on Fifth Avenue. The other taxi turned and stayed with us. We drove up Fifth Avenue for at least a dozen blocks, with the other taxi behind us all the way. Our cabby turned left and pulled over in front of a grand hotel. The other taxi stopped at the intersection, and after waiting for a break in traffic, turned down the same street. I stepped out of the cab and eyed the other taxi, half expecting it to pull in behind us. Instead, I watched as it slowly rolled past, then sped up down the block.

CHAPTER 6

I stood on the sidewalk in a silent daze, while my companions, unaware of my observation, solicited the assistance of the bellhops. They were halfway to the entrance when I heard JB's voice behind me. "Are you coming Conrad? What's keeping you?"

With my mind elsewhere, I followed our entourage, bellhops and all, through the front entrance. A doorman in regal uniform welcomed us to the plaza, and we entered a palatial lobby with plush furnishings and marble columns that rose to a decorative ceiling adorned with the sparkling light of crystal chandeliers. At the front desk, we checked in and signed the hotel register. The hotel was happy to make accommodations for the Professor, affording him a connecting room. JB inquired with the clerk concerning our boat passages, and a well-attired man behind the counter stepped forward.

"Allow me to be of assistance gentlemen. I am Mr. Strathmore, the manager," He said with a welcoming smile. He looked at our names in the register. "Ah yes, the hotel is holding two passages on the liner America for you. You may pick them up upon your departure in the morning. Please enjoy our hospitality for tonight and have a pleasant evening. Your rooms are on the ninth floor and have a commanding view of Central Park. If I can be of service, just ring the front desk."

"Please take these gentlemen to their rooms," he said, handing the keys to a bellhop.

We boarded an electric lighted elevator enclosed by dark wood paneling and furnished with brass handrails; and with the turn of a lever, the operator started our ascent to the ninth floor, where the bellhops conducted us to our accommodating suites. Once inside, they opened the connecting doors between the rooms and politely asked if we needed anything else, before departing with a generous tip from JB.

I hid the case under my bed; and after a bit of unpacking, we decided to order a late supper from room service. While we waited, we discussed what plans we should make concerning the tablet once we were aboard ship. The Professor advised placing it in the ship's vault. That way, we would be free to move about the ship without the burden of having to keep an eye on it. As for any danger that might present itself, we would just need to be vigilant. JB and I agreed with his reasoning, and we considered the matter resolved.

Half an hour had passed when a knock at the door announced the arrival of room service. I answered, and a waiter wheeled a dinner cart into the room. He removed the sterling domed plate covers, releasing an appetizing aroma, and arranged the place settings on a table.

"Just leave the cart in the hall when you're finished," he said.

JB signed the bill, and anticipating a welcome interval of repose, we sat down to enjoy a fine meal; but the day still held yet another unforeseen surprise. As JB opened his cloth napkin, a folded piece of paper fell out and dropped into his lap.

"What's this?" he remarked, picking it up and unfolding it.

Once opened, it was about the size of a postcard. Puzzled and speechless, he stared at it for a few moments and then handed it to me without saying a word. I was fully expecting it to be a written note, but it turned out to be something entirely different. It was a drawing – an ominous design composed of symbols and geometric shapes. Two concentric circles bordered a band of inscrutable writing that ringed a triangle. Positioned in the apex of the triangle, a menacing eye projected its gaze, and below the eye, in the center of the triangle was a square with three symbols within: an oil lamp, a hand, and a circle with a protruding line. I held it up to the light, but the parchment revealed no watermark; and failing to otherwise make heads or tails of the thing, I handed it to the Professor.

He donned his spectacles and scrutinized the drawing for some time. Our meals grew cold, as JB and I, preoccupied with this new development, eyed him in anticipation.

"This is an allegorical design of magical significance, and it was made with a grave and sinister purpose in mind," he grimly assessed, leaning back in his chair. "These occult runes summon destruction, while the remainder consists of symbolic representations. The circle symbolizes eternity, no beginning, no end, and encompasses the macrocosm, the whole of the complex cosmos. The triangle represents the number three, symbolizing the spiritual element. At the top of the hierarchic order is the omnispective eye, not portrayed as the all-seeing eye of providence, but as I have seen in the works of forbidden cults. Below, the square portrays the material dimension in which we reside, and I fear the symbols within are representative of the three men sitting at this table. Let us speculate. The lamp is a symbol pertaining to knowledge – a professor perhaps? The hand – could it be the hand of healing, the hand of a physician? And the last symbol depicts a magnifying glass, the tool of a detective. This thing is designed for no other purpose than to bring some dreadful malediction upon us, and if I am not mistaken, it has been drawn in blood. Whoever the maker, he possesses extensive knowledge of the black arts. I would highly advise against eating or drinking anything from the cart."

By now, JB was in a state of utter dismay. His eyes grew wide with panic. "They know where we are. They're going to get us – just like they got Drafe. What are we going to do Conrad?"

I put a reassuring hand on his shoulder. "For starters, we're not going to lose our heads over some bad doodling," I calmly said. "A piece of paper can't hurt you. I need you JB. And I need you in an objective frame of mind."

"You're right," he remorsefully said. "But I don't mind telling you I'm scared – really scared. Now I know how Drafe must have felt."

"Don't trouble yourself," I said. "Today's events were enough to frazzle anyone's nerves. We should be safe once we're out of the country. Besides, a transatlantic voyage and some fresh sea air will do us all a world of good."

"Mr. Blake is absolutely correct Doctor," the Professor said, exhibiting his peculiarly sympathetic smile. "We must maintain our composure and remain objective. This may simply be a means to rattle us, and nothing more. However, I have to admit it did the trick," he confessed, his smile fading.

I requested another look at the damnable thing, and once it was in my hand, I walked over to the nightstand by the bed, put it to the match, and dropped it in an ashtray.

"So much for the boogie man," I said.

Deep crimson flames sputtered and sparked, and emitted wisps of acrid smoke that swiftly filled the room.

"That could have repercussions," the Professor warned, getting up to open the window.

As the smoldering remnants crumbled into ashes, a blast of bitter cold air came streaming through the open aperture. The curtains billowed, and the frigid gust whiffed through my hair, chilling me to the bone and sending a shudder coursing through my veins from head to toe. The Professor opened his mouth to speak, but I stayed his words with a look.

"Just a burst of December wind, nothing more," I adamantly declared, and I shut the window.

Looking at his pocket watch, the Professor remarked as to the hour and recommended the remedy of sleep. Our untasted fares were returned to the cart, which was wheeled out into the hall; and after locking all the outer doors and securing the windows, we retired to our respective rooms for the night, leaving the connecting doors open. I tucked my Luger under the pillow before getting into bed; a smart man hedges his bets, and I was not taking any chances.

My mind raced. Sleep escaped me. This was one of the most bizarre cases to cross my path, and I was in it up to my ears. My thoughts were racked with speculation as I kept reviewing the elements of it over and over in my mind. It all boiled down to the tablet. What was so important about an etched block of stone? Thinking back on the day, I wondered if today's events were a portentous token of what lay ahead. Despite my stoic façade, I was becoming increasingly concerned for my own welfare, as well as my companions.

I mulled things over for what seemed like hours. Finally, I started to drift off, but peculiar scratching sounds emanating from JB's room brought me to full alertness. I got on my feet, donned my robe, and stealthily tread a path through the darkness. As I neared JB's room, the sounds became more audible and distinct. Pausing in the doorway, I heard a harsh grating – a clawing – and it was coming from the window! The sounds sent shivers up my spine, like the scraping of nails on a chalkboard, and soon another sound was distinctly apparent amidst the grating – the sound of flapping wings. But what shocked me was the staggering sight of a stirring bestial shadow silhouetted on the shade. I wondered if it could simply be the shadow of a bird magnified by the moonlight, but the sheer size of it made that supposition highly improbable. Disturbed by the awesome sight and the growing sounds, I frantically clambered in the dark to find the light switch. The window creaked and snapped, and I thought surely it would break open at any moment, when, by sheer luck, my fingers tripped the switch, illuminating the room, and the sounds abruptly ceased.

Out of bed and in his nightshirt, JB stood paralyzed with his back riveted against the wall, his brow overlaid with beads of perspiration, too terrified to utter a word. I put my finger to my lips, indicating silence, and waited for a moment, but the only audible impression was the late autumn wind whistling in the window. Suddenly, I realized that my Luger was still in its place under the pillow. Nevertheless, I gathered my fortitude and approached the window. Eyes wide, JB shook his head back and forth in quick motions with a look that begged me to stop. Swallowing my spit, I opened the shade and breathed a comic sigh of relief as I gazed at the reflection of my own unshaven mug in the window. I thought JB would fly into a panic when I opened the window and poked my head out to have a look. Initially, only the night and the city lights presented themselves, but then I noticed them – inexplicable gashes on the sill and frame.

"There's nothing here," I said, not wanting to alarm JB any further.

He went limp and slid down the wall to a sitting position with his knees up.

"What's all the hubbub?" the Professor asked, now standing in the doorway.

"I'm investigating a noise we heard coming from the window," I said.

"Is the Doctor in distress?"

"He'll be all right. Would you come over here please? There's something I'd like you to take a look at."

The Professor came over to the window, and I pointed out the marks.

"What do you make of this?" I asked.

He examined the sill and frame, and what he saw brought an expression of consternation to his face. He took one glance at JB and then looked at me with a twinge of fear in his eyes. "I'm not sure what to make of them. They appear to be claw marks," he whispered.

After having viewed the deep parallel gashes myself, I simply nodded concordantly.

JB must have overheard. Dispirited, he held his head between his hands. "They're going to get us. That's how they got Drafe. They're going to get us, just like they got him. What have I gotten myself into? Oh, what perilous state of affairs have I gotten us all into?"

I knelt down beside him. "Sometimes life deals you a bad card," I compassionately said. "It's how you play your hand that counts.

Nobody has got us yet, and rest assured they're not going to. JB, I want you to remember you're not alone. We're in this together. I give you my word, that if anyone endangers your life, they'll have to get through me first." Whimsically I said, "I'm sure that we're making too much of this. It was probably just a flock of pigeons pecking at the window."

But I knew what I had heard and seen, and it was no pigeon.

JB came to his senses and stood up. "I think I'll be all right now. Thank you for your kind reassuring words and your attempt to allay my anxiety," he said soberly. He looked at me out of the corner of his eye. "But we both know that wasn't a flock of pigeons in the window. You'll never convince me of that."

The Professor closed and latched the window, while JB walked over to the desk and picked up the telephone receiver.

"Who are you going to ring?" I asked.

"I'm going to ring Mr. Strathmore, and arrange for a change of rooms," JB replied.

"That won't be necessary. Besides, there are just a few more hours 'til daylight. I'll switch rooms with you, if it will make you feel more at ease."

"That would do fine," he assented with a sigh, placing the receiver back in the cradle. "No matter though, I don't think I'll be able to sleep a wink for the rest of the night," he said, lowering himself into the desk chair.

"Do you have a sedative in your bag? That might do the trick."

"Yes. It's over there," he said, pointing to the bureau.

I fetched his bag, while the Professor poured a glass of water. JB removed a corked vial from the bag and dissolved a measure of the contents in the glass.

"The problem is, I'm afraid to go to sleep," he said, staring with apprehension at the concoction in his hand.

"Nothing is going to happen, and if it does, I'll be in the next room," I assured him.

He tipped the glass to his lips, and while he imbibed the concoction, I excused myself to my room, ambled over to the bed and casually slipped my Luger into the pocket of my robe.

I returned to the doorway with my hands in my pockets. "Let's get some rest," I said.

I switched rooms with JB and waited for their lights to extinguish before turning out my own. I did not go to bed. Instead, I settled into a chair to wait out the night. After a while, JB's rhythmic breathing indicated he was in a peaceful slumber. At times I felt drowsy and began to nod off, but the Professor's occasional snoring always stirred me to consciousness again.

All was quiet for quite some time with only the occasional footfalls or voices passing in the hallway; until one time, the footfalls came to a halt outside the door. The silhouettes of two feet broke the sliver of light under the door, casting parallel shadows on the floor. I got up and took up a position to one side of the door, my bare feet moving silently across the carpet. I stood ready and silent, my hand in the pocket of my robe gripping the handle of my Luger. The keyhole went black. Was someone spying through the keyhole? After a few brief moments, a faint light reappeared in the keyhole, followed by a jiggling of the doorknob. I knew what was coming next and acted to prevent it. I braced myself against the door and inserted my room key in the lock, holding it in place to thwart any intrusion from the opposite side. The click of the key sliding into the lock alerted the intruder to my presence; the shadows under the door disappeared, and the cushioned clamor of footfalls briskly receded away.

Deciding not to give chase, I returned to the chair and remained at my post, keeping vigilant watch until the first glimmering rays of sunrise struck the shades. By then, I was physically and mentally exhausted. My thoughts were fragmented and my faculties had waned considerably. I took a cold bath and shaved. The razor in my unsteady hand nicked my face in several places. I donned a fresh suit, packed, and when the time came, roused my companions from sleep. JB took one look at my haggard face and saw through my façade.

"You stayed awake all night, didn't you?" he asked.

"Yes, and I'm in no mood to quibble about it. We've got a boat to catch. I'll arrange for a taxi," I said.

While JB and the Professor prepared for the day, I rang the front desk and arranged for a taxi to drive us to the pier. I asked the operator to connect me with Boston and gave Cindy a ring to tell her we had arrived and everything was ok, but there was no answer. It being early, she probably had not arrived at the office yet, and I considered it no cause for worry. We decided to forego ordering breakfast on the premise that it might be an unwise invitation for a repeat of last night's episode.

When all was ready, I rang the front desk, and shortly thereafter, a couple of eager young bellhops showed up at the door. Under the scrutiny of my watchful eyes, they went about their business gathering up our baggage. Downstairs, I purchased a newspaper at the stand in the lobby and scanned the surroundings, while JB settled our bill and paid for our passages at the front desk. The doorman bid us a cordial good morning as we stepped out into the bright sunshine, and then he ushered us to a taxi waiting at the curb. The bellhops loaded up our baggage, JB tipped them, and we set off for the pier.

The cabby steered along city streets buzzing with traffic. Manhattan's vertical structures blotted out the morning sun, and as we passed by, they drifted off behind us, one being replaced with another. I gave the cabby the once over and then gazed out the back window, looking for any evidence of a tail. Nothing conspicuous presented itself, so I settled into the seat and relaxed for the remainder of the drive.

At the pier the liner America came into full view. She was an eyeful, a noble behemoth of a vessel with her proud stacks reaching to the sky. We weaved our way through the throng, boarded the gangplank, and an assistant purser gave us directions. JB and I had adjoining staterooms and the Professor's cabin was a short distance down the corridor. I asked the Professor to join us once he had unpacked, then opened the door and stepped into my stateroom. Despite its regal appearance and private bath, the first thing I noticed was a welcoming bed beckoning me. I locked the door and plopped the case on the foot of the bed. Exhaustion had taken its toll. Beat and played out, I loosened my tie, tumbled onto the bed, and collapsed into unconsciousness.

CHAPTER 7

When I returned to the waking world, time had changed everything. The last glimmering rays of the setting sun softly filtered through the curtained aperture, dimly illuminating the room with a soft gold and red hue. The bed swayed in a slow, gentle motion. My feet were no longer propped up on the case. In fact, it was gone altogether. Where the case had once been was now an empty space. I leapt up in alarm and immediately took in my surroundings at a glance. Nothing appeared to be amiss. My suitcase had been placed atop the bureau, but the case containing the tablet was nowhere to be seen. The door connecting JB's room was open and the lights were out.

Not knowing what to expect, I passed through the connecting doorway and turned on the lights, illuminating an empty room. JB's traveling trunk was open, a black bow tie hung from a hook on the mirror frame, and his tuxedo lay neatly upon the bed. Despite the normality of outward appearances, was all as it seemed to be? Returning to my room, I spied a piece of writing paper atop the bureau. A handwritten note on the ship's stationary read: "Conrad, The case has been securely placed in the ship's vault. The Professor and I have gone out to promenade on deck and tour the ship. We shall not be terribly long – JB." It was unmistakably JB's handwriting, and a whirlwind of harrowing thoughts dismissed themselves.

Hungry, I went in search of a cup of coffee and a bite to eat. I accosted a passing steward, who politely recommended the Terrace Café for its view and gave me directions. On the way, I happened to pass by a nightclub named the 'Blue Trumpet Lounge'. From inside, the symphonic sounds of a piano tweaked my ears. A tranquil classical melody was being played masterfully. The sweet tones piqued my curiosity, and I took a detour through the door into an establishment devoid of patrons.

"We're not open for business yet," said the man behind the bar.

I set my eyes on the source of the tender music. Sitting behind a grand piano was Dr. JB Hawkins, his long slender fingers gliding over the keys like a skillful skater on a frozen pond, his arms ebbing and flowing with the gentle rhythm of the music. The professor was sitting on the piano bench beside him, his eyes closed, and his head mildly swaying. JB acknowledged me with a smile and a nod, all the while continuing to play his melody. I approached and stood by the piano until he had finished his piece.

"I find it to be an efficacious remedy for relaxing the nerves," he said, after the last note had drifted away.

The Professor raised his eyelids and was a bit startled to see me.

"So you're awake I see," he said. "He makes the piano sing marvelously, wouldn't you say, Mr. Blake? What bravura, I never knew the Doctor had such talent."

"He does at that," I said assertively.

JB toyed with the keys. "Here's one for you," he said, and then he let loose with a short ragtime rendition.

"Did you find my note?" he asked, taking his hands from the keyboard.

"Yes I did."

"You were dead to the world. You even slept through the lifeboat drill."

"It was upon the good Doctor's recommendation that we let you sleep," the Professor said. "As for the case, I can assure you it is secure. The Doctor rented a safe deposit vault. It will require both the Doctor's key and one held by the trustee to access it, as well as the Doctor's signature. By the way, I understand that you remained awake the entire night on our account – quite commendable of you."

JB reached into the pocket of his trousers and presented me with a key.

"I think you should be the one to hold onto this," he said, handing it to me.

"I was on my way to get a bite to eat," I said. "Would you both like to join me?"

"The dining saloon will be serving dinner soon. Why don't you join us?" JB asked.

"That's the best offer I've had all day. You got yourself a deal," I replied.

The Professor opened his pocket watch. "And it's about time we were getting ready."

That night we lived the life of Reilly. Champagne and liquor flowed like water, and we enjoyed a sumptuous meal. We shared a table and light conversation with Edgar and Harriet Vandegraf, an amiable middle-aged couple on their way to spend the holidays with their son and daughter-in-law living in Sussex. They would be seeing their grandson for the first time, and Mrs. Vandegraf was obviously overjoyed at the prospect. Mr. Vandegraf and the professor both shared a passion for the game of chess and agreed to a match at sometime during the voyage. After dinner, we returned to JB's stateroom, where we whiled away the evening in good spirits, consuming several nightcaps and playing card games.

As a precaution, I slept with my Luger under the pillow again, but the dark shades of night passed quiescently. When I awoke, the bright golden rays of the morning sun filled the room, giving me the impression that all was well and any danger was behind us.

As I shaved, the mirror told me that the laceration on my cheek was healing nicely. The bump on my head was receding too. I donned casual attire and wore the sweater Mrs. Coggins had knitted for my birthday. JB knocked at the door connecting our staterooms, and presently he stood in the doorway, looking well rested. In a pleasant disposition, he bid me good morning with a smile. He said he was going to drop in on the Professor and would meet me shortly for breakfast.

As he exited, he turned in the doorway. "You said we'd be safe once we were at sea. By all indications, it seems you were right," he said.

Upon leaving my stateroom, I stopped to lock the door; and as I reached my hand into my pocket to retrieve the key, my fingers touched a folded piece of paper. At first I thought it might be a laundry ticket or a note I had forgotten, but its peculiar texture had a familiarity to it. With great trepidation, I pulled it out. The paper was of the same color, grade and texture as the one with the drawing we had received two nights ago at the hotel. I unfolded it, and my heart skipped a beat as I gazed upon an identical drawing. Resolving not to let a piece of paper intimidate me, I gathered my wits and shoved it back into my pocket. En route to breakfast, I stepped outside to the railing, wadded it up, and tossed it overboard.

In the dining saloon, JB and the Professor were already seated at a table, conversing and drinking coffee, and I joined them.

"Good morning, Mr. Blake," the Professor said amicably. "Did you sleep well?"

"Well enough, thank you."

As I took a seat, JB looked at me with concern. "You look troubled. Is everything all right?" he inquired.

"Everything's fine," I calmly said, pouring myself a cup of coffee from the sterling pot on the table.

Their demeanor and conversation during breakfast exhibited all the essence of normality. It was quite apparent that I was the only one to receive the ominous message. I pondered how and when it had been planted and deliberated whether or not to reveal this recent discovery to my companions. After debating between my concern for their safety and the need to avoid causing any unnecessary anxiety, I decided to keep silent for the time being.

JB and the Professor shared their itineraries for the day. The Professor planned to visit the ship's library and spend a quiet day in his room with a good book. Being Sunday, JB wanted to attend mass in the ship's chapel, and then enjoy an invigorating swim in the indoor pool before lunch. Before departing our separate ways, we agreed to meet for lunch at the Terrace Café.

Deciding to take a sobering promenade on deck, I returned to my stateroom to fetch my coat. Outside the door, I thrust my hand into my pocket and struck upon an all too familiar object – a folded piece of paper. Perturbed, I drew it forth and unfolded it. Except for being crinkled, it was the same paper, the same drawing! How did it get there, and how could someone have slipped it into my pocket without me noticing? To be the same one was impossible. Earlier, I had watched with my own eyes as it disappeared amongst the rising and ebbing swells, certain to be left far behind in the wake. Were my senses playing tricks on me?

I poured myself a shot from the bottle on the bureau. The uncanny aspects of this quandary puzzled me deeply; and alone in my stateroom, I ruminated on it for some time. No plausible answers came to mind; and the more I deliberated, the more I realized the need to share this recent development with my companions. And I knew to whom I should speak with first – the Professor.

I found him in his stateroom, sitting in a comfortable chair and reading a leather-bound volume.

"Why hello Mr. Blake. Please have a seat," he said, looking up over his spectacles. "Is there something I can do for you?"

Maintaining my composure, I pulled out the chair from the writing desk and sat down without saying a word.

He looked at me inquisitively. "What is it Mr. Blake?"

"This," I simply said, taking the paper from my pocket and laying it out on the desktop.

He closed the volume and came over for a closer look.

"I found it in the pocket of my trousers earlier this morning when I departed for breakfast."

He looked at the enigmatic drawing and raised one eyebrow. "Great Caesar's ghost!" he exclaimed, and then with a pensive expression, he backpedaled to his chair and eased into it. "Does the Doctor know of this?" he asked.

"No – not yet. I thought it would be prudent to discuss the matter with you first. As far as I'm concerned, it's a harmless doodle. What I'm itching to know, is who planted it? I speculate that it must have been planted while we were at dinner last night, which leads me to believe the anonymous sender is on board, and that is cause for concern. However, something uncanny occurred that left me scratching my head, a paradox that defies deductive reasoning."

"I see. Pray continue," he said.

"I'm sure you noted that the paper is creased and crinkled."

"Yes I did."

"Well, that's what has me puzzled. When I first discovered it, it was cleanly folded. On my way to breakfast, I crumpled it up into a wad and tossed it overboard. I saw it plunge into the sea with my own eyes; but when I returned to my stateroom after breakfast, it was still in my pocket, folded like before, and crinkled as if it had been wadded up. I have interacted with no one but yourself and JB thus far today. Whomever it is, must be a magician, because I can't figure out how they're doin' it. This sort of thing seems to be your bailiwick, Professor. What's your opinion?"

"First, I'm not sure I share your assertion in regards to the innocuous nature of the malevolent charm."

He paused for a few moments, stroking his beard in thought.

"Allow me to hypothesize," he continued. "I suggest we try an experiment, which will prove beyond peradventure whether or not this is the same charm you discarded earlier. If so, we are dealing with stronger magic than I first supposed. I will escort you to the railing at the far end of the stern. There you will discard it as before, both of us witnessing the act. We will then return here and wait for a period of time. How long was it between the time you discarded it and when you rediscovered it?"

"About three quarters of an hour, I'd say."

"Then that is how long we shall wait, checking the contents of your pockets periodically during the interim. We'll see what develops, then proceed from there."

He paused and gave me a look that solicited a response.

"I can't think of a better means to answer the question," I said. "At this point, I'm game for just about anything."

"Then let's be about it."

We departed, and after stopping by my stateroom to fetch my coat, made our way to the stern of the vessel. Standing at the railing, with a cold North Atlantic wind buffeting our faces, we executed the Professor's scheme. I drew forth the drawing and a two-bit coin. I crumpled the paper around the coin to weight it down and then cast it into the churning wake. We both observed its descent and subsequent immersion in the swirling foam, then we returned to the Professor's stateroom, all the while being cognizant of our surroundings and vigilant not to come in close contact with anyone.

Inside the Professor's stateroom, we shed our coats, and I settled into the chair at the writing desk. The Professor detached his pocket watch from its chain, opened it, and set it on the desktop.

"Note the time. We shall wait approximately fifteen minutes. I believe that should be sufficient time before initially testing our hypothesis," he said, and then he lowered himself into his chair.

Minutes passed like hours as I listened to the ticking of the watch. Looking at the face to note the passage of time, I noticed an engraved symbol on the inside of the watch cover, a golden cross with a red cross in its center set against the background of a rose bloom and encircled by an inscription in Latin, which read 'Frater Crusis Rosae'.

"Almost time," I said, interrupting the uneasy silence.

"How much time is left?"

"Two minutes."

"We'll wait."

They were two of the longest minutes I could recall. My mouth was dry as a desert; I was keenly aware of each breath I drew and every beat of my heart was made manifest.

When the minute hand finally marked the allotted time, I stood up. "Time's up. Let's get this over with," I said.

"I suggest you commence with the pocket where you first discovered the charm," he said with a most inquisitive expression.

My heart raced furiously as I slowly slipped my hand into the pocket of my trousers. Anticipating to find only my room key, my composed demeanor changed to a state of consternation and disbelief, and the Professor's eyes widened, as I pulled out and unfolded the same crinkled piece of paper. A two-bit coin fell out and dropped to the floor.

"It is as I feared," the Professor said.

Flabbergasted, I let loose with a heavy sigh and sank back into my chair. I offered the charm to him for examination, but he refused to touch it and asked me to lay it on the desktop.

He produced a magnifying glass and scrutinized the markings closely. "If I am not mistaken, the deviations in the blood-drawn lines are identical," he said.

He handed me the glass.

"See for yourself," he said. "This is the exact same charm we received at the hotel. Which means the sender may or may not be on board."

"But I burned the thing."

"Apparently, that was ineffective against its magic. You were also the last one to touch it."

"What's that got to do with it?"

"That is precisely why it invariably returns to you."

"You've got to be kidding," I said.

"No, Mr. Blake, I am quite serious," he said, returning to his chair.

His words left me perplexed. The Professor's rationale was a departure from my line of reasoning, but I recognized the need to remain objective.

"What sort of people are we dealing with here?" I asked.

"We are dealing with nefarious minds devoid of sane reasoning, at least as you or I understand it to be, and one cannot fathom the workings of such minds. No benevolence or good can come from delving into the black arts. Black magic is rooted in the darkest levels of the mind. Thus, in my opinion, they are individuals consumed with a desire for power, and their motives can only be evil. We both know what they're after, and I believe it is imperative that we prevent them from obtaining it."

He gazed at me over his spectacles with resolute eyes. "Mr. Blake, I have a supposition in reference to the charm. Would you like to hear it?"

"I'm all ears, Professor."

He stood up, and began slowly pacing back and forth, his hands grasping the lapels of his suit jacket.

"It is an instrument of summoning – a beacon. Think of it as a lighthouse, which as seen from the ethereal, lights a course to our physical plane. A balefire luring some malignant supernatural entity to its intended victim like a moth to a flame."

He stopped pacing and looked squarely at me.

"Based upon this premise and my knowledge of the subject-matter, I dare say that you, Mr. Blake, will be first to fall victim," he said, and he continued his pacing.

"I will admit something uncanny is going on," I said skeptically. "But I'm not going to be frightened by a bunch of hocus-pocus. I've been in tighter jams than this, in which the danger was real."

"I make no pretense. I assure you the danger is quite real," he said earnestly. "In fact, if my supposition is correct, we are all in grave danger, for the charm's magic is intended to befall all three of us – you, me, and the good Doctor. You will simply be the first to be subjected to its malevolent power."

"So when do you suppose this so-called entity is going to nab me?"

"I cannot be certain, but the longer the charm is in your possession, the greater and more imminent the danger becomes."

The Professor was a man of sound intellect and not a novice on the subject. My intuition told me it would be wise to heed his words.

"What if you're wrong about me being the first?" I asked.

"I have made a conjecture based on supposition. It is possible that one of us may be targeted randomly. But I am fairly certain of the charm's primary purpose."

He ceased his pacing, then turned and looked at me as if he had already deduced my next question. Before I could open my mouth to speak, he answered it for me.

"You can relax your concern for the Doctor. He is in the chapel attending mass and should be safe for the time being."

"Is there no respite from this thing?"

"Yes. Its power can be exorcised."

"How?"

He returned to his chair, reclined back and stroked his beard.

Looking at nothing in particular, he said, "If my memory serves me correctly, I recall a litany or incantation which will render its power impotent. Unfortunately, I cannot recall the exact text and I do not have the pertinent reference materials with me. Even if I did, it requires a material component, one which we do not possess – holy water."

Those last two words jogged my memory, and the drive back from Cambridge came to mind.

"Dr. Hawkins has holy water," I said with an expression of recollection.

"Are you certain?"

"On the drive back from our first meeting at the museum, JB asked to stop at St. Mary's. A priest he spoke with gave him a vial of it."

"Does he have it with him?"

"Most likely."

"We must be certain. It would constitute our trump card. Mr. Blake, we might yet be able to achieve our aim of obliterating this cursed thing," he stated.

A pensive expression fell over his face, and after a brief period of silence, he continued, "We must act with expedience. May I suggest a course of action?"

"By all means," I said agreeably.

"Find the Doctor and stay with him. The chapel would be a good place to start. Ascertain if he has the vial with him. In the meantime, I will see what the ship's library has to offer. Then I will meet you and the Doctor for lunch at the appointed time."

"Very well, Professor, we'll play it your way."

"I would advise you to keep to public areas and be on your guard. I cannot emphasize enough the danger you face. We are dealing with forces greater than ourselves, and which cannot be combated by conventional wisdom."

I checked the chapel, but the Catholic services had since ended and JB was nowhere in the vicinity. After stopping by his stateroom, I finally caught up with him at the indoor pool. I called out to him, trying to project my voice over the clamor of echoing voices. He emerged from the water and toweled off.

"That was quite refreshing," he said.

"Can we go to your stateroom? There's something I need to discuss with you in private."

"Why certainly," he said with a perplexed expression.

He retired to the locker room to change and returned fully dressed. I had already resolved not to insult his intelligence by employing any pretenses, and made no effort to hide my disquietude.

"Are you all right?" he asked as if I were one of his patients. "You have the same forlorn look you had at the breakfast table."

"There has been a development that you need to be made aware of," I said with downcast eyes.

As we made our way to JB's stateroom, he carried a somber, perplexed demeanor and made no inquiries. I was the first to break the silence.

"How well do you know Latin?" I asked in an effort to distract his thoughts.

His expression changed to confidence, and he looked as a man about to impart expert advice within his purview.

"I would say fairly well," he replied. "I studied it in college, and I am well-versed in Latin terminology pertaining to medicine and biology."

"Can you tell me what 'Frater Crusis Rosae' means?"

"If I am not mistaken, those words translate to 'Brother of the Rosy Cross'. Where did you hear or read that?"

"It's engraved on the inside of the Professor's watch cover. Does it pertain to some kind of society or association?"

"Your guess is as good as mine. I haven't the foggiest."

"He's a bit of a mysterious fellow, isn't he?"

"He does have a mysterious air about him at that. But I know enough to regard him to be a venerable and reposeful man."

"You're right on both accounts. He is a man possessing good qualities."

Once inside JB's stateroom, I asked him to have a seat and poured him a drink. He said he didn't drink this early in the day, but I handed him the glass anyway and told him to make an exception.

Stillness pervaded the room as I pondered the best way to break the news. JB was getting anxious waiting for me to answer the question that was written all over his face. I could not concoct a better way, so I gave it to him straight. Showing him the drawing, but not allowing him to touch it, I informed him of all that had transpired earlier in the day. I gave him a comprehensive account, including my conversation with the Professor and his supposition in regards to the drawing. As I spoke, a look of despondency fell over his face, and he silently stared into his glass. When I had finished, he slowly shook his head.

"Take heart," I said. "The Professor has a scheme to rid us of this nonsense once and for all. Do you have the vial of holy water Father Higgins gave you?"

"Yes," he said, setting the glass on the bureau, its contents unconsumed.

"Good, the Professor says he'll need it."

"I have it right here," he said, and he retrieved the vial from a compartment in his traveling trunk.

As prearranged, we met up with the Professor at the Terrace Café. He was seated at a table, sipping a cup of tea and snacking on buttered crackers. I informed him of the good news, but that didn't seem to change the look of disappointment on his face. JB produced the vial and handed it to him.

"Conrad has told me everything," he calmly said.

The Professor briefly examined the vial and its contents. After a taste and couple of queries, he was convinced that it was genuine.

"This is all good and well gentlemen," he said, returning the vial to JB. "But unfortunately the ship's limited library is woefully inadequate for our purpose. I'm afraid we will have to wait until our arrival in London. I'm sure the library at the British Museum will have the necessary reference materials. Furthermore, my credentials may enable me to obtain a pass to the library at the Royal Society."

"Professor, if it's a book you're looking for, I know someone who may be of assistance," JB revealed. "After Mass, I had the most delightful conversation with Father O'Flaherty. He has a private collection in his rectory containing many rare volumes, several in the original Latin, and an extensive section on theology."

"Would you arrange an introduction?" the Professor asked.

"Most certainly."

"Do you think he would allow me to browse his collection?"

"I don't see why not."

The Professor's look of disappointment evaporated. "Dr. Hawkins, you just may be the harbinger to our salvation," he said.

"If you would like, I could introduce you promptly after lunch," JB said in his urbane manner.

"That would be just fine."

"You do seem to come through in a pinch," I said, wearing a smile.

As we dined, I admired the view of the vast expanse of water and sky afforded by the café's large windows. The Professor queried JB concerning the titles in the priest's collection, and one in particular seemed to strike a note. When we adjourned, the Professor and JB headed off to pay a call on Father O'Flaherty. I thought it best not to be overbearing and chose not to accompany them. The Professor advised against me being alone, but I assured him that I would be fine.

"We shan't be too long," JB said as we parted company.

In my room, I passed the time playing solitaire. After several games, I went into the bath to pour a glass of water; and standing at the sink, I gazed in the mirror. It was then that I began to behold a most shocking sight. A dark blotch, as black as ink, appeared in the center of the mirror and started to swell. Fluctuating and wavering, it transmuted into a billowing sinister cloud that spread over the entire surface of the glass, blotting out the reflection of my astonished visage; and as I stared in disbelief, an unearthly cold clutched my soul with a shivering sense of dread. The surging billows contorted into nebulous shapes and then coalesced to form a grotesque, grisly image. Nothing I had undergone before could have prepared me for what I now saw. Three eyes opened – crimson eyes of fire with black centers shaped like the diamond eyes of a serpent. They set their hellish gaze upon me and leered at me with intense malice. The distinct outlines of three cavities became apparent and manifested into three gaping mouths bristling with serrated rows of elongated razor sharp yellow teeth or fangs, each one tapering to a sharp point. A disgusting thick green phlegm-like secretion dripped from its crimson red lips and the corners of the cavities. The hideous image gnashed its teeth and snarled at me. "What the blazes," I exclaimed, half expecting the menacing figure to lash out from the mirror, and then to my utter astonishment an array of snake-like tentacles lunged forth in an effort to seize me. I could have dropped on the spot, for all the strength ran out of my body with a rush. Wholly disconcerted, I recoiled before the infernal fiend, staggered back through the doorway to the bath, and slammed the door shut. I gripped the knob tightly, but the perspiration on my palms caused it to slip in my grasp. A whirlwind of commotion came from within the bath, and the door began to rattle and shake. My first instinct was to retrieve my Luger from the top drawer of the bureau, but the Professor's words flashed in my mind – "we are dealing with forces which cannot be combated by conventional wisdom". I retreated and pressed my back against the door to the corridor. The door to the bath began to buckle outwards. The wood and frame stridently creaked and groaned, the hinges snapping. Another rush of dreadful terror swept over me with uncanny swiftness, and my heart raced as I fully anticipated facing a malign force bent on nothing less than my ruin.

I felt a jarring from the door behind me and became acutely aware of a knocking from the other side. In a state of alarm, I spun around and flung the door open. There stood the Professor with a leather-bound tome tucked under his arm, and JB standing beside him. On the verge of collapse, I leaned against the doorframe drenched in a cold sweat, a blank stare on my face and abject terror in my eyes. The Professor shoved the tome into JB's arms and rushed past me. He moved swiftly to the convulsing door and braced up in front of it with the temerity of a man endowed with great fortitude. Zealously and vehemently, he rhythmically chanted strange mysterious words while making signs and gestures. A deathly wail howled from within the bath and then waned away; the tumultuous commotion ceased, and all was quiet. The Professor breathed a heavy sigh, and completely taxed of his mental and physical strength, slumped into a chair. JB set the book down and came to my side.

"Never mind me," I said. "See about the Professor."

I shut the door, and in a state of sheer consternation, lowered myself into a chair. "Is it over?" I asked the Professor.

"For now, but it will inevitably return," he replied. "It seems the propinquity of the attack was more imminent than I anticipated."

JB went into his stateroom and returned with a glass of water, which he handed to the Professor. The Professor said there was no need for concern; he just needed some time to regain his strength. Once JB was satisfied with the Professor's well being, he focused his attention on me.

"I want you to relax," he said in his typical settling bedside manner.

"I kept hoping it was a bad dream and I would wake up," I said. Instantly, I realized I had used the same words JB had spoken that night at the flophouse. "I'm sorry JB. I had my doubts, but now I believe you."

"There's nothing to forgive," he said propitiously. "I still find it all hard to believe myself."

The Professor asked me to give him the details of my experience, but I had no desire to recount the ghastly episode. Even with coaxing on his part, I remained close-lipped.

"Let's just say I had a harrowing encounter with JB's baleful spectre and leave it at that," I said.

"When will it return?" JB asked.

"There is no telling," the Professor replied. "Therefore, time is of the essence. Mr. Blake, I have good news."

"I could use some."

"In Father O'Flaherty's collection, I found a volume which shall bring an end to this implacable madness. Within it is the incantation and adjuration that will deliver us from this plight. Furthermore, I have acquired all the pertinent materials in addition to the holy water. All I need now is a quiet place where I can be alone to study. It might require some deal of time, and I think it best if I remained nearby. May I use your stateroom Doctor?"

"Certainly," JB replied.

"Before I leave you gentlemen, one matter remains to be resolved," the Professor said.

He opened the door to the bath and invited me to have a look. What I saw sparked the shocking revelation of the incredible event that had so recently unfolded before my eyes. The bath was a shambles. Shards of mirror littered the floor along with strewn items and fixtures, and the sink had been wrenched from its fastenings.

"You see, Mr. Blake, you have no reason to question your sanity," he said, and the sincere manner in which he spoke had a reassuring effect.

The Professor patted his pockets and gathered up the book in his arms.

"Dr. Hawkins, I'll need you to keep Mr. Blake company. Feel free to disturb me if necessary. Now, if you gentlemen will please excuse me," he said, and he withdrew to JB's stateroom, closing the door behind him.

JB and I settled in and struck up a conversation. We talked on a myriad of topics, except for the subject at hand, as if avoiding it would make it go away somehow. For the longest time all was predominately quiet from within JB's stateroom. Sometimes I could hear the Professor pacing and reciting. Eventually he emerged with a quantity of paper in his hand and handed several sheets to each of us.

"The incantation is in the form of a litany," he stated. "I have transcribed your responses. Each of you has an identical set. You will need to memorize the ordered phrases, which are written in Latin." He turned to JB. "Mr. Blake will need coaching on the pronunciations, and I leave that in your capable hands, Doctor. It is imperative that the words are pronounced correctly. Any deviation may diminish the efficacy of the incantation. I will return for you in approximately one hour."

He excused himself and returned to JB's stateroom.

For the benefit of my understanding, JB translated the meanings, and we practiced the phrases repeatedly until they became almost elementary. When the Professor finally reemerged, the sun had dipped below a deep blue horizon.

"The time has come gentlemen," he said. "Are you ready?"

We passed through the connecting doorway into JB's stateroom, and the Professor closed the door behind us. He instructed me to move the writing desk to the center of the room. Upon the surface, he placed a saucer and surrounded it with three thick candles in a triangular arrangement. He placed the holy water and the tome in front of him and opened the book to a marked page. With a piece of chalk he drew two encompassing circles on the floor around us, one drawn inside the first. Between the circles, he empowered the perimeter with enigmatic words, symbols, and scribbles; including four Hebrew letters and a phrase in Latin 'Dominus adjuter meus,' and each cardinal point he marked with the sign of the cross. After this, he reinforced the spiritual barrier with sprinklings of holy water and salt, all the while repeating,

"O Lord, we fly to thy power. O Lord, confirm this work." Lastly, he lit the candles in final preparation. Twilight had dwindled into evening, and the flaring candles now provided the sole source of illumination. All about was swathed in luminescent tinctures of yellow and gold intermingled with leaping shadows.

"Mr. Blake, please unfold and place the charm on the saucer," the Professor instructed.

I produced it from my pocket and did as he requested.

"Gentlemen, please retain your copies of the responses and use them lest you stumble. Throughout the incantation, I will recite my part and then you will jointly recite your response. I will nod my head to cue you for your responses. Are you prepared?"

JB and I simply nodded concordantly.

"I know the Doctor to be a solemn believer. Are you a believer Mr. Blake?" the Professor inquired.

I hesitated on my response. Seconds withered away as I contemplated my answer.

"Are you a believer in the redeeming power and grace of the Almighty?" he emphatically asked again.

"Yes – yes I am," I responded.

"Good. Then we shall begin," he said, giving me an approving nod.

The Professor began his recitation. When he had concluded his part, he nodded for our response. JB and I spoke in unison, and I articulated the pronunciations as best I could. As we uttered our response, the Professor sprinkled some of the blessed liquid on the charm. The droplets sizzled and foamed upon contact with the parchment, and the candle flames flickered despite the absence of a draft. The Professor continued to recite and prompt us for our responses. He retained a steadfast composure as he spoke in a resolute voice, placing adjuratory emphasis on certain words and phrases.

I looked up to see the faces of my companions faintly illuminated in the dancing candlelight. Out of the corner of my eye, I caught sight of a deformed black shadow on the wall not attributable to any of my present company, and I became keenly aware of a malevolent presence. I could see by their troubled expressions that my companions perceived this ominous manifestation as well. During our next response, the Professor once again sprinkled the parchment with holy water, producing a similar caustic reaction as before. The flame light dimmed, and dark sinewy tentacular shapes stretched out from the threatening shadow. Twisting and winding, the sinister black tentacles coursed over the surface of the walls, floor and ceiling, and twined and merged until they had enveloped the entire room, shrouding it in an eerie, unnatural darkness. An icy cold permeated the room, and the only impression my eyes now received was that of the three flittering flames emitted by the candlewicks.

With but one more response remaining, the Professor finished his discourse. Silence ensued as he waited for us to begin. I usually awaited JB's lead, but the only sound emanating from his direction was that of the papers quivering in his hands.

Seconds passed.

"Your responses, gentlemen," the Professor sternly called out in the dark.

I started my recitation and JB followed suit, but his voice was subdued and lacked its previous fervency. The Professor splashed the parchment with holy water for a third time. Vehemently, he spoke the final words of adjuration. As he uttered the words, the temperature rose, the dreadful darkness receded, and the candlelight once again projected its comforting illumination. A fuming mist encompassed the parchment. The putrid smoke trailed up and evaporated, and I watched the parchment dissolve until no trace of it remained. Subsequently, a peaceful calm pervaded the room.

CHAPTER 8

Blown by the wind, a stratum of fleecy white puffs whisked across a crystalline blue sky as if from the gentle strokes of a painter's brush. JB Hawkins breathed in the brisk invigorating ocean air as he strolled about on his morning constitutional. Promenading on deck, he bid a cordial good morning to those passengers he happened by, occasionally remarking about the weather, and sometimes striking up a conversation.

During his excursion, he chanced upon a slender young woman leaning with her back against the railing, the lapels of her long coat flapping in the stiff blustering breeze, and one hand pressed atop her felt cloche hat to prevent it from flight. He tipped his hat and bid her fair regards in his urbane manner.

"Excuse me sir, do you have the time?" she asked.

He paused to politely respond, and was smitten the moment he beheld her captivating visage as soft and beautiful as a morning sunrise. His eyes met hers, and when he gazed deep into those alluring emerald eyes, he became completely entranced. Enthralled, he stood silent, staring earnestly in admiration, only jumbled words came to mind and his lips failed to utter a sound.

"Do you happen to have the time?" she mildly asked again with a bit of a brogue.

With flushed cheeks he looked at his watch and shyly replied, stumbling on his words.

"I'm Sadie – Sadie Morrell," she said, offering her hand.

He cordially took her delicate hand wrapped in a soft leather glove, and collecting himself, reciprocated, "Enchanted – JB Hawkins, and the pleasure of our meeting is all mine."

What does JB stand for?" she asked with a warm, playful smile and inquisitive eyes.

"Jonathan Bedford."

"Well Jonathan Bedford, it's been very nice meeting you, but I'm afraid I have to run now. Thank you for being so kind."

"Please wait," he urgently said as she walked away. "Will I see you again?"

She turned back and gave him an inviting look. "I'll be at the ballroom tonight around eightish. You can look for me there."

She left him with a smile on his lips, and he watched until she had passed out of sight through a doorway into the bowels of the vessel. He stood leaning on the rail, gazing out at the vast waters to dream. Her visage was manifest in the clouds, the sky, the rolling swells, and even in the faces of the strangers he passed en route to his room. The magic of love had woven its spell.

JB met the Professor and myself for lunch, and after cordially regarding us, he quietly stared off into the distance with carefree eyes, his thoughts adrift in a daydream. Silently he sat, seemingly unaware of our company.

"How was your walk?" I casually asked, trying to get his attention.

His lips curled up into a smile, producing dimples on his cheeks, and a twinkle flashed in his eyes.

"Splendid – absolutely splendid," he said lackadaisically, continuing to look afar off.

It did not take a psychiatrist to explain his rapt condition. His face bore all the telltale symptoms of a lovesick schoolboy.

"Who's the dame?" I bluntly asked, cracking a smile. "The one that's got you flustered."

"She's an enchanting creature with the most charming brogue, and I'm thoroughly infatuated with her. I can't stop thinking about her," he said in a dream. "She takes my breath away."

"Does she have a name?"

"Her name is Sadie. I met her during my stroll this morning. It was as if fate had orchestrated our meeting. Alas, she had some pressing errand or engagement, and our conversation was all too brief, but I plan on seeing her again. She said that she'd be at the ballroom tonight around eight and invited me to meet her there. Would you both care to join me? It would give me great pleasure to introduce you."

"She must be extremely attractive for her to leave such an impression on you. This is a woman I've got to meet. How about it Professor?"

"I'm afraid my dancing days are a bit over," the Professor replied. "But I would also like to meet this young lady who has taken the Doctor's heart away."

"That settles it," I concluded.

That evening, JB got all gussied up in decorous fashion with his hair slicked down. He barely touched his dinner that evening. He was antsy and impatient all through the meal.

Arriving at the ballroom, we passed through a large entranceway flanked by twin open doors and stood upon the landing of a grand staircase that descended down to the gay social gathering below. Dark-wood banisters sloped down the sides of the wide carpeted steps to scroll around two lampposts sporting ornate candelabrums with electric lights encased in frosted glass globes. Opulent crystal chandeliers hung from a patterned ceiling, their sparkling brilliance reflected in the prodigious, framed mirrors mounted on wood-paneled walls. In one corner a resplendently ornamented Christmas tree rose to a prominent height. The elegantly and colorfully dressed socialites only added to the lavish display. The room swayed with the music of an orchestra donned in white jackets, and the dance floor swirled with the graceful motion of the dancers in a waltz. A man with a pencil moustache wearing a tuxedo greeted us at the foot of the stairs and ushered us to an empty table.

"Is she here?" I asked JB when we were seated.

"No, I don't see her."

JB glanced to and fro, and he watched the entranceways with restless anticipation. He purchased a bottle of champagne; we had drank a toast, and were casually enjoying a glass, when he remarked, "There she is." His head tilted upwards and his eyes gazed aloft. I turned to look and eyed a striking vixen standing at the top of the grand staircase with all the poise and presence of royalty. She was one sultry dame in every sense of the term, a ravishing redhead with fine, silken hair draping her shoulders like a train. A ringed black hat adorned with a curved red feather crowned her head, and a red sequined dress accentuated all her feminine features. A fur stole caressed her all but bare shoulders, and her hands were sheathed in long red silk gloves. On top of that, she was decked out in a string of pearls and a diamond bracelet that could buy and sell me. Half the heads in the place turned as she sashayed down the steps in red heels, one hand gliding along the rail, the other clasping a cigarette holder.

She paused on the bottom step and coolly looked about the room seemingly seeking a familiar face. JB stood up to draw her attention, and their eyes met. She minced in our direction like a cat on the prowl, and as she approached our table, her slender, shapely figure moved in seductive ways that made my head spin.

"I'm so pleased you decided to come. You look so handsome and dapper in your tux – positively chic," she said to JB with a delightful smile and a luster in her eyes.

"As do you – you look quite lovely, and that's a very attractive dress you're wearing," JB replied, somewhat bashful, his cheeks painted with the color of a blush.

The Professor and I courteously stood up.

She looked at each of us in quick succession with scrutinizing eyes. "Are these gentlemen friends of yours?" she asked.

"Allow me to introduce you," JB said.

When she cordially presented her hand to me, I caught a whiff of her enticing fragrance. Something about it was vaguely familiar, but I just could not place it.

"My stars, a Professor no less," she said, presenting herself to him. She sidled up to JB and tenderly intertwined his arm in hers. "It seems I find myself all alone. The acquaintance I was to meet doesn't appear to have shown up. Will you be so chivalrous as to be my escort?" she requested, innocently batting her eyes.

"Most certainly – it would be my undying pleasure," he said, beaming with pride. "Would you care to join us for some champagne, or would you rather dance?"

"Oh, the orchestra is striking up a new number. I love this piece – please, let's dance," she said playfully. Leading him off to the dance floor, she turned back toward us. "You won't mind if I borrow him for a while – will you?" she cheerfully asked.

She appeared to be light as a feather in JB's arms, and they twirled and glided across the floor in poetry to the music as if floating on a cloud. A smile never left JB's face, and he seemed to be having the time of his life.

"A delightful and attractive young lady, isn't she?" the Professor casually remarked.

"I have to agree with you there."

"Seeing this pageant display brings back fond memories of my wife. She loved to dance, and many an evening we danced the night away," he said lamentingly.

"You speak of her in the past tense, Professor."

"My Emily passed away some years ago during the influenza epidemic of 1918."

"But you wear a wedding band."

"She is a part of me, and thus I wear it to remind me that her love will always be with me. One day we will be reunited for eternity. That is assured."

"Well, Professor, for what it's worth, here's to your beloved Emily," I said, raising my glass.

"Thank you for the sentiment," he said, and we drank a toast.

After several dances, JB and Sadie returned to our table. JB pulled out a chair for her to sit down and then poured her a glass of champagne.

"Did you enjoy your dance?" the Professor asked.

"Superlative – he's such a marvelous dancer and says the sweetest things," Sadie said, looking at JB with a smile on her lips and a glow in her cheeks.

She seemed to manipulate the conversation by keeping to small talk and making innocent inquiries. JB's lips were flapping, and once I gave him a sidelong glance. I made a couple of guileful attempts to ask probing questions, but she skirted each with the mastery and tact of a politician. She sipped her champagne, and when her glass was drained, whisked JB off for another dance.

I could not waltz a lick, and there we sat, the Professor and I, a couple of wallflowers soaking in the atmosphere. The Professor enjoyed the reminiscent dancing and music, while I was content to sip champagne. A gentle hand touched my shoulder and I heard the kindly voice of Mrs. Vandegraf.

"Good evening, Mr. Blake. I see you're taking pleasure in the voyage."

"Having a ball," I said, concealing my sarcasm with a smile and a pleasant tone.

The Vandegrafs exchanged cordial greetings with us and sat down for a sociable chat. Throughout the conversation, I mostly smiled and nodded, putting a word in here and there. The ambience was all well and good, but it wasn't my cup of tea. I needed to loosen my tie, and when the opportunity arose, I politely excused myself, leaving the Professor with the affable Vandegrafs.

It was too early to retire to an empty stateroom, so I made my way to a place that I thought would be a little more up my alley – the 'Blue Trumpet Lounge'. I passed inside, and ambled up to the bar in a setting blurred by drifting tobacco smoke and heavy with the smell of spirits. Small tiffany table lamps dimly lighted the tables, and blue shaded sconces cast a sapphire glow over the loungers. The air was saturated with the swinging tones of smooth jazz played by the 'Red Onion Jazz Boys', coupled with lively voices and laughter. I perched myself on a stool, and the bartender mixed me a manhattan. Mindful that I should keep my wits about me, I slowly savored my drink while taking in the gala scene. Pyrotechnic horns and a sizzling piano had the place hopping to tunes like 'Drop That Sack'. Half the patrons in the joint got up to dance the Charleston when the musicians played 'Static Strut', and a couple of numbers later, a chorus of inebriated voices erupted in a sing-along during 'Bye, Bye, Blackbird'. The place reminded me of Mahoney's, the speakeasy I frequented back home in Boston. I started to relax, gradually letting my guard down. Against my better judgment, I ordered another manhattan, and for a while, I almost forgot about the events of the past few days.

Upon exiting, I craved a breath of fresh air after that smoke-filled environment, so before retiring to my stateroom, I stepped outside on deck into the night air. It was an invigoratingly brisk December night, and the North Atlantic wind whipped across my face and through my hair. A bright luminescent halo ringed the moon and a thousand stars twinkled like lanterns in the heavens. I leaned against the rail, taking in the sights and thinking of home.

Some distance from me, I noticed a couple emerge from a doorway. Hand in hand, they walked over to the railing and turned to face one another. Illuminated in the glow of the moonlight, I saw the faces of JB and Sadie. He removed his jacket, draped it around her shoulders, and she slipped her arms into the sleeves. Gazing at one another, they stared deeply into each other's eyes. She slowly closed her eyelids, and slightly parting her enticing lips, she tempted him to kiss her. Falling under the spell of her appealing charms, he gently placed his hands about her waist and softly touched his warm lips to hers. As their lips conjoined, she reached up and amorously caressed his cheeks and neck, then freely and affectionately wrapped her arms around him. He held her close, and entwined in a loving embrace, they shared a prolonged moment of fervent passion.

Lost in rapture, they failed to notice me; and I retreated through the nearest doorway, leaving them to their desires. Back in my stateroom I lay awake in bed for a time, never hearing any audible signs of JB's return.

The morning sun pushed its rim above the horizon, emblazoning the canopy of clouds in a foreboding pastel shade of crimson. JB slept in, and I had breakfast in the company of the Professor. It was not long before the subject of Sadie entered the conversation.

"What's your impression of her?" I asked.

"Quite the charming and personable young lady," he returned with a positive assessment. "It's a shame you left when you did. You missed a delightful time. I found her company most refreshing, as did the Vandegrafs. She was even gracious enough to spare room on her dance card, granting me the privilege of a dance."

"Didn't you find her a tad forward?"

"Overly friendly perhaps, and I can't say as I find any fault in her behavior, after all, the Doctor is a handsome young bachelor. He seemed to be rather enamored with her."

"Can you give me any particulars about her?"

"The inquisitorial detective being true to his profession," he said with a chuckle, reclining back in his chair. "To put it concisely, what I gathered from the conversation is that she is a dilettante traveling to Europe to view the works of the great masters."

"Anything else?"

"No, not that I recall, but I'm sure the Doctor would know more than I."

In the late morning, sullen dark clouds canvassed the sky, blotting out the warming sun. The black mass poured forth a torrent of hard rain, and coupled with a frigid gale wind, the sea unleashed its implacable fury. Raging swells rose to towering heights and thrashed against the hull of the indomitable vessel as it carved a path through the turbulent, mountainous waves.

The Professor and I were in the clubroom playing backgammon when the squall brewed up. My chair swayed in a slow continuous motion, and after a time, I began to experience an uneasy queasiness.

"You look a little green around the gills," he Professor commented. "Perhaps this dreadful weather has a grip on you."

Waves of nausea churned my stomach, and I rose to leave, a movement that only exacerbated my squeamishness and returned me to my chair. A bit concerned, the Professor obligingly offered to escort me to my stateroom. The deck below my feet rolled from side to side as I maneuvered along the corridors, and consequently I clutched the rail to steady myself. Upon entering the stateroom, I ran to the bath and disgorged the contents of my stomach, then immediately took to my bed.

The Professor fetched JB to my bedside. JB asked what my symptoms were; and after I gave him a rundown of my complaints, he examined me.

"Would you like to hear my diagnosis," he asked.

"Let me have it," I groaned in reply.

"I'm sorry to say that your dysphoric symptoms are due to an acute case of naupathia."

"For cryin' out loud JB, what the heck does that mean?" I gruffly spouted in an irascible state.

He placed a gentle hand on my shoulder. "In layman's terms you're seasick – 'under the weather', so to speak," he said in a calming voice.

"Oh, is that it? I thought I'd been poisoned or something."

"No, nothing that severe, and I can promise that you'll survive."

He dissolved bicarbonate in a glass of water and gave it to me to drink.

"This will help to quell your stomach," he said, and then he administered chloroform to ease my discomfort and help me sleep. "I'll be spending the afternoon with Sadie and we plan to have dinner together this evening. I'll check in on you from time to time to see how you're getting along. For now, try to sleep. Hopefully this terrible weather will abate soon and you'll be back to your old self."

He left me in the company of the Professor, who vigilantly sat in a chair by my bed that afternoon, quietly reading a book.

JB returned later that afternoon accompanied by Sadie. As JB brewed another ebullient potion, she sat on the edge of my bed and compassionately held my hand.

"I'm so sorry to hear that you've taken ill Mr. Blake. I do trust you'll be feeling better soon," she sympathetically said.

*   *   *

Sadie and JB shared an intimate romantic dinner that evening. Long after the dessert plates had been taken away, they drank wine, talked and held hands across the table. Their conversation consisted mostly of tender words interrupted by long moments of silence, in which they desired nothing more than to gaze at each other. Looking into her lustrous emerald eyes, he was lost in a realm of fancy, and his heart melted like butter over a hot flame. He wondered how he could have merited the affections of a young woman with such beauty and benevolent charm.

As the evening drew to a close, they strolled arm in arm, eventually stopping outside the door to her stateroom. She asked if he would like to come in, and once inside, she helped him off with his jacket. Taking her in his arms, he felt her warm voluptuous body, as she pressed snug against him. She wrapped her loving arms around his neck and tenderly urged him closer to her inviting lips. Their lips coupled in a long fervent kiss, and he delicately caressed the soft alabaster skin of her cheek, while she loosened his tie and unbuttoned his collar and shirt. Assuring him that she would be right back, she went into the bath and left him alone for a brief interval to dream. She emerged with only a silk robe covering her bare skin. Before he could utter a word, she put a silencing finger to his lips, then affectionately took him by the hand and led him to the bedside. She loosened the sash and enticingly unveiled her nakedness, allowing the robe to slide over her sleek sensuous shoulders and fall to the floor. She slipped under the bed sheet, and reclining back upon the pillows, she invited him to join her. His senses seduced, he abandoned himself to temptation; and they spent the night writhing in a tempest of sensual passion, awakening from joyous dreams in each other's arms the following morning.

*   *   *

For days the storm raged relentlessly. Primarily confined to my sickbed, I lived on dry toast and broth, and during the process lost several pounds. JB spent every waking moment with Sadie, and the Professor stayed close at my side for the most part. For the sake of precaution, the vault key hung from a shoestring around my neck, and my Luger lay secretly at hand.

With plenty of time on my hands to mull things over, my mind was again racked with questions and speculation. I tried to retrace Drayfus' steps. His papers indicated that he was most recently in London, England. If he was associated with the Royal Society in London, as denoted in the London Times article, it stands to reason that he would have sought the assistance of his colleagues. Did he come in contact with Sir Gunston Mallory? He did have Mallory's book and card in his possession. Someone must have interacted with Drayfus and know something. And if Drayfus had colleagues in London, why then did he leave England for Boston? Was it a homecoming, or was he fleeing from the same staunch pursuers that now dogged our steps? One thing was certain though, with the tablet in our custody, sooner or later our adversaries would have to play their hand and tip me off as to their identity. Although they had not made their presence evident, were they aboard ship, just keeping tabs on us and biding their time?

Late on the third day of heavy seas, JB came in to check on me, as he periodically did.

"How's the patient?" he asked with genuine warmness and concern.

"Like you said – I'll live"

"Unfortunately, it seems our arrival will be delayed. Reports of iceberg sightings forced the captain to steer a more southerly course. However, I have good tidings for you. According to the latest report, they expect this inclement weather to break by nightfall and anticipate calm seas ahead."

"That's darn good to hear. It's been a rocky ride, and I'll be glad when it's over. I can see that you're enjoying the voyage at least."

"Except for the weather, ever since we removed the dark cloud of that malevolent charm from over our heads, it's been a pleasant trip, and meeting Sadie has made it all worthwhile."

"You two certainly have been spending a lot of time together. She must be traveling with friends or relations. Has she introduced you?"

"No, not yet. She's traveling alone for the transatlantic voyage, but she plans to stay with friends in London."

"You don't intend on her traveling with us to London, do you?"

"I've been meaning to ask you. I was hoping you wouldn't mind."

"Actually, that would complicate things and make for a sticky situation," I remonstrated. "How well do you know this girl?"

"Well enough to know I'm madly in love with her. And I am Conrad. I adore her. She's everything I've ever dreamed of. I think she's the one."

"The one what?'

"The one I want to marry."

"You can't be serious. You met her only a few days ago. I hope you didn't tell her the underlying reason for our voyage," I said, giving him a stern gaze.

He averted his eyes, reluctant to respond. I waited, but no answer was forthcoming.

"You let the cat out of the bag, didn't you?"

"What would you have me do – lie to her?" He retorted, shrugging his shoulders.

"Yes," I bluntly said. "Now, what exactly did you tell her?"

"I told her about the tablet, and that we were taking the artifact to the Royal Society for evaluation," he said guardedly.

"Is that all?" I pryingly asked.

"You're suspicious of her, aren't you? I can see it in your face and in your eyes."

"It's in my nature to be suspicious," I said.

"Well in this instance, I think your recent bout with the sea has seriously affected your judgment!" he indignantly deprecated with a vexed expression and a touch of anger in his voice.

"Don't get your dander up. I meant no offense. The last thing I want is a rift between us. Look JB, if she's on the up and up as far as you're concerned, that's all right with me," I propitiated. "But for our sake and hers, I wouldn't tell her any more than you already have."

His anger defused, he resumed a reposed manner and sat down on the edge of the bed. Stooped forward with his hands on his knees, he was silent for a few brief moments, then turned his head to look me in the eye.

"I don't want to be an alarmist, but something happened this morning that I should make you aware of," he said in earnest. "Sadie and I went for a swim. When I returned to my locker to change, it was quite apparent that someone had gone through my belongings, and my pockets were turned out."

"Was anything missing?"

"No, nothing was stolen."

"Apparently, robbery was not the motive, but I have a good notion what they were looking for."

"What's that?"

"This," I said, displaying the key dangling from the shoestring around my neck.

"That would mean – you don't suppose that…."

"That our nefarious stalkers are aboard this ship? I do, indeed," I said, completing his thoughts.

"And all this time I thought we had left them behind in New York," he said as a look of despondency flushed his face.

"They're persistent, I'll say that for them."

"I'm going to have to leave you for now. I have a date with Sadie for dinner."

He stood up to depart.

"JB, be especially careful and take heed not to drop your guard," I said.

"I won't," he assured.

That night the skies cleared and it was smooth sailing for the remainder of the voyage. Early on the day the liner was due to dock in Southampton, JB called on Sadie, but his solicitous knocks on her door went unanswered. He returned later, but still roused no response. With time running out, he frantically searched everywhere for her. He ran into the Vandegrafs and asked if they had seen her, they had not.

He burst into my stateroom while I was packing. "I can't find Sadie. I can't find her anywhere," he said in a panic. "Has she been here looking for me?"

"No, she hasn't," I replied.

"I just don't understand it."

"Don't trouble yourself; she's bound to turn up. Right now, you and I need to retrieve the tablet from the vault."

Ultimately the time came to go ashore. When we were about to debark, JB entreated us to wait just for a while, and we lingered and watched the scads of passengers funneling onto the gangplank until the stream had trickled down to a few stragglers. JB's head sank down in anguish; and placing a consoling hand on his shoulder, I gently urged him onward. The Professor and JB stepped onto the gangplank ahead of me, and before making my descent, I briefly paused to look down at the throng on the pier below. I descried a Rolls Royce beyond the multitude. A chauffer was holding the door for a red-haired vixen. As she climbed into the back seat, I caught sight of her face. It was, unmistakably, Sadie Morrell.

CHAPTER 9

JB brooded in silence, while the cabby drove through the bustling streets of Southampton en route to the train station. Thus far, I had been close-lipped about my observation at the pier, and thought it best to keep it that way. At my request, we took a short diversion and stopped at the cable office. As the taxi pulled over to let me out, a Rolls Royce, identical to the one Sadie got into earlier, pulled away from the curb in front of us and merged into traffic.

Inside, I dictated a telegram destined for Boston.

Cindy

Arrived in Southampton STOP Situation looks promising STOP Will keep you posted STOP

- Conrad

After writing it down, the clerk neatly stacked it atop another wire request. I caught a glimpse of the other message under mine, but time and my angle of view prevented me from reading the text. However, I was able to make out the initials of the sender – SM. Before I could conjure a ruse to distract the clerk, an operator stepped up and whisked away the completed forms.

At the depot, we boarded a train bound for London, and as the train rumbled along the tracks, a darkening sky unleashed a slow drizzle that developed into a steady monotonous rain. Rainwater rippling and flowing over the surface of the glass blurred the passing scenery. JB stared moodily out the window, and the only sounds that broke the silence were the drops splattering against the pane. After what seemed an eternity, he slowly turned to look at me.

"I was hoping she would be at the station. I wonder what happened?" he somberly said, a watery glaze over his eyes.

"Who knows," I said, giving him a sympathetic smile. "Right now we have important enough business to attend to. Maybe you should be focusing on that."

"I guess you're right," he said resignedly, and he resumed gazing out the window.

The Professor napped most of the way, and JB remained reticent. We traveled through the counties of Hampshire and Surrey, arriving at Victoria Station in Westminster that evening. The taxi ride took us along vibrant boulevards and winding streets lined with a mix of stately structures that displayed an artful blend of the old world and the new. At Piccadilly Circus the cabby turned down Piccadilly and drove a short distance to the Piccadilly Hotel. The Professor had recommended it due to its proximity to the Royal Society.

We passed through a wide entranceway in a privacy wall and into a courtyard enclosed on three sides by an august building of white brick that ascended to a lofty sloped roof dressed with dormer windows and a cupola topped by a weathercock. After signing the register, we settled into rooms overlooking the courtyard and the rooftops beyond, from which plumes of smoke belched from countless chimneystacks.

Church bells rang out the next morning, their tones resounding throughout the old city. It was a beautiful but crisp day, and I spent most of it cooped up in my room safeguarding the tablet. JB and the Professor took a leisurely stroll through St. James Park and up the mall to Buckingham Palace. That evening, after a meal of mutton and bread pudding, we planned our next move and resolved to solicit the Royal Society the next day in hope of arranging a meeting with Sir Gunston Mallory.

Majestic Burlington House stood just a few blocks away; and heartened by a bright morning sun, the Professor and I set out with high hopes, leaving the tablet in the care of JB. Arriving, we entered through a pair of stout black doors with brass knobs into a broad entrance hall. Two polished gentlemen standing nearby were in the midst of a discussion, and ceasing their conversation, they set their gaze upon us. A crooked man with white wavy hair and a long face notched by sunken cheeks took more than a curious notice of us and approached, his spindly bowlegs moving at a shuffling gait.

"A pleasant day to you, gentlemen. Welcome to Burlington House. I am Cecil Smyth of the Royal Society. Might I be of assistance?" he said with a distinct accent and a hospitable grin.

"I am Professor Chadwick Hanson of Harvard University and this is Mr. Blake," the professor said, courteously presenting his card. "We are seeking an esteemed Fellow of your Society, Sir Gunston Mallory. Might you know how we can contact him?"

The crooked man's face lit up. "He is here now in the library. May I state the nature of your call?"

"It is a scientific matter, requiring his knowledge and expertise," the Professor replied.

Smyth ushered us to a nearby door and into a well-furnished room off the hall.

"Please have a seat and make yourselves comfortable. I will inform Sir Gunston you are here," he said, and he shuffled out of the room.

Smyth returned, accompanied by a distinguished-looking man wearing a blue crested blazer, white dress shirt and gold ascot. His clean-shaven face had chiseled cheeks and a square cleft chin, and a sharp slender nose descended from between piercing gray eyes. His short brown hair was parted at the side and a tinge of gray accented his temples. We stood up, and Smyth introduced him as Sir Gunston Mallory.

Expressing a genial smile, Mallory extended his hand to the Professor. "Professor Chadwick Hanson, I presume. I've been – it's a pleasure to make your acquaintance, sir," he said, firmly shaking his hand.

"Yes, I am Professor Hanson, and this is Mr. Blake," the Professor said, gesturing to me. "We apologize for calling unannounced and appreciate you sparing your time."

"A pleasure Mr. Blake," Mallory said, shaking my hand.

"Likewise," I replied.

"I see you've already met Mr. Cecil Smyth, our eminent secretary," he said, giving the crooked man a friendly pat on the back.

"Thank you, Sir Gunston. Now if you gentlemen will please excuse me," Smyth said, and he shuffled off.

"May I retain your card Professor?" Mallory asked.

"By all means, please do," the Professor replied.

"I have never visited your prestigious university; however, I am acquainted with its illustrious reputation as an institution of higher learning. What is your capacity with the Peabody Museum?"

"I am the assistant curator."

Impressed, Mallory said, "I understand the museum boasts a fine collection."

"The finest and most comprehensive in North America," the Professor asserted.

"Our secretary tells me you have a scientific matter to present. This is indeed an honor and my services are at your disposal. Let me take you to a place where we can speak in private without interruption."

He conducted us to a sunlit meeting room with tall windows. A long teakwood table surrounded by matching high-back chairs stretched out before us, and a fire burned within a white marble fireplace, its crackling flames warming the room. Mallory strode up to the chair at the head of the table, and standing behind it, he rested his palms atop the back.

"Do not titillate my curiosity any further, gentlemen. Please enlighten me as to the matter which has brought you such a long distance," he said.

"Mr. Blake has in his possession, an artifact with markings that I am unable to decipher. Allow me to show you," the Professor said, and he produced a rubbing of the tablet from within his tweed jacket and unfolded it on the table.

Mallory stepped up, and placing his hands on the table, he leaned forward over the rubbing. As he surveyed it, his eyes grew wide and the corners of his mouth turned up in a slight curl.

"Outstanding – absolutely outstanding!" he remarked. "The inscriptions are indeed impressive, and these runic markings are quite intriguing."

"Yes, they are unique. I've never seen anything like them," the Professor commented.

"I have," Mallory proclaimed, turning to the Professor. "I came across markings bearing a remarkable resemblance to these amongst ancient ruins I discovered on the slopes of a mountain rising above the banks of the River Sanga in the remote African hinterland. It's most fortunate you chose to consult me, and I'm delighted that you did. While this is a good representation, some of the images and symbols are not well-defined," he said, waving his hand over the rubbing. "Where is the original? I would very much like to examine it."

"It's back at our hotel," the Professor replied.

"Would you bring it here?" Mallory asked. "I will gladly place my motorcar and driver at your disposal."

"I thank you for your generous offer, but that won't be necessary. We are staying but a short distance away at The Piccadilly. If

Mr. Blake has no objections, we can return with it forthwith," the Professor said, looking at me for concurrence.

"No, I've no objections," I said amenably.

"Splendid," Mallory remarked.

"Would you mind if I remained here with Sir Gunston?" the Professor asked me. "I'm interested in hearing his interpretations."

"That's okay Professor, no sense in us both going," I said.

When I reached my room, I gave the prearranged knock and opened the door. JB was casually seated in an easy chair facing the entrance, smoke curling up from the pipe in his hand. The nickel-plated .45 lay conspicuously on the table beside him.

"Any news?" he asked.

"The best – not only was Mallory there, he wants to see the tablet. The Professor showed him a rubbing of it, and he recognized the runes. He's giving the Professor the scoop right now. Come on, I'll introduce you," I said, retrieving the tablet from its hiding place.

We walked down the sidewalk at a fast pace, both of us eager to get the answers we came for. Upon entering the meeting room, we found Mallory engaged in an edifying discourse, and the Professor listening intently, his forehead wrinkled in mindful consideration.

"Ah, here we are," the Professor said, taking notice of us.

I introduced JB as an integral member of our party, and Mallory gave him a complaisant reception. I laid the case on a window seat, unlocked it and lifted the lid. At Mallory's request, I picked up the tablet, infolded in a quilted cloth, and set it before him on the teakwood table.

"May I do the honors?" he asked.

"Be my guest," I said.

Mallory unfolded the cloth, and his eyes flashed with enthusiasm at first sight of the tablet.

"Yes," he barely whispered under his breath.

He inspected it assiduously, making learned comments here and there and caressing the surface with his hand.

"These runic markings on the sides are indeed identical to those I found amongst the ruins I spoke of. They are even fashioned in the same style," he said, lifting his eyes from the tablet.

Mallory flipped the tablet over, and an inquisitive smile crossed his face.

The Professor imparted his thoughts. "As I expressed earlier, I am fairly certain that this is an astronomical chart. However, its arcane purpose eludes me. It is notably accurate in all respects except one. I cannot identify the star represented by the hollow cavity amidst the group that comprise the constellation of 'The Serpent'," he said, pointing to the specific spot.

"I cannot purport to be an adept astronomer, but I would have to agree that your tenet is correct," Mallory said. "As to the hollow circle you refer to, its anomalous character distinguishes it from the other inscriptions representing stars, and thus it may be attributable to something entirely different. However, if it does represent a star, that presents a conundrum." He stood upright and placed his hand atop the back of the chair beside him. "The ruins I explored in Africa were the structural remains of a lost city, presumably dating back to antediluvian times or even earlier, and it is my firm belief that this artifact was crafted by the very same civilization that built those structures, for it bears striking similarities in many respects," he demonstratively stated. "Therein lies the conundrum. I am curious to learn how so early a civilization could have knowledge of a star that modern astronomers have yet to discover. Such knowledge would be indicative of a scientifically advanced society, wouldn't you say? And the existence of this chart alone is evidence of that. I would like to conduct an experiment, if I may. One that will render certain whether or not my inference is valid."

"What would that entail?" asked the Professor.

"Something quite simple really. Do either of you gentlemen happen to have a compass handy?"

"No," the Professor replied.

"Nor I," JB said, and I responded by simply shaking my head.

"If you will excuse me, gentlemen, I will return shortly," Mallory excitedly said, and he exited the room.

Mallory had no more than closed the door behind him, when I turned to the Professor. "So Professor, what did Sir Gunston say while I was gone?"

"We conferred on several particulars. Most especially, Sir Gunston expounded on a fascinating theory he holds in regards to the runes. His hypothesis is predicated on the premise that they are not a written language, but are instead a cryptic mathematical code," he imparted. "He was relating his underlying thesis to me when you entered. He took thorough notes and made copious sketches while exploring the ruins he discovered. Since his return, he has been working diligently to decipher the code, and apparently is on the verge of a profound breakthrough."

"So what are you saying? They're numbers?" I asked.

"Something like that, but not only numbers, they comprise mathematical signs as well. Quite an interesting theory, don't you think?"

"I'll say."

"I wonder what the experiment is? And I can't imagine what a compass has to do with it," JB remarked with curiosity.

"I'm sure we'll find out soon enough," the Professor said.

We chatted for another minute or two, at which time the door opened and Mallory entered, compass in hand.

He stood at the end of the table. "Now, gentlemen, for the moment of truth," he said, raising his eyebrows.

He set the compass on the table and fixed his eyes on the dial, watching for the needle's reaction. The needle swung on its pivot and pointed directly at the tablet. He turned the compass clockwise, then counterclockwise, but no matter which way he turned it, the needle always pointed to the tablet. He took up various positions around the table, and each time the compass needle pointed inerringly at the tablet. Lastly, he set the compass on the surface of the tablet. Initially the needle wavered back and forth in increasingly wider arcs, and then my eyes grew wide with amazement as it spun round and round. Mallory's grin spread from ear to ear upon seeing the marveled expressions on our faces.

"Most extraordinary!" uttered the Professor.

"Yes, Professor – most extraordinary. It was the same with the ruins of the lost city – a compass was useless. If it had not been for my native guides, I would have become easily disoriented and possibly lost. The stones comprise an ore that exhibits a magnetic property. The intensity of the field is stronger than the meridian but sufficient to attract only small objects consisting of paramagnetic metals."

"May I take the liberty?" the Professor asked, reaching for the compass.

"Of course, I would be disappointed if you didn't."

The Professor picked up the compass and stepped into the hallway. Through the open door, I could see him orienting himself, trying to get a steady bearing. Satisfied that the compass was working properly, he reentered the room, closing the door behind him, and slowly approached the table, his discerning eyes riveted on the dial. He then repeated Mallory's experiment with the same results.

"I believe it is safe to conclude that this tablet was quarried from the same source as the stone blocks used to erect the edifices that compose the ruins," Mallory said with certitude. "I am convinced of its authenticity, it is exact in all respects to the samples I collected. I donated several to the British Museum here in London. Perhaps I could have their top geologist make a comparative match, with your consent of course. I'm certain he would be most interested. Shall I arrange it?"

Before any of us could reply, a knock came at the door.

"Excuse me, gentlemen," Mallory said, and he went to answer.

He half opened the door, and we heard the voice of a man in the hall. "Pardon the intrusion Sir Gunston, Malcolm Broderick to see you. He states you have a lunch appointment."

"Thank you. Tell him that I'll be with him straight away," Mallory replied.

He closed the door and took up his previous position at the table.

"I apologize gentlemen, but it seems our time has been cut short. I have an appointment, which I must keep, and I have so many unanswered questions, as I'm sure you do. I invite you to be my guests and dine with me at my club this evening. We can continue our discussion in a more relaxed atmosphere over a snifter of brandy and a cigar, perhaps," he said with a warm persuasive smile.

"We'd be delighted," the Professor replied without hesitation.

"Shall we say six o'clock?"

"That would suit us fine," the Professor said agreeably.

"It's the Athenaeum. The address is Waterloo Place. Allow me to write it down for you."

Mallory removed a piece of stationery from a drawer in a credenza. He penned the address and a note in an eloquent flowing script.

20 December, 1926
The Athenaeum
Waterloo Place
107 Pall Mall

Miles,
This will introduce Messrs. Hanson, Blake and Hawkins. Please admit these gentlemen as my guests.

GM

He folded and creased the paper. "Give this to the man at the door," he said, handing it to the Professor. "As for transportation, I will despatch my driver to pick you up at your hotel. In the meantime, would you assent to leave the tablet here? In addition to the geologist I spoke of, there are two other learned gentlemen whom I would have examine it. One is the Director of Antiquities at the British Museum and the other is a Fellow of the Royal Astronomical Society here at Burlington House. Their opinions would be most valuable. This is indeed a priceless artifact, and you have my word that it will be treated as such."

The Professor shot me an impelling look.

"I think that would be prudent," I agreeably replied, deeming that we could not leave it in our hotel room this evening and trusting this place to be safer than most.

"Splendid," Mallory said.

He politely ushered us out. "Good day, gentlemen – until this evening," he said, standing on the threshold.

Strolling back to our hotel, I could not help but express my gnawing apprehension regarding the tablet.

"I think we might have made a mistake," I remarked.

"What's that?" JB asked.

"Leaving the tablet."

"There is no cause for worry, Mr. Blake," the Professor said. "I assure you it could not be in better hands"

"I'm sure it will be all right," JB corroborated.

*　　　*　　　*

That afternoon as I was leaving the hotel, I recognized a man seated in the lobby, seemingly reading a newspaper. He had a bushy moustache, thinning red hair, and he was wearing an inverness. I had seen him several times during the transatlantic voyage, and I even recalled seeing him on the train in New England. Folding his paper, he stood up as I exited. I climbed into a taxi and directed the cabby to take me to the office of The Times. I gathered it was not just a coincidence when the man flagged the next taxi and followed. Fortuitously, the shadowing taxi became entangled in traffic, and when I arrived at my destination it was no longer in sight.

Researching back issues at the office of The London Times, I found the two articles that Harold Drayfus had clipped and copied them verbatim. Accompanying one article was a photograph picturing the members of the Bradford Expedition. Luckily, the photograph was on file, and with some gentle persuasion, I obtained a couple of reproductions. I searched for any other mention of the Bradford Expedition and any events that I could tie to Drayfus, but came up empty. In an issue dated last June, I stumbled upon a curious article involving Mallory's ancestral estate.

Atmospheric Phenomenon Emblazons Sky

An unusual atmospheric phenomenon occurred the night of June 21st in the skies over the village of Blytemoor in Kent. A number of witnesses reported brilliant dazzling lights, emanating from the vicinity of Blytemoor Manor, set the sky ablaze with a radiant red and amber hue. Villagers, believing that a fire was consuming the manor, rushed to the scene. Instead of finding the manor house engulfed in flames, they stared in shock and amazement as an immense conglomeration of iridescent globes danced and hovered in the air above the manor house. Some of those witnessing the sight ran away in abject terror, while others fainted, and frightened horses disregarded their masters and bolted in panic. Blytemoor Manor is the ancestral estate of Sir Gunston Mallory. Meteorologists are baffled, and no comment has been forthcoming from Sir Gunston.

I returned to my hotel room with barely time to spare, and I was still struggling with my bowtie when JB knocked and entered. He said that he and the Professor were going down to the lobby, and to come down as soon as I was ready. Not two minutes later, the front desk gave me a ring to inform me that my ride was here. I grabbed my coat and hat, and dashed down the stairs to the lobby. JB and the Professor were standing at the front desk in the company of a chauffeur dressed in a double-breasted gray uniform.

"Here's our other party now," JB said as I approached.

The chauffer introduced himself as Nigel. "Shall we go, gentlemen? Best to be punctual."

We followed him to a shiny black Bentley standing at the curb, and he held the door as we climbed in.

It was but a very short drive down Piccadilly and then Regent Street to Waterloo place. The chauffeur pulled over in front of a stately building facing the square, got out and opened the door for us.

"Sir Gunston awaits," he said.

We advanced up to a door crowned by a pediment and stood before it in the lamplight. The Professor pulled the cord, ringing the bell, and an impeccably dressed man wearing white gloves answered. He stood perfectly erect in the doorway and surveyed us.

"Can I help you, gentlemen?" he asked solemnly.

The Professor politely introduced our party and presented him with Mallory's note.

"We are here on the invitation of Sir Gunston Mallory," the Professor communicated.

"You're expected, gentlemen," the man said, cordially admitting us.

He ushered us into the dining room, where men were seated in leather armchairs, talking and taking their meals in a refined atmosphere. A cozy fire warmed the room. Mallory sat alone at a table by the fireplace, and he stood up as we approached.

"Good evening, gentlemen, so good of you to come," he said with a genuine smile, and he gestured for the Professor to sit at his right. "Thank you, Miles, that will be all," he said, addressing the impeccably dressed man, who rigidly bowed and withdrew.

A waiter came to the table cradling a bottle of wine and presented the label to Mallory.

"A cabernet from my personal stock," Mallory said.

After Mallory had tasted the vintage and given his approval, the waiter poured the wine, and JB pleased our host by complimenting him on its exquisite taste.

"I suggest we defer that which is foremost on our minds until after we have eaten. I would like the opportunity to better make your acquaintance," Mallory said amiably.

He asked if we were enjoying our stay in London and pointed out the more notable locations of interest. JB remarked about the climate, comparing it to New England, to which Mallory jested that Britain has no climate, it just has weather.

The waiter returned to serve the first of several courses. Between courses the conversation picked up again, and Mallory told us about his club, professing that all its members were patrons of the arts, science and literature.

"We have an excellent library with an extensive collection containing numerous rare volumes, including an unabridged edition of *The Golden Bough* by Sir James Frazer," Mallory said, directing his words to the Professor.

"Impressive," the Professor remarked, his interest piqued.

"You're most welcome to make use of our library facilities as my guest while you're in London."

"Yes, thank you. I would very much like to browse your collection."

"Remind me later to give you a pass. I can also arrange for you to obtain a pass to the reading room at the British Museum," Mallory congenially said.

"I'm overwhelmed by your kind consideration and hospitality," the Professor said, filled with gratitude.

"My dear fellow, one day I may visit the halls of your honorable institution, and I will look to your hospitality," Mallory said with a touch of humility.

Our host asked the Professor subtle questions about his academic work as a curator and instructor, and had him talking on various particulars of Harvard and the Peabody Museum. Addressing JB, he showed sincere respect for his humanitarian profession and seemed enthralled with his work as a medical examiner. Mallory himself spoke of his proud ancestry and related some of his forebears' more notable exploits with the narrative skill of a masterful storyteller. Throughout the meal, I kept my mouth closed and my ears open. I observed our host closely, and his mannerisms had all the air of a well-bred man beyond reproach and in his own element.

Our sumptuous meal consumed, a waiter presented us with a box of fine cigars, and another waiter followed with four snifters of brandy on a silver tray. Mallory and the Professor each took a cigar, and JB declined, preferring to fill his pipe.

Mallory swirled the brandy in his glass. "Gentlemen, allow me to propose a toast – 'to the discovery of the past, may it enlighten our future'," he said.

"Well said," the Professor concurred, and we each drank a swallow.

Mallory reclined back and cradled his glass, occasionally swirling his brandy, the fire's reflection instilling a luster in his eyes.

"I'm very pleased that you chose to bring the artifact to the Royal Society. Which leads me to ask the question that has been haunting me since our meeting this morning. How did you come upon such an extraordinary piece?" he asked, his eyes trained on me.

"Suffice it to say, an anthropologist affiliated with Harvard University left it in my care. Unfortunately he couldn't be here. His name is Dr. Harold Drayfus. Perhaps you've met him? He had your card," I replied, sidestepping the pertinent issue to ask a burning question.

I thought I detected a flash of recognition in his eyes, but he responded to the contrary.

"No, I can't say as I've met the fellow. He had my card you say?" He paused for a moment to ponder. "Well, he could have derived it from a number of sources. It's a shame he never contacted me. I would have welcomed the opportunity to speak with him. Now tell me Mr. Blake, how and where did Dr. Drayfus originally procure the tablet? The answer is imperative," Mallory earnestly inquired.

"He didn't say exactly. However, he had been doing fieldwork in Central Africa."

"And his proposed route and destination would have placed him in the same geographical area where you discovered the ruins," the Professor added. "Which lends significant credence to your correlation between the tablet and the ruins. As a matter of fact, after our earlier discussion, I consider it highly probable that Dr. Drayfus recovered the tablet from those very same ruins."

JB remained silent, and his eyes traveled back and forth between speakers as he casually puffed on his pipe.

"That's good of you to say, Professor. It certainly confirms my assumptions. Can you tell me anything more specific?" Mallory probed further.

"No. Dr. Drayfus met with an untimely tragedy before he could convey any details," I evasively replied.

The Professor added no comment to my response.

"Did he keep a journal?" Mallory asked.

"Not that we're aware of," I replied.

"How queer," Mallory remarked. "You would expect such a man to keep a journal. Nevertheless, I must congratulate you. The tablet is nothing less than a genuine link to the past – a find of monumental proportions. I can't begin to emphasize its implications. It could herald the discovery of a lifetime. Coupled with my findings thus far, it is substantial proof of the existence of a highly-developed ancient Central-African civilization, whose origin and culture have yet to be determined," he staunchly said. "A conference is being held at Oxford next week. I will be giving a lecture, in which I plan to disclose my findings before some of the most erudite scholars of our time. This may be presumptuous on my part, but I would like to unveil the tablet at that lecture along with my other evidence. It would do much to convince even those with the narrowest of minds," he said egotistically. Relaxing his demeanor, he added, "Of course you'll need to be present, so that I may give proper recognition. What say you, gentlemen?"

All eyes were cast upon me.

"What do *you* say, Professor?" I asked, deferring to him.

"It so happens I will be attending the same conference, which makes your proposal feasible," he said to Mallory. "But before we can give you a definitive answer, we would need to discuss the matter between us. In addition, I would want to review your notes and findings with you if I am to lend my endorsement."

"Quite understandable," Mallory said. "Then I take it you have no immediate objections. As far as the prerogative to review my notes – you shall have it. Divulging my findings is but a small price to pay.

However, the bulk of my notes are at my family estate of Blytemoor in Kent."

"I'm hosting a dinner party Wednesday evening," he said after a perceptive pause. "It's a gathering of friends and learned colleagues, and I invite you to come and partake of some holiday cheer. In fact, I insist you come. I think you'll find it to be a most insightful evening, and I can place the entire next day at your disposal."

"I don't know what to say," the Professor said with an incredulous expression.

"Say yes," Mallory entreated.

"What I think the Professor is trying to say is – we'd be delighted," JB interjected. I could only agree after JB's acceptance. It seemed our course was set.

"Jolly good! Jolly good indeed!" Mallory exclaimed. "That leaves just one amenity to attend to."

He drew out an invitation from the pocket of his suit jacket, filled in our names, and handed it to the Professor.

"You'll need directions of course," he said, and he wrote them on the back of his calling card. "Your hotel can make the arrangements for you. Should you need to contact me in the interim, the number for my London residence is on the card. I'll arrange to have someone meet you at the railway station in Charing to take you to Blytemoor. I'm afraid I am unable to extend you accommodations at this late date. There is a public house in the village named The Crooked Crow. You can secure lodgings there. The innkeeper's wife makes a marvelous steak and kidney pie. The time you're to be expected is on the invitation. I'll send my car around shortly before to bring you to the manor."

Mallory leaned forward. "I should have achieved a solution to the markings on the tablet by the time of your arrival. With the solution, I'm confident that I will be able to determine its purpose," he resolutely stated. "I'll need your rubbing Professor. It will do much to avail my progress."

"Consider it yours, Sir Gunston. I can always make another," the Professor obliged.

"In the meantime, I highly recommend that you permit the Royal Society to retain the tablet," Mallory advised. "It is currently stored with other priceless treasures and artwork at Burlington House. The building houses several learned societies, their libraries and museums, including the adjoining Royal Academy of Arts. I assure you it is quite safe. There are more than adequate safeguards and the facilities are patrolled by private guards – all of whom are men of reputable report.

"Of course you may retrieve it at any time during normal business hours if you wish," Mallory continued. "I've left instructions with Mr. Cecil Smyth to deliver it to you upon your request."

"All things considered, I think that would be wise," the Professor concurred. Turning to me, he asked, "Don't you think so, Mr. Blake?"

Uncontrollable events were unraveling at a rapid pace, and I had to make a hard decision without the luxury of time.

"All right – for the time being," I reluctantly agreed.

"Then it's settled," Mallory said, smiling and nodding approvingly. "It's going to be a pleasure collaborating with you, Professor. Gentlemen, you couldn't have come at a more opportune time. It is what the Matoomba call 'Maju' – divinely bestowed luck."

Mallory set his snifter on the table and stood up.

"It's been a pleasure, gentlemen. I apologize, but I'm afraid our time is drawing to a close for now," he said, snuffing out his cigar in the ashtray. "I'll have my driver take you back to your hotel. I look forward to our next meeting."

We rose to our feet and exchanged the usual amenities. When Mallory extended his hand to the Professor, he covered the handshake with his other hand, and his lips slowly spread in a reposeful smile. As they shook hands, the Professor perked up and his face bore an expression of realization, as if he had suddenly become cognizant of something he was previously unaware of.

"Oh yes, I almost forgot," Mallory said.

He asked the waiter to retrieve a sheet of stationery, on which he wrote a note giving the Professor access to the club's library.

"Please have Miles inform my driver that my guests are leaving," he said to the waiter.

We retrieved our coats and hats and found Mallory's chauffeur and Bentley waiting out front.

"Did you gentlemen enjoy your evening?" the chauffeur asked once we were under way.

"Yes, we had a most enjoyable evening – an extremely good-natured gentleman, Sir Gunston," JB replied.

"That he is," the chauffeur remarked. "I count myself fortunate to be in his employ."

Returning to our hotel, we picked up our keys at the front desk and boarded the elevator. The operator pushed the lever, and after a slight jolt, the cage began to ascend.

"I guess this means we'll be going to Oxford with you Professor," I said.

"I can't see any other way," he accorded.

"I was hoping that Sir Gunston might provide some information on Drayfus. Still, I got the sense that he knew more than he let on. He seemed guarded in his replies."

"Sir Gunston? Nonsense – a genteel man of his stature – what reason would he have to hide anything?"

"I don't know. Like I said, it was only an impression. By the way Professor, I noticed you didn't mention the Bradford Expedition."

"I saw no reason to," he said.

Yet I knew he had intentionally avoided the subject, as did I.

"On a positive note, it looks like our concerted efforts so far are paying dividends," JB piped in. "At last we're going to discover the tablet's purpose."

"If Mallory's findings are correct," I said.

"We'll find out in the coming days when I've reviewed his notes," the Professor stated.

The operator brought the elevator to a halt and opened the accordion doors.

"Oh, I've been meaning to tell you Professor – I dug up several articles at the office of The Times this afternoon. Two in particular were amongst Drafe's possessions," I said as we casually walked down the hall to our rooms.

"Yes, I remember you telling me during our voyage. I'd like to read them if I may."

I drew out the copies of the articles from my coat pocket and gave them to him. "They all mention Mallory, and I think you'll find one rather peculiar," I said.

We came to the Professor's door, and deciding to call it a night, he turned in. JB and I continued on to our respective rooms down the hall. Before inserting my key in the lock, I looked over at JB, who was standing at his door, now looking forlorn and depressed.

"You look troubled. Is something the matter?" I asked.

He cast his eyes downward and let out a deep sigh. "I was just thinking of Sadie. I know I should put it behind me, but I can't seem to get her out of my mind."

I felt like a heel for not telling him what I had seen in Southampton.

"Get some sleep, you'll feel better in the morning," I assured him.

They were not the most sincere choice of words, but I was not sure what to say, and it was too late to retract them.

He lifted his eyes and turned to face me. "I'll be all right," he said. "I just need time. The Professor gave me some kind words of advice yesterday that helped considerably. He's a wise man, the Professor."

With that, he bid me a good night and passed through his doorway.

*   *   *

Recalling that first night when it all began, I stopped and returned the room key to my pocket. I took out my notebook and flipped to a page. I had written down the name of the London nightclub printed on the matchbox I found in Drayfus' suit pocket – Regal Diamond Club, Grosvenor Square, London, Tel: Mayfair-3477. I looked at my watch. It was not that late. I concluded that this was as good a time as any to pay the establishment a call, and I was no doubt dressed for the occasion. Departing the hotel, I surveyed the lobby for any sign of the red-haired man. He was not present, and I wondered about his identity. Who was he, and what part did he have to play in the affair?

At the club a doorman screened me before granting me admittance. A brass plaque by the front door read – 'suit and black tie required', and a lit-up billboard advertised 'Frank Starlata and the music of Jake Hilton's Kit Cat Band'. An upscale clientele occupied a majority of the tables, which were arrayed around a crowded sunken dance floor, and a half-moon shaped bar in the background circuitously stretched round the periphery. A man at the podium ushered me to an empty table, and when a young waiter came around I ordered a manhattan.

Sipping my drink, I soaked in the surroundings, and when I felt the time was right, I made my move. I strolled over to the bar and flagged the bartender's attention with a five-pound note.

"What can I get for you, guv'ner?" he eagerly inquired.

"A minute of your time."

"You can have two if you like," he said, gazing at the money.

I took out a photograph of the Bradford Expedition and pointed to Harold Drayfus.

"Do you remember seeing this man in here?" I asked. "It would have been some time back, probably a month or so."

"No," he said, shaking his head.

"Take another look," I petitioned.

Squinting his eyes, he subjected the image of Drayfus to closer scrutiny.

"No," he repeated somewhat apologetically. "I can't recall the face. A lot of faces come and go here. It would be difficult to remember them all. Perhaps he was here on my night off."

I pocketed the photograph and passed the money across the counter to him.

"Thanks anyway. Should you remember, I'm sitting right over there," I said, pointing to my table.

The waiter made his way around again to my table, and I ordered another manhattan. When he returned with my drink, I placed a couple of one-pound notes on his tray and motioned with my finger for him to come closer. He leaned forward, and I discreetly took out the photograph and placed it on his tray. Pointing out Drayfus, I asked if he recognized the man. Obliging, he looked intently at the photograph, and after a few moments an expression of awareness flushed the young man's face and his eyes flashed with recognition.

"Yes, I remember him – an American chap. He was in here several weeks ago," he said, handing back the photograph.

"Was he alone?"

"No, he was sitting at a table with one of our regular patrons."

"Can you give me this patron's name?"

"Oh no sir, I'm not at liberty to divulge the names of our valued patrons."

"Would a bigger tip incite you?" I asked, placing more money on his tray.

He sighed, quickly looked about him, and leaned slightly forward.

"Philip Malfort – a man with a most notorious reputation," he said just audible enough for me to hear over the clamor and music.

"Does he come on any particular night?"

"No, but he usually comes in at least once a week."

"Do you know where I can find him?"

"That's him now," the young man replied, pointing toward the entrance with his eyes.

I looked over to see a heavyset man with an obvious devotion to rich food. A sweet honey clung to his side, her silk dress accentuating voluptuous curves, and two well-dressed ruffians stood in the background. I turned to address the waiter, but he was gone.

The headwaiter directed the heavyset man to a table nearby, and the two goons sat down at a table adjacent to his. Not imagining a better opportunity, I got up and approached the large man.

"Mr. Malfort?" I inquired.

"I beg your pardon."

"You're Mr. Philip Malfort, aren't you?"

"That depends on who wants to know," he said warily.

"My name is Blake. Might I have just a minute of your time?"

"What business do you have with me?" he asked, sizing me up with a look.

"I'm looking for answers, and I understand you can help me."

The girl kissed and nibbled his ear as I spoke, distracting his attention.

"You've got brass, I'll say that much for you, and you're no police inspector, that's bloody well apparent. I happen to be feeling rather generous tonight, Mr. Blake. Why don't you sit down?" he said, motioning for me to be seated. He gave me a stern look. "You've got one minute," he said in no uncertain terms.

Again I took out the photograph, and laying it in front of him, I pointed to Drayfus. "Have you met this man?" I asked. "He's an American named Harold Drayfus."

He briefly studied the face in the picture.

"No," he flatly replied, pushing the photograph back toward me and looking away.

"Are you sure?" I implored, pushing the photograph under his nose.

A slight fear shown in his eyes, it was not ostensible, but it was there just the same.

"I'm positive," he returned without even taking another look.

"Just take a closer look. That's all I'm asking."

Vexed, he snatched up the photograph and snapped his fingers.

"Your minute is up," he indignantly said.

In no time the two goons were on either side of me.

"This chap is on his way out – assist him," Malfort dictated. "I advise you to watch your step," he said to me, tearing up the photograph.

The two goons lifted me from my chair and unceremoniously conducted me to the front door, where they shoved my coat and hat in my arms and promptly ejected me from the club.

I stoically straightened myself and donned my hat and coat. I had been thrown out of worse places. I flagged a taxi and left with more questions than answers.

Entering my room, I switched on the lights, not knowing what I might find. I locked myself in, and while preparing for bed, I mulled over the events of a long day. I figured the tablet was safe at Burlington House. At least if our antagonists came looking for us, they would not find it. I wondered why our pursuers had not made a significant move yet. It had been two days since our landing in Southampton. I thought for sure they would have made some attempt by now. Then it hit me, and what had been only a hunch was now becoming clear as glass. I could sleep soundly tonight.

CHAPTER 10

Overcast skies brought a gentle snowfall that ushered in a new day. A soft blanket of snow canvassed the streets and rooftops of the old city, and the picture from my window had been repainted in mundane shades of gray and white. The Professor left shortly after breakfast with the intention of riding the tube to Bloomsbury and visiting the British Museum. Having time at my discretion, I visited the office of the Daily Telegraph and the American Consulate that morning; and in each case, I left disappointed. Later, JB talked me into accompanying him, and we hopped a double-decker to Soho.

The district was alive with the holiday spirit, and the gathering snow adorned the windowsills and storefronts on streets lined with a disparity of fashionable shops, restaurants and theatres. During our excursion, I took the opportunity of picking up a few items, namely a flashlight and compass, as well as some Christmas presents. I purchased a decorative scarf for Cindy, a cameo broach for Mrs. Coggins, an anthology of Dickens for the Professor, and at a tobacconist – a pouch of tobacco for JB that later turned out to be imported from Virginia. With darkness falling, we returned to our hotel and met the Professor for dinner. Afterwards, I picked up a detailed map at the front desk, and we packed for the next day's journey.

We boarded a morning train to Ashford where we caught the next train to Charing. Wisping puffs of steam and coal smoke flowed past the window, and flurries drifted down from dreary skies. By midday the clouds broke, enabling the sun's rays to come streaming through, and bright sunlight reflected off the snow that blanketed a peaceful countryside.

Standing on the platform at Charing Station, we scanned the scene for anyone there to meet us. Through the thinning crowd, I descried a short man in a woolen pea jacket holding up a thin wooden plank with the Professor's name on it. His neck was wrapped in a long knitted scarf, and a cloth cap sat cocked on his head.

"There's our man," I said, pointing to the man with the sign.

We headed in his direction with a porter in tow pushing a trolley laden with our baggage. As we approached, the man lowered the sign.

"I am Professor Hanson," the Professor informed him.

He looked at us through eyes that had seen many a season. His scruffy timeworn face had wrinkled leathery skin, red puffy cheeks, and a protruding chin. When he parted his sunken lips to speak, spacious gaps from missing teeth distorted his pronunciations.

"Name's Barnesby," he said indifferently. "I was sent here by Sir Gunston to fetch you to Blytemoor. Them your bags?" he asked with a crotchety gruffness.

"Uh – yes," JB hesitantly replied.

"Best be comin' along then," he said half-heartedly, gesturing for us to follow, and he began to walk away.

We looked at each other with confounded expressions, and I shrugged my shoulders.

Around the corner stood a tall grey hitched to a sturdy cart.

"Owin' to the recent weather, it's the best you're goin' t'get t'day," Barnesby said, seeing the expressions on our faces.

He helped the porter load our baggage on the cart, and we climbed onto the hard bench seats. The crotchety old-timer mounted the front seat, and snapping the reins, called out, "Get along, Chancey."

Once beyond the boundaries of Charing, the grey, with his head bucking to the rhythm of his stride and his nostrils expelling clouds of vapor, pulled us at a steady gait for several miles along a snow-covered lane that passed over gentle rolling hills and through lonely lowlands and barren woods. We emerged from a grove of aged, misshapen oaks into an expansive white glade. A brisk breeze stung my cheeks and whisked the glittering flakes into whirling funnels. The cart descended a slight grade, and the wheels rumbled over the planks of a bridge that crossed a shallow gurgling stream. A stone wall now paralleled the lane, and ahead the village of Blytemoor jutted out of the landscape, a secluded cluster of tumbled cottages huddled by the edge of a wood. In the distance a church spire towered over the snow-capped roofs.

We rolled into the village, and the old-timer steered the horse along narrow winding streets surrounded by antiquated half-timbered and stone buildings. He nodded or tipped his cap to the few townsfolk we passed, who silently acknowledged his greeting and then gawked at us until we had well gone by; after which, they vanished like shadows through some doorway or around a corner. Anonymous eyes curiously peered out from behind closed windows. We spanned an all but deserted open square dominated by an old stone church, and Barnesby turned down a lane off the square. He halted the cart in front of the last vestige of comfort and shelter before the lonely lane trailed off into a desolate wood, a two story rustic stone building with diamond-paned windows and a roofed bretesse projecting from the corner of its upper story. A weather-beaten sign displaying a black bird and the words 'Crooked Crow' hung from over the entrance.

Barnesby climbed down and traversed the trodden path to the doorstep.

"Best be comin' inside," he said, knocking the snow from his black boots.

With that, he unlatched the stout oaken door and disappeared through the portal.

"He's not much on words," JB remarked. "What about our bags?"

"Leave 'em," I said, and I hopped down.

The door remained open and clamorous voices echoed from within. As I crossed the threshold a hush fell over the room and the tavern became quiet as a tomb. The only sound that rose to my ears was the crackling and snapping of the log fire. Several townsmen were gathered at the bar. The innkeeper, a large robust man with rolled up shirtsleeves and a soiled apron stood behind the bar opposite the group. Except for the innkeeper, the patrons all averted their gaze. Barnesby warmed his bones by the fire, and two locals seated at a table stared down into their tankards.

"Come in gents," the innkeeper invitingly said.

By now my companions were standing behind me. JB shut the door, and we stepped up to an empty stretch of bar.

The innkeeper came over and stood across the bar. "You'll be needin' lodgings I gather," he said.

"Three rooms, if you have them," JB spoke up.

"I'm sure we can accommodate you gents," the innkeeper said, pulling out a register and setting it in front of us. "Now let me see," he said, doing arithmetic on his fingers. "For three rooms, that comes to one quid, two bob and sixpence per day – to be paid in advance."

"We'll be staying at least two days," the Professor said.

The innkeeper counted on his fat fingers again.

"That'll be two quid and five bob," he levied.

JB laid two one-pound notes and a crown on the countertop. "I believe that's the right amount," he said.

The innkeeper scooped up the money, stuffed it in a metal lockbox, and asked us to sign the register.

"Americans I'd say by the likes of you," he said with a friendly disposition.

"Yes – we're Americans," I said.

"By jove, I knew it," he remarked, cracking a smile. "Where from?"

"Boston, Massachusetts," JB replied, signing the register.

After looking at our names in the register, the innkeeper said, "Emmett's my name. If you gents need anything just let me know. We'll put you up right; I trust you'll find the hospitality to your likin'. My wife'll show you to your rooms." He turned his head and called out, "Aggie!"

"Do you have a telephone?" I asked.

"No – the only telephone is at Blytemoor Manor," the innkeeper replied.

A door from behind the bar opened, and my nose caught the delicious aroma of something cooking. A buxom woman emerged, wiping her hands on her apron. Her graying blonde hair was tied up in a bun and frazzled loose strands dangled over her brow.

"What's all the bloody fuss? I've got me hands full right now," she said somewhat put off, giving us the once over.

"We've guests, woman. I need you to show these gents to their rooms," the innkeeper said.

"I shan't be long," the woman called back through the half open door.

She smoothed out her dress and straightened her hair.

"If you gents'll follow me," she said, lifting up the bar gate.

"I'll be getting' your bags," Barnesby said, now heading for the entrance.

The woman led us up a flight of well-worn steps to an upstairs hallway and opened four doors.

"Take your pick, we don't usually have guests this time of year,' she said.

She opened another door, revealing a water closet containing a large pitcher and washbasin next to a hand pump, a primitive privy, and a claw-foot bathtub.

"If you want the tub filled with bathwater, tell me ahead of time," she decreed. "If you want it hot, that's extra."

We made our choice of rooms, and she inspected them, making sure each was amenable. She retrieved three sets of towels from the hall closet and laid them on our beds.

"Breakfast is included in the cost of your rooms. I serve it promptly at eight and you'll be takin' all your meals downstairs," she said before leaving us.

"Yes ma'am," I found myself blurting out.

Barnesby carried up the bags, and then he and the innkeeper hauled up JB's traveling trunk. JB tipped them, and as they turned to go, Barnesby said to the innkeeper, "I'll be havin' that pint now."

Sitting on the soft bed in my room, I took in my immediate surroundings and realized the only sources of illumination when darkness fell would be the oil lamp and candles on the bureau. A sudden wave of isolation swept over me – no electricity, no telephones and no motorcars.

I did not bother to unpack. Instead, I went downstairs to the tavern and sat at a table in the inglenook.

"What'll you be havin'," the innkeeper asked me, and I requested a pint of his ale.

An attractive golden-haired girl of about eighteen performed her duties behind the bar. The innkeeper called her Elsa; and speaking in tender tones as a father would speak to a beloved child, he directed her to bring me a pint. Her unspoiled beauty exuded a youthful innocence, but something about her was peculiar. She filled a tankard from a tapped barrel and brought it to my table as if in a trance. She uttered no word, and no soul seemed to stir behind her vacant blue eyes. The locals assembled in the tavern spoke with a colloquial dialect in subdued voices, and only waves of vague murmurs and half-lost echoes reached my ears. The repressed atmosphere momentarily changed when every patron in the tavern perked up and took notice of a motorcar that passed by the inn on its way down the lane leading to the wood, followed by sidelong glances at me. Despite the cozy setting of the inn, a disquieting uneasiness gnawed at me, as if my keen intuition was trying to tell me something, something ominous, something dire.

My companions came down and joined me for a while, then retired upstairs to prepare for Mallory's upcoming dinner party. I, instead, lingered in the tavern and tried to dismiss the persistent impending feeling that hung over me like a dark cloud. I realized I was in no mood to attend a high-class affair and made the decision not to go. I would be out of place anyway, and there would always be tomorrow I rationalized.

JB later returned, looking sharp and decked out in decorous fashion.

"Here you are," he exclaimed. "Our ride will be here any time now. You should be dressed."

"I'm not going," I flatly told him.

"What do you mean you're not going? You're expected," he emphatically said.

"Just what I said – I'm not going."

Over JB's shoulder, I saw the professor descending the stairs with hat in hand and wearing his overcoat.

He walked up beside JB. "Are we all ready?" he asked.

"He says he's not going," JB said. "Maybe you can talk some sense into him, Professor."

"What's this – you're not going? Why?"

"I have my reasons."

"I'm not going to try to persuade or compel you Mr. Blake, but I do wish you would reconsider," the Professor said.

"You can fill me in when you get back."

I saw the lights of a motorcar outside the window, and soon Mallory's chauffeur appeared in the doorway. Disappointed with me, JB shook his head. He asked the chauffeur to wait, and he went to fetch his coat and hat.

"I was instructed there would be three of you," the chauffeur said when they were ready to depart.

"One of our party has chosen not to come," JB replied, giving me a look askance.

I watched as they got into the black Bentley and it traveled down the lane into the woods.

* * *

The Bentley's headlights illuminated the roadbed through the gloom as the motorcar traveled along a solitary lane that meandered its way through a dense host of grim and ancient oaks standing vigilant by the roadside. After the Bentley rounded a bend, the roadside trees fell away and the lane traversed a misty bog. The chauffeur turned off and drove through an open iron gate flanked by two weather-stained rampant lions upon tall stone pedestals. He proceeded down a long drive lined by hedgerows and then steered around a circle with a fountain at its center, icicles dripping from the rim. Outlined against a wintry moonlit sky and still much as the Elizabethan builder had left it, stood the castle-like manor house of Blytemoor, with its bartizans, oriels and gothic mullioned windows. Gargoyles watchfully guarded from their perches, and ivy-covered gray stone walls emitted an eminent prestige that bore the elegance of an era gone by. The windows on the first level were brightly lit and silhouettes moved about on the other side of the dull glass. The chauffeur let them out, and then he drove down a path off the circle that led to a converted carriage house, where several motorcars were parked.

JB and the Professor walked across a stone bridge that spanned a wide moat; the snow-covered frozen surface of the moat gave it the deceptive appearance of only a shallow depression. They then crossed a lamp-lit terrace to arrive at a pair of stalwart doors laced with ironwork and decorated with pine wreaths. One of the doors opened and a solemn butler welcomed them. They entered a large, lofty entrance hall ornamented with paintings and portraits, and a grand staircase rose to a balustraded gallery overlooking the hall. Two princely suits of armor stood at attention like unsleeping sentinels, the polished plate glistening in the light of the chandelier. A servant took their coats and hats, and the butler ushered them to a set of open double doors.

Standing in the doorway, they looked about a tastefully furnished, spacious drawing room. More than a dozen smartly dressed guests, mostly men, were milling about or conversing in small groups. The gentle rambling tones of a piano intermingled with their voices. Black velvet curtains with gold fringe, drawn back and tied, adorned the windows, and a garland garnished the mantel. A large punchbowl rested on a long sideboard along with plates of hors d'oeuvres. Male servants in white tie and black tails, carrying silver trays with hors d'oeuvres or crystal cups filled with eggnog, circulated amongst the guests.

Mallory was in the midst of graciously entertaining his guests, and taking notice of JB and the Professor, heartily greeted them.

"Merry Christmas, gentlemen. Welcome to my home, I'm very pleased you've come."

"Merry Christmas," JB and the Professor chimed in return.

"Where is Mr. Blake?"

"He's feeling a bit under the weather this evening," JB evasively replied.

"I'm sorry to hear that. I hope it's nothing serious."

"No – nothing serious."

"That's a ruddy shame, I had counted on the three of you," Mallory said disappointedly.

He turned to the butler and instructed him that there would be one less for dinner.

"Please allow me to introduce you to some of my other guests," he said, a smile returning to his lips.

Making the rounds, Mallory courteously presented them to the other distinguished guests: Lord Thomas Mansfield, fifth Earl of Foxford, and Lady Mansfield, Malcolm Broderick of the British Museum, Professor Wendell Scott of University College, Mr. Arthur Winthrop, a newspaper publisher, Sir Timothy Bradshaw, Member of Parliament, and a Mr. A.E. Waitley among others.

"You're the Harvard Professor who is collaborating with Sir Gunston. Jolly good show on your part," Professor Scott remarked when introduced to the Professor.

Soon they were an integral part of the affair; the Professor involved himself in a discussion on metaphysics with Mr. Waitley and another gentlemen, while JB, employing his urbane Boston manner, mingled amongst the company.

The butler called the gathering to dinner, and they all filtered into a prodigious dining hall, heavily raftered with huge stout beams of age-darkened oak. A long solid table that could easily seat two-dozen prominently stretched out along the center of the long expansive chamber, the table settings illuminated by candlelight. Tapestries draped the walls, and a noble coat of arms was conspicuously displayed above an imposing fireplace, a roaring fire burning within the hearth.

Place cards indicated the seating arrangements, and JB and the Professor found themselves seated near the head of the table.

After an extravagant dinner, the men remained in the dining hall to smoke their cigars while the ladies retired to the drawing room. Mallory took JB and the Professor aside into the entrance hall to inform them of good news: he had achieved a profound breakthrough. Exhibiting an exuberant optimism, he asked if they might speak for a few moments in private. They readily obliged, and Mallory conducted them down an extended dark hallway to a remote door in a wing of the manor house. He pulled a key from his pocket, slipped it into the antique mechanism, and opened the door, revealing a dimly illuminated interior.

"After you, gentlemen," Mallory said, gesturing for them to enter.

They stepped into an office furnished with all the marks of aesthetic distinction. A desk lamp resting atop a broad expansive mahogany desk proved to be the source of illumination. The curtains were drawn closed, and a second door that perhaps led to an adjoining room provided the only other egress. Mallory closed the door behind them and casually locked it.

"I don't wish for us to be disturbed," he clarified, allaying any apprehension on their part.

He ushered them to two leather wing chairs positioned in front of the desk and hospitably bid them to please sit down and be comfortable.

He walked around behind the desk and opened the top drawer.

"Gentlemen, this is a matter which can no longer wait," he earnestly said.

He reached into the drawer and calmly drew forth a loaded Webley revolver, and taking a perfectly composed stance, he pointed the barrel directly at them. Shocked, JB and the Professor sat wide-eyed in bewildered surprise, and when Mallory slammed the drawer shut, they shuddered in their seats. Mallory's demeanor instantly altered to that of a vile serpent, and he looked at them with cold harsh eyes. His lips creased his face in a wicked grin, and he let loose a sinister chuckle.

CHAPTER 11

No sooner had the Bentley carried my companions away than all eyes in the tavern were cast upon me. Looking back at the simple townsmen, their faces racked with travail, I realized it was not curiosity that impelled them. A nameless fear lurked in the recesses of their souls and was clearly present in their eyes and in their disconcerted expressions, and their perturbing stares provoked an apprehension in me.

"Won't you be joining your friends?" the innkeeper asked from behind the bar.

Before I could respond, the door to the inn swung open and a rush of cold night air blew in. A man stepped inside, and after pushing the stout door closed, he removed his overcoat and scarf and hung them on a peg by the door.

"There's an icy chill in the air tonight," he said.

He had curly gray hair, bushy muttonchops and a wise face, and his collar indicated that he was a man of the cloth. He immediately became aware of the ill mood pervading the room and took notice of me.

"Good evening, friends," he congenially said to those gathered in the tavern.

"Good evening, Vicar," replied a chorus of voices.

The Vicar turned to me. "Ah, we have a visitor in our midst. Good evening," he greeted me with a bow of his head.

I nodded in response. He walked over to the fire to warm himself, and as he did, he gave a reassuring look to his parishioners, who returned to their drinking and communing. Rubbing his hands by the fire, he looked at me with a sincere smile and a kindness in his eyes.

"Will you be havin' the usual, Vicar?" asked the innkeeper.

"Yes please," replied the Vicar.

He approached my table and introduced himself. "I'm Reverend Travis. May I join you? You look as if you could use some company."

"Conrad Blake," I reciprocated, motioning for him to be seated.

He lowered himself into the chair across the table. "I'm the shepherd of this suspicious flock," he said. "You'll have to forgive them, for they are very wary of strangers, especially those visiting the manor."

"What makes you think I'm here to visit the manor?"

"News travels fast in the village of Blytemoor." A queer inquisitive expression suffused his face. "You're not English," he said, stating the obvious.

"No, I'm an American."

I took a swig of ale and evaluated him with my eyes. His eyes exhibited a gleam that was not a reflection from the fire, and I realized that I too was being silently scrutinized.

"Have you known Sir Gunston long?" he asked in a casual way.

Although presented casually, the question was no doubt direct. Something about his kindhearted disposition and trusting smile persuaded me to answer.

"Not really, I made his acquaintance two days ago."

He slowly shook his head and sighed. "Where might I ask?" he questioned with genuine concern.

"At the Royal Society in London. My companions and I consulted him in regards to an academic matter," I disclosed.

"Have you been in England long?"

"Less than a week."

"Were those your companions I saw getting into Sir Gunston's motorcar?"

"Yes, they left to attend a dinner party at the manor."

"Will you not be joining your companions then?" he inquired with a noticeable curiosity.

"No, I bowed out."

"You were wise to do so. Do you not know what night this is?"

It had to be a trick question. "Sure, Wednesday night," I said sarcastically.

He reclined back in his chair, and his inquisitive expression changed to discernment.

The innkeeper brought a mug of steaming liquid to the table and set it in front of the Vicar.

"Ah, nothing like hot-buttered rum to warm the soul," the Vicar remarked, his eyes sparkling with delight.

"Will you be havin' somethin' to warm your belly?" asked the innkeeper.

"I have a taste for Aggie's steak-and-kidney pie. Have you any?"

"Comin' right up," the innkeeper said, a bit puffed up with pride.

"Thank you Emmett," the Vicar returned.

"Will you be wantin' anythin'?" the innkeeper asked me, and I requested another pint.

"What did you mean when you said I was wise not to go?" I curiously asked the Vicar when the innkeeper had withdrawn.

"You do not know the history of the manor then."

"No."

He leaned forward, looked at me with those kind eyes, and spoke in a benign voice. "I want you to consider me a friend, and what I tell you now, I tell you as a friend. The manor holds many dark secrets and has done so for centuries. Many generations of the Mallory family have come and gone since the manor was built some three and one-half centuries ago. But always there remains a prevailing evil that overshadows it. It is primarily on the nights of the solstice and the equinox that this dark power manifests itself. It is the house of the devil, and the devil is its master. Your friends were ill-advised to go there."

He lowered his voice a degree, and at times his speech fluctuated with a noticeable emphatic inflexion.

"Sir Mortimer, the builder and first to occupy the manor had a frequent guest, a man he had met at the Royal Court." His voice sank to a whisper as he spoke the name – "John Dee."

Firelight danced in his eyes. "This man was the Royal Astrologer to Her Majesty Queen Elizabeth. He was a depraved man, an alchemist and professed sorcerer. When he had fallen out of favor and lost the protection of the Queen, the populace stormed his house and put it to the torch. On nights during his visits, strange lights emanated from the manor, and dreadful sounds, carried on the wind, resounded through the nocturnal air. Young women and girls from the village disappeared and were neither seen nor heard from again. Blytemoor was a village in constant mourning. This depraved sorcerer imparted arcane knowledge to Sir Mortimer, forbidden lore delving into sacrilegious pagan rites devoted to the secret worship of blasphemous deities. Since that time, the evil spawned within those walls has passed from generation to generation. Even the family has suffered from its virulence. Each lady of the manor died or disappeared under mysterious circumstances, usually shortly after giving birth – always to a male child. Lady Margaret, the wife of Sir Reginald, Gunston's grandfather, died in a lunatic asylum, and two of his known mistresses committed suicide. Sir Reginald lived to a ripe old age, outliving his son, who was killed in a freak riding accident. It was not until his death that the prevalent evil subsided, releasing its oppressive grip that had held the villagers captive for so many years, and a sense of normalcy finally reclaimed Blytemoor. Tales of those dark times are still told by those old enough to remember. Legend has it the manor stands upon the very entrance to hell itself. Sir Jonathon, Gunston's elder brother, inherited the title and estate after the death of his grandfather. He was a benevolent man who bestowed good will on the villagers. He, his lovely wife and son attended church regularly, and are the only family members to set foot within the walls of my church during my tenure, and I have been Vicar of this parish for over forty years. His wife, Lady Annabel, died of an unexplained malediction, and she alone lies buried in hallowed ground in the churchyard. Other than Sir Jonathon and his son Edward, who are buried somewhere in Africa, all of the Mallory ancestry are interned in the family mausoleum on the estate. With little exception, everything I have just told you stems from personal experience or is written in the church records, and some of the entries penned in the records by my predecessors are most disturbing. As for Sir Gunston, he and his grandfather were quite close, and it appears he has chosen to follow in the footsteps of his forebears. For since his return from Africa, the evil has been rekindled, and the potency of that ungodly power has resurged again. See that innocent golden-haired child behind the bar?" he said, motioning with his eyes. "She is a pitiful victim of its recurrence." He paused to take a swallow from his mug, and before I could digest his words, he warned, "Tonight is the night of the winter solstice. Heed my advice and leave Blytemoor while you can."

If not for the uncanny events of the past two weeks, I would have normally regarded his yarn as superstitious folklore. He had spoken with such grave resolve that I was compelled to believe him. His next words only served to fuel my suspicions.

"It might interest you to know that another American was here some time back and stayed at this very inn. He was a historian, I believe. He came to my church and asked to study the church records. I granted him access, whereupon he spent hours pouring over them. One day a motorcar came from the manor to fetch his belongings. He was being put up in the manor they said. He did not return to my church and that's the last I heard of him."

"Do you remember his name?"

Summoning his memory, he rolled his eyes up for a moment. "It seems to have slipped my mind, but I recall that it started with a "D", and he called himself Doctor."

"Drayfus – Dr. Harold Drayfus?"

"Yes, that's it," he declared, a light of recollection in his face. "Do you know him?"

"My companions know him quite well. When was this?"

"It was early autumn I recall."

My intuition now shouted at me, and I concluded that my hunch was right: we were in a rigged game. JB and the Professor had walked into the lion's den of their own accord and I had let them. A sense of disquieting guilt and dread I had never known before seized me.

In alarm, I sprang to my feet. "Where is the manor? How do I get there?" I demanded.

"After all that I have told you? Please sit down – do not be rash. I entreat you not to go. You will only be placing yourself in danger."

"What do you expect me to do? Just sit here while my friends may be in danger?" I emphatically asked, lowering myself into my chair.

"I will not be a party to your fate," he somberly said, his head bent and a tinge of cowardice in his voice.

"What about the fate of my friends? Doesn't it say in that good book of yours something about laying your life down for your friends?" I reproved.

"Yes it does – John fifteen, verse thirteen," he conceded, propping up his composure.

Look, just point the way – I'll walk," I insisted.

"It's too far to go walking alone in the dark of night. In good conscience I could not allow you to do that. If you must go, you'll be needing suitable transport and a guide, someone to show you the way."

"You, Reverend?"

"Alas no, but I know your man. Are you willing to pay a good sum?"

"Whatever it takes – name it."

"Wait here," he requested.

He rose up, walked over to Barnesby, who was engaged in a game of darts, and whispered in his ear.

Barnesby's eyes widened with a flabbergasted expression. "Not on your life I won't – not tonight!" he exclaimed.

Again the Vicar whispered to him. Barnesby squinted his eyes and rubbed his chin in contemplation.

"Only if you go with me Vicar," he stipulated. "I'll be needin' your company on the way back."

The Vicar tried to reason with Barnesby, but he would not budge, and eventually the Vicar resigned to his stipulation. He brought Barnesby over to my table, and they sat down.

"So you want to be taken to the manor, do you? Well my price is twenty quid," Barnesby assessed, levying an exorbitant sum, expecting me to decline.

His face expressed disbelief at my answer.

"I'll give you twenty now and five more when we get there."

"All right then, I'd like to finish me pint first," he reluctantly said in agreement.

"I'll need to retrieve my coat and some things from my room. That should give you enough time," I said.

As I climbed the stairs, the innkeeper brought a plate of food to the Vicar, and the three of them muttered amongst themselves.

Inside my room with the door closed, I placed my suitcase on the bed and opened the lid, exposing my Luger tucked in its holster. Steadfast in my resolve, I donned the holster over my thick woolen sweater, and my trench coat safely concealed the pistol's presence. I gathered up several necessary items, including a flashlight, and stuffed them in the pockets of my trench coat. Before going downstairs, I went into JB's room and took the bottle of chloroform from his medical bag. I returned to the tavern to find the Vicar gobbling his meal and Barnesby swilling down the last drop from his tankard.

"Time to go – you ready?" I asked stolidly, laying the agreed sum of money on the table.

They both looked at me with reluctant faces. "As ready as I'm goin' t'be," Barnesby replied.

Barnesby went to hitch up the cart, and by the time he returned, the Vicar had finished his fare and drained his mug. He wrapped himself in his coat and scarf, and we stepped outside into the open air.

It was a cold, crisp night and a bright rising moon sailed amidst sparse drifting clouds. A biting breeze nipped at my flesh, and I turned up the collar of my coat, pulling it taught. The Vicar and I climbed into the back of the cart, and he settled into the seat opposite me.

"Tonight of all nights. Madness, that's what this is – sheer madness," Barnesby grumbled under his breath as he mounted the front seat; an unlit lantern rested on the seat beside him. "Get along, Chancey," he called out with a gentle snap of the reins.

The cart rolled up to the edge of a dark impenetrable wood, and we passed into another realm. Giant majestic oaks and elms hedged in the narrow lane, and as the horse plodded along, they encroached in behind us, seeming to bar any retreat. Their bare gnarled branches reached out to create a confining arched canopy, and the moonlight filtering through their twisted limbs shrouded the way in a sea of gathering shadows. The clip-clop of the horse's hooves and the crunching sound of the wheels rumbling over the earth and stone bed gave respite from the eerie stillness. Barnesby nervously hummed a tune, and at the slightest noise, he straightened up and took notice. The Vicar sat silent and wide-eyed, constantly looking about and over his shoulder as if he expected some malignant menace to pounce out of the shadows.

We rounded a bend and came to a point where the Vicar spoke up. "Remember that sweet girl at the inn? One night, when the moon was full, her father Emmett, the innkeeper, arose to investigate a noise. He discovered her missing from her bed and the window wide open. He and his wife Aggie desperately searched the inn and the grounds, but to no avail. They enlisted the aid of others including myself, and we set out to comb the village and the countryside. Many hours later, we found her wandering aimlessly along this very stretch, that blank stare in her eyes. Since then, she has neither uttered a word nor a sound."

"A pathetic sight she was," Barnesby remarked and turned his head to spit.

The bleak wood gave way to a dismal bog, and a mantle of rising mist cloaked the ground in swirling white vapor. Evanescent lights like flickering candles would appear off in the mist, hover for a fleeting moment, then extinguish. Hollow murmurs filled the air, and I could have sworn my senses were playing tricks on me, but one look at the Vicar told me he heard them too. The boundary of the lane became indistinguishable and Barnesby halted to light the lantern. He held it aloft as he cautiously proceeded onward.

"Don't you worry none, Chancey knows the way," he assured.

The murky haze veiled our surroundings and at times obscured my vision such that I could barely see the horse's flopping mane.

The mist receded and a tall hedgerow now edged one side of the lane. Barnesby brought the cart to a halt.

"This is as far as I dare tread, and not for a king's ransom will I venture farther," he asserted.

"I don't see any signs of a manor. Where is it?" I asked.

"The lands of the estate lie on the other side of this hedgerow and yonder lies the manor house," the Vicar replied, pointing.

Making a quick assessment of the situation, I determined the hedgerow to be insurmountable.

"How do I gain entrance to the grounds?" I asked.

"The main gate is up the road a furlong."

"Is there another way?"

"Not unless you want to risk traversing the moor."

"Take heed lad and don't go treadin' the moor," Barnesby warned. "Many a lost soul's bin swallered up in the mires of that festerin' dreg."

"What about up the road beyond the gate?"

"The hedgerow continues on a ways," the Vicar answered. "Then a tall iron fence bristling with spikes borders the south side of the inner acreage. There's a postern gate a good stretch down the fence near the stables, but it's kept locked with a heavy chain, and the dogs are sure to be out."

"Vicious animals they are – powerful beasts that'll tear your limbs off and rip you to shreds," Barnesby remarked, putting in his two cents.

It seemed my options were limited and each fraught with hazards.

I thanked them both for braving the night on my behalf and for their candidness. I paid Barnesby the additional amount I promised him and gave a couple of bills to the Vicar.

"Consider it a donation. I can always use help from the man upstairs," I said.

"Remove your hat and bow your head," the Vicar instructed. "For tonight you may face the devil himself."

He laid a hand on my head and uttered a solemn prayer over me, then traced the sign of the cross atop my head and pronounced the words "Dominus vobiscum."

I replaced my hat snugly.

"God go with you," he said, placing a hand on my shoulder.

I hopped down, and the Vicar climbed onto the front seat next to Barnesby. Barnesby passed the lantern to the Vicar, and then he turned the cart around.

"Good luck lad," he said.

The Vicar turned and waved as the cart ambled away to be swallowed by a curtain of mist. The sound of the wheels died away and the diminishing glow of the lantern was all that remained.

Alone, I strode up the lane toward the main gate, the light of a cold moon illuminating my way. Heeding Barnesby's warning, I dismissed any notion of traversing the moor. The dispiriting nature of it lingered fresh in my mind. Ahead, a pair of stone lions rising above the hedgerow marked the location of the gate. Sticking close to the wall of prickly foliage, I slunk up to the first stone pillar. Above my head, a roaring lion poised on its hind legs stood like a dutiful sentry. A thick heavy chain and padlock secured the two hinged iron gates. Peering through the bars, I looked down a wide dark corridor hemmed in between two high walls of clipped hedge running parallel to the drive. In the distance I could see the rooftop of the manor, and the tips of its turrets and chimney tops silhouetted against the wintry sky.

Afar off down the drive a light appeared. It hovered a few feet above the ground and then grew brighter as it moved up the drive toward me at a slow and steady rate. I kept a keen and curious eye on it as it came ever closer, until the source of the strange light became apparent, and I discerned it to be a lantern. Illuminated in the lantern's glow, a footman in tall boots walked at a steady gait, a shotgun tucked under his arm. Plodding along at his side was a hulking black and tan brute of a dog. The footman continued to head straight in my direction; and to avoid the chance of revealing myself, I slipped back out of sight, retracing my steps. Cloaking myself in the shadows, I hid in the recess where the hedge buttressed against the pillar. The footman's heavy footfalls neared, and the dog's panting became audible. My heart beat fast as they drew near to the gate. The gate chain rattled and coiling wisps of vapor from the dog's breath floated past on the breeze as he sniffed the air, and I knew he was close. The beast growled and began to bark ferociously. “What is it, Lucifer? What’s out there?” the footman inquired.

CHAPTER 12

His eyes fixed on the instrument of death in Mallory's hand, JB tightly clutched the arms of his chair, and dumbfounded, shrank back into it. The Professor looked up at Mallory's smug face and perceived a latent evil lurking behind those cold, cruel eyes.

"I demand to know the meaning of this outrage!" he vehemently insisted.

Mallory chuckled scornfully.

"What insidious perfidy is this? Do you intend on shooting us?" the Professor asked, maintaining a stoic composure.

"Oh please, Professor, nothing so crude as that," Mallory chided, relaxing his threatening demeanor. "I have something a little more sophisticated in mind. I'm having a special gathering tonight, and you're going to be the guests of honor."

He picked up a small sterling bell from atop the desk and rang it. From behind JB and the Professor came the sound of a door opening, followed by a single set of footfalls drawing near and the panting of a dog.

Perilously close came the sounds, and then a young black-skinned African man garbed in western dress stepped into view, accompanied by a powerful brindled mastiff. A colorful cap without brim or visor adorned the man's head and covered his brow. He carried a tea service, which he gently placed atop the corner of the desk, and then he spoke a command word to the dog, who sat and quietly kept a vigilant eye riveted on JB and the Professor. JB fidgeted in his chair, and his movements induced the animal to show his teeth and snarl. Fearful that the beast might strike, the Doctor stiffened in place, and he became as rigid as an image in a photograph.

The Professor's eyes grew wide with recognition as he looked up at the face of the African man. "The steward on the train!" he uttered aloud.

Recognizing the very man he had seen in the window at the flophouse, JB sat speechless with an expression of terrified alarm. The African man stood stolid and silent.

"I believe a proper introduction is in order, gentlemen," Mallory said with an inflexion of satire in his voice. "Allow me to present Manbootu, a revered member of the Matoomba tribe. He is what his tribe calls a Shamba, an individual of eminent power and prestige. Within his tribal hierarchy he commands as much authority as the chief. He possesses a most distinguishing trait, which gives him extraordinary powers of perception and clairvoyance – a sixth sense, if you will. Show them, Manbootu."

Mallory's lips contorted into a sardonic grin as Manbootu removed the cap from his head, revealing a freakish deformity – a third eye centered in his brow. The eyelid raised and the leering eye shifted its penetrating gaze between them, its ocular movements independent of the other two eyes. JB gasped, and averting his eyes, he turned away. The Professor, undaunted and ever a man of science, curiously regarded the anatomical anomaly with inquisitive amazement.

"You see, gentlemen, your irritating interference and meddling have come to an end," Mallory said contemptuously. "As for Mr. Blake, I'll deal with him in short time, mark my words. That detective will regret the day he blundered across my path. He'll be joining you soon enough. A simple ruse shall lure him here."

"What makes you think Mr. Blake is a detective?" the Professor asked. "He never mentioned his profession and neither did we."

"I am quite well-informed, and I know all I need to know concerning Mr. Blake and yourselves. The morning we first met at Burlington House I was expecting you, for your coming was foretold to me. And I will say I found you easily duped and ensnared – quite the gudgeons," Mallory said with a flare of condescending arrogance.

Mallory stepped around to the front of the desk, pausing briefly to affectionately pat the dog. He leaned back against the desk and lowered the revolver, allowing it to rest against his thigh. Exhibiting a cold confidence, he placed his other hand on the desktop and tightly curled his fingers around the edge.

"I do however want to thank you for returning my property, gentlemen. The tablet is now secure within these walls," he said.

"Your property? What do you mean your property?" the Professor inquired, somewhat puzzled.

"Yes Professor – my property!" Mallory proclaimed with indignation. "Stolen by that impertinent thief, Harold Drayfus, and for his meddlesome interference, he suffered the consequences, as will you. You Americans – such an incorrigibly stubborn and persistent lot."

"So Mr. Blake's suspicions were correct. You knew about Harold all along, and being the perpetrator behind his demise, you acted under false pretenses, hoodwinked and outright lied to us. And what of the Bradford Expedition? Did you murder them too?" the Professor adamantly decried.

"The bloody buffoons stumbled upon me and almost ruined everything. They needed to be silenced," Mallory retorted.

"Then I take it we are to be silenced as well?" the Professor imputed.

Dismayed by what fate may lay in store for them, JB awaited Mallory's answer with fearful anticipation.

"I can't afford to do otherwise. You are aware of the tablet's existence. The risk of any further interference on your part must be eliminated, and your silence guaranteed, at least until its purpose is fulfilled, and that time is nearly at hand. In the meantime, you will enjoy the hospitality of my dungeon. It is quite medieval. As an archaeologist, Professor, I'm sure you'll find it most intriguing, and you'll have plenty of time to study the stonework. Even if you should find a means of escape, as Drayfus did, you will either suffer his fate, or spend the remainder of your wretched, piteous days in an asylum for the insane, there to rot as the last remnants of your sanity is wrenched away."

"Good lord man, what are you insinuating?"

"All in good time Professor, all in good time."

"You'll never get away with this despicable act."

"On the contrary Professor, you underestimate me, and let me remind you that my title and credentials coupled with an esteemed reputation make me a man who is practically beyond reproach. Even if you gained the opportunity to tell anyone, your story would be so chimerical that no one in their right mind would ever believe it, certainly not the police."

JB observed Mallory's shifting countenance and altering demeanor, and as a physician, noted the Englishman's unpredictable state of mind with grim concern. The man before him now was a far departure from the man they had dined with just earlier.

The Professor made a last ditch appeal for a reprieve. "Apparently we are at your mercy. You are obviously a refined man of notable intellect, and I appeal to reason. Allow us to return from whence we came, and this incident will be considered forgotten. I assure you nothing will be said, and as for the tablet, you may retain it without fear of reprisal. You have our word on it," he propitiated.

"Yes Sir Gunston, you have our word on it," JB readily concurred.

Mallory chuckled for a moment, then abruptly ceased. His eyes flashed with malice. "Your word as gentlemen and scholars," he coldly scoffed. "An honorable sentiment, but it will not avail you."

Despondent, JB looked up into the malicious eyes of a callous man bereft of mercy and compunction.

"For you to go to such lengths, the tablet must be a relic of paramount importance," the Professor stated. "Tell me Sir Gunston, what purpose does it serve? What meaning have you derived from its markings? I'm genuinely interested to know. Since we are to be imprisoned against our will, and in all probability murdered, you should have no apprehension in assuaging the academic curiosity of an old scholar seeking the truth."

Mallory's lips curled back in a condescending grin. "What makes you any different or better than the majority of my so-called peers, a swaggering collection of narrow-minded archaic fools, who haughtily fancy themselves to be enlightened and erudite, but could neither recognize nor grasp the truth if the most palpable evidence of it was to fall in their laps," he petulantly said. "Their practical intellect presumes all things to have fixed dimensions, properties, causes and effects, and they rule out as incredible all that cannot be explained or understood by the doctrines of prevailing dogma and theory. To them, all things must reconcile to their settled order of nature."

The Professor gave no ostensible reaction to Mallory's remarks.

"You will find me to be in the qualified minority," he firmly stated. "Try me, prove me, impart to me that knowledge which is so momentous as to outweigh a man's life and well-being. You must have some inward importunate yearning to impart it to objective ears, and you'll find mine most receptive."

The Professor settled back in his chair, rested his elbows on the arms, and clasping his hands together, assumed an attentive posture as if he was attending a seminar or lecture. Knowing full well the dangerous game he was playing, he dared not show the trepidation and fear that gnawed at his insides.

"Pray tell, Sir Gunston, edify me – enlighten me," he requested with deference. "I entreat you not to leave me in the dark."

Mallory's wide bulging eyes receded, his flushed cheeks faded to a normal pallor, and he cracked a smile. He surveyed the Professor with discerning eyes as if he were rendering judgment.

"I suppose it would be rather cruel to leave you floundering in the dark Professor, at least not yet anyway, but I caution you, one should be careful what one wishes for," he admonished. "Yes, Professor, I will prove you, and we shall see if your unimaginative mind can fathom the truth. And you may find its bitter fruit distasteful."

He picked up a shelled nut from a shallow silver bowl on the desk, plopped it in his mouth and chewed it in irony. The crunching noise seemed intolerable in contrast to the otherwise deathly silence and grated on the nerves.

The Professor gave Mallory an impelling look of impatience, and Mallory smiled like a cat toying with its prey.

"First and foremost, I know full well the purpose of the tablet and the markings on its face," Mallory declared. "In fact, I have possessed the knowledge for quite some time. I have in my possession, a hermetic tome containing a wealth of untold secrets. The abstruse words and symbols upon its pages are as old as time itself, and its recondite ciphers and cryptic passages are keys to unlocking the mysteries of the universe. Its name I will not disclose to you, though you may be aware of it. Doctor John Dee, a learned sage and noted astrologer in the sixteenth century, transcribed the work into the Old English. He was a renaissance man ahead of his time, yet debased and derided by an ignorant, superstitious populace. He bestowed a hand-written copy to my ancestor and instructed him in deciphering its abstract text. It has since been handed down through the generations to me. Only a few copies are known to still exist. My fool of a brother almost burned it after the death of my grandfather, and would have done so, had I not been there to prevent him. Within the binding, lies the revelation of the runes and the interpretation of their arcane meaning."

"I am aware of both the man and the unholy, blasphemous tome of which you speak," the Professor acknowledged. "And I earnestly warn you – monstrous consequences await those who covet to possess forbidden knowledge and power, for diabolical things lurk in the shadows of death, waiting to seize the souls of those who trespass in forbidden realms."

"Superbly remonstrated, Professor," Mallory said with a laugh. His eyes flared wide. "But that pertains only to the weak-minded," he emphatically said. "Even as a boy, I was drawn by the allure of its enigmatic contents, and at my grandfather's side, I boldly dared to solve the riddle of its mysteries. My steadfast efforts did not go unrewarded, for through diligent study and application I elucidated the text, and became endowed with a superior understanding of the mystic secrets of the universe and all they hold. I learned of the Elder Gods before time, supreme beings of cosmic origin. The runes appertain to a god who sleeps, abiding in the shadows on the fringe of reality between dimension and time, eagerly awaiting his hour of awakening. He communicates with his minions through the medium of dreams, and I have heard his calling."

"I implore you not to speak his abominable name," the Professor petitioned.

"He has many names, Professor. In Zoroastrianism, he is known as Ahriman. In the language of the Matoomba, his revered name is 'Zaku-Tog' – the sleeping god, a name spoken only in sacred ritual."

The desk lamp flickered, and the temperature momentarily plummeted to such a degree that their warm breath emitted wisps of vapor.

"Generally, he is referred to as 'Bonwoni Monu-Tog' – god under the mountain, a name I disclosed in my book. You see, Professor, I ventured to Africa with foreknowledge, my express design in mind masked by auspicious reasons."

The Professor interjected. "To search for the ruins with the aspiration to find and acquire the tablet," he deduced.

"More than just that Professor, but you're catching on nicely."

Slackening his posture, Mallory slightly leaned to one side and continued his discourse. "Permit me to give you a little background. We first encountered the Matoomba on the second day after having transgressed into their valley. On that morning, drums resounded throughout the jungle and our guide insisted that we turn back. But we had found a path, and were making good progress in our endeavor to reach the Sanga River. Undaunted, I urged that we press onward. We had struck camp and were under way, when without warning,

Matoomba warriors arrayed in fearsome costumes and paint, assailed our beleaguered party as if out of nowhere. Several of the bearers fell mortally wounded, pierced by spears like pincushions. It seemed fate was about to dash all my ambitions; and in the pandemonium that followed, I thought it an inauspicious end to an all too arduous journey. Then a peripeteia occurred that only fate could orchestrate. During the scuffle my shirt was torn open, exposing my bare chest and a medallion that hung from my neck, a gift bequeathed by my grandfather. Whereupon, at the sight of it all commotion ceased, and the warriors confronting me recoiled with wide eyes and cried out. I held it up, presenting the embossed symbol on its face. One, obviously the leader, for his commanding manner and adornment distinguished him from the others, came forward for a closer examination. He gazed intently at the medallion and then looked me in the eyes. I maintained a steady composure and showed no fear. Turning to address the warriors, he barked out a series of orders, and we were taken to their central village where I was presented to the chief and a tribal priestess. The priestess wore stunning regalia and an amulet, both bearing the identical symbol as that on the medallion, which I discovered to be a symbolic representation of their most hallowed deity. They believed me to be an emissary of this deity, and thus I was able to persuade them to spare the lives of my brother, nephew and our guide, whose skill as an interpreter was invaluable. The other members of our party were not so fortunate and met with a most horrid and untimely end. I bided my time while learning all that I could with expedience, and then the day came when a fateful event occurred that ensured my place in the tribe and paved the way for destiny. To put it succinctly, I rescued the life of Manbootu here," he said with a gesture toward the African man, who smiled and gave an affirmative nod. "As a reward for my magnanimous deed I was inducted into the tribe, with all the rights and privileges appertaining thereto, and in accordance with tribal custom, given a status equivalent to being a godfather to Manbootu – a role I took to heart. After being indoctrinated in tribal language and custom, and fully accepted as a member of their society, I learned of their intimate knowledge of the ruins and thus seized opportunity. The rest I'm sure you can surmise, Professor."

"Yes, It's becoming quite clear to me now," the Professor said.

"And now I shall impart that which you so ardently seek," Mallory said. "The tablet was forged by a primeval race with a superior knowledge of the sciences and the stars, and it has an ancient and guarded purpose. It shall not be allowed to ignobly rot in a museum, to be gawked at by a nescient public. The tablet is more than just symbols and pictures. It is a tool – an instrument – a cipher key. One of two keys actually, and the other is very nearly within my grasp. A key not unlike the one I used to open the door. Except this key will unlock a gateway to the mystery of the ages and usher in a new era. Even if you could interpret the runes, by adhering to the sequence as presented on the tablet, the translation would seem like nonsense. But when aligned with their counterparts, the cipher becomes intelligible."

"And where are these counterparts?" the Professor slyly asked.

Mallory paused to consider an answer.

"The ruins perhaps," the Professor inquired further.

"Perhaps, Professor – perhaps," Mallory allusively replied.

His countenance shifted and he gazed at the Professor with piercing eyes. "Now if you will afford me no further interruptions," he sternly reproved.

Utter silence ensued, broken only by the tick-tock of the clock on the wall, its pendulum swinging back and forth. Mallory's vexed expression melted away and he resumed a more placid state. The Professor respectfully gestured for him to continue.

"If you could only fathom the depth of its significance. The tablet is not limited to one purpose, this enigmatic wonder – this marvel of the ancients, is more than simply a key, it was forged with a foresight that only superior intellect could inspire," Mallory prated. "It is a prophetic relic which foretells the occurrence of a forthcoming astronomical event, marked by the appearance of a brilliant star blazing in the night sky. Astronomers the world over will gaze at the heavens in wonder, and chronicle it as a momentous phenomenon. In the course of this cataclysmic event, powerful cosmic forces shall be set in motion, causing an upheaval in the heavens and splitting a rift in the fragile fabric that weaves the macrocosmic barrier. And in that hour of reckoning, I shall employ both keys in conjunction to unlock the gateway bridging dimension and time, and call forth the one of old, awakening him from the slumber of eons. No longer imprisoned and bound by the shackles of heavenly restraint, his immortal spirit once again free to roam this physical plane, he shall abolish the idols of what a decadent, corrupt and supercilious mankind so pridefully refers to as western civilization, and stem the polluting human tide of ethnocentric pestilence which is spreading to every corner of the globe and inevitably beyond. Kings, potentates and the governments of mighty industrial nations will topple under his heel, and a new world order shall be established under his omniscient dominion. The curtain is closing on the age of man. As it is written, so shall it be. On an apocalyptic scale in proportion to your biblical revelations, this world will experience wrath and cataclysmic upheaval, such as mankind has never known. Like the lancing of a boil, the earth shall cut away and spew out the festering illness of humanity along with all its lucripetous machinations. The world will serve a new master, and sanctioned by his approbation, I shall be at his right hand, basking in the radiance of his eternal throne, there to see it all come to fruition. The time is close at hand when the stars will be in perfect harmony and alignment. Thus the prophecy shall be fulfilled, and I will be the instrument of its fulfillment. He shall call forth his minions and servants out of the dark, hidden places in the earth and muster them at his feet. They shall crush the egotistical will of mankind and efface the icons of his religions. I will be part of a new beginning – a new cosmos – a new world in harmony with the earth and the stars, and I shall be exalted in the heavens! And for their steadfast belief and obeisant worship, the Matoomba people will be lifted to high places."

Mallory paused to collect himself.

"Your bombastic discourse is more than sheer eccentricity," the Professor denounced. "Such radical convictions could only stem from a deranged mind consumed with a lust for power. Yours, Sir Gunston, are the heretical and maniacal ravings of a megalomaniac," he categorically stated.

Mallory leaned forward, his eyes flared wide with reproof. "Is it maniacal to embrace the truth? Is it madness to hold destiny in the palm of your hand? I shall be as a god!" he proclaimed. "Sic itur ad astra."

"Are you equating yourself with the architect of the universe?" the Professor solemnly asked.

"There is no architect of the universe, at least as you perceive him," Mallory retorted. "He is a fallacy – a figment of man's imagination to satisfy his need to fill a spiritual void and rationalize that which cannot be explained. It is the elder gods who reign over the cosmos. The ancients knew and revered them. The Mayans, the Aztecs and the builders of Stonehenge all offered blood sacrifices."

The clock chimes tolled the quarter hour, and Manbootu motioned to direct Mallory's attention to the tea service. Mallory looked at him with a grin and a devilish gleam in his eyes.

"Why gentlemen, where are my manners? Your tea is getting cold," he said sarcastically.

The African man gracefully poured two cups of tea and served them to JB and the Professor. The cup rattled in JB's unsteady hand as he stared down at the rippling dark liquid.

"It's a special brew containing an extract of the lotus plant – a particular species indigenous to Equatorial Africa," Mallory said. "One which is extremely environmentally sensitive, and having no tolerance for this temperate climate. Most of my attempts to transplant it failed, but with the right cultivation and sedulous care I was able to get a few to grow in my greenhouse – a feat I am proud of. The only other living specimens in the British Isles are at the Royal Botanical Gardens in London."

The Professor sniffed the aroma of the tea and the scent stirred in his mind a recent memory.

"It's not poison, I assure you. It won't kill you, but if you don't drink it, I will," Mallory stated, cocking the revolver. "Drink up, gentlemen," he pressed. "Don't insult my hospitality."

JB grimaced with disgust upon imbibing the tea, and the Professor reluctantly lifted his cup to his lips and drank.

"It has a bitter taste, but is quite effective, and in a short time you should be experiencing the soporific effects," Mallory apprised. "Soon gentlemen, you will know what makes a man afraid of the dark, for there are things most terrible lurking in the dark corners and recesses of your minds."

He pressed them to take another swallow, then another, and observed with expectancy.

After a time, he leaned slightly forward and riveted his eyes on the Professor. "There are things within our earthly realm, that if known, would send a wave of controversy crashing through the scientific world, and shatter most existing theories, most especially those pertaining to the origin and evolution of mankind and his place in the order of the cosmos."

As the Professor listened to Mallory's inane prating, his surroundings became blurred and surreal as if looking through a glass of water, and his ears received a cacophony of distorted sounds and obscured words. JB was rendered unconscious, his eyes still open, fixed, and staring into oblivion. In a futile effort the Professor tried to resist the disorienting potency of the tea, but inevitably succumbed. Slurring his words, he uttered, "You're mad." A curtain of darkness now veiled his vision. His body went limp, and he drifted off, lapsing into the shadows of a nightmare.

CHAPTER 13

Recumbent on his back, the Professor lay upon a block of cold stone and gazed up at a star-spangled violet sky with a thousand twinkling crystals dangling in the heavens. Shadowy waves of grass glistened in the soft moonlight, and a strange, yet sweet, pleasant odor hung in the air. His mind fused with wondrously boundless thoughts, he conceived of traveling to the stars with nothing more than the simplicity of his own willful desire to propel him. For a time, he gazed in wonder, his mind consumed with contemplation.

His ears received the faint sound of chanting – a chorus of many voices. The stars floated freely, swirling and shifting in the heavens, and then coalesced into the outline of three eyes arrayed in a triangle. Ignited by a scintillating spark, they burned with a tempest of raging hellfire and black abysmal pits devoid of all light loomed within the center of each fiery ferment. Filled with insidious evil passion, they riveted their gaze upon him. Aghast, he watched as the horrid spectacle descended from the sky, growing larger as it loomed closer and closer, and all the while the chanting chorus filled his ears with strange inscrutable words.

The moon turned to blood, casting a crimson hue on the land. The mantle of lush grass wilted and withered away to dust, to be replaced by twisted thorny brambles, and the landscape transmuted to a lonely sea of desolation broken and blotched with jagged crags erupting forth from an infernal ground.

Feelings of terror and dread flooded his being, and his thoughts centered on making a mad dash to escape some perceived impending doom. But in his effort to move, the synapses failed, and he discovered all his voluntary motor functions below the neck to be completely inoperative. He lifted his head to find himself clad in only his trousers. Slithering snake-like tentacles sprouting forth from the surrounding earth constricted his limbs and torso, lashing him to the cold gray granite. Floating balls of fire now hovered a few feet above his head and feet, the sinister blazing eyes encroached ever closer, melding into one great eye, and the relentless chanting continued.

Shifting and altering, his surroundings melted away like colors running down the canvas of an oil painting, and a very different scene unfolded before his astonished sight. Where once the balls of fire had hung suspended, flames now lapped up from red-hot coals burning in two braziers, and what had been a thousand twinkling stars were now the lambent lights radiating from scores of flickering candles arrayed in tiered rows. Illuminated in the dim dancing light, a darkened chamber came into view, a stone vault in which he realized he was not alone amidst the nebulous shadows. Coming into focus and silhouetted against the candlelight, obscure figures cloaked in purple ecclesiastical vestments embellished with golden symbols were assembled in the chamber, their nameless faces veiled and hidden by the shadows of their hoods. The eye now leered down from an embossed relief behind a stone altar. A magnificent carbuncle set in the center of the iris glimmered and sparkled in the soft undulating radiance of the flames, which cast an iridescent amalgam of golds and reds blended with shadow rippling over the interior of the unholy sanctum. Revolting and abhorrent carvings covered the base of the altar, and upon it, arranged in a triangle, stood three gold candlesticks fashioned like intertwining snakes. Two of the candles emitted red flames, and the wick of the elaborately molded third burned with an ominous black flame. At the center of the candlesticks rested a bronze vessel; wisps of smoke coiled up from the burning salts within, permeating the chamber with a strong spicy fragrance. A bejeweled silver chalice and an open tome also occupied a place on the altar. The breathing walls and ceiling were decorated with painted murals depicting horrid monstrous beings that appeared to move with animation, and the surface of the vacillating columns was composed of unctuous black and green scales seeping with viscous fulsome slime.

In an eminent place at the altar, a prominent figure wearing a chasuble with blasphemous markings presided over the profane ceremony. Standing with his back to the Professor and his arms raised in adulation, he led the assembly in a ritualistic intonation. *"Gloir Lakatu. Gloir Yog Soth Toth. Yog Soth Toth itur ad astra. Nich'naach toth koth karna-mor. Lok-tee karna-mor. Hebron-zed Yog Soth Toth. Hebron-zed Lakatu. Lakatoooo! Lakatoooo! Necrophillum Lakatoooo!"*

As the chanting reached a crescendo, everything in his view suddenly crashed in a whirlwind of images, and a new picture emerged from the crumbling remnants. He beheld a great city situated on a recessed plateau encircled by the towering ridges of a lofty mountain. Its colossal edifices erected of glossy black stone were of strange geometric design with beveled planes meeting at oblique angles, the layout and arrangement of the structures indicative of some underlying significant purpose. At one end of a grand avenue stood a tall obelisk reaching to the sky. At the other end stood a towering structure of pyramidic shape; sculpted busts, their ghoulish features manifesting a fiendishly cruel and frightening countenance, bordered the wide over-sized steps that ascended to an august temple bathed in a phosphorescent celadon light, its walls and flat roof translucent in the glowing aura. In a columned basilica out of the bowels of hell, he descried a multitude of foul alien beings obeisantly worshipping an abominable shadowy inhuman image seated in all its majesty on a monumental throne of bone ornamented with human skulls. The shrill of chaotic piping filled the air, and the gesticulating mass of disciples thrashed and flailed in a tumultuous sea of frenzy before the diabolical deity, which in the Professor's discerning perception personified the embodiment of all negative emotions, and he detected the presence of pure systemic evil. Shocked, he shut his eyelids in an effort to wipe out the appalling picture from sight, but to no avail, for his retinas still received the harrowing impressions.

In a terrifying journey beyond the endurance of the mind unprepared for its rigors, he experienced a feeling of falling into an abyss; and all began to spin in a maelstrom of shapes, colors and sounds, until at last he found himself back in the gloomy confines of the iniquitous chamber, laying prostrate on the stone as before, once again in the presence of the assembled idolaters. A shimmering medallion attracted his swimming vision, a medallion worn by the priestly figure now at his side. The unholy priest pulled back the hood of his garment, uncovering his head; and through a bleary haze, the Professor identified the face of Gunston Mallory, and the fiery reflection in Mallory's cold gray eyes imbued a devilish luster. The Professor mustered his faith and called out to his redeemer for deliverance, but his lips uttered no words – only a silent scream. Mallory's facial features twisted in a cruel expression, and he chuckled scornfully at the Professor's feeble attempt to speak.

Out of the shadows, a spectral robed figure emerged, his hooded garment ornamented with a single omnispective eye. Approaching, he glided across the floor as if riding on a cushion of air and came uncomfortably close to the Professor's side. He removed his hood, and the Professor gazed upon the deformed loathsome visage of the African man – Manbootu. A sense of dread rose up from the very marrow of the

Professor's mortal being, and he perceived himself to be the sacrificial victim in some diabolic ritual. He tried to turn away; but it was too late, he had looked into those mesmerizing eyes and was transfixed by their hypnotic gaze. He found himself locked in a mental struggle for control of his very mind and soul. Entranced and spellbound, he succumbed to an irresistible potent power. His willpower abandoned him, and all stored within the farthest reaches of his mind was laid bare before the probing intruder – his innermost thoughts, ideas, aspirations and fears.

Mallory turned back toward the nearby altar, and with both hands, he raised the bejeweled chalice aloft. He adamantly spoke, his words repeated by a resounding chorus of voices. *"Gloir Lakatu. Hebronzed Lakatu. Lakatooo! Lakatooo! Necrophillum Lakatu."* A loud clap of thunder ensued, and the very stones beneath quaked in the rolling rumble. All the while, Manbootu maintained eye contact with the Professor, his expression stolid, his preternatural eye glaring with intense concentration.

Holding the chalice, Mallory returned to his place at the Professor's side; and Manbootu began to utter strange mystifying words, which had an anesthetizing effect upon the Professor. Caught in the grip of a dark power, the Professor grew languid and helpless. In full realization of his hapless, dire circumstance, he relinquished any remaining recalcitrance, and consigning himself to fate, he prepared to meet his maker. Breaking eye contact, Manbootu released his transfixing hold and made a sign with his hand on the Professor's chest; voices in the background softly chanted in a methodical repetition of indiscernible phrases. His eyes wide and focused, Manbootu lifted up his hand, then thrust it downward toward the area marked by the invisible sign, and plunged his hand deep into the Professor's chest cavity. The Professor gasped in anticipation of the expectant pain, but in defiance of physical law, the hand passed through the flesh and ribs as if it was ethereal. The Professor experienced a tugging sensation, then stared in speechless horror and amazement as his still beating heart was plucked out before his very eyes. Mallory presented the chalice cupped in his hands to Manbootu, who squeezed the vital organ like a sponge, draining the bright red liquid into the chalice.

A hooded acolyte came forward cradling a doll about the size of a ventriloquist dummy and made of reeds sown and tied together with vines. The doll, which had an uncanny resemblance to the Professor, was attired in his spectacles, bowtie, pocket watch, and a little jacket made from the fabric of his clothes. A small sack made of animal hide hung from a leather strand around its neck. Manbootu parted the reeds and inserted the extracted heart into the torso of the doll. Mallory held the chalice aloft and zealously spoke a foreboding invocation accompanied by loud chanting from the unholy assembly. The blood in the chalice began to bubble with effervescence. Manbootu turned to face Mallory, took the chalice in his blood-soaked hands and drank. The acolyte placed the doll upon a small table near the altar. Atop the table sat a second doll resembling Doctor Hawkins and adorned with various articles belonging to him.

The Professor closed his eyes again hoping the dark curtain of his eyelids would blot out the macabre scene, but received no respite. He only succeeded in substituting one terrifying vision for another. The starlit night sky reappeared. Luminous bright lines connecting the stars delineated the depiction of a vast expansive web being woven across the heavens by a great celestial spider. One by one the stars rapidly blinked out. A dark shaft opened beneath him, and the Professor plummeted into the abyss.

Screaming, he awoke in a cold sweat on a sullied straw-stuffed mattress, his body shivering from the clammy chill in the air. Gathering his wits, the Professor sat up and surveyed his surroundings to find himself a prisoner, alone in the confines of a dank and dreary cell dimly lighted by a single candle and heavy with the odor of dampness and decay. A stout metal door with a wicket that opened from the other side provided the only egress from the small cell inclosed by four stone walls. The only items for warmth and comfort were a tattered blanket at the foot of the mattress, along with his shirt and shoes. Of one thing he was certain – with no window to see the sun, when the candle burned out he would be shrouded in pitch-black darkness.

CHAPTER 14

Hidden in the shadows, I flattened my back against the pillar. By the thunderous uproar the ferocious beast was raising, I knew that he had ferreted me out, and only the locked gates restrained him. My heart pounded and a bead of sweat trickled down my temple. I quickly considered equally undesirable alternatives. I could ill-afford a contentious encounter at this stage of the game, nor could I risk any action that would alert the footman to my presence.

The footman turned up the flame and stuck the lantern through the bars, illuminating the lane and surrounding area outside the gate.

"What's all the bloody fuss about boy? Dere's nothin' out dere," the footman remarked.

Despite his effort to quiet the animal, the beast continued his relentless ruckus.

"All right – all right," the footman said, yielding to the dog's persistence.

I heard the clinking of keys and thought the jig was up for sure. Putting one foot forward, I shifted my weight in preparation to make a run for it, but my luck had not run out yet. At that moment, a rabbit sprung out from the hedge, darted between my legs and scampered across the lane, disappearing into the gloom beyond the glow of the lantern.

"All that over a rabbit," the footman commented aloud over the dog's incessant racket. "It's just a rabbit. Now quit your yappin', Lucifer, and come on. We've rounds to keep," he sternly ordered.

With a forceful tone, he gave the dog a firm command, which was clearly not in English, and the brute ceased with a whimper. He called the beast to his side, and I breathed a heavy sigh of relief as their footfalls faded and the lamplight receded away.

When the danger had passed, I contemplated my rationale for being here. What was I doing? Had I let the Vicar's tale incite me to rash and impulsive action? No, I convinced myself. My blood was boiling, and I smelled the unmistakable scent of foul play. But what was the nature of Mallory's game and what were the rules? That is what I wanted to know and intended to find out. Apparently, he took great measures to protect his privacy. Barnesby had not exaggerated in his description of the vicious animals that prowled the grounds.

Keeping a level head, I hatched a plan. Having no proof that my companions were in any danger, I heeded patience and decided to wait for a while. If my companions did not emerge within a reasonable amount of time, I would pay Mallory an unexpected call, and it was not going to be social or polite. Across the lane stood a line of ancient oaks, and one with a wide trunk and low branches opposite the gate made a suitable post from which to keep watch. After a considerable period, the footman had not returned, nor had my companions emerged. My patience wearing thin, I looked at my watch and deemed that a reasonable amount of time had lapsed.

I was deliberating my next course of action, when a single light, emanating from down the drive, pierced the darkness and moved toward the gates. As it drew near I could make out the figure of the footman, a shotgun tucked under his arm, and thankfully he was alone this time. Upon reaching the gates, he set down his lantern and sifted through keys dangling from a large metal ring. After unlocking the padlock and unlatching the bolt, he swung the gates wide, then leaned against one of the pillars and casually lit a cigarette.

Shortly thereafter, I heard the rumbling engine of a motorcar, and a pair of headlights illuminated the drive. A few moments later the headlights of another motorcar followed. Anticipating my companions' safe return, I breathed a sigh of relief, and under the light of a sailing moon, I observed both vehicles as they exited the gate and turned onto the lane; neither were the Bentley, and my sense of relief rapidly turned to apprehension. A lone driver operated the first motorcar, and I clearly did not recognize the two occupants of the second. None came thereafter, and my heart sank when the footman closed and locked the gates. He strode back from whence he came, and the glow of the lantern was swallowed by the gloom.

For an interval I lay in wait until I was fairly certain that no more departing guests were forthcoming; and as I committed myself to action, I observed and experienced a most extraordinary phenomenon. Before my astonished sight, an ominous dense cloud descended from the night sky and hovered about fifty feet above the manor. Iridescent bright lights pulsed and flashed in and about the undulating mass, which continually altered in shape. A bolt of lightning shot down, striking a spiring rod mounted atop the conical roof of a corner turret. The casements of the manor erupted in a burst of brilliant colors and a booming clap of thunder resounded in a reverberating wave that made me instinctively duck. In the thunder's wake a powerful blast of wind swept across the estate and past me. The hedges rustled violently, and the mighty oak I sought refuge behind bent and creaked in the forceful gale, its branches swaying and flailing. Chaotic voices whispered on the wind, and I covered my ears in an attempt to drown them out.

Eventually the raging wind subsided and I dared to take a peek. The billowing and surging cloud varied in shape and size as it contracted and expanded, its luminescence lighting the firmament for miles in shades of red and amber, and a rainbow of colors intermittently streaked across the sky. The shocking sight rattled my rational mind and made my blood run cold. I averted my eyes, but after a vision of such bewildering magnitude I could not erase the irrepressible impression, and felt as if a chunk of my sanity had been chiseled away. Trying to fathom it all, I recalled the earnest words of the Vicar – "For tonight you may face the devil himself."

Flooded with a dire sense of urgency, I focused on my primary objective, and taking the direct approach, I went to work picking the padlock securing the front gates. In no time the lock was open and the chain removed. The long dark drive extended on before me hemmed between two tall, thick palisades of clipped hedge, and slinking along in the shadow of the hedge-wall, I advanced down one side of the drive toward the manor house.

As I cautiously edged closer, the strange cloud became more distinguishable. It was like nothing I had ever seen before – a conglomeration of iridescent spheres shifting, coalescing and forming anew. My eyes widened in amazement at the unearthly sight of it. One of the larger spheres welled up with an intense radiance; a bolt of lightning shot forth and struck the rod atop the turret with a flash that momentarily blinded me. A resounding boom followed and the earth shook beneath my feet. Suddenly all hell broke loose, and a gust of gale-force wind funneled down the drive, knocking me flat on my back. The wind abruptly ceased, and propping myself up on my elbows, I shook my head in utter disbelief as I watched the bubbling mass roll into one giant translucent sphere and ascend to the heavens at incredible speed. In the blink of an eye it disappeared amongst the infinite points of light.

Gathering my wits and fortitude, I picked myself up off the snow-covered ground and proceeded onward. The curtain walls of hedge came to an end, opening to a circular drive, and the castle-like manor house stood in full view against the backdrop of the wintry night sky. Under the moonlight it was more than haunting; angry-faced gargoyles cast their fearsome countenance, and darkened casements stared down from weathered gray stone walls with a cold grim essence that made the gothic structure seem alive. A wheel-rutted path led off the circle to a detached garage and stables just beyond. A light shone in a ground story window of the garage, and several motorcars were parked in a row outside. In the other direction lay an expanse of gently rolling ground scattered with trees, which stood like an array of tall dark sentinels guarding against any intruder who dared encroach upon the estate. Before me loomed the manor.

Every fiber in my being told me that something was terribly wrong. One thing was for sure, my companions were in that dreadful place and I was determined to get them out. Knocking at the front door was out of the question. I would have to seek a more clandestine means of entry. Not relishing the prospect of an encounter, I determined the most advantageous route, and set off to circumvent the manor in the opposite direction of the garage and stables. Darting from tree to tree, I made my way around to the side of the manor, where I eyed a parapeted balcony protruding out from the second story and a trellis climbing the wall next to it. I wondered if the trellis was sturdy enough to support my weight, but deemed it too risky. Maybe a better way would present itself.

I had reached the boundary of safe cover provided by the trees, and before abandoning their shelter, I perked up my ears and scanned the open terrain. I detected no sign of man nor beast, and the only impression my senses received was the foul stench of the moor drifting on the chilling breeze.

As I crept stealthily across the snow-blanketed lawn, a sound not of my own making made my heart leap. I stopped dead in my tracks and remained absolutely still. Again I heard it, distinct and behind me, the patter of feet treading on the soft mantle of snow accompanied by heavy breathing. I spun around in alarm; and at the periphery of the trees stood the form of a huge mastiff, his sinister eyes and sharp teeth glistening in the moonlight, and his fuming nostrils snorting wisps of vapor. For a few moments he viciously snarled and growled as we stood face to face, and then he lunged out of the shadows and charged headlong at me, his muscular limbs propelling him swiftly across the snow. I was caught in the open with nothing but a scant chance of escape. I tried to remember the strange command the footman had spoken at the gate, but could not recall it in the heat of the moment.

Hitting upon a scheme, I immediately put it into action. Standing firm, I took the bottle of chloroform and a handkerchief from my pockets. Quickly, I uncorked the bottle and doused the cloth with the anesthetizing liquid. Before I could brace myself for the attack, the hostile beast leapt upon me, and I instinctively held up my arm in defense. His powerful jaws latched onto my forearm like a vice, and the impetus of the charge knocked the uncorked bottle from my hand and sent me reeling backwards. I tumbled to the ground with the beast on top of me. His sharp canine fangs perforated the sleeve of my leather coat, puncturing into my flesh. It was all I could do to keep from crying out in anguish as his gnashing teeth ripped and tore at my arm. Still holding the handkerchief in my other hand, I shoved it in the brute's face and smothered his snout. Shortly, the animal went limp, releasing his bite, and I rolled his heavy frame off of me. I sprang to my feet, and was astonished at the immense size of the now unconscious beast. He was more a monster than a dog. Without hesitation, I took out a blade and slew the sleeping giant.

Scanning the ground around me, I discovered the bottle tilted downward in the snow. Practically all the chloroform had drained out, leaving only a few useless drops. My arm throbbed painfully and trickles of blood dripped from my fingers, staining the white snow with droplets of red. I unbuttoned my coat and gingerly slid my arm out from the sleeve for a better look. The mastiff had inflicted a nasty wound, and with little time to spare, I wrapped it tightly with my scarf to stem the bleeding.

I was fitting my arm back in the sleeve when out of the corner of my eye I caught sight of a shape rising above a knoll a short distance away. The figure of another huge mastiff stood prominently in the moonlight from his vantage point atop the rise. He clearly saw me and commenced to bark savagely. I considered making a mad dash for the trees, but he could cut me off before I reached them. My mind raced, and quickly taking stock of the immediate surroundings, I eyed the closest and most apparent means of escape – the trellis. I turned to make a run for it, and he stormed down the grade to give chase. Coattails flapping, I bolted for the trellis as fast as my legs could carry me. As I neared the wall, the ground sloped downward into a depression that encompassed the manor; and behind me, the enormous hellhound had narrowed the gap and was practically on my heels.

Hard-pressed, I bounded full-tilt down the slight incline into the wide trench and found myself in for a rude awakening. Beneath the masking carpet of snow lay a sheet of ice. I had inadvertently stumbled onto the slick frozen surface of a moat. My feet almost flew out from under me, and losing my footing, I struggled to regain my balance. The slippery sheet of ice cracked and splintered beneath me. In a race to reach the safety of firm ground on the opposite side, I hastily shuffled across the fragile layer of thin ice, which fractured under the weight of each step. Hell-bent on making chop suey of me, the fiendish hound was still in hot pursuit, and when his huge paws hit the ice, his momentum sent him sliding into a spin with legs outstretched.

Narrowly avoiding serious mishap, I reached the far edge, and hurriedly scrambled up the bank and across the narrow strip of solid ground between the wall and moat. Undeterred, the malignant beast rose up on his legs and was off to the races like a thoroughbred out of the starting gate; but with little traction, he was going nowhere fast and making slow headway on the slippery surface, the brittle ice snapping and popping under his massive frame. Much to my bitter dismay, he managed to make it across, and once on solid terrain, he took off like a speeding locomotive.

Getting a foothold, I began scaling the vine-covered trellis with the staunchly pursuing hellhound biting at my heels. As I hoisted myself up beyond his reach, he vaulted upwards with all the power of his hind legs and his snapping jaws seized the cuff of my trousers. I held on with all the strength I could muster as he clung on tenaciously. The latticed woodwork creaked and groaned, and started to give way under the strain. I kicked and stomped furiously in a frantic effort to extricate myself from the pernicious baggage dangling from my pant leg. I heard a snap, and just as the trellis was about to break and send us both toppling, the fabric of my trousers ripped, and he plummeted the short distance to the ground with the piece of torn cloth still locked in his jaws. He slid down the snow-covered bank onto the already weakened and fragmented layer of ice. The ice split asunder and splintered into chunks, and the massive beast plunged into the murky frigid water with a splash. He frantically flailed and clawed at the broken edges in a desperate struggle to clamber out. Exhaustion and the freezing water eventually took their toll, and he sank below the dark surface of the moat.

Wasting no time, I scaled the rickety trellis up to the balcony. I reached out, and securing a handhold, climbed up and wormed my way between the merlons topping the wall. Atop the balcony, I had a fairly commanding view in the moonlight, and could see the body of the first mastiff lying on the bed of snow. A vast flowing sea of dense vapor was rolling in from the moor, creeping across the surreal landscape like the tide, and in a few minutes would envelope and temporarily hide the evidence of my recent handiwork.

French doors provided access to the balcony, but were latched and bolted from the inside. What lay behind them was a mystery; drawn black curtains prevented even the slightest hint of the interior beyond. I removed one of my gloves, and pressing it against the glass to muffle the sound, punched out one of the panes with the butt of the flashlight. Broken shards hit the floor with a sharp tinkle, possibly alerting anyone within earshot. Undaunted, I reached in, unbolted the doors, and quietly slipped inside behind the curtains.

All was silent; and slightly parting the curtains, I peeked out. A long darkened corridor stretched to a candlelit gallery and grand staircase. Walnut paneled walls were arrayed with doors at irregular intervals and ornamented with ornately framed portraits. A suit of armor stood nobly atop a pedestal, and the distant flittering candlelight cast streaks of bronze racing over the dark-stained wood.

Stepping out of my hiding place, I crept up to the nearest door, turned the knob and opened it. I switched on the flashlight and scanned the darkness to survey a large bedchamber opulently furnished with antiques. The canopied four-poster bed was neatly turned down, and a suitcase lay tucked under a highboy. Apparently, Mallory had afforded a number of his guests with overnight accommodations. That would explain the departure of a mere three.

Keeping to the recesses of the doorways, I furtively crept down the wide corridor, checking doors as I went and discovering several other bedchambers in the same inviting state of fastidious preparation. The pieces did not fit. Looking at my watch, I noted it was well past midnight. Where was everybody? The place seemed deserted, and as I neared the gallery and stairs the only sound was the occasional creak of a floorboard. No indication of any holiday festivities was detectible: no clamor of voices, no music, nothing. The place was quiet as a tomb.

Draped from ceiling to floor, an elaborate tapestry decorated a section of the wall. It rendered a depiction of Adam and Eve standing under the tree in the garden tasting the forbidden fruit, while a beguiling serpent coiled around a branch looked on with a smirk of self-satisfaction. Something about it was peculiar. Looking intently, I noticed minute movements in the fabric, which billowed and wavered almost imperceptibly as if from a draft. Curious, I looked behind it to discover that it curtained a spacious arched opening. I slipped behind the tapestry, switched on the flashlight, and peered into the black hole. A perpendicular hallway ending in a pair of doors extended toward the rear of the manor. Beneath the doors gleamed a faint sliver of light.

If it was worth concealing, it was worth investigating, and I nimbly crept down the hall. I planted my ear against one of the doors, and hearing nothing, I tried the knob; but as anticipated, the doors were locked. Peeping through the keyhole revealed little more than a furnished chamber bathed in the soft radiant glow of firelight with no sign of occupancy. Manipulating the antique lock was easy, and with the right tool I picked it in no time. The well-oiled hinges emitted nary a sound as I opened the doors just wide enough to permit me to cautiously slip through.

Rows of inlaid shelves well stocked with numerous volumes rose to the tall ceiling of the elongated rectangular chamber, with access to the top shelves afforded by a ladder that rolled along a rail. A low fire crackled and popped in the hearth of an imposing stone fireplace, and a pair of sculptured gargoyle heads adorned the corners of the mantel. In a prominent place above the mantel hung a full-length, life-size portrait of a dashing man in black velvet and lace. His slick raven-black hair draped his ruffed collar, and a stiletto moustache and goatee accentuated sharp facial features. His cold piercing eyes stared insolently down at me as if I was some menial servant in need of correction. The sky above him was overcast with gray sullen clouds, yet I perceived a strange shadow in the background not cast by the subject. A brass nameplate divulged the name of the sinister man depicted in the portrait – Sir Mortimer Mallory. A set of wing chairs and a couch were arranged before the fireplace, and a long table stretched down the length of the room. Atop the table crouched the ebony statuette of a criosphinx, and an obsidian crystal ball rested on a decorative tri-pronged stand ornamented with monstrous demonic figures in relief. A volume on ancient mysticism lay open on the table, and on a lower shelf I noted a complete collection of the works of Charles Darwin, including *The Origin of Species* and *The Descent of Man*, along with a collection of works by Charles Lyell. Other titles included – *The Cult of the Nyaking and the Divine Kings of the Shullock*, by C.G. Seligan and *Impressions of West Africa*, by T.J. Hutchinson. Here and there magnificent pieces of African art were displayed, and intricate masks decorated the walls like trophies, each exhibiting a shockingly terrifying countenance. At the far end of the chamber a set of black velvet curtains were nearly drawn. Centered in front of the curtains stood a large mahogany desk with a throne-like chair behind it, and the elaborately carved symbol of an eye adorned the back of the chair. I recognized the symbol the moment I laid eyes on it, for it was identical to the one on the cursed parchment we had received in New York. All my suspicions were confirmed, and I knew without a shadow of a doubt that my comrades were in grave danger.

Heading for the desk, I spanned the length of the chamber with the harsh eyes in the portrait appearing to follow my every move. The simple lock securing the top desk drawer was no deterrent, and rummaging through the contents, I uncovered another strand in an already convoluted web. Tucked inside were two opened envelopes postmarked Venice, Italy, and a copy of a telegram sent to Venice, dated today.

The telegram read:

To: Count Francis Borgia

Acquisition of journal is essential STOP Obtain by whatever means STOP Leaving on morning train for Dover STOP Will contact you upon arrival in Venice STOP

Sir Gunston Mallory

I read each letter in chronological order, the most recent dated about a week ago.

My Dear Sir,

I have obtained the ship's log of "The Corsican" and have thoroughly read its contents. It is written in the vernacular Italian of the seventeenth century, but I had no difficulty in the translation. The log entries bear evidence that her captain may have been more of a pirate than an explorer commissioned by the Doge. Several passages make significant reference to the item we so earnestly seek; however, I was unable to uncover any definitive knowledge, and the log holds no additional value to our quest. This is a most unfortunate disappointment, since it did not come cheap.

Barsucci is currently attempting to locate the journal of Captain Matteo Veneti. In the absence of any pertinent facts in the log, I am certain that the answers lie within the journal's pages. If the journal still exists, I am confident of Barsucci's ability to locate and obtain it.

I will contact you when I have received word of the journal. Notify me of any change in plans. Glory to the Gods. Necrophillum Lakatu.

Faithfully yours,
Count Francis Borgia

My Dear Sir,

Success! Barsucci has located and purchased the journal from a collector. I have seen it this day, and although he allowed me only a glimpse of the text, I believe it to be genuine. It bears the timeworn marks of age, but otherwise it has endured the ravages of time, and is in good condition.

Barsucci left on an important business matter and stated he would return in a fortnight. His departure was imminent, and he had not yet determined a price. He will notify me immediately upon his return, and settle on a price at that time.

I cannot verify it, but I have the distinct impression there may be other suitors. I am well acquainted with Barsucci. He is a shrewd businessman, who would not pass up an opportunity to make a higher profit.

Necrophillum Lakatu.

Faithfully yours,
Count Francis Borgia

P.S. In addition to the journal, Barsucci has a rare tome in pristine condition that would be most instrumental and worth procuring.

I had neatly replaced the items and shut the drawer, when the sharp grating of stone grinding against stone startled me. To my surprise, a section of wall by the fireplace opened. Hearing voices, I quickly ducked behind the curtains into the alcove of an oriel window.

Reflected in the window, a partial view of the room was visible through the gap in the curtains. Into the view stepped Mallory cradling a large tome in his arm, followed by a young African man wearing a colorful cap that clashed with his conservative English attire. He carried two peculiar dolls in male dress, one of them wearing spectacles resembling the Professor's.

"All is prepared for our immediate departure. We must reach Dover in time to catch the morning ferry to Calais," Mallory said. "Now that our guests of honor are cloistered away under lock and key, we'll have no further interference on their part. In little more than a month's time they'll have been rendered mad as hatters and quite certifiable. The complete and utter erosion of one's mental faculties is an agonizing thing to experience," he continued with morbid satisfaction.

Mallory's words were deeply disturbing.

He pressed the spine of a book, and it sank into its slot on the shelf. He pushed against the bookshelf, and a section of shelves in front of him pivoted in place, revealing a small hidden room into which he entered.

The African man set the dolls on the table. "What of Mr. Blake?" he inquired.

"I'm confident that the individual I dispatched will take care of the job well enough," came the reply from beyond the opening, followed by a sardonic chuckle.

While patiently waiting for Mallory's return, the African man casually looked in my direction. His eyebrows tightened in an inquisitive expression and he riveted his gaze on the curtains. Had he somehow detected me? My pulsed raced, and I dared not even breathe.

After a brief period, Mallory reemerged without the tome and closed the secret portal. "Bring our two duffers," he said, jokingly referring to the dolls; and opening the door to the hall, he exited the room expecting his African ward to follow. But the African man stood firm, and his attention remained focused on the curtains that concealed my presence.

He removed his cap, exposing an eye in his forehead. My rational mind vehemently argued the validity of what my eyes proclaimed to be real; it was just as JB had described, and I almost let out a gasp at the incredulous sight of it. The monstrous eye stared intently at the very spot where I was hiding. It was as if the curtains were invisible and he could plainly see me; and then he began to approach.

CHAPTER 15

My heart beat furiously, and reaching inside my coat, I gripped the handle of my Luger. Time passed like an eternity as the African man's steps carried him closer and his reflection in the window loomed larger and larger.

"The Rolls is waiting sir, and the trunk you requested is in the grand foyer," came an unfamiliar voice from the hall.

"Thank you, Dudley," Mallory returned. He called back through the doorway, "What's keeping you? Time is pressing. We must be on our way."

Distracted, the African man halted and turned away. He looked back in my direction momentarily and then left the room, picking up the dolls on his way out. The door closed, and relaxing my grip on the pistol, I exhaled a heavy sigh as a key turned in the lock.

For a brief time I stood motionless, listening to the crackle of the fire while I considered my next move. I was playing it by ear, but that was nothing new to me. Right now, finding JB and the Professor was my primary concern. It was a dangerous proposition, but I figured that if I followed Mallory and his cohort, stayed out of sight and within earshot, I might learn more and discover the exact whereabouts of my companions.

I emerged from my hiding place and traversed the length of the room under the watchful eyes of Sir Mortimer. Listening intently at the door, I strained my ear for any audible impressions, but received none, and the keyhole was dark. After skillfully manipulating the lock, I gently opened the door and slipped out into the unlit corridor. Feeling my way along the wall for guidance, I stealthily crept the distance to the tapestry.

Distant inarticulate voices were discernible from the other side. Taking a risk, I sidled between the tapestry and wall and poked my head out. The voices emanated from the direction of the candlelit galley, and as I drew closer to investigate, I recognized the distinct sound of Mallory's voice resounding up the grand staircase. I peered around a corner and looked through the balustrade down into a large foyer.

Four men occupied the foyer below. The mysterious African man placed the two dolls in an open trunk, then closed and latched the lid. Nigel, the chauffeur, stood dutifully by while Mallory addressed a butler. The case containing the tablet rested on the floor beside Mallory.

"See to it that my guests are made comfortable. They will be departing in the morning after breakfast. Please have a sumptuous buffet prepared for them," Mallory instructed, sheathing his hands in a pair of gloves. "Dudley, you have loyally served this household in an exemplary manner as did your father," he commended. "Pending my return, I entrust Blytemoor Manor to your capable hands."

"Thank you, Sir Gunston," the butler returned. "No need to worry about a thing, sir. A safe journey to you, and I look forward to your homecoming."

Mallory picked up the case, and the chauffeur and butler carried the trunk out the front door, followed by Mallory and his African cohort. The door remained open behind them, and then I heard a motorcar being started. Soon the rumble of the engine died away, and the butler returned alone, closing the large stalwart door behind him. He spanned the foyer, disappearing from my sight.

My companions were prisoners somewhere within the manor – but where? I had a valid suspicion that secret door in the library would be a good place to start, and I retraced my steps.

Running my fingers along the joints between the stone blocks, I traced the outline of the secret portal by the fireplace, and having located it, I methodically searched the surrounding area for the mechanism to open it. Inspecting the fireplace and mantel, I reached inside the gargoyle's open mouth and touched a metal ring. I pulled it, and a narrow section of the wall slowly opened with a scraping groan.

I stepped through the secret aperture into a darkened narrow corridor and switched on the flashlight. The corridor extended a short distance to a descending stairwell that coiled its way around a newel; and near the opening, an unlit candle lantern hung beside an iron ring fastened to the wall. Conjecturing the ring to be the mechanism to operate the door, I gave it a tug, and the heavy door ground shut, sealing me in. It set within its jambs with such precision that only the illusion of a blank wall remained.

Deeper and deeper the spiral stairs led me, each wary footfall solemnly resounding in the distance. Musty odors drifted up from below, and moisture oozing down the face of the smooth cut stones glistened in the beam of the flashlight.

At the bottom, two doors confronted me. One, a locked metal door with a barred wicket, gated a passageway that extended into obscurity. The other, an unlocked wooden door opened to a small room with an alcove in one wall. A wooden bench rested against the wall across from the alcove, two purple vestments elaborately embroidered with gold thread hung on brass pegs, and a bracket on the wall held an unlit torch.

Examining the room's interior, I noted a peculiar oddity. One of the stone bricks bordering the alcove had a worn edge where it abutted the next stone, and a hairline cleft ran along the joints. I wrested the stone loose, and it swung open on a pivot to reveal a hidden cubbyhole that held a lever. The mechanism ratcheted by degrees as I worked it to the opposite setting. Gears in motion sounded from within the stonework, and the recessed wall yawned open.

Ducking my head, I passed through the aperture into a large darkened chamber that had the semblance of a temple: a temple in which dark blasphemous rites are practiced. An altar inscribed with runic markings and decorated with fiendish carvings stood before a gigantic eye in relief with a magnificent ruby set in the center of the eye. A large rectangular stone block, with shackles fastened at the corners, rested near the altar. Bloodstains marred the top surface, and cut grooves for channeling blood outlined the perimeter. Two ranks of columns supported the ceiling, their exteriors carved in a reticulated snake-scale pattern. Painted murals depicting hideous monstrous beings covered the walls and ceiling, and the marble floor tiles were arranged in a cryptic pattern. A pair of tall arched doors constructed of stout timbers marked the sole apparent entrance. Two large metal rings, each fashioned in the likeness of a coiled snake, served as door handles.

The stone vault held a disquieting sinister aura and an icy chill pressed close. Soft inscrutable mutterings haunted the shadows, brief whispers floating out of the emptiness, first here, then there; but when I strained my ear or shined the flashlight the illusion evaporated, only to arise again elsewhere. An electric surge of fear quickened my heart and caused the hairs on my neck to stand as rigid as serried needles. The next moment I was running for the doors, and grasping one of the rings, I pulled with a pumping rush of adrenalin. The great door gaped open; and without regard, I hastened through the gap to the other side, shutting the door behind me.

Quickly surveying my surroundings, I found myself in a vaulted antechamber where the whisperings no longer haunted me. Numerous embroidered purple vestments hung from lines of pegs, a padlocked cabinet stood against the masonry, and an archway breached the wall ahead. With no other route, I passed under the arch and proceeded down a vaulted hallway extending to a series of steps that led up to a strong door.

Manipulating the archaic lock proved to be difficult; nevertheless, persistence paid dividends, and the ponderous door stridently squeaked on its hinges as I forced it open to unveil a lofty chamber. Stone stairs ascended along the wall to a landing and door above, and two stout oaken doors on my level barred what lay beyond.

Faced with a choice, I was considering which course to pursue, when the moving catch on the door above forewarned me of unwelcome company. I extinguished the flashlight and sank into the recess of the nook below the landing. The door opened, and the soft radiance of a lantern bathed portions of the chamber followed by footfalls echoing off the stone steps. The ever-shrinking shadows threatened to expose me as I watched the butler descend the stairs. Failing to notice me, he halted in front of one of the oaken doors, set the lantern down, and pulled a ring of keys from his pocket – keys that I desperately wanted.

Tempting fate, I stole up behind him as he fiddled with the keys and then inserted one into the lock. He must have sensed my immediate presence, for his head spun around, and he gasped in wide-eyed surprise. Before he had an opportunity to cry out in alarm, I grabbed him by the arm, slung him around with all my might and slammed him into the wall face first. He hit with a dull thump and crumpled to the floor. In a split second I was on him, and grasping his collar, I demanded to know the whereabouts of JB and the Professor. Rattled and dazed, he mumbled incoherently, and feebly lifting his hand, he pointed toward the door with the key in it. His eyes rolled back in his head, and he collapsed into unconsciousness. Acting quickly, I opened the door and dragged the butler's limp body through the doorway into a damp cellar containing racks stocked with wine bottles and casks; and after shutting myself in, I bound the butler's wrists with his shoestrings and gagged him with his handkerchief.

Tucked away between two large casks stood a narrow door made of solid planks and laced with ironwork. One of the keys turned in the lock, and employing the weight of my shoulder, I pressed the reluctant door open. Taking the lantern in hand, I ventured into the darkness.

Steps descended to a dungeon passage that stretched its way to a door and then disappeared beyond a veil of ink.

I opened the door to reveal an expansive room outfitted with long tables, cabinets, and machines fitted with gauges, dials and gadgets. Atop the tables were a diverse collection of glass jars, beakers, retorts and alembics, some empty and others containing liquids of various tinctures or salts. Electric lights hung from the ceiling. Near the center of the room stood an examination table equipped with heavy leather straps. A row of cryptically labeled bulbous glass jars containing mixtures of salts lined a shelf; and on one wall, a cast iron hatch covered the soot-stained opening of an incendiary oven.

After a short span, the passage widened to a small empty chamber, then resumed on the other side of a portcullis operated by a winch. Beyond the barrier, bands of shadow cast by the bars ran the length of the short passageway, which ended at a half open door, and four stalwart doors with sliding wickets stood interspaced along both walls.

I cranked the winch, raising the creaking gate of iron bars. Beyond the half open door lay a silent darkened void, and as I warily approached it, an offensive odor filled my nostrils. The big door groaned as I opened it wider and held the lantern in the doorway. Illuminated in the glow was a ghastly chamber of horrors fitted with abominable implements of torture.

Just then, a faint voice reached my ears. Then I heard it again, more distinct and recognizable. It was coming from behind one of the stalwart doors, and I raced to it.

The words were clear and concise now. "Is someone out there? Who is it? Who's out there?"

My nerves thrilled with anticipation as I slid the wicket open and spoke into the narrow slit. "Professor?" I inquired in a hushed voice.

Peering through the wicket, I could barely discern the Professor's drawn face and disheveled appearance by the dim candlelight in his cell.

"Heaven be praised – it's you, Mr. Blake! I must say you're a most welcome revelation!" he rejoiced at hearing my voice. "I don't know how on earth you found me, but I thank God you did."

"Where's JB?" I earnestly asked in a raised volume that conveyed channeled echoes fading down the passage.

"In here," came a somber voice from behind the door across the hall.

"Hold on, I'll have you both out in a minute," I assured.

I fumbled with the keys, trying one after another. One of the larger keys worked with success, and the cell doors gave way, creaking and groaning on their hinges. Liberated, the Professor grasped my hand, shaking it heartedly.

"There'll be time for amenities later," I said. "Right now, we've got to get out of here."

JB's sunken eyes were glazed and his haggard face had an ashen pallor. It was fear I read in his face – a deep, paralyzing fear. He placed his hand on my shoulder to steady himself. With the other hand he pulled open his unbuttoned shirt, exposing a gruesome scar on his chest.

"Look – look what they've done to me," he stammered out in a raspy voice.

He placed my hand on his chest.

"No heartbeat – no pulse – nothing. They abstracted my heart – ripped it from my chest cavity," he raved forlornly.

His skin was cold and clammy, and to my utter astonishment, I felt no heartbeat – none at all.

Looking at the Professor, JB woefully wailed, "Are we to end up like Drafe? Say it isn't so, Professor – say it isn't so! Tell me it was all a dream."

The Professor answered with silence, unbuttoning his shirt to reveal an identical scar.

"No! No! No!" JB repeated over and over.

"Quiet," I admonished.

He abruptly ceased his babble, a tear welled up in his eye, and he completely broke down, sinking to his knees. Embracing my leg, he sobbed on my trousers.

"Forgive him Mr. Blake, for we have both undergone an ineffably horrifying ordeal," the Professor compassionately pleaded. "Come, there's something I wish to show you."

I helped JB to his feet, giving him my best reassuring smile. He gathered himself and then sat on the ragged mattress, stooped over with his hands on his knees and his head bent. The Professor led me into his cell where he directed me to move the shoddy wooden bed frame.

"Feast your eyes on that," he whispered.

Etched in the stone floor were lines in verse:

As I sleep, my darkest dreams stalk the night
My blood runs cold from terror and fright
That which I most fear
Dreadfully draws ever near
On the back of my neck, I feel its icy breath
Then I awaken, one step closer to death
Trapped in a tomb with walls of stone
There is no one else, I am all alone.

HD

Below the initials, two barely discernible lines were scrawled:
The eye opens the path
The charnel house is the way of escape

HD – initials I recognized with utmost certainty. Ostensibly the words seemed to be nothing more than insignificant prattle, but I deduced those last two scrawled lines to comprise a cleverly hidden message, and I had a darn good supposition as to what it alluded to.

"Clear confirmation that Harold Drayfus was confined in this very cell. Sir Gunston divulged as much to us," the Professor apprised. "He, Mr. Blake, is the culprit who orchestrated Harold's demise. He crafted a deceitful, insidious scheme to lure us into a trap, thence dispense with us in the same manner. The tablet holds a grim, arcane purpose, which he possesses full knowledge of. He plans to use it as an instrument to realize his maniacal, nefarious vision. The man is utterly mad," he stated categorically.

I simply nodded in agreement, for his words verified even my most remote suspicions.

Hastening to make good our escape, I led them along the passage back to the wine cellar. We crept past the still unconscious butler, and then following my earlier route, we fled down the vaulted hallway to the great doors of the unhallowed temple. Calligraphically inscribed in the archstones above the doors were the words "Enter Ye Who Seek and Serve".

I pressed my weight against one of the massive doors, and we passed into the disquieting atmosphere of the temple. JB took one look at the interior and stopped dead in his tracks. Eyes widening, his face burst into an expression of frightful realization, and he recoiled back through the doorway.

"This is where it all took place," the Professor said.

He went to JB's side, urging him onward with gentle condoling words. JB reluctantly reentered the chamber, moving at a slow and wary pace. Wide shadows cast by the columns continuously bowed and shifted in the moving lantern-light, passing over the pictorial walls and ceiling like darkening spectres. As we neared the altar, elusive, grumbling murmurs harassed our ears. JB's eyes were wide as saucers, and the Professor tried to maintain his composure, but his disconcerted expression betrayed him. Even I was spooked by the unsettling nature of the place.

"We must leave this cursed place," the Professor stressed.

I pointed, directing them to the secret portal at the side of the chancel, and I hastened them to the opening and ushered them through. JB almost hit his head in his rush to cross the threshold. Once inside the small vestry, I pulled the lever, closing the portal and shutting out the disturbing voices.

JB and the Professor continued to follow my lead, and we funneled into the spiral staircase.

"That way takes you up to the library," I said, pointing up the stairwell. I shined the light through the barred wicket in the metal door. "This way I'm not sure of, but if my guess is right, it leads to the mausoleum," I said.

"What makes you draw that supposition?" the Professor asked.

"Deduction," I replied. "The writing in your cell – those last two lines alluded to directions. Take the first one – 'The eye opens the path'; I've got a hunch that the ruby in the eye triggers the portal from within the temple. The second refers to a charnel house, and I happen to know there's a mausoleum somewhere on the estate, probably somewhere close to the manor. We have only two paths, one of which I am certain of its destination; the other must lead to the charnel house and escape."

"You mentioned a library," he said. "During our ordeal in the temple, Mallory recited from a tome on the altar." He described the tome, asking if I had per chance seen it.

"Yes, Mallory had a book like that."

"Does he still have it? Do you know where it is?" he rattled off in quick succession.

"It's in a secret room off the library. I hope you're not thinking about going back for it, because we don't have time for that."

"He's right, Professor, let's get out of this awful place," JB spoke up with a dire sense of urgency, giving me a nudge as if it would expedite matters.

"I cannot explain fully here and now, but it is imperative we return for it. We must have it if we are to undo what has been done. Otherwise, the Doctor and I will experience the gradually degenerating, malevolent power of the imprecation, inevitably to be robbed of our sanity without recourse. The curse must be lifted before the nerve-shattering effects leave an indelible scar on the mind. In addition, we would consequently deprive Mallory of an invaluable tool," the Professor adamantly argued with grave, compelling resolve.

Rather than expend precious minutes in debate, I yielded. "All right, follow me."

Up the coiling steps we climbed, our footfalls resounding in rhythmic echoes, and atop the stairwell, the short narrow corridor ended in a solid stone wall.

"Step back," I said, and I tugged on the iron ring.

My companions' eyes filled with astonishment as the wall yawned open with a scraping groan. Upon entering the library, I extinguished the lantern, leaving the room bathed in the soft dim glow of a dying fire. Gold lettering on the spines of numerous volumes shined with a dazzling glint, and the repugnant masks on the walls were like an assembly of demons in the fluttering shadows.

"JB, I want you to listen at the door and alert us if anyone's coming," I directed.

"I can manage that," he asserted, now somewhat composed, until he passed by the portrait of Sir Mortimer and looked up into those sinister piercing eyes.

"Over here," I said, motioning for the Professor to follow.

I went straight to the section of bookshelves that Mallory had opened. "It's one of these, I'm sure," I said, seeking the book Mallory had pressed. "Yes, here it is."

I pressed against the spine of the book, and the bookshelf pivoted as I gave it a shove, revealing the secret entrance to a hidden room.

"You're a credit to your profession, Mr. Blake," the Professor stated.

In one corner of the small room, a spiral staircase ascended to a makeshift observatory. A cabinet stood against the wall, and on a podium rested a ponderous, folio-sized, bound manuscript, entitled *Necronomicon.* The Professor's eyes flashed with recognition and incredulous awe upon seeing it.

"The genuine article, penned by Dr. John Dee himself," the Professor emphatically remarked, caressing the cover.

Inside the cabinet was a cache of several large leather-bound, timeworn texts with non-English titles – *Libor Ivonis, Magus, Unausprechlichen Kulten, Grimorium Verum, Libor Trium Verborum, Lemegeton,* and *Testamentum* among others.

"All rare volumes delving into the arcane black arts and alchemy," the Professor apprised. "Disregard them. This is the one we want," he said, lifting up the manuscript from the podium and cradling it in his arms.

Having nabbed our prize, our thoughts returned again to escape. After snatching the letters and telegram from the desk drawer, I pivoted the bookshelf back in place, and we disappeared through the secret portal by the fireplace and hurried down the corkscrew stairs to the solid metal door. The ring of keys provided the means, and the squeaking barrier opened to a tunnel that extended beyond where the blackness swallowed the light.

My companions had insufficient clothing to shield them against the cold night they would face once outside, and thinking quickly, I fetched the two robes from the vestry.

"Put these on," I said. "They're not much, but it's better than nothing."

Gratefully, yet reluctantly, they donned the robes, and we pressed on at a swift pace, deep into the abysmal reaches of the dark confining tunnel. In the continually receding darkness, forbidden reaches seem to beckon us forever, until finally the tunnel came to an end, and an iron ladder fastened to the wall rose up a vertical shaft to a trap door.

I scaled the rungs, and daring to raise the heavy trap door, I emerged from the shaft to find myself inside a marble crypt. Pale moonlight passing through a pair of grated gates dimly illuminated the interior. Rows of brass plaques denoted the entombed members of the Mallory family, and a sarcophagus conspicuously rested on a thick slab at the center of the vault. Engraved on the lid was the name of the interned – Sir Mortimer Mallory – but no dates or epitaph accompanied the name.

JB called out my name from below. "This is it," I said, directing my voice down the shaft.

The Professor struggled his way up the ladder carrying the cumbersome manuscript under his arm, followed by JB toting the lantern. I extended them each a helping hand as they reached the top, and then I lowered the heavy door into its seat. The brass plaques now shone like gold in the glow of the lantern. The Professor's eyes scanned the crypt, and gently nodding his head, he turned to me, one corner of his mouth curling up in a half-smile.

I pointed out the name engraved on the sarcophagus. "The old boy himself. The same one depicted in the portrait hanging in the library. The Vicar gave me a brief rundown on the family history back in the village."

Suddenly, JB's attention was drawn to the floor. Droplets of crimson red dripped from a trickling flow coursing down my finger, splattering against the white marble. The wound, which I had thus far disregarded, now panged with an unbearable throbbing.

"Looks like I'll be needing your skills, Doctor," I said stoically, attempting to allay any concern.

Outside the grated gates, insurmountable walls of clipped hedge delineated a snow-covered path.

"Look, footprints in the snow," JB observed.

Sure enough, a set of impressions made by a single pair of shoes started just outside the gates, descended the steps at the entrance to the mausoleum, and led away down the path to be swallowed by a mantle of wispy vapor. The single set of tracks indicated the recent passage of someone leaving, but otherwise the soft blanket of snow lay undisturbed without any sign of approach.

"Maybe the old boy got up and walked away," I joked.

"I find it perturbing," the Professor said.

I found it a bit baffling myself, especially since a padlocked chain secured the handles on the other side of the gates. To my bitter frustration, I could not get my hand through the grating to reach it. JB however, was able to thread his slender hand and wrist betwixt the latticed metalwork and maneuver the lock close to the grid, making it feasible for me to insert a key. I tried every key on the ring capable of fitting the keyhole, but every attempt failed; and although my companions said nothing, their disappointment showed in their dejected expressions.

"There's always alternatives," I confidently said, pulling out my trusty tools.

JB held the lock steady, and I went to work while my companions watched with eager anticipation. Their despair rapidly melted into a well of relief when I skillfully picked the lock.

"You're a man of unusual talents," the Professor remarked when the lock sprang open.

No longer impeded, we stepped out into the open air, and JB extinguished the lantern, shrouding us in the dull gray shades of moonlight. Tall walls of hedge dictated our path, and we had not gone far when an opening in the hedge-wall revealed an identical parallel path walled in by rows of hedge. It was then I realized we were in a labyrinth, and I advised we follow the trail of footprints, which proved to be more difficult than anticipated. The imprints lay partially screened under a veil of mist, and we made slow progress, constantly stopping to search for the trail. Winding this way and that, the tortuous tracks guided us through an elaborate hedgerow maze containing blind misleading alleys and dead ends, eventually coming to an entrance marked by a barred iron gate embellished with scrollwork.

Beyond the gate, a tiered cobblestone walkway lined with yews ambled up a gentle slope to wrap around the side of the forbidding manor, which stood in dark silhouette against the moonlit sky. No lock secured the gate, and unhindered, we cautiously proceeded up the walk, cloaked in the moving shadows of the rustling yews. When we reached the crest of the rise, the garage and stable complex came into view, and further on lay the long drive that stretched to the front gate and freedom.

"This way," I said, leading them onward.

All seemed still, when suddenly I detected a hint of movement close by, a stirring in the shadows. Training my eye, I caught the glint of two menacing eyes peering out from the darkness and discerned the outline of a dark familiar shape. My companions were unaware of the impending danger, until a deep rolling growl drew their attention.

"Run!" I cried, grabbing them by their robes and propelling them in the direction of the nearest refuge – the garage.

The malicious beast lunged out of the shadows and bolted into full stride, giving chase. The Professor's short legs stumbled as I virtually dragged him along, darting between two parked motorcars and racing for one of the pairs of hinged bay doors. The vicious brute was closing fast. Things looked bleak amidst an uncertain outcome; and with not a moment to spare, we rushed inside and shut the doors against a charging assault.

Barking ferociously, the animal raised an uproarious ruckus. While I was trying to think of a way out of our dilemma, a light appeared under the door to the adjoining building. Trapped, we were in a nasty predicament, and adverse circumstances now dictated drastic action. The Bentley was parked inside the bay, and hopping in behind the wheel, I ordered my companions to get in. They complied without hesitation, climbing into the back seat as I cranked the starter. I put the stately motorcar in gear, revved the powerful engine, and popped the clutch. The hardy machine lunged forward, crashing into the bay doors and flinging them wide. We shot out of the garage, and I turned the wheel sharply, narrowly avoiding a collision with a parked sedan. I steered onto the rutted path and hit the gas, gaining momentum. The unwieldy vehicle swerved and fishtailed as we rounded the circle and turned down the long drive, the persistent hellhound in hot pursuit the whole way, barking and yelping.

I shifted gears, picking up speed and distancing ourselves from our pursuer. Pressing my luck, I drove at a dangerously rapid clip, my companions riveted to their seats; and in the distance, the front gates stood sturdy in the gleam of the headlights. Unexpectedly, the footman emerged from the shadows. Shotgun in hand, he stepped onto the drive and motioned for us to stop.

"Brace yourselves," I warned, pressing down hard on the accelerator, the engine roaring.

My companions were utterly stunned at the realization of my reckless intentions. The footman leveled the shotgun, pointing it directly at us.

"Duck!" I cried as the shotgun discharged with a flash and a loud report.

Flying pellets shattered a headlight and hit the windshield, splintering the glass. I popped my head up to see the footman diving into the hedge as we sped by, barreling headlong toward the iron gates. We rammed the gates at breakneck speed, the rugged vehicle slamming into them with a thunderous crash and the crunch of crumpling metal, splitting them wide and rending them from their hinges. Hitting the brakes, I fought to maintain control as I steered between two giant oaks and came to a sliding stop in the open field beyond the gates.

"Anyone hurt back there?" I asked.

"Just bumps and bruises, but I'm not sure about the Doctor," the Professor responded.

"JB? Are you all right?" I asked concernedly.

A lack of response prompted me to look back. JB sat paralyzed, rigid in his seat, breathing hard and fast with a blank stare on his face. Suddenly, a blast sounded, immediately followed by the nearly simultaneous tinks of shotgun pellets hitting the metal paneling of the Bentley.

Sparing no time, I put the vehicle in motion. The collision had knocked out the remaining headlight, and driving by the dim light of the moon, I could barely see what lay ahead. The mantle of mist gave the illusion of riding on a shadowy sea of white vapor, and all that jutted out of the landscape appeared as dark ill-defined shapes floating on its surface. Accelerating, I drove parallel to the lane for a distance, guided by the straight row of oaks, the heavy vehicle bouncing over the bumpy ground. Gripping the unsteady wheel tightly, I veered onto the lane, nearly sideswiping an oak.

When I was certain we had attained a safe distance from the gate, I stuck the flashlight out the window, directing the beam ahead. The hedgerow and oaks marked the boundary of the lane for a stretch, then fell away. As we began to traverse the moor, the thick layer of low-lying miasmatic mist masked the lane, making it almost indiscernible and perilously difficult to navigate.

I was beginning to think we might make it, when our luck ran out and the cruel hand of fate intervened. The engine began to clunk and sputter, hissing steam spewed from the radiator, and then the right front tire blew out, causing me to lose control. The vehicle swerved off the lane, pitched to one side, and came to an abrupt stop in a mire. The dying engine belched its last throes and conked out.

"Looks like we'll be walking from here," I said.

Abandoning the Bentley, we sluggishly trudged through the foul muck to the lane and the safety of solid ground, and I warned them to keep to the lane as we proceeded to cross the ghostly moor. Whispering murmurs rose up with the rising gases, and strange blinking lights like fireflies appeared in one direction and then another, as if to intentionally mislead even the most wary traveler, insidiously drawing him to his doom. JB followed closely in my footsteps. The Professor apprehensively looked to and fro, holding fast to the tome in his arms as if it contained the wealth of the world.

The dispiriting moor edged up to a host of towering trees, and we passed into the dark forbidding confines of the dense wood. Cold, tired and huddled together, we continued on along the lonely winding lane, our way now shrouded in a tangled web of contorted shadows. In their hooded robes, my companions resembled a couple of grim reapers stalking the night. Intermittently, the hoot of an owl broke the eerie silence. The misty haze enveloped our surroundings, cloaking them in obscurity and retarding the beam of the flashlight, such that it barely penetrated the murky gloom. Bare gnarled branches like sinewy claws seemed to reach out from nowhere, grasping at us. The unnerving atmosphere had me on edge and kept me in a constant state of watchfulness. I, like the Vicar, half-expected to be waylaid by some sinister lurking threat.

Finally the menacing trees parted, and the comforting sight of the inn enlivened our spirits. The lamp by the front entrance still burned like a beacon, and eager to seek refuge from the cold night, we quickened our pace. All the windows were darkened, save one – the window of my room.

Once inside, my companions shed their robes. The glowing coals of a smoldering fire faintly lit the empty tavern, and the room smelled of stale smoke. We made our way upstairs, and standing in the darkened hallway, we looked with perturbed curiosity at the sliver of light under my door.

"Shhh," I quietly sounded, and I nimbly crept toward the door with my companions pressed in close behind me, our efforts at stealth frustrated by the creaking floorboards. I motioned for them to stand on either side of the doorway, then crouched down and spied through the keyhole.

Seated in a chair was a man wearing an inverness with his hands in the pockets. The lighting and limited view prevented me from making out the identity of the interloper or discerning if there were more than one. Rising up, I put my finger to my lips, sternly urging silence, and drew out my Luger. The pistol in my hand demonstrated to my companions the gravity of the situation, and the eyes on their troubled faces widened at the sight of it.

Hoping for some element of surprise, I quickly turned the knob, flung open the door, and stormed into the room. Unstartled, the interloper looked up at me with a dour expression. He had receding red hair and a luxuriant moustache covered his upper lip; his lustrous eyes glistened with keen, scrutinizing intelligence beneath bushy eyebrows. He was the same man I had seen in the lobby of the Piccadilly Hotel. The one who had tried to tail me on my way to the office of The Times, and the same one I had seen on the train to New York as well as the boat. My suitcase lay open on the bed, and our passports were arranged on the bureau next to a lighted oil lamp.

"Get your hands out of your pockets. Put them where I can see them!" I barked, aiming the pistol square between his eyes.

"Mr. Conrad Blake, I presume," he said unflinching, removing his hands from the pockets of his coat and resting them on the arms of the chair. His accent was distinctly British, and his unexpected cool, confident demeanor perplexed me.

"Now, who the devil are you?" I demanded.

"I am Inspector Lionel Geoffries of Scotland Yard," he replied matter-of-factly.

CHAPTER 16

I was dumbstruck. Keeping the pistol trained on him, I demanded the interloper prove his words. By now, my companions had entered the room, and were curiously eyeing the so-called inspector with suspicion.

With poise, he slowly reached inside his coat. "It seems we have a common interest, Mr. Blake. Are you acquainted with a countryman of yours named Harold Drayfus?" he casually inquired, displaying his credentials, which appeared to be quite valid.

His question left us stunned.

"If you're going to shoot me, have done with it, man. Otherwise, put that pistol down," he said authoritatively.

Tucking my Luger away, I wrestled with the answer to his question. "Yes, I know who he is," I answered guardedly. "Now what's this all about?"

"It concerns your affiliation with Harold Drayfus. Be at ease gentlemen, and please allow me to explain. I am not here to arrest or apprehend you. On the contrary, I am here to reconcile the truth."

"Then start explaining," I curtly said, parking myself on the chest at the foot of the bed.

Cold and spent, JB and the Professor wrapped themselves in a couple of extra blankets, then sat on the bed, looking intently at the inspector with anxious expressions.

"Dr. Drayfus solicited me, stating that his life was in danger, and made several traducing accusations regarding Sir Gunston Mallory," Inspector Geoffries began with a solemn inflexion. "The most damaging allegation purported Sir Gunston to be a murderer. Drayfus stated to have been a member of an expedition sponsored by the Royal Society, and he showed me a clipped article from The Times and a photograph to prove it. He boldly asserted that while deep in the African interior, Sir Gunston took a direct part in murdering the other members of his party, whom he said met with a most horrid end. All to guard a secret – a secret which Drayfus knew. According to his account, he and their guide, a man he called "Brandy", avoided the others' fate by supposedly escaping into the jungle. Furthermore, he claimed to have been held a prisoner in the dungeon of Blytemoor Manor, where he was subjected to torture, and from which he also supposedly made good his escape. It was with an air of skepticism that I took his statement, and rightly so, mind you. However, I have learned in my profession that the truth is not always credible and is sometimes hidden in the improbable and obscure. Facts are stubborn things, and can be stranger than fiction.

"I found Sir Gunston to be in London at the time," Inspector Geoffries continued. "And with utmost misgivings, I called on him and questioned him regarding the allegations. Sir Gunston utterly repudiated them as fanciful aspersions, making the counterclaim that Drayfus had betrayed his hospitality by stealing a priceless artifact, of which he gave a description. He demanded that I arrest the man forthwith and recover it, further charging that the man was one for the asylum. Faced with weighing contradictory statements, I had little choice but to place credence in the word of Sir Gunston, him being an irreproachable man of high stature. Determined to uncover the truth, I went to Drayfus' lodgings, to find only the evidence of his expeditious departure. His abrupt flight implied guilt on his part and served to corroborate Sir Gunston's testimony. Armed with a warrant, I traced Drayfus to Liverpool, where he hopped a tramp steamer bound for Boston before I could apprehend him. Undeterred, I booked the next available passage and followed. Upon my arrival, I intended to present my warrant to the local authorities, but in trailing the man, I discovered that my quarry had other pursuers, and events unfolded rapidly."

He reclined back in the chair. "I observed you and Dr. Hawkins that night at the dilapidated lodging house on the Boston waterfront," he said, focusing his gaze on JB. "Tuesday, December 7th, it was. I remember it well, because I saw things that night that defied the physical laws of nature. Knowing you to be in possession of the stolen item, and perplexed as to your motives, I bided my time while following you full circle. Once within the jurisdiction of my authority, I was still curious as to your intentions, and thus I refrained from apprehending you for the time being, preferring to keep you under watch. I thought the case closed when you returned the item – a fact Sir Gunston verified. However, I deemed his explanation to have certain flaws, which left nagging unanswered questions. The kind of questions that compel an inquisitive man to delve further, and I am firmly certain that your version of affairs will do much to clarify matters."

Long seconds passed as a hush fell over the room.

The Professor leaned forward, his voice penetrating the silence like a pebble dropped into a deep well. "I am Professor Hanson of Harvard University and a colleague of Dr. Drayfus. I can attest for a fact that everything he told you is true," he categorically affirmed.

"Darn right it's true," JB indignantly piped in with a vindictive scowl on his face.

"Sir Gunston is a treacherous madman," asserted the Professor. "He is the one you should arrest. He divulged in his own words that he was responsible for the deaths of the members of the Bradford Expedition. He admitted his complicity in the murderous deed while threatening the Doctor and myself at gunpoint. He insidiously lured us to the manor on the pretext of a cordial invitation to dinner last evening; then he forced us to drink a narcotic-laced tea, after which he perpetrated hideous unspeakable violations upon our persons and locked us away to rot in a dank cell with scant means of comfort. If it had not been for the intrepid efforts of Mr. Blake, the Doctor and I would still be languishing in that horrid dungeon."

The Professor's ardent resolve lit a spark in Geoffries' eyes. "Indeed – most interesting, please go on," he said with an intrigued expression.

"As to the priceless artifact," the Professor continued. "It was never our intention to return it. We were not aware that it might be stolen, and under the firm impression that Dr. Drayfus had every rightful claim to it. We sought out Sir Gunston for a consultation concerning it – not to return it. For this purpose we granted it on loan to the Royal Society. But once he had us alone in a remote room of the manor, he proclaimed it to be his property, while brandishing a revolver, and adamantly stated in no uncertain terms that our involvement and knowledge of it needed to be silenced. He even had the effrontery to disclose the despicable fate he had planned for us. As for Harold, any question of guilt on his part is no longer relevant, for he is no longer of this world, and it was that reprehensible devil incarnate who orchestrated his mortal demise. Sir Gunston stated, and I quote, 'for his meddlesome interference, he suffered the consequences, as will you'. I will testify to these allegations in any court, and the Doctor can corroborate my testimony, as I his."

"I appreciate your candor, Professor," Inspector Geoffries said with a gentlemanly nod. "It seems some of your statements bear striking similarities to those made by your countryman. Do you have anything further to add, Dr. Hawkins?"

JB reticently hesitated. "No, not really. The Professor covered the salient points," he replied.

"I suspect I shall be obliged to have a look at this dungeon of Sir Gunston's. Yes – we will all pay a call on Sir Gunston in the morning, and get to the bottom of things," Inspector Geoffries said resolutely. "I trust you are amenable to that, gentlemen."

"You won't find him at the manor," I said matter-of-factly. "He and another man – an African man, left for the coast."

"That would be Sir Gunston's ward," Inspector Geoffries acknowledged. "England has an extensive coastline. Can you give a more specific destination?"

"Presently – Dover." I hesitated briefly, and then I filled in the rest. "They intend to take the ferry to Calais en route to Venice."

Geoffries cast a discerning eye upon me. "Nevertheless, we shall pay a call at the manor tomorrow," he resolved. "The hour is late, and I believe that will be enough for tonight. We shall sleep on the matter and convene in the morning for breakfast. At that time, I shall want to hear further details. I've procured lodgings in this quaint establishment, so it seems I am your neighbor," he said, rising from the chair. "Good night, gentlemen," he cordially bid, and he excused himself, closing the door behind him.

I keened my ear for the anticipated receding footfalls, but none followed. For a period we sat quietly, allowing time to elapse; after which, I gingerly removed my coat, exposing the bloodied scarf wrapped around my aching forearm.

"Goodness, gracious," JB remarked concernedly. "I'll get my bag," he said, and he hastened to fetch it.

When he opened the door to exit the room, he was a bit startled to discover Inspector Geoffries standing in the hallway just outside the door.

"Pardon me, sorry to have given you a start," Inspector Geoffries said, peering through the opening. "It seems I dropped something, but I have it now. Good night, Doctor," he said elusively, and he retired to his room.

After JB left the room, I turned to the Professor. "Where's the book?" I asked, noticing it to be nowhere in plain sight.

"I slipped it under the bed while you were scrutinizing the inspector's credentials," he replied.

JB returned with his medical bag and then went into the bath, reappearing shortly thereafter carrying a basin and pitcher of water. He gently unwrapped the scarf, and I peeled off the sweater Mrs. Coggins had knitted for me. It was in sorry shape, and I wondered what I was going to tell her. She fretted over me enough as it was.

"You've got some nasty puncture wounds and lacerations, but nothing too severe. None appear to require stitches, and barring any infection, they should heal up in time," JB diagnosed, examining my injuries. "Would I be wrong to presume that you tangled with the vicious animal that chased us?"

"An example of Mallory's hospitality," I said stolidly. "You've had a taste of it."

JB cleaned and dressed my wounds with skillful hands, administering an astringent and antiseptic. "This is going to need changing on a regular basis," he instructed, tying off the bandage.

As the lamp oil burned, we compared notes in hushed tones. The Professor related all the sordid details of their ordeal at the hands of Mallory and of his mad machinations. In turn, I clued them in on what I had seen, heard and experienced, including the Vicar's tale, and shared the letters and telegram I had discovered in the library. With dawn approaching, we wrapped things up and got our stories straight, then retired for what remained of the night.

I was utterly played out – my mind muddled; and once the lamp was extinguished, I lay in darkness, a cold wind whistling in the window. I was not sure what to make of the inspector. He had not been entirely forthright, and had left unfilled gaps in his story, yet he had provided several missing pieces of a twisted puzzle. He had mentioned the name "Brandy" – the unidentified name on the handwritten note I had found amongst Drayfus' effects. I finally knew the man's connection with Drayfus and the part he had played. If anything, Geoffries was astute. Whether he would turn out to be an ally or a detriment was still to be determined. Overcome by exhaustion, I lapsed into sleep.

Deep in the realm of dreams, I was abruptly awakened by a bloodcurdling scream – a cry of extreme anguish. I sprang to my feet in alarm and rushed into the hall. Simultaneously, the Professor emerged from his room holding an oil lamp, his unnerved expression exhibiting shock.

"Was that you?" I asked.

"No, it came from the Doctor's room," he replied with strong concern.

We burst into JB's room. He was lying on the bed clutching his throat, his wide eyes glazed and bulging, his face turning blue. I hastened to his bedside and literally had to pry his hands from around his neck. He grasped my collar, choking and fighting for breath, his pleading eyes staring into mine. We propped him up, and the Professor slapped him hard on the back several times. His eyes closed, and he went limp in my arms, releasing his grip; then suddenly, his eyes reopened and he sprang to life, a bewildered and frightened expression on his face. He sucked in a great draft of air, and began breathing heavy and fast. As his breathing slowed, a normal shade returned to his cheeks.

"Are you ok?" I earnestly asked.

Appearing a bit confused, he gazed back over his shoulder at the Professor, then turned to look at me, his eyes wide with terror. "They get you – they get you in your dreams – nightmares – just like Drafe said," he emphatically stammered in a trembling voice, his eyes growing even wider.

"What's all the bloody ruckus?" came the innkeeper's voice from the hall.

It was then I noticed the imposing figure of Inspector Geoffries standing in the doorway; behind him, the innkeeper was looking over his shoulder.

"Can I be of assistance?" Inspector Geoffries asked with genuine concern.

The Professor moved to interpose himself in the doorway.

"Sorry to have disturbed you. Our companion has had a bit of a shock. He's all right now. Please return to your beds. We'll attend to him," he politely said, slowly closing the door to shut them out.

Holding the knob, the Professor leaned back against the door and exhaled a heavy sigh. He waited until the footfalls had waned away and then furtively peeped out into the hall, finding it empty.

He gently closed the door again and pulled up a chair by JB's bed. "My good Doctor," he said with weary, sympathetic eyes. "It is imperative that you impart to me your experience, for what has befallen you will inevitably befall me. Do not hesitate to tell me everything – leave nothing out," he said reposefully.

JB looked at the Professor with a forlorn expression, his eyes imbued with a dancing luster from the flickering flame of the oil lamp. He spoke in broken phrases and with a grave inflexion. "I had a nightmare – not just any bad dream – a nightmare of horrific proportion – so vivid – so terrifyingly real." He paused, a spark of genuine fear in his glassy eyes. "I was lost – lost and alone – deep in the confines of a tenebrous wood of giant dead and petrified trees bristling with immense thorns that could impale a man. Thick swirling wisps of miasma wafted up from a barren ground threaded with a creeping chaos of gnarled roots and twisted bare briars. The noxious vapor filled my nostrils with the foul stench of rancid decay, gagging and sickening me. A layer of sullen red clouds blotted out the sun and cast a crimson radiance over the surreal infernal landscape. I called out. In response, a cacophony of shrieks and weeping wails resounded in the distance, the anguished cries of mortal souls in torment. A clap of thunder boomed, the ground shook, whereupon, out of nowhere appeared before me a dark faceless phantom, which called my name in a low guttural voice. His malevolent countenance embodied my most secret fears, for he plucked them from my innermost thoughts, casting the most shocking, horrid impressions in my mind. Gripped by extreme terror and panic, I turned and fled. Desperately seeking any escape, I ran hither and thither, slicing my ankles on the thorny growth. With a crash of thunder, the crimson clouds unleashed a showering torrent of blood, which rained down from the sky, soaking me to the skin – and all the while, relentlessly pursued by the wraithlike phantom – its icy breath on the back of my neck as cold as death. My feet sank deep into the gory muck, making each step an arduous undertaking and slowing my pace to a staggering crawl. An amorphous black shadow eclipsed the land, carrying with it a rush of whispering voices advocating my doom. With the dizzying voices whirling in my head, I madly trudged onward, expelling every measure of strength in my frantic efforts. Spiny ophidian vines sprang forth from the infertile dirt, grasping at my ankles – causing me to trip and stumble. Ensnaring me, they coiled and slithered about my legs and torso. Wrestling to free myself, I grabbed, pulled and writhed, but my struggles were futile; and binding my arms, the strong coarse vines rendered me helpless. Deeper and deeper they dragged me down into the blood-drenched soil, which opened up to swallow me like a ravenous monster. Before my head went under, I cried my last, but my screams were drowned amidst the tormented wails and merciless utterances. The earth smothered me – buried alive, I was shrouded in utter blackness, immobile and gasping for air. If you hadn't awakened me when you did – Oh, I dread the thought!"

"It has begun already," the Professor said with a sigh of dismay, his eyes cast downward.

"Is there nothing that can be done, Professor?" JB asked in despair.

"I'm afraid this is beyond my knowledge."

"Nothing – nothing at all?"

"There is hope yet, Doctor, for somewhere in that blasphemous codex lies the dark spell that binds us, of that I am certain. I have already spent the better part of an hour pouring over its pages, earnestly searching, but its staggering contents are cumbersome and abstruse. However, the incantation, once found, may hold a means to remedy our condition."

"I'm sure the Professor can find a way, if anybody can," I reassured JB.

JB entreated us not to leave him alone or let him fall asleep again; and at the Professor's suggestion, we gathered in his room to wait it out until dawn.

Time passed slowly as I sat in a chair in a drowse, trying to stave off sleep. The Professor delved into the pages of the tome, while JB, in his nightshirt and wrapped in a blanket, paced back and forth like a pendulum. Every so often he would urgently inquire of the Professor as to his progress, to which the Professor would give a simple negative response, or reply, "Patience, Doctor, patience."

CHAPTER 17

Outside the window, the dark gloom faded to ever lightening shades of blue as the first golden rays of the sun streaked over the horizon. The disheartening shadows of night dissolved as the sunlight brightened the room, competing to outshine the lamp's flame. With a yawn, the Professor looked at JB's pocket watch, which lay open beside the book. Commenting on the time remaining until breakfast, he suggested we adjourn to get ready.

As I prepared for the day, I wondered what developments might unfold over the course of the next several hours. I concealed the bandage as best I could. The surging pain of my wound served to remind me of the previous night's hectic events, and I was not looking forward to a return trip to the manor. Mallory and his cohort were gaining precious distance, and my intuition told me that we should be catching the next train for Dover, but I doubted our chances of giving Geoffries the slip. On a positive note, Mallory was absent, and without his glib tongue to refute our seemingly incredible story, we stood better odds of swaying the inspector to our side.

I met my companions in the hall, and together we proceeded downstairs to the tavern. Geoffries was already seated near the fireplace at a table arrayed with four pewter place settings, spreading jam on a piece of toast. A fire blazed in the hearth, its warming flames chasing the morning chill away. Geoffries bid us a cordial good morning as my companions and I approached and sat down. We were all burned to a frazzle, and our dampened dispositions showed on our drawn, haggard faces.

The innkeeper emerged from the kitchen. "Mornin', gents, breakfast will be out in short order," he said, wiping his hands on his apron. "Elsa," he called back through the door. "Best be servin' our gentlemen guests now."

The golden-haired girl with vacant eyes came out with a teapot and pitcher of milk, which she placed on our table. She returned to the kitchen and reemerged adroitly balancing a platter of scrambled eggs and sausage and a tray with bowls of piping hot porridge. Utterly silent, she performed her simple chores in an impassive daze, and gave no notice or response when JB thanked her.

Not having eaten since midday yesterday, I lapped up the porridge hungrily and ate more than my fair share from the platter. JB had little appetite, and he pushed the eggs on his plate around with his fork. His mood openly reflected the discomforting anxiety that clung like a wet blanket and weighed heavy in the air. Geoffries sensed it, and genially offered a few conciliatory words of small talk to alleviate the tension. For the time being, he seemed content to postpone his impending questions.

Our fare finished, the youthful beauty emerged to whisk away the plates and bowls. When she had finished, the innkeeper approached our table.

"Nothing like a hearty breakfast," he said. "I trust everything was to your likin'."

"Yes, thank you," Geoffries politely replied. "I especially enjoyed the strawberry jam."

"My Aggie did put up a good batch this year. I'll let her know," the innkeeper said, quite pleased.

Geoffries gave him a dismissing look, and the innkeeper promptly excused himself, returning to the kitchen. Except for Geoffries and us, the tavern was empty. He nonchalantly scooped up a spoonful of sugar and stirred it into his tea. The fire crackled and popped as we sat silently in nervous anticipation, awaiting his next words.

His knotted brows gathered more heavily over his keen eyes. "A case so ostensibly simple, yet boundlessly perplexing. The more I delve, the more questions that arise," he said, reclining back and sipping his tea. "Mr. Blake, I'm sure a man of your profession can appreciate the intriguing nature of such a conundrum."

"It would pique my curiosity at any rate," I said.

He looked at each of us in turn, then slightly nodded and sighed. "There's a strange, sordid business afoot, of that I am certain. Last night, our good host was telling me all sorts of mighty queer goings on at the manor, and I myself saw the night sky ablaze with a spectacular light – an unnatural light it was – and that crashing thunder." He paused to catch our reaction. "I also observed the disheveled condition in which you returned from the manor, and your soiled shoes clearly indicated that you had been wandering about out of doors and had most likely traveled some distance on foot. Whatever is going on, I'm bound and determined to get to the bottom of it. Now gentlemen, there are several points of your testimony which need refining, and it would do you well to be forthright."

"You shall have our complete cooperation, Inspector," the Professor said agreeably.

"Thank you, Professor Hanson. That's what I'm counting on," he said.

Focusing his initial attention on the Professor, Geoffries took out a notebook and pencil. He reiterated the particulars of the Professor's previous statement and reviewed it with him, detecting for inconsistencies, but the Professor remained steadfast in his responses. JB fidgeted with his signet ring, sometimes nodding in affirmation, and occasionally exchanged glances with me.

"The invitation Sir Gunston extended to you, was it verbal or written?" Geoffries asked.

"Written," the Professor replied.

"Do you still have it?" Geoffries further inquired, jotting down a note.

"No, the butler retained it."

"I see. Now, sir, as for these violations which you say Sir Gunston perpetrated, I'll need you to be more specific," Geoffries probed.

Suddenly, JB's face erupted in an expression of indignation. "You want to know what he did! I'll show you what he did – I'll show you!" he raged, his burning eyes fixed on Geoffries. "Look at this!" he demanded, opening his shirt to expose the gruesome scar on his chest.

Geoffries' eyes grew wide at the sight of it, and his facial features scrunched with repugnance.

"I have a similar mutilation as well," the Professor stated. "Would you care to see it?"

"No, that won't be necessary. I've seen enough," Geoffries replied.

He shifted in his chair and resumed his neutral demeanor. "There is one further matter, however," he said, directing his attention to me. "I presume you were included in Sir Gunston's invitation as well, Mr. Blake. Am I correct?" he speculated.

"Yes," I succinctly answered.

"Then how is it you were not there to share in your associates' grim fate, yet aided in their escape?" he queried, thoughtfully looking at me like a chess player awaiting his opponent's move.

"I was delayed and showed up some time later. When I arrived, I found things amiss and pressed the butler for answers. I twisted his arm so to speak," I responded frankly.

"I see – I see indeed. And how did you learn of Sir Gunston's travel plans?"

"Like I said, I twisted the butler's arm."

He released his riveting gaze and cast his eyes upon my injured arm. Although the wound was well hidden, he seemed to be aware of it nonetheless, and his contemplative expression suggested that he was formulating another question; but whatever was on his mind, he kept it to himself.

He tucked away his notebook, and after draining the last sip from his cup, he patted his lips with his napkin. "Very well, gentlemen, I have all I need for now," he said, glancing at each of us. "I've made arrangement for our transportation to the manor. We shall reconvene here at ten o'clock – less than an hour from now," he mandated, looking at his pocket watch.

Excusing himself, he rose from his chair to take his leave. He paused at the foot of the stairs. "In the meantime, gentlemen, I advise you not to leave the confines of the inn," he said, and he ascended the staircase.

"He's a hard one to figure," I said when Geoffries was out of earshot.

"Do you think he believes us?" JB asked.

"Can't say for sure, but I think so – especially after your ardent demonstration. It had an effect on him, that's for certain," I replied and turned to the Professor to get his thoughts on the matter.

Distrait, he stared ahead at nothing in particular, seemingly oblivious to his surroundings. Perceiving my gaze, he stirred to awareness. "If you'll please excuse me, I think I'll use the time allotted to our benefit. There's much to be done," he pensively said and retired upstairs to his room.

My belly was full and my eyelids were heavy. "No offense JB, but I need to catch forty winks," I said, standing up to leave the table.

"By the way, I forgot to thank you for rescuing us," he said sincerely.

"Anytime," I returned, expressing a reassuring smile.

I left him alone in the tavern; and once within the quiet confines of my room, I closed the shades and tumbled onto the bed, where I drifted into an uneasy slumber.

Roused from a half-dream by a sharp rapping at my door, I sat up with a start. From beyond the window rose the dulled voices of two men conversing in the street below. From the hall came the voice of the Professor telling me the time had come. I shook off the daze and peered out the window to see Barnesby's horse and cart, and I observed as he and the Inspector stepped inside the inn. Again, the Professor spoke through the door, his words more urgent this time and soliciting a response.

"I'll be right down," I acknowledged.

When I arrived downstairs, my companions were gathered with Geoffries at the front door, and Barnesby was warming his bones by the fire.

Geoffries exhibited a smile of contentment upon seeing me. "Ah, good," he remarked. "We'll be going now, Mr. Barnesby," he directed, speaking to the crusty old man bent over the fire.

Geoffries held the door as we all funneled out of the tavern. What had been a bright morning sun was now dimmed by an opaque sky smeared with brooding clouds shaded in darkening tones of gray and indigo.

"Good to see you agin' yank," Barnesby muttered as he passed by me on his way to mount the front seat.

We climbed aboard the cart and set off down the meandering lane into the thick, desolate wood. In the daylight, the aged trees no longer cast their sinister spell of foreboding gloom; in contrast, their massive trunks and towering branches possessed a venerable charm, yet still exuded an uninviting presence, and held an ancient reverent power that made me feel insignificant. Barnesby uttered nary a word, and holding the slackened reins loose in his hands, he restricted his eyes to the lonely lane ahead. The horse pulled us along at a slow and steady gait, his plodding hooves beating a clopping rhythm, and sunrays piercing a brief rift in the canopy of clouds splashed patches of brilliance amidst the shifting shadows.

The barren wood gave way to the expanse of the moor. Tufts of marsh grasses and rushes stood among scummed mud-pits and foul quagmires. Tire marks indicated the spot where the Bentley had veered off the lane, but the wreck was nowhere in sight.

Leaving the moor behind us, we approached the rampant lions that marked the front gate. The gates stood open, hanging crookedly on their hinges, and Barnesby turned down the long hedge-lined drive toward the manor. As we rounded the circle in the shadow of the imposing castle-like structure, I took a gander at the garage. The motor cars that had been parked there the previous night were gone. Through a pair of open bay doors I descried the damaged Bentley with its crumpled fenders and splintered windshield, and the butterfly hood was open. A man holding a grease-stained rag emerged from within the bay, and taking notice of us, he swung the doors shut, screening the Bentley from sight. Barnesby halted at the stone bridge that spanned the moat, and we climbed down from the cart.

"If it's all the same to ya, I'll be stayin' right here," Barnesby unconditionally declared, a hint of fearful apprehension evident in his eyes.

"Suit yourself, Mr. Barnesby," Geoffries conceded.

With Geoffries at the head, we started across the bridge that spanned the moat. The Professor placed a restraining hand on my arm to retard my pace, and we lagged behind Geoffries and JB.

"I've made a positive discovery. I'll inform you later," he said in a hushed tone.

Geoffries rapped loudly with the knocker. Shortly thereafter, one of the doors opened, and the butler stood solemnly in the doorway, impeding any ingress. He silently surveyed us with a stern expression. His bruised forehead was wrapped in a bandage and his eye was blackened. Geoffries announced himself and inquired if Sir Gunston was in.

"No, Sir Gunston is away. There's no one here for you to see," the butler stolidly stated.

"And whom am I addressing?" Geoffries asked.

"Dudley, sir. I am the butler of this household," he courtly responded.

"Then Dudley, it'll be you I shall be conducting my business with. It's a trifle chilly here on the doorstep. May we come inside?"

Yielding, the butler stepped aside, motioning for us to enter. He gave me a scowl as I crossed the threshold, and Geoffries noticed it.

"I don't see as how I can help you," he said, closing the door.

"On the contrary, my good man, I believe you can be most helpful. Do you recognize these gentlemen?" Geoffries asked, gesturing to us.

"No," the butler flatly replied, poker-faced.

"Never set eyes upon them?"

"No – not that I can recall."

"Indeed," Geoffries remarked. "They supposedly attended a dinner party here last night."

"Sir Gunston did entertain yesterday evening, but I can assure you they were not among the guests."

"May I see the guest list?"

"Do you doubt my word, sir?"

"Your word is not in question. I simply wish to see the guest list – if it's not inconvenient," Geoffries retorted assertively.

The butler stalled, and as he deliberated on his response, a bead of sweat trickled down his temple. Eyebrows slightly raised, Geoffries cast an impelling gaze at him.

"Wait here," the butler solemnly decreed, and relenting, he turned on his heels and strode away.

During the butler's absence, Geoffries walked about the entrance hall, his examining eyes soaking in everything. The butler returned with the list, which he handed to Geoffries. The bottom of the page had been seemingly creased and torn away.

Geoffries scanned down the list, and when his eyes reached the uneven edge, his lips crinkled in a bemused suppressed smile.

"How did you sustain such a beastly injury?" he inquired on a tangent, handing back the list.

"I – I tripped on the stairs," the butler answered, taken off guard.

"Now, my good man, I'd like to have a look at your cellar."

Stunned, the butler stood speechless.

"You do have one, don't you?" Geoffries persisted.

"Well – well yes," the butler stammered out. "But this is a private home, sir, and I will not have a pack of strangers gallivanting about this house as if it were a spectacle open to the public. Now I must bid you good day, sirs," he sternly said.

"You can indulge me now, or I can return later with a vast retinue of police, the lot of them swarming and combing over this property," Geoffries threatened.

The butler swallowed his spit. "Follow me," he said reluctantly.

He conducted us into the bowels of the manor to a stout door, which opened to a landing, and beyond, a series of steps disappeared into the darkness below. He lit a lantern, and we descended into a lofty subterranean chamber with three doors. As I looked about the chamber, its cold stone walls bathed in the fluttering radiance of the lantern, my nerves were tweaked with an overwhelming sense of déjà vu.

Thus far I had remained silent on the sidelines. "That's the way," I volunteered, pointing to a door.

"Open it," Geoffries said authoritatively to the butler.

"Why that's nothing but the wine cellar," the butler protested.

"Open it," Geoffries firmly repeated.

The butler sifted through a set of keys on a ring, and inserting one in the lock, he opened the door.

"As you can plainly see, this is where Sir Gunston stores his private vintage," he said, holding the lantern aloft to illuminate the musty cellar lined with casks and dust-covered bottles.

"Over there," I said, urging Geoffries onward.

He took the lantern from the butler and followed me to the narrow door laced with ironwork.

"Through there," I said.

Geoffries tried the door without success and then instructed the butler to open it. The butler unwillingly complied, and the heavy door groaned on its hinges as he put his weight against the strong planks.

With Geoffries leading, we proceeded along the lower passage, the butler protesting all the way.

"Before we go any further, I think you'll find what's behind that door to be most interesting," I said, drawing Geoffries attention to the only door along that stretch of passage.

Geoffries pressured the butler to grant us entrance; and once inside, I switched on the electric lights, illuminating the extensive array of accoutrements that made up a well-equipped laboratory. The butler implored Geoffries not to disturb anything as the inspector toured the room, examining this and that. The examination table fitted with leather restraints particularly attracted his fascination, along with the cast iron hatch covering the incendiary oven.

He opened the hatch and sifted through the ashes with a poker. "Hmmm, what have we here?" he remarked upon discovering bone fragments amidst the powdery residue; and with careful precision, he placed them in an envelope.

While Geoffries was preoccupied, the Professor went about with inquisitive curiosity. He skimmed through papers with scribbled notes and perused the various bottles, jars and vials, reading the labels in an attempt to determine the contents of each. One vial in particular caught his eye, and when he thought no one was watching, he removed it from the shelf and slyly slipped it in his coat pocket. He had not noticed me standing behind him, and upon turning around, he realized I had witnessed his uncharacteristic act of pilfering. He offered no excuse, just a silent expression of indifference. Knowing he must have good reason, I let the matter drop and said nothing.

Once Geoffries was satisfied with his findings, we continued onward down the passage to the portcullis that barred the only way. Geoffries peered through the bars to see what lay beyond within reach of the lantern's light.

"That part dates back to when the manor was first built. It hasn't been used for over a century," the butler dryly asserted.

As he spoke, I was already cranking the winch to raise the creaking gate; and when the way was open, the Professor directed Geoffries to the dungeon cells in which he and JB had been held prisoner. Geoffries put a handkerchief over his nose to filter out the stale, disgusting odor that now permeated the air.

"Within this cell lies undeniable proof of my words, as well as those of Harold Drayfus," the Professor categorically stated, standing before the threshold of his former prison.

After the butler had reluctantly unbolted the door, the Professor ushered Geoffries into the dank confining cell.

"On the floor under the bed you'll find writing etched in the stone by Harold Drayfus," he said, and he requested Geoffries help in moving the shoddy wooden bed frame, which had been moved back into place.

"Blimey," Geoffries exclaimed upon viewing the inscribed message and initials.

"How would I have knowledge of this, if I had not been here?" the Professor proposed, presenting a logical question.

"You have a valid point there," Geoffries replied in agreement. He knelt down for a closer inspection. "The initials certainly match, and it also appears that this was done fairly recently," he expressed as he examined the cryptic verse.

He moved on to the cell across the hall, where he found a monogrammed gold cufflink, which JB verified as his. At that point, the butler began to lose his stolid composure, and he shrugged his shoulders in ignorance when Geoffries gave him a sharp look askance.

Geoffries checked the other cells, and he eventually came to the heavy door at the end of the passage. The sight of what lay beyond appalled him – a sadistic chamber, which contained a ghastly array of vile medieval instruments dedicated to the infliction of horrific pain and torture.

"Original fixtures – antiques from the turbulent days of King Charles, nothing more," the butler professed.

Intrigued, Geoffries inspected several of the pieces. "Interesting – this equipment has been maintained," he said, projecting his thoughts aloud.

Having seen enough, we returned back along the passage and through the wine cellar to the lofty chamber.

"There's one other thing you should see, Inspector," the Professor said. "The place where we were violated." He pointed to the strong door that led to the profane pagan temple. "Through that door."

Objecting profusely, the butler refused us entry. Geoffries snatched the key ring from his hand, and soon we were heading down the vaulted corridor to the great doors of the temple. I pushed against one of the ponderous doors, it yawned open, and we passed into the interior of the unholy sanctum with Geoffries holding the lantern aloft. A cold chill shot down my spine as if it was hollow and someone had filled it with ice. As before, hollow whispers echoed throughout. JB covered his ears, and Geoffries too was clearly affected by the unnerving atmosphere. He took awe-stricken notice of the murals, and how the hideous, monstrous figures they portrayed appeared to stir and move, and at second glance had repositioned themselves.

Directing Geoffries toward the altar, the Professor led him to the sacrificial stone with its bloodstained surface and shackles dangling from the corners.

"Fastened to this block of stone, we suffered horrible indignities," he emphatically stated. "The chafe marks on our wrists and ankles alone will bear witness to that."

Suddenly, I realized the butler was no longer with us, and I looked around to discover that he was conspicuously absent. Sensing treachery, I slipped away from the group into the shadows. From my cloaked position, I observed as the butler emerged from the edge of the lantern light. With revolver in hand, he furtively approached the others gathered about the stone. Distracted, they failed to notice him drawing near amidst the rippling shades of dancing light and darkness.

He halted several paces from them. His eyes shifted back and forth. "Where is Mr. Blake?" he demanded, immediately capturing their attention.

My startled companions froze at the sight of the leveled revolver in the butler's hand.

"Are you daft, man?" Geoffries exclaimed, remaining steadfast and undaunted. "Put that pistol down if you know what's good for you."

"Fools, you'll never leave here alive," the butler grimly stated.

CHAPTER 18

His eyes flaring with malice, the butler uttered a stream of strange, inscrutable words. More audible grew the chaotic mix of mutterings, which melded into one coercive chorus of voices invading my mind. Geoffries clapped his hands to his ears, and he staggered backwards, shaking his head. JB sank to his knees, and it took all the mental fortitude I could muster to retain my senses.

Having left my Luger behind, I was powerless to match the firepower of the butler's revolver. But the desperate situation called for immediate action; and drawing upon that last measure of inner strength, I rushed out from my place of concealment, barreling headlong at the butler. Hearing my swift footfalls and glimpsing me out of the corner of his eye, he reacted quickly. He whirled to face me and pulled the trigger. A flash erupted from the muzzle, and the report resounded off the walls of the temple. Suddenly a sharp pain seared my side like a hot poker. Undaunted, I ducked my head, the driving force of the charge hurling me forward. In the next instant, I rammed into him, spearing him in the chest and grappling my arms around his waist. He reeled from the impact, staggering backwards. Exerting every ounce of muscle, I propelled him straight at the pillar in our path and slammed him against it. He hit with a smashing thud, his head smacking the hard stone. Dazed and stunned, he expelled a groan; and before he could recover, I punched him several times in the stomach and diaphragm, each blow provoking a guttural sound. Rising to full height, I drew back and delivered a sound right cross to his jaw, which sent him ratcheting sideways, and he fell to his hands and knees, dropping the revolver.

Holding his gut, he scrambled to retrieve the gun, and I moved to intercept. He reached out to grasp it, but just as his fingers touched the handle, I kicked it away, and it skated across the floor into the shadows. I hoisted him to his feet by the scruff, and holding him steady, socked him square in the face. Losing control of my anger, I furiously pounded him to a pulp. I had him against the wall about to deliver the coup de grace, a bashing haymaker, when a hand gripped my arm to stay the blow.

"He's had enough," the Professor declared.

His words brought me to my senses, and restraining the rage, I released the butler. A bruised and bloodied mess, he slid down the wall, crumpling into a heap on the floor. Geoffries and JB appeared on the scene, and Geoffries retrieved the revolver.

Although diminished, the disconcerting murmurs were still present.

"Let's get out of this place," JB said, noticeably shaken.

"I'm for that," Geoffries wholeheartedly concurred.

Geoffries and I got the butler to his feet; and supporting his arms, we half-carried him as we exited the temple post-haste and proceeded back along the vaulted corridor to the lofty chamber. As we started up the stairs, I could no longer disregard the stinging pain that nagged me, and grimacing, I clutched my side.

"What's wrong?" JB asked.

"I took a slug – but I don't think it's bad."

I'll be the judge of that," he said as he gently pried my hand loose, revealing a bullet hole in my trench coat. When he opened the coat, the Professor exhibited an expression of genuine concern.

"We need to get you someplace where I can have a proper look at this," JB said with a degree of urgency.

They escorted me to a drawing room in which comforting daylight shone through tall windows. JB had me lie down on a couch, and Geoffries sat the battered butler in a chair before the astonished faces of several curious servants. Displaying his credentials, Geoffries informed them of his identity.

"I'll need some hot water and bandages," JB petitioned, examining my wound. "You're lucky, Conrad. The bullet only grazed you."

"You heard the man," Geoffries barked, prodding one of the servants to meet JB's request.

While JB patched me up, Geoffries queried those servants present. They all choked on their responses and pleaded ignorance under the stern gaze of the butler. After JB had finished with me, he turned his attention to the butler, and always the compassionate humanitarian, treated his inflictions with the same assiduous care he would afford any patient.

Geoffries was cognizant of the butler's influence and cut short his questioning. Frustrated, he lifted the butler from his chair, and we gathered to leave.

"It's the choky for you – make no doubt about it," Geoffries said, dragging the butler out the front door.

Upon our return to the village, Barnesby halted in front of the inn to let us off. Geoffries intended to continue on to Charing, as the village constable had no facilities to incarcerate the butler. After which, he planned to return to the manor with several bobbies and submit the servants to further questioning, as well as conduct a thorough search. He instructed us to prepare signed written statements, which he would collect and review later.

As I climbed down from the cart, the butler shot me a cold glance of contempt, his face contorted in a seething expression. "Wait 'til the awakening!" he scornfully cried, and then he laughed mockingly as the cart rolled away.

Once inside, we went straight up to JB's room so he could properly dress my wound. As JB practiced his exceptional skill, the Professor imparted that positive discovery which he had so vaguely informed me of earlier that morning.

"I have encouraging news," he apprised. "After leaving you this morning, I renewed my earnest search for the vile spell that binds the Doctor and I – and I uncovered it. Mind you, its text and symbols were difficult to decipher, and in the time allotted, I was hard-pressed to fully construe its contents. Nevertheless, I came across a passage that instructs one how to negate the spell's virulent effects. However, two crucial components are required – one being the dolls – and the other the lotus extract, which we now have," he disclosed, pulling from his pocket the small bottle he had purloined from the laboratory.

"Those dolls are on their way to Venice," I pointed out.

"Then that is exactly where we must go – and with all haste," the Professor earnestly stated.

Furnished with this striking revelation, we decided to depart for Charing first thing in the morning and catch the next train for Dover, regardless of Geoffries' involvement. It was then I suddenly realized my motives in this case had changed from investigation to vindication.

Together, we corroborated on our written statements for Geoffries. Keeping to the basics, I short-changed my story a bit, glossing over or omitting certain particulars that might incriminate me or give the impression I had lost my marbles; but my companions found it sound and synonymous with their accounts.

Requesting solitude, the Professor resumed his research, while JB and I whittled away the time in the tavern and took a stroll through the village. As we meandered down narrow streets, the village had an attractive, almost dreamlike quaintness. All the same, a latent dark secret lay buried in the mortar and hidden behind closed casements on tumbled gables – a fearful secret that manifested itself in the silent faces of the villagers we encountered, who took immediate notice of us and crossed to the opposite side of the street, some acknowledging us with a polite nod. At the church we paid a visit to the Vicar and perused the same records Drayfus had examined. Many of the entries denoted births, deaths and marriages, but others, more notably the older ones, read like a surreal folktale.

Geoffries returned late that evening, his arrival heralded by the lights and rumbling of a motorcar. We convened in his room, where he collected and reviewed our statements.

"These seem well in order," he said when he had finished. "They'll do in lieu of your personal witness. Your testimonies, although incredible as they may seem, ring true in my opinion. There's a strange, sordid business afoot all right, and it involves more than murderous complicity. I wish to thank you gentlemen for your cooperation and assistance. You have been exceedingly forthright and helpful – and Mr. Blake, your actions this day are no doubt commendable. I have the distinct impression you'll be leaving on the morrow, and I've a firm notion as to where you're going – Venice, if I'm not mistaken. In any case, I'm not going to lift a finger to stop you. I, however, must return to London to sort out the matter."

"I admit you're correct as far as our destination. The fact is, we have unfinished business with Mallory," I divulged.

"I too want to see justice done, but unlike you, I have procedures I must adhere to. Let me assure you, I have every intention of going to Venice myself and taking the man into custody. I would like to know that I can count on your assistance in the undertaking."

"You shall have it," I pledged, and my companions expressed their agreement.

"I suggest you stay at the Hotel Domenico on the Ruga Due Pozzi while in Venice, and I'll contact you by telegram as soon as I can," he advised.

After ironing out some details, we shook hands and said goodnight.

* * *

Abruptly awakened from a restless sleep in the middle of the night, I opened my eyes to the startling sight of a dark figure looming over me and the glint of a straight razor poised to slit my throat. Shining in the darkness, glaring eyes burned with malicious intent. Instantly, I grasped the assailant's wrist to stay the blade. Leveraging his weight, he pressed downward, and I felt the sharp edge against my exposed flesh. A constricting hand seized my throat, and I struggled to catch my breath while now employing both hands to hold the blade at bay. The razor shook in his hands as I gradually forced it away. Pressing hard, he renewed his efforts – the blade drawing closer, and all the while his crushing chokehold was suffocating me. My heart racing, I slipped one hand under the pillow, while straining with the other to stave off the unthinkable. Desperately, I groped for my Luger as the cold steel came within a hair's breadth of my neck. Searching frantically, my hand found the pistol, but as I gripped the handle, a sudden realization struck me – with no round in the chamber, I would have to cock the toggle bolt, and for that I needed two hands. Keeping my head and rapidly considering options, I speedily withdrew the pistol, and wielding it as a blunt weapon, I delivered a hard blow to his head. Stunned, he reeled sideways, releasing his lethal grip, and I heard a thud as he hit the floor.

I sprang out of bed, and after fumbling in the dark with a box of matches, I lit the oil lamp and turned up the flame. My shaving kit was open atop the dresser – the razor missing, and my attacker lay sprawled on the floor next to the bed. Kneeling down beside him, I illuminated his face and gazed in utter astonishment at what I saw.

CHAPTER 19

In the lamp's glowing radiance, I recognized the well-defined features of my attacker. It was the Professor! Blank and vacant as if in a trance, his open eyes stared into oblivion, and his face had a ghostly pallor. His hand still clutched the handle of the razor, and I took it from his grasp. Despite his deathlike appearance, he exhibited signs of life, for his chest rose slightly with each shallow breath. Initially, my attempts to rouse him evoked no response, when suddenly his eyes closed, then reopened. His eyes fluttered several times, and he looked up at me with the most perplexed expression.

"What on earth?" he blurted in a state of bewilderment. "Why, this isn't my room," he said in a somewhat faltering voice, now coming to grips with his surroundings.

"No – it's mine," I said.

"What am I doing here? And why, pray tell, am I on the floor?" he demanded to know.

"Frankly Professor, I'm not sure myself."

"I seem to have hurt my head," he said, sitting up and rubbing his temple.

"That's because I hit you."

Shocked, his eyes widened in an expression of consternation that sensed betrayal. "You did what?" he exclaimed.

"I had to. Fact is, you tried to slit my throat with this," I said, showing him the razor.

A change came over him. He seemed his normal self again, and I helped him to his feet. Feeling a little disoriented, he lowered himself into a chair.

"So you say I tried to slit your throat," he pensively said, appearing quite distressed.

"As crazy as that may seem – it's true."

He stroked his beard in contemplation. "Forgive me, for I was not consciously aware of my actions. I was deep in the abyss of slumber, under the controlling influence of a dream that apparently had the power to induce somnambulism. A nightmare of terrifying magnitude, the vivid reality of which I was compelled to acknowledge, and the only means to escape the terror was to slay the monster in my dream. You,

I'm afraid, must have been the illusionary manifestation of that monster. There can be no other explanation."

His eyes were trustful and his words sincere. He was also a man not prone to whimsical flights of imagination. When considering the uncanny circumstances and harrowing events that had thus far plagued us, it made perfect sense. I placed a conciliatory hand on his shoulder.

"Please don't ask me to recount the details," he requested. "Suffice it to say, only time will efface the unspeakable impressions that will no doubt haunt my waking hours as well. We must dispel the power of this potent black magic before it destroys us all, for it seems not even you are safe from the reaches of its vile devastating grip."

"Keep heart, Professor. We'll beat this thing, and who knows, we may just even the score in the process," I said with determination. "Go back to bed, and no hard feelings."

As he stood to leave, he actually appeared frightened at the prospect of returning to his bed. "I advise you to lock your door," he said, profoundly concerned.

"I'll do that," I assured, and I saw him to his room.

Before returning to my room, I quietly checked on JB and found him sleeping soundly. As I locked my door, the very notion that my own companions might pose a potential threat greatly disturbed me. Struggling with that disquieting thought, I climbed into bed and slept with one eye open for the rest of the night.

Next morning, the Professor was reticent and looked as if he bore the worries of the world upon his shoulders. After breakfast, Barnesby took us to Charing. Geoffries accompanied us and saw us to the rail station, where he bid us Godspeed and a merry Christmas. It was, after all, Christmas Eve.

Upon our arrival in Dover, I sent a telegram to Cindy.

New developments STOP Heading for Venice STOP Will keep you posted STOP Merry Christmas STOP

Conrad

We crossed a stormy English Channel by ferry to Calais and purchased tickets for the next train to Paris. Not surprisingly, the

Professor spoke fluent French, which facilitated matters. Traveling along the rails through the north of France, we enjoyed a comforting measure of solace within the confines of our private compartment. JB puffed on his pipe, while a serene countryside passed across the window like a moving picture. Obsessed, the Professor absorbed himself in the pages of the tome, pouring over its cryptic passages and copying down the annotations Mallory had written in the margins to augment his notes. Now and then, the Professor would make comments to himself, or his eyes would flash with a scintillation of discovery, after which, he would usually jot down something in his notebook. He made no mention of the previous night's incident, and neither did I.

At the rail station in Paris, we procured private staterooms on the express leaving the 27th for Venice and Constantinople. Undecided on where to stay, we took the suggestion of our taxi driver and stayed at a small family-run hotel owned by his brother-in-law. Although lacking in some of the more refined amenities, it abounded in hospitality.

We shared a bottle of wine with our dinner that evening, and as JB slowly sipped his wine, he reminisced with a far-off look in his eye.

"I was to spend Christmas at my sister's this year. I can picture it so clearly, the room bathed in the warm glow of the soft firelight, a cold wind howling at the window, my brother pouring the wine and my sister gently stroking the cat in her lap, the dog resting peacefully on the braided rug before the fire, and my nephew's face beaming with delight, a smile of anticipation and wonder on his lips."

He instilled a sense of homesickness in us all, and later I retired to bed with thoughts of Boston on my mind.

That night, instead of dreams of sugarplums dancing in their heads, horrible nightmares tormented my companions, and I was up half the night for their sake – and mine. I blamed myself for their ill fortune. If only I had acted on my hunches and kept them from attending that dinner party at the manor, I thought in hindsight.

Christmas morning came, announced by a rising sun sprinkling flecks of gold upon the maze of rooftops. What would normally be a joyous holiday was met with dampened spirits, and my companions' haggard faces told the story.

JB insisted on attending Mass. "We can use all the help we can get," he urged.

Although the Professor was not Catholic, he concurred, and they set out with the hotelkeeper and his family for the neighborhood church, leaving me behind to watch over the tome. Before they left, the Professor adamantly warned me against gazing at its maddening contents; but as the time passed, my curiosity got the better of me, and I opened it. Its strange, inscrutable passages spoke of unspeakable and abominable things. Appalled, I slammed it shut lest it corrupt my mind.

Upon their return, JB presented us each with a package to unwrap. Mine contained a pair of leather gloves with fleece lining, and the Professor received a silver-plated fountain pen. In turn I passed out the gifts I had purchased for them in Soho. At first, the Professor was a bit overwhelmed, but then his gratitude changed to remorse.

"This is most thoughtful of you, gentlemen, but I regret that I have nothing to give in return," he said. "Ah, but wait, I may have something after all."

From his suitcase he retrieved a brass chess knight and a well-worn leather volume.

"I was awarded this for my victory in a chess match back in my younger days," he said, handing me the chess piece. "I consider it to be a token of good luck. May its magic now work good fortune for you. The base is hollow and can be accessed by unscrewing the bottom. It may come in handy should you wish to conceal something small in size." To JB he gave the book. "It is a collection of poetry, into which I have retreated countless times, always finding solace."

"But these are your cherished keepsakes," JB said, and I too was moved by the Professor's sentiment.

Later that afternoon, the hotel owner invited us to have dinner with him and his extensive family, which turned out to be a pleasant exchange of cultures. For a time, the congenial atmosphere proved to be an uplifting distraction from our current troubles; but as sunlight dwindled into twilight, the impending night struck my companions with an overpowering sense of dread. An expression of unbridled fear was clearly evident on JB's face. Back and forth he paced the floor of my room, running his fingers through his hair and smoking his pipe incessantly.

Sleep eventually found my companions; and amidst the foreboding shades of night, deep in the secret world of dreams, they again wrestled with their darkest fears, and I was powerless to relieve their torment.

Two days later aboard the train, their sunken eyes and reticent mood exhibited the outward signs of their ordeal; and every night the awful dreams haunted them, each having the detailed misery of some prolonged nightmare, and each one more terrifying than the last.

On a cloudy day, as the train lumbered over the Italian Alps, I knocked on JB's door and entered without waiting for a response. I discovered him seated on his bed, his sleeve rolled up and his medical bag open beside him. A tourniquet constricted his arm. He did not regard me, but instead concentrated on his present task; and with syringe in hand, he self-administered a hypodermic injection.

"Don't look so surprised," he said after withdrawing the needle. "Don't you understand? I've got to stay awake. I can't endure another night. I can't – I won't!" he exclaimed. "Now I know why Drafe beseeched me for stimulants – his desperate need to stay awake. I didn't know it then, but I know it now. They get you in your dreams. They get you in your dreams just like he said! Even awake, I sense their vile presence – watching – waiting," he stammered in a faltering voice, his wide eyes shifting this way and that in an excited state of paranoia.

Reaching out, he clutched my sleeve and pulled me closer, his wild eyes like those of a madman staring into mine. "They're coming – coming for me – tonight. But I won't let them. No – I won't let them," he explicitly declared, his lips quivering in agitation.

"Get a hold of yourself, Doctor," I admonished.

His excited emotions cooled, leaving him like a receding tide, and remembering himself, he reverted to his normal stature. He looked up at me, his apologetic eyes entreating understanding.

"Don't' worry. We're going to beat this thing," I said encouragingly. "The Professor's cooking up the means, and I've got a plan."

That evening, the three of us convened in the dining car. Throughout the meal, the Professor was unusually reserved, while JB was a bundle of electrified nerves. After the dinner plates had been whisked away and the coffee poured, the Professor brought up the subject, which by now had taken up residence in the forefront of our thoughts and minds.

"I have something of grave importance I must share with both of you," he grimly announced with an inflexion that denoted a deadly seriousness. "We must find the dolls and obtain them by any means with extreme haste. I cannot emphasize enough the dire need to accomplish this. The very sanity of the Doctor and myself weighs in the balance, for the debilitating effects of the curse are cumulative, and will become permanent unless removed in time. And time is something I'm afraid we have little of. With each wretched nightmare, our most ingrained fears further manifest, dragging us deeper into a realm of madness, eventually to spiral into an abyss from whence there is no return – to be rendered pitiful, feebleminded idiots fit for nothing, destined to rot in an asylum. Our only recourse is to refrain from sleep. Even awake, the Doctor and I will retain a dreamlike state, and those faculties we so heavily rely upon will not be as acute."

He paused to reflect on his next words.

"That is not the only crisis that confronts us," he continued. "I have made a profound and most frightening discovery in my research. Suffice it to say, that if Sir Gunston is allowed to succeed in his machinations, it will spell doom for the human race and the world as we know it. He is not alone, mind you. Others are aiding and supporting him in the achievement of his aims – of that I'm certain; and all the powers of hell are abetting him, striving to reap the fruition of his efforts. That, gentlemen, is what we are up against."

He was talking in riddles, and under normal circumstances I would have ordinarily considered the last part of his discourse absurd, but these were not normal circumstances. "So what exactly is Mallory's master plan, Professor?" I asked, still retaining a bit of skepticism.

"To put it succinctly, he intends to awaken a sleeping god. Like the beast of Revelations, this foul, corrupt being will wreak terrible chaos and upheaval, and crush mankind under his thumb. Mallory stated that his name in Zoroastrianism is Ahriman. Zoroastrianism is an ancient Persian religion first promulgated by the prophet Zarathustra, or Zoroaster in the Greek, and is today regarded mainly as mythology. In the heart of this mythology, Ahriman is the evil one, the destructive spirit, and is served by a host of demons. Ohrmazd, the creator of the universe and the two worlds, both spiritual and material, put Ahriman to sleep for three millennia when he chanted the *Ahunvar* – the true speech or word of truth. The actual name of this being – this destructive spirit as revealed in the *Necronomicon* I will not utter. According to its blasphemous text, which I suffered to read and decipher, his awakening is forthcoming, and the foreshadowing events enabling this to occur draw nigh. An astronomical sign will indicate when the conditions are right. This I have determined to be the purpose of the astronomical chart on the tablet, for the Necronomicon's text alludes to the tablet and contains a rudimentary sketch of its star chart. Based on my research thus far and my knowledge of the stars, I conjecture that on the next solstice, the heavens will be in perfect alignment, setting the stage for the resurrection of evil."

"You can't be serious, Professor," I said. "You don't really believe all this, do you?"

"Yes, I do indeed," he stated adamantly.

JB looked as if he did not know what to believe, and I was concerned that the Professor might be going off the deep end.

"I wouldn't worry too much," I assured. "The next solstice is six months away, and by then Mallory will have been brought to justice. I'll see to that if I have to haul his carcass all the way back to England and drop him off at the doorstep of Scotland Yard. He can't very well do any harm from inside a jail cell, now can he? As for getting the dolls, I've a plan. You told me Mallory was looking for some kind of key. Granted, he knows what that key is, but like us, he doesn't know where it is. According to his correspondence with Count Borgia, he desperately wants to procure the centuries old journal of a sea captain from an antiquities dealer named Antonio Barsucci. But the journal itself is not what he's after – it's what's in it. If my hunch is correct, somewhere in the journal lies the secret to the key's location, and in all probability what the key is. All we need to do is get our hands on the journal first and find the key before Mallory, then use it as a bargaining chip for the dolls. And I know just where to start," I confidently said, opening my notebook and showing him the page with Barsucci's business address and telephone number. "Should we need to take a more direct approach, we pay a call to the address on the telegram Mallory sent to Count Borgia. But I've a sneaking suspicion we won't have to go looking for them, they'll come looking for us."

"That's a most dangerous game you propose to play, Mr. Blake," the Professor deemed.

"Have you got a better idea?" I retorted.

"For the life of me – no."

JB stared silently into his coffee with troubled eyes, his hands quivering with a nervous jitter, his thoughts a mystery.

Stopping only to replenish the supply of coal and water, the train traveled the expanse of rail across Northern Italy toward Venice. In the passing view, picturesque villages staggered up hillsides and nestled in valleys, and towering slopes adorned with a blanket of snow touched the sky.

Upon reaching the Adriatic coast, the locomotive conveyed us over the Ponte Della Liberta, which stretches across the crystalline waters of the Venetian Lagoon, linking the island city with the mainland. In the distance, gothic church domes and spires rose above a tumbled cluster of tiled rooftops. As the train rolled into the station, a sign read: Stazione Ferroviaria Santa Lucia.

Stepping out onto the platform, we were beset by a wet chill that seemed to seep through even the thickest layer of fabric. Outside the station entrance, a flock of gondoliers solicited for passengers like taxi drivers waiting for a fare, their gondolas lining the edge of a broad canal bustling with boat traffic. A stout young man with olive skin accosted us, his wide-brimmed black hat adorned with a red ribbon. He spouted a few phrases in Italian, and although I could not understand a word, his gestures communicated the meaning.

"Unfortunately, my Italian is a bit rusty, nevertheless he says his name is Luigi and he'll take us anywhere we desire to go in the city," the Professor informed. "Sono Americano. Parla inglese?" he said, responding to the gondolier.

"Si, I speak a little English," the gondolier said with a thick accent.

"Good. We want to go to the Hotel Domenico," JB requested.

"Si, si, niente – come, I take you," he replied, motioning for us to accompany him.

We loaded our luggage and ourselves into his more than accommodating gondola; and employing a single oar, the gondolier slowly propelled the flat-bottomed boat through the heart of the city, along the wide, bending length of a Grand Canal, its waters glistening with a speckled brilliance in the bright sunlight. On either side, grand palaces with loggias overlooked the canal and traced a magical outline against a cobalt blue sky.

"Venice has a vast repertoire of churches and museums exhibiting marvelous examples of renaissance art," the Professor passionately stated.

"We're not here for sight-seeing. We've got important business to attend to," I reminded him.

"Yes, it's a pity," he said wistfully. "But I must at least make an effort to visit the Biblioteca Nazionale Marciano. Initially founded in 1362 by Petrarch, the library contains a vast collection, including many rare volumes and literary works dating back centuries. I may be able to find material essential to our objective."

"In that case, I think that's definitely worth working into the picture," I assented, focusing a keen eye on the gondolier to see if he might be eavesdropping.

The gondolier turned the boat and steered down a narrow canal; and after turning again, he rowed a steady course for a stretch along a waterway tightly hedged by continuous buildings with shuttered windows and railed balconies. The boat flowed beneath several arching footbridges, finally easing to a stop at a landing. A place-name read: Ruga Due Pozzi.

"The Hotel Domenico," the gondolier said, gesturing to the nearest structure, which stood nestled in a corner where the canal turned sharply at a right angle, its frontage facing the street above. "I wait here. Hotel get your bags," he said with an honest smile.

The Professor left us waiting while he held a brief conversation with the gondolier in the man's native tongue. At the conclusion of their talk, he handed the gondolier a sum of money, and the man nodded in affirmation.

"What was that all about?" I inquired of the Professor as we ascended the steps to the street above.

"Luigi might prove invaluable as a guide, and thus I retained his services as such. I asked him to return in a couple of hours. That will give us time to unpack and have some lunch," he replied.

"Good thinking," I said.

We casually entered the small hotel lobby and checked in at the desk. As I signed the hotel register, the clerk removed an envelope from a cubbyhole on the wall behind him.

"Mr. Blake, we received word of your arrival," he said to my surprise. "I have a telegram for you."

As he placed the envelope in my hand, a familiar voice came from behind me – a voice that grated the length of my spine.

CHAPTER 20

Hardly believing my ears, I turned around to match the face with the voice. JB wheeled about and stood motionless for a moment, his facial features frozen in an expression of incredulous recognition that quickly changed to elation. There stood Sadie Morrell, wrapped in an elegant fur coat, and looking like a picture in a top-drawer magazine.

"JB Hawkins, you handsome devil. I thought I'd never see you again," she said forlornly, her eyes reflecting the wistful yearning of a wounded heart.

Before JB could gather his wits to utter a word, she flew to him, and passionately embracing him, kissed him square on the lips. Beguiled, he succumbed to her bittersweet charms and reciprocated with equal passion.

"Why didn't you contact me in London, my darling?" she softly demanded, looking deeply in his eyes.

"How was I supposed to?" he questioned, somewhat puzzled.

"Didn't you get my note? I gave it to a steward to deliver. I received urgent word from family friends in London and had to depart immediately upon docking. It was all in my note, including the address and telephone number where I would be staying."

"I never received it," he stated with heartfelt sincerity.

"You never got my note?" she expressed again with a tinge of saddened betrayal. "Well that explains everything. Oh, my darling, I thought I'd lost you; but no matter now. I never gave up hope; and here I am in your arms again, and I never want to leave. I should never have left our fate in the hands of another."

"I, too, wondered and hoped, and I'm so glad that it was all a misunderstanding," he said in a conciliatory tone.

He kissed her softly, and they held each other close as if they would never let go. What smoldering embers remained were now rekindled and fully aflame. But I was not buying any of it. The scene read like a staged act in a play, and her story was too convenient. I stuffed the telegram in my pocket.

"My dear Professor Hanson, how good it is to see you again – and Mr. Blake," she said, now politely regarding us with a pleasant smile. "What brings you to Venice?" she inquired with a playful inquisitiveness.

"It's a magnificent city. One worth seeing," I quickly replied, concocting a vague answer. "And yourself?" I asked, immediately returning the question.

"I'm a lover of art, and there's no city like Venice to see the great works of the renaissance masters."

"I agree," the Professor said with a touch of alacrity. "I myself am somewhat partial to Tintoretto. His paintings possess a strong effect of light and shadow, and the drama portrayed in his scenes can be extremely moving. And of course, one must acknowledge Paolo Veronese. Though not Venetian, he painted some of his greatest works here. The church of San Sebastiano is noted for its many works by Veronese. Which artist might you favor, Miss Morrell?"

"I'm not a connoisseur, just an enthusiastic admirer," she lightheartedly responded, skillfully skirting the heart of the question.

"After checking in, we plan to have some lunch. Perhaps you would care to join us?" the Professor cordially proposed.

"Yes, you simply must join us," JB insisted.

She accepted with fervid eagerness. "I can't think of anything I'd rather do more. The hotel restaurant serves a delightful regional fare," she said.

"Then it's settled," JB said, his face beaming with unrestrained joy.

"You two go ahead," I said. "The Professor and I will settle in and meet you later."

Sadie took JB by the hand and led him to the dining room. They had no more than disappeared from view when the Professor anxiously inquired about the telegram. I opened it, and we read the contents together. It was from Geoffries, informing that he had obtained a warrant and would be arriving any day.

Our accommodations were on the second floor and consisted of a common drawing room adjoined by bedrooms and a private bath. A balcony off the drawing room overlooked the restful waters of the canal.

After finding a suitable hiding place for the tome, we retired downstairs to the dining room, where Sadie and JB were picking up where they had left off. JB was suffering from a complete relapse, having all the outward symptoms of lovesickness. During lunch, his eyes rarely left her. She, of course, was her usual cache of polite talk, weaving her charms so artfully that even the Professor fell under her spell. JB excitedly informed us that Sadie was staying at this very hotel; and although it did not strike him or the Professor as odd, I considered it a remarkable coincidence.

Despite JB's blissful expression, he could scarcely hide the traces of fatigue and strain that marked his facial features. "I haven't been getting much sleep as of late," he simply replied when Sadie concernedly noted his condition.

She suggested they take a leisurely stroll to Saint Mark's Square and along the waterfront after lunch to catch up on lost time. "We can make an afternoon of it, and maybe visit the church of San Zaccaria," she enthusiastically proposed. "It's decorated with an array of magnificent paintings, most notably Bellini's 'Madonna and Child with Saints', and I understand the prophet Zachariah from the Bible is entombed there as well."

"He is indeed," the Professor concurred. "His body was donated to Venice by the Byzantine emperor Leo V, and has since been laid to rest in the church that sanctifies his name. As the father of John the Baptist, his remains are considered a sacred relic," he freely expounded.

Silently deliberating, JB spooned sugar into his already sweetened coffee. He shot me a glance, to which I responded by simply nodding agreeably.

"You two enjoy yourselves. I'm sure you have a lot to talk about. The Professor and I will manage all right," I said, forcing a smile.

*   *   *

With an uneasy expectancy and a scheme, the Professor and I set out for Barsucci's that afternoon. Our hired guide was waiting; and as Luigi ushered us aboard his gondola, the Professor gave him the address. The sleek boat glided atop the water like a swan as our gondolier steadily sculled along a maze of serene waterways. We eased up to the edge of a walkway and came to a stop by a bridge that crossed the canal. A place-name identified the street that bridged the canal – Strada Nova. Luigi pointed out the first in a row of jumbled buildings on the far side of the bridge as the address we were seeking.

I wait here," he said with a reassuring gesture.

The Professor and I left our guide and walked up a slight incline to a wide street bustling with foot traffic and lined with a disparity of shops. As we crossed the bridge, I checked out our intended destination, noting the building's points of entry. The casements at street level had been bricked up to the transom, leaving small arched windows at the top to admit sunlight, and a porticoed entrance at water level afforded accessibility only by boat. A gold-lettered sign above the door greeted us as we entered.

The Professor approached the man behind the counter, and speaking in Italian, asked if he was Barsucci, to which the man replied negatively. The Professor inquired if he might speak with Mister Barsucci, and the clerk informed him that Barsucci was out of town, but was expected to return later that night or tomorrow. Declining to give his name, the Professor stated that the matter could wait until tomorrow. His imperfect accent, however, most likely exposed his American heritage.

During their conversation, I browsed about the shop, examining the interior. The front room displayed an array of antiquities and knickknacks; and a set of stairs rose to an upper level, its use impeded by a velvet rope strung across at the base. Through a broad archway, scant sunlight dimly lit a room furnished with shelves containing numerous musty volumes, and in the far wall stood a single door.

Turning to leave, the Professor prompted me to follow, and we exited into the street, where he divulged the pertinent points of his conversation with the clerk. I was pleased to hear that our initial venture had born fruit. He had acquired a key piece of information, and as we walked back to the waiting gondola, I expressed my thoughts.

"We must act tonight, before Mallory has a chance to purchase the journal from Barsucci," I resolutely stated.

The Professor seemed to know what design I had in mind, and he presented a more rational option. "What if we purchase it first?"

"An attempt to purchase it might result in a bidding war, in which Barsucci comes out the winner, and Mallory has considerably greater financial resources. Besides, we don't want to tip him off that we're in Venice, not yet anyway."

"So what exactly is it you propose we do?" he asked, broaching the inescapable subject.

"This calls for a more subtle but direct approach. If my hunch is correct, and I'd bet my bottom dollar on it, the journal is somewhere in that shop. I have every intention of returning tonight and heisting it – and you're going to help me."

He stopped dead in his tracks. Momentarily silent, he contemplated, his conscience wrestling with the idea. "That's a rather drastic measure, don't you think? One which could put us in prison," he remonstrated.

"Consider the alternative," I emphatically stated, looking him square in the eyes. "Do you want those dolls or not?"

He sighed. "I'll do what I can," he said, agreeing with a degree of reluctance.

"Besides, somebody's got to identify the goods."

"And what about the Doctor?"

"No need to involve him."

We boarded Luigi's gondola, and he conveyed us back to our hotel. With a cash incentive, he agreed to meet us again at midnight.

That afternoon, the Professor and I navigated our way on foot to the Strada Nova, and followed it to Barsucci's shop. We repeated the trip several times, finding the shortest route and familiarizing ourselves with it should unforeseeable circumstances dictate an alternate way.

JB never showed up for dinner; and by the time ten o'clock rolled around, we had become quite concerned. My inquiries at the front desk yielded no answers; unfortunately, the clerk had recently come on duty. He provided me with Sadie's room number, but numerous knocks on her door roused no response. Inevitably, the hour arrived when we could wait no longer, and had to make the difficult but unavoidable decision to act on our plan.

True to his word, Luigi was diligently waiting; and waterborne, the Professor and I set out in the middle of the night for Barsucci's to perpetrate an illicit but necessary deed. Beset by a damp chill, we gradually moved along at a slow but sure pace, the close-knit, rambling buildings hemming us in like the walls of a canyon. Irregular rooftops traced a broken outline against a starlit midnight sky, and intermittently, lighted casements projected their gilded reflections upon the dark water, its placid surface rippling from the rhythmic lapping of the oar.

The Professor leaned closer to me. "What if it's not there?" he whispered with a sense of doubt.

"It has to be," I confidently returned.

"How can you be so sure?"

"Trust me – it's there."

As we neared our destination, I tried to focus on the task at hand. JB never lingered far from my thoughts, and I could not repress the worrisome apprehension welling up in me.

The Professor directed Luigi to drop us off at the porticoed entrance and then instructed him to return in thirty minutes. He seemed a bit puzzled by the request, but agreed. After watching the gondola disappear from view, I turned to inspect the stout door secured by a heavy padlock; and cloaked in the shadows, I went to work picking the lock while the Professor kept a lookout. The lock yielded to my efforts, and we furtively slipped into the black interior.

Switching on a flashlight, I scanned our surroundings, revealing a storeroom filled with a conglomeration of packing crates, boxes and articles of furniture. Exposed pipes ran along the ceiling, and a staircase angled up to a landing. Next to me, a long rectangular wooden box of otherwise small dimensions rested atop another crate, its hastily placed lid slightly askew. Curious, I removed the lid, uncovering a rolled up canvas.

"It's a painting," the Professor expressed. "Shall we dare to take a peek?"

He began to unroll the canvas, unveiling the artist's signature in the bottom corner, and as he exposed more of the painting, his eyes widened in astonishment.

"The renowned artist who painted this masterpiece, Jean Baptiste Greuse, flourished between 1750 and 1800," he remarked. "If this is a genuine original, which I believe it to be, it should be hanging in a museum, not in a private collection."

"This Barsucci character must deal in some heavy loot, and not all of it above board," I commented. "Put it back – time is pressing, and that's not what we came for. In any case, I don't think we'll find it in here," I said, combing over the contents of the room with the flashlight beam.

The Professor stuck close on my heels as we ascended the stairs to the landing where a single door marked the way. With a bit of tinkering, I successfully worked the old lock, and we passed into a spacious room, which I immediately recognized from our previous visit. Books of every size and sort lined the shelves, and glimmers of moonlight struck the timeworn, tiled floor. On the far side, a broad archway opened to the front room of the shop.

We cautiously proceeded toward the archway, our footfalls against the hard tiles seeming to resound volumes in the silent dark. Upon entering the front room with its display of antique wares, the Professor gasped at seeing the glint of a face peering back out of the darkness. Turning quickly, I passed the flashlight beam over a collection of carnival masks hanging on the wall, their eyeless, pagan countenance staring at us like the faces of malevolent spirits. For a moment the Professor stood rigid, and then coming to grips, he relaxed his posture while letting out a sigh of relief.

Continuing on, we made our way past the rope barrier and up the stairs to the second level. Upstairs, a hallway presented a choice of several doors, and one bearing the label 'A. Barsucci', sealed our decision. The lock was no match for my skill, and gently opening the door, we stepped into a sizable office in which drawn dark curtains blanketed the windows. A broad desk, upon which sat a telephone, stretched out before a plush leather chair. Decanters of liquor and a set of glasses on a silver tray rested atop a credenza, and a file cabinet stood against the wall. An ashtray on the desk contained the remains of a recently smoked cigar, and the stale odor of tobacco clung to the air. A variety of museum quality items adorned the room, including a suit of armor dressed in a Knight Templar's tunic and a Gutenberg Bible in a glass case. Paintings decorated the walls, and a prodigious mirror hung in an elaborate frame.

In the top drawer of the desk, I found several pieces of unopened mail and a folded note with a crest pressed into the unbroken wax seal. Discovering a false bottom, I uncovered a little black book containing names, numbers and addresses, including that of Count Francis Borgia and the name of his yacht, the "Anaconda". The contents of the remaining drawers yielded no clues as to the whereabouts of the journal, and the disorganized files in the cabinet, largely in Italian, were no help either.

"It's got to be here somewhere," I whispered to the Professor. "But where?"

I went about searching the rest of the office, looking for a payoff – and found it. Hinges connected the mirror frame to the wall, and with little effort, the entire mirror and frame swung open to reveal a wall safe behind.

"Bingo," I remarked under my breath. But my initial enthusiasm was short-lived, for a combination lock secured the safe, and I was no safecracker.

In the midst of deliberating the next course of action, I felt the Professor's hand on my shoulder. "Listen," he said. "Do you hear that?"

Outside the window the rumbling of an engine heralded the approach of a motorboat. At first I gave it little concern, but then the engine slowed and sputtered to a stop. We hastened to the window, and parting the curtains, gazed down at the canal. A motorboat carrying two men eased up to the porticoed entrance below. The pilot was a man of small stature, wearing a fur-collared coat, while in contrast his companion was a much larger man. The night shadows and the brims of their hats hid even the faintest glimpse of their facial features. The larger man hopped onto the landing to moor the small craft, and then together they struggled to unload a crate.

Jumbled curses rose up from under the portico, and I knew they had gained an obvious awareness of the missing padlock.

"I think it's time to go," the Professor urged.

"The game's not over yet," I said, hitting upon a scheme, which I immediately put into execution. "Wait here," I instructed.

Allowing no time for a response, I left him with a dumbfounded expression and rushed downstairs to the shop. After snatching a couple of carnival masks, I hurried back to the office to find the Professor in a state of agitated anticipation.

"Put this on," I directed, handing him an elaborate gold painted mask.

He shot me a silent questioning eye.

"No time to explain," I pressed. "They'll be coming up here any time now."

"Am I to understand that you propose we remain here and risk being discovered?"

"Actually, I'm counting on it," I said confidently. "I need you to put on the mask and sit behind the desk."

Again he shot me a questioning eye.

Two sets of approaching footfalls rose up the stairs, one much heavier than the other.

"Just trust me," I earnestly requested with a sense of urgency.

"This goes against my better judgment," he muttered as he donned the mask, and reluctantly complying, he did as I had directed.

After donning my own mask, I quickly but furtively placed myself against the wall beside the door, so that when it opened, it would initially hide my presence; and I waited like a fox in the dark for our pigeons to enter the roost. My heart beat furiously as the footfalls drew ever nearer and stopped just outside the door. A key turned in the lock, and as the knob began to turn, I grabbed a small statue from its pedestal and kept it ready.

The door swung open and I heard two men funnel through the doorway, switching on the lights as they entered. The big lug stepped into view, and my heart sank at seeing the Glisenti automatic pistol in his hand. He failed to notice me, his attention drawn by the Professor. A whirlwind of foreign exclamations erupted from the smaller man, and I sprang into action, slamming the door shut. The larger man wheeled about in alarm, his astonished eyes gaping wide as the statue came down on his forehead with a crash that sent breaking shards sailing in all directions. He went limp and collapsed, dropping the pistol and hitting the floor like a heavy sack of potatoes.

Making a move for the pistol laying on the floor, I noticed the little man had recovered from the initial shock of surprise, and was fumbling to withdraw a small caliber pistol tucked in his belt. I rushed him. Grasping his forearm and wrist before he could level the weapon, I twisted his arm around behind his back and wrenched it until he released the pistol with a groan. The little man squirmed and struggled, kicking his legs up and making every defiant effort to free himself, but I had a good hold on him and he was going nowhere. He began to call out, but before he could utter another syllable, I tightly clasped my hand over his mouth. He tried to bite me, which forced me to wrench his arm further, causing him to let out a muffled cry of pain.

"Stop struggling or I'll break your arm," I asserted, upon which he ceased all resistance. "Do you speak English?" I demanded in a hushed tone.

He shook his head no.

"I think you do," I stated positively. "Now I'm going to ask you just one more time. Do you speak English?"

Again, I wrenched his arm – this time to the breaking point. In whimpering anguish, he nodded affirmatively, and I relaxed the pressure.

"Cry out and you're a dead man," I assured in no uncertain terms and then slowly removed my hand from over his mouth.

I spun him around and shoved him back first against the wall.

"Who are you? What do you want?" he fearfully asked, a tremor in his voice.

His panic-stricken eyes grew wider as I picked up his popgun and cocked it. Keeping it trained on him, I stoically approached to within an uncomfortably close distance, and plucked his hat from his head, tossing it aside.

"Please don't kill me," he pleaded.

"Put your hands on top of your head," I sternly ordered, poking the barrel in his ribs.

Consigned to the realization of the moment, he obeyed, and I began rifling through his pockets.

"Did the Baron send you?" he probed in a blind attempt to learn the reason for our intrusion.

"Maybe," I tauntingly responded.

"It's not my fault. I can explain," he rattled off. "I was unaware at the time that the painting might be a reproduction. My agent in Trieste was dealt a clever forgery. Even I was fooled. I swear it on my mother's grave," he claimed. "But I have since located the original. Tell him I can get it. I just need a few days," he babbled on.

"While that sounds like an intriguing story, that's not why we're here," I said, relieving him of a thick billfold from the inside pocket of his suit jacket.

Stepping back, I took my first good look at the man before me. He was a short man of slight build, wearing a dirty white suit under his fur-lined overcoat, and the collar of his white shirt sported a red bow tie. His receding dark hair was combed over in a failed attempt to hide his balding olive-skinned head, an untrimmed moustache covered his upper lip, and his beady eyes gave him the distinct look of a weasel.

The billfold contained a considerable sum of cash in a variety of currencies and his identification papers bore the name of Antonio Barsucci. Having verified the identity of the little man, I tossed the billfold on the desk and returned my attention to the goon still motionless on the floor. His pistol still lay where it had fallen, and I picked it up and slipped it in the pocket of my trench coat.

After opening the elaborately framed mirror, I grabbed Barsucci by the scruff of his collar and led him to the combination wall safe.

"Open it," I curtly demanded.

At first he hesitated, clearly contemplating some excuse, but the cold pistol barrel against his temple was an inciting motivator. He spun the dial, first left, then right, then left again, and did it so rapidly that I failed to note the exact number each time the dial stopped. With a bit of further prodding on my part, he reluctantly turned the lever, giving it a tug, and the solid door swung ajar.

Directing the Professor to take a look, I planted Barsucci in the chair and kept him covered while the Professor searched through the contents of the safe.

"Keep quiet if you want to stay alive," I warned Barsucci during the wait.

Finally, the Professor turned around, holding a timeworn leather-bound volume in his hands. Afraid he might speak, I put my finger to my lips, indicating silence, for thus far, Barsucci had heard only my voice.

"Is that it?" I asked, and he nodded affirmatively.

Seemingly relieved, Barsucci chuckled mockingly and shook his head in disbelief, as if our purloined prize was worthless. Nonetheless, we paid his ploy no heed, and I proceeded to gag him with his handkerchief and tie him to the chair with curtain cords. Barsucci now securely restrained, I set about hog-tying the unconscious goon.

My watch indicated that our allotted time had ticked away. Confident that Barsucci and his cohort could stir up no further mischief for the time being, we made our way back downstairs to the porticoed entrance by the canal, discarding the masks as we went. When we reached the landing, I was struck by the dumbfounding realization that Luigi was nowhere in sight. I cursed under my breath at having been left to hang in the breeze, and as I considered other means of a getaway, the idea of stealing the motorboat did not seem half bad.

"Where is he?" I asked in frustration, looking at my watch.

"There he is," the professor announced in a low volume, pointing into the night.

The shape of a gondola emerged from under the bridge, becoming visible in the moonlight, and as it came closer, I recognized Luigi at the oar. He steered the ebony boat alongside the entrance, and we hopped in. The gondola carried us away upon the waters, fading into the shadows and making good our escape.

"I'd say we got the proverbial drop on those two," I said in sport, trying to lighten things.

"I may not agree with your methods, but I have to admit they were effective," the professor acknowledged.

Entering a darkened hotel lobby, we discovered the electric power to be out. An apologetic desk clerk furnished us with candles to illuminate our way.

"When do you expect the power to be restored?" I asked.

"That's the trouble. They can't seem to find the problem. But I'm sure we'll have it fixed soon enough," he replied.

Thus by the soft, fluttering radiance of candlelight we navigated the stairs and upper hall to our suite. All was quiet—too quiet; and as I turned the knob on an unlocked door, an overwhelming sense of trepidation gripped me.

Ice cold was the air in the drawing room. Wisps of vapor floated on my breath in a frigid foreboding atmosphere. An unnatural darkness cloaked everything, pressing in around us and dimming the warm glow of the candle flame. Amidst the darkening tide, an unmistakable diabolic presence assailed my senses, sending a dreadful chill down my spine – a chill that made my very soul shudder.

The Professor's face burst into an expression of alarm. "What in heaven's name?" he blurted out, looking in the direction of the balcony doors, his eyes wide as saucers.

Straining to see in the flittering amber hue of the repressed candlelight, I stared in bitter astonishment as long fingerlike shadows seeped through the seams of the balcony doors, growing and reaching. Their contorted skeletal features ebbed and flowed as they coursed over the walls, ceiling and floor. Stunned by the unsettling, incredulous sight which held me fixed, I closed my eyes for a brief moment, but upon reopening them, the phantom illusion remained. Like oil through a funnel, the menacing shadows converged on the door to JB's room, penetrating the keyhole, slipping through the porous cracks, and oozing between the sliver of space under the door.

Suddenly stricken with the awareness of imminent danger, I shook off the malaise and raced headlong for the door. Not knowing what awaited me, I flung it wide and charged into the room. JB lay crossways on the bed, fully clothed and fast asleep, his body writhing in the throes of a nightmare. The window was open, allowing in the cold night, and the parted curtains billowed in a winter breeze.

Like gushing streams of murky water, the elongated black fingers surged swiftly toward JB. They constricted him in a death grip, binding and choking him. He gagged and struggled for breath. I tried to help him, jostling him and clawing at the threat, but despite my desperate efforts, I could not fight an unearthly force without substance. The door slammed shut, and a sudden gust of wind blew out the candle, plunging me into blinding darkness. The doorknob rattled, and the Professor called out from the other side, unable to gain entry.

CHAPTER 21

In the midst of those fateful moments as my eyes adjusted, I discerned a man's head in the window silhouetted against the moonlight. Instantly, elements of JB's story at the flophouse rushed to the forefront of my mind. Acting on instinct, I hastened to the window, and there I came face to face with the three-eyed African man. His eyes were riveted in intense concentration and his lips faintly chanted a strange incantation. Defying gravity, he rode upon the air with no visible means of support, his bowed legs giving the impression of him straddling some spectral beast out of Hell – the whole incredible appearance magnified by the sight of a hideous bat-winged shadow dancing on the surface of the canal below.

Scrambling for viable options, I drew the flashlight from my coat pocket and shined the beam in his eyes, but out of nowhere an unseen force snatched it from my grasp. His transfixing gaze unbroken, he disregarded me and continued his chant with unwavering determination. JB's dying gasps pressed me to reckless action, and lunging forward, I reached out to seize the fiend, but he was just out of arm's length. In my mad efforts to get my hands on him, I leaned further and further out the window, until with one good stretch, I clutched his collar and pulled him closer; but by now I was precariously kneeling on the windowsill. I clasped my fingers around his neck and began to tighten my grip, turning his obscure words to garbled utterances.

"Let him go, you contemptible bastard! Let him go!" I cried.

That got his attention. He shifted his focus to me, and those hypnotic eyes looked directly into mine with malignant intent. I tried to avert my gaze, but some potent mystic power held me spellbound; and mesmerized, I stared back into the pits of Hell. Locked in a battle of wills, I mustered every ounce of fortitude to combat the onslaught, but his telepathic ability was too strong, and I felt my mental faculties being drained away like beer from a thirsty man's glass. My thoughts no longer held dominion over my physical operations, which failed to obey my commands. It was as if some intruder had invaded my brain, and was pulling the strings to my motor senses. I found my fingers loosening their grip, and subsequently my hands released their grasp altogether. It was then I realized I had extended myself too far; and teetering without a handhold to support me, I fell forward, plummeting downward and plunging head first into the cold drink.

Water and blackness surrounded me, clinging garments weighted me down, and I was lost as to which way was up. As I sank deeper, my ill-spent life flashed before me like a movie reel in fast motion. But I was not ready to make a permanent call on St. Peter; and laboring to save myself, I shed my trench coat and shoes as if discarding a ball and chain. Faint and desperate for breath, I thought my lungs would burst when a glint of ruffling light revealed the surface, and I swam in a frantic dash toward hope.

Passing beyond the limits of my endurance, I strained to hold my breath, when just at the moment I could hold it no longer my head popped through the surface. Deprived of oxygen, I sucked in volumes of fresh December air while fighting to keep my head above water. Sheer walls rose on either side of the canal, offering no easy deliverance, and the nearest landing was at least a hundred feet away around the corner.

Flustered, but no worse for wear, I looked upwards, expecting to see the African man, but he had mysteriously vanished into the night. Electric light now illuminated JB's window, indicating the power had been somehow restored. Amidst the sound of lapping water, I faintly heard the Professor's voice. Soon he appeared in the open window, leaning out and calling my name with a note of grave concern, his echoing cries seeking a response.

"I'm all right," I yelled back.

"I'll get help," he loudly assured.

"No, stay there!"

Numb with cold, I strained to move my extremities; and it was sheer determination that carried me to the Rue De Pozzi, where I hauled my drenched body out of the freezing, murky waters.

Dripping wet, I crossed the hotel lobby under the curious eyes of the desk clerk and hurried up the stairs to our suite. I entered an empty drawing room, dimly lit by the light projecting through the open door to JB's room.

"Professor?" I called out.

"In here," came the reply from beyond the open door.

The grim tone in those two words sent me rushing to the source. The Professor at his side, JB lay as if lifeless on the bed, his open eyes staring into oblivion.

"He's alive, Mr. Blake. For that, heaven be praised," the Professor informed with disconcerted reserve. "But he's incoherent and inconsolable, and I am unable to revive him from his insensible state."

JB's blank expression was painted with a ghostly pallor and his shallow breathing erratic. Bending over him, I spoke his name, trying to rouse some response, but only muttering mumbles rolled off his barely moving lips. I passed my hand in front of his face several times without evoking any reaction; his eyes still remained fixed.

"Almighty God help us. Father in heaven we beseech you," the Professor solemnly petitioned aloud.

Cool droplets falling from my soaked garments softly spattered upon JB's face, sending glistening wet trails trickling down his pale cheeks and across his forehead. His eyelids fluttered and color returned to his cheeks.

He looked up at me with glassy eyes seeming to recognize me, then spoke in a weak voice. "Conrad, is that you? I can't see you clearly."

"Yes, JB, it's me. I'm right here," I assured.

He feebly took hold of my lapel as if to verify the reality of my presence. "Don't let them get me, Conrad. Don't let them get me," he implored with a note of extreme despair.

The words no more left his lips than his eyelids closed. He released his grip and lapsed into unconsciousness; however, his steady breathing and peaceful appearance gave every indication that he was now deep in a restful sleep.

"I strongly suggest that you change into some dry clothes before you catch your death, Mr. Blake," the Professor advised. "No need to worry, I'll look after the doctor."

Powerless to do anything for the moment, I deferred to the common sense in his words. The still open window allowed in the night chill, and I shut it tight. As I drew the curtains, a perplexing question rolled over and over in my mind, and upon exiting the room, I stopped cold and turned in the doorway.

"What is it?" the Professor asked, seeing the expression of flummoxed frustration on my face.

"How did they know, Professor? How did they even know we were in Venice, let alone knowing exactly where to locate us?"

"I have to admit it's rather uncanny and most disturbing. I would suppose they possess some supernatural omniscient power or have access to such knowledge by means of divination."

"Perhaps, but I've a notion there's nothing supernatural about it," I speculated, and leaving him to ponder the issue, I went to change.

After freshening up and donning a new set of clothes, I again entered the drawing room, switching on the lights. There on the coffee table stood two wine glasses and a half empty bottle of red wine with the cork partially inserted. What ostensibly appeared to be the signature of a romantic interlude tweaked my inquisitive senses, and I examined the glasses with a scrutinizing eye. One had traces of lipstick on the rim, and the other had an almost indiscernible powdery residue undissolved amidst the remnant of wine at the bottom. A torrent of suspicion cascaded into the well of my thoughts, funneling to one conclusion.

Heeding precaution, I checked the remaining rooms to find nothing amiss, and the arcane tome still occupied its hiding place. Although I doubted what good it would do, I made sure the windows and entranceways were locked shut, and then I rejoined the Professor in JB's room.

"How is he?" I asked.

"Sleeping calmly, and I'm most relieved to see you're doing all right. A myriad of distressing thoughts plagued me when I opened the door to discover you absent and the doctor prostrate on the bed," he said with genuine regard. "What happened in here? I'm most curious to know."

I related all the grim particulars of my harrowing encounter with the African man. He listened intently, his intellect digesting every extraordinary morsel. When I had finished, he sank into the armchair, and for a few moments he seemed lost in pensive rumination.

He looked at me, his lustrous eyes filled with solemn resolve. "We face diabolic forces wielded by the infernal workings of nefarious minds empowered with black magic. Ours is a precipitous state of affairs. We must be careful, Mr. Blake. From here on, we must be very, very careful," he counseled.

"I think the danger has passed, at least for now," I said assuredly. "Why don't you get some sleep, and I'll sit up with JB."

"Frankly, I'm frightened at the prospect of sleep," he confided. "But I can't stave it off forever. Inevitably, exhaustion will overtake me, and I will again sink into a sea of unspeakable horrors. Last night I had an awful dream of incredibly vivid magnitude, in which I was lashed to a post by a multitude of constricting serpents, the creeping mass writhing and slithering over every inch of my body. Around me stood a hooded company bearing torches, and at the virulent command of a hissing voice, the serpents turned to fire. Scorching flames licked at my flesh, enveloping me in a searing inferno. In a feverish pitch, I awoke in excruciating pain, and although in a state of conscious awareness, I could still smell the acrid stench of burning tissue. I'm afraid that a time will come when I won't wake."

He rose from the chair with a sigh and reluctantly edged his way out of the room. Shortly thereafter, he returned with a blanket and settled back into the chair. "If it's all the same to you, I'll bed down here for a while," he said.

I planted myself in a chair at JB's bedside to keep vigilant watch. Soon, the Professor nodded off into a reposeful slumber, and the guttural rhythm of his snoring amply served to keep me alert. As the lingering minutes passed, I mulled over the whirlwind of surprising and shocking events that marked our first day in Venice. The suspicious substance in JB's wine glass darkened the shadow of my distrust of Sadie. There was something to be said about a young woman traveling alone, and none of it good. Somehow, someway, for whatever reason, that wily dame had a part to play in the whole horrific affair – of that I was now convinced.

Dawn's ever brightening sunlight brought with it a comforting sense of relief, and I eagerly embraced the morning with a welcoming spirit. Golden drops of sun sprinkled the walls and fell upon the Professor's face, awakening him. For a few hours of respite he had slept without incident and appeared somewhat refreshed for it. Seeing the haggard signs of weariness that marred my face, he kindly offered to relieve me; and with his promise to apprise me of any significant developments, I retired to my bed for a period of much needed sleep.

When I returned to the waking world that afternoon, I found the Professor hard at work translating the journal and JB conspicuously absent. Absorbed in his task, the Professor failed to notice my approach, and he practically jumped out of his skin at the sudden awareness of me looking over his shoulder.

"Goodness, you gave me such a start!" he exclaimed with a sigh.

"Where's JB?" I asked.

"Out for a walk. Sadie's with him, so he's in good company," he casually conveyed. "You were fast asleep, and we chose not to disturb you."

My guts sank into a pit of gnawing apprehension. "Is he aware of what happened last night?"

"Yes – I informed him. It pained me to do so, especially since it exacerbated his already increasing neurotic state. To be honest, I dare say the doctor may not last much longer."

"And the journal, does he know about that too?"

"Oh yes, I was working on it when he got up. It was welcome news to him, and I have good news for you as well. My efforts thus far have borne fruit. Upon these brittle pages are the memoirs of a most interesting man. Although the paper is discolored with age, the ink has passed the test of time, and the handwriting is still legible. It appears Captain Matteo Veneti was quite the mariner and adventurer, and the account of his last voyage holds many revealing facts regarding that which Sir Gunston seeks." His eyes shined with the excitement of discovery and revelation. "It is a diamond, Mr. Blake – a diamond of sizeable proportions," he imparted, his voice electrified with animation.

"Bigger than the Hope diamond?"

"Much bigger. Even larger than the legendary ruby of the Great Mogul."

"That's some diamond. Where do we find it? How do we get our hands on it?" I eagerly asked in rapid succession.

"I have yet to uncover that knowledge, but there is still more text to pore over."

"Well keep at it," I said encouragingly. "I've got to go out for a while."

The wine bottle and glasses were gone, and I queried the Professor about them on my way out.

"The maid took them away when she came in this morning," he replied.

I assured him that I would not be too long and locked the door behind me upon leaving.

After getting directions from the desk clerk, I set out for the cable office. The route took me past Barscucci's establishment, which was open for business. On the way, I stopped at a shop on the Strada Nova and purchased a new leather trench coat. Although it was slick and a good fit, it would take time to break in. Continuing on, I traveled a thoroughfare bustling with a flurry of people, yet I felt distant and alone, and I longed for home. I had so much to say, but the telegram I sent to Boston was all too short.

Cindy
Have arrived in Venice STOP Things are heating up STOP
- Conrad

On the way back to the hotel my thoughts centered on the Professor's preliminary findings. The idea of an immense diamond of great wealth intrigued me. When I returned to the hotel, the setting sun had dipped below the rooftops, and a tide of darkening shades of violet ebbed across the sky, bringing with it the twilight.

Inside our suite nothing was amiss. The Professor was still engrossed in the journal, furiously scribbling notes. I found JB seated on his bed. He was just buttoning his cuff when I walked into his room, and a syringe lie atop the nightstand. His once contagious smile and charming demeanor had all but vanished, replaced by the ugly scars of relentless stress.

"How long can you keep that up?" I asked concernedly.

"As long as it takes. I've got to stay awake," he stressed, replacing the syringe into his medical bag beside him. "I can't withstand another night – not like last night. So vivid – so real it was. They almost succeeded in my destruction. Then in the midst of my darkest despair, I saw the image of your face, and the horror ceased. At first I thought it a dream, but the Professor told me what really happened. It seems I again owe you a debt of thanks."

"We're all in this together, and no one's going to get you as long as I'm around to do something about it," I reassured him. "We missed you at dinner yesterday evening. We were worried about you. We waited around, but you never showed."

"Sadie and I had dinner at a quaint little café. I'm sorry to have caused you concern, but I was caught up in the moment. I wasn't thinking. In fact, my mind is so flustered lately that I can't think straight anymore, and finding Sadie again has made things so complicated. I can't hide it from her – but I can't tell her the truth either," he confided, slouching forward with downcast eyes.

"Was it her you shared the bottle of wine with last night?" I subtly probed, treading on thin ice.

"Yes. It was against my better judgment, but I feel so comfortable when I'm with her. After only one glass I was feeling the effects, and in my exhausted condition, it must have been the catalyst that precipitated my physical breakdown. From now on it's coffee – lots of coffee. I barely remember her helping me to bed – and then the tortuous terror started all over again."

"I don't know about you, but I'm starving. What do you say we catch an early dinner?"

"I don't have much of an appetite right now. You go on ahead. I'll get something later."

"Suit yourself."

Obsessed with the completion of his task, the Professor preferred to have his meal sent up to the room, and thus I departed to dine alone in the restaurant downstairs. As I began to descend the staircase to the lobby, I spotted Sadie at the front desk. Her attention drawn by the desk clerk, she failed to notice me, and I backtracked out of view. Peering from my concealed position, I observed and listened.

"You have a message, Miss Morrell," the clerk said, retrieving an envelope from a cubbyhole behind him.

She cordially thanked him and opened the envelope. After reading the contents, she stuffed it in her coat pocket, then turned and walked out the front door.

That night I found sleep unattainable. A bundle of nerves, JB paced the floor incessantly, and the Professor burned the midnight oil. For a long time, the Professor immersed himself in quiet study. Then painstakingly working on some problem, he grew frustrated, mumbling comments to himself. More than once he removed his spectacles and rubbed his tired eyes.

Suddenly without warning he sprang from his seat, journal in hand. "That's it!" he excitedly exclaimed. "How could I be so slow-witted? The answer's so simple!" he said with unrestrained elation, holding the open journal up to a mirror.

Intently gazing at the page's reflection, he silently read to himself as JB and I waited in anxious anticipation.

"What is it?" JB eagerly asked, no longer able to contain himself.

"A riddle – a riddle in prose," the Professor replied, his eyes flashing with renewed enthusiasm. "And written in Old English, not Italian."

A fountain of questions hung on my lips as he casually placed the open journal on the writing desk. Without divulging the slightest hint, he sat at the desk and began to transcribe what he had just read.

"Grant me but a few moments gentlemen, and I will soon assuage your curiosity," he said, scribbling furiously with his new silver fountain pen.

When he had finished, he stood up and leaned back against the desk, with one hand clutching the lapel of his jacket. "Before revealing the contents of the riddle, I must acquaint you with some crucial background knowledge that we might better solve its clues together. I ask you to bear with me, for I feel it important," he said, and he commenced to tell us an intriguing tale.

"In the year of our Lord 1603, when Venice was still an influential power, Matteo Veneti sailed his last voyage. After several earnest petitions, he persuaded the Doge, Leonardo Dona, to grant him a commission to seek out the legendary city of Medra, which, according to earlier Portuguese explorers, lies somewhere in the bowels of the African continent. To fulfill this arduous undertaking, he was given the captaincy of a grand vessel, the 'Corsican'. He had once seen the city's location on a map drawn in 1570 by the Flemish cartographer Abraham Ortelius. The map, entitled 'Africae Tabula Nova', placed Medra along the west bank of the mighty river Niger, close to where the waters emptied into a great basin in the interior.

"Thus he set course for the Gulf of Guinea with a handpicked crew and the most current charts he could lay his hands on. Being an opportunist, he acted more like a privateer than an explorer on the first leg of his voyage; and considering himself sanctioned for his actions, he took the liberty on more than one occasion to seize a hapless merchant vessel displaying the flag of a rival state or enemy nation. The ship's hold laden with goods and the crew in high spirits, he contemplated returning to Venice, when the ship became embroiled in a fierce storm off Cape Verde, and good fortune turned to bad as he ordered the reluctant crew to jettison most of the cargo overboard in a desperate effort to remain afloat and weather the storm.

"Narrowly having avoided calamitous ruin, he anchored in a cove to make badly needed repairs. The ship seaworthy again, he sailed onward to the Gold Coast, always keeping the safety of land in sight. Provisions ran dangerously low, and twice he sent foraging parties ashore, but both failed to return. Given the present mood of the crew, he dared not risk sending another party, and he set an immediate course for a Portuguese colony on Princess Island. As the ship sailed into the Bight of Benin, the men watched the last remnants of shoreline disappear with the waning twilight. Calm winds made for slow headway, and the crew was subsisting on half rations by the time the island was sighted in the distance.

"They remained at the colony for several days while replenishing supplies. During this time, a trader relayed to Veneti a tale pertinent to his quest – a tale that titillated his ears and whet his appetite for adventure. The trader told of friendly natives on the mainland who spoke of a fabled city built by an ancient race that lies in the interior beyond a mountain range from which the sun rises. The city rests on a high plateau towering above a river the natives call the Sanga, and its ruins contain the riches of the ages. But the pass to reach the city was jealously guarded by a man-eating tribe of devils that ruled the valley below. They possessed a magnificent gem endowed with magical powers, and any who dared encroach were said to either have their flesh devoured or be cast into a 'pit of screaming souls.'

"Believing the object of this tale to be the lost city of Medra, Veneti set sail for the African mainland with renewed resolve. Landmarks described by the trader guided his way along the coast to the mouth of a wide river, which he followed inland. Further up river, navigation proved difficult, as treacherous currents and lurking shoals hampered progress. Eventually, they reached an impasse where they had to weigh anchor.

"Veneti formed a party consisting primarily of his most hearty crewmen, and the next morning he led them into the impenetrable jungle. Day after day, they trudged onward into remote uncharted reaches, battling the unforgiving elements and hostile natives. The grueling journey exacted its toll, and by the time they reached the base of a majestic mountain range several of the men had perished, while others were delirious with fever. Confronted with seemingly insurmountable mountains, his men pleaded and argued with him to turn back, but Veneti remained steadfast in his resolve, and with bold assertions on his part, the men begrudgingly pressed on. Those who persevered the perilous climb to the opposite slope gazed down in wonder on a lush tropical valley; and through his telescope, Veneti descried a distant river and three mountains nestled together on the far side of the valley, their distinctive features fitting the trader's description.

"Fueled by a lust for treasure, they disregarded the Trader's warning, and casting vigilance aside, they descended headlong into the valley. That night, the men bedded down to dreams of wealth and grandeur. But the next morning, as the sun rose higher in the sky, their nerves were battered by the rhythmic beat of drums resounding throughout the jungle – first from one direction, then another. When the drums ceased, an eerie silence ensued.

"Not long thereafter, a rustling in the brush perceived by all ignited their senses to an acute state of alertness, and each glimpse of some elusive foe was immediately communicated to the others. One startled fellow fired his wheel lock pistol at a hidden menace, the loud report stirring a flock of birds to scatter in flight. It soon became apparent that an ever increasing number of natives were stalking them. Swift and agile, fearsome warriors stealthily moved amongst the trees and brush, keeping their distance and never presenting themselves to be a viable target for either firearm or crossbow. Vastly outnumbered and now boxed in on three sides, Veneti's beleaguered men continually sought the only avenue of escape; and after a time, they came to the demoralizing realization that they were being systematically channeled in one direction – deeper into the heart of the valley.

"Encumbered by accouterments and baggage, the men failed in their exerted effort to outrun the gauntlet. Exhaustion met with despair as the jungle receded and they came to the edge of a wide clearing. A herd of goats grazed on the verdant sloping landscape, and at the edge of a broad river stood a sprawling metropolis of thatch-roofed huts enclosed by a wooden palisade.

"Veneti and his men decided to take their chances in the open, where they could at least see their staunch enemy, and they proceeded out into the expanse. To the rear and on their flanks, scores of painted black-skinned warriors wielding spears and decorated shields emerged from the jungle, and as the horde closed in, a harmony of loud horns sounded from within the village. The men prepared for a desperate last-ditch stand, when the gates opened wide, and a lone figure adorned in leopard hide gestured for them to enter. With no other option available, they had little choice but to enter into the jaws of fate. Gathering inhabitants created a lane along which they were paraded to a courtyard at the center of the village, a multitude of gawking eyes dogging their every step, and from behind them, the warriors funneled through the gate in a military style procession.

"Veneti's party was presented to the chief and subjected to the perturbing trial of a witchdoctor, who regarded them with awe and reverence. Their fair skin, their strange garments bristling with breastplates and helmets, and their weapons, all invoked fear, curiosity and wonderment. In a gesture of good will, Veneti had a small chest brought forth containing appeasing gifts, including a hand mirror, which fascinated the chief. Veneti's men were then bestowed with greatness and treated as honored guests. That night they attended a tribal ceremony in their exalted honor and witnessed a bizarre pagan ritual, involving the gruesome acts of human sacrifice and cannibalism.

"After Veneti managed to communicate their intention to find the lost city of Medra, the man in leopard skin, along with a small entourage of warriors, took them across the river and led them up the steep slope of one of three mountains. According to the literal translation of the journal, they entered the mouth of a lion and passed through two perils before reaching a plateau upon which stood an ancient city forgotten by time – an acropolis of empty avenues, plazas and colossal structures of strange geometric shapes constructed of immense stone blocks. They ascended to a platform atop a step pyramid at the city's center. Near the edge of a pit filled with billowing celadon mist, they were shown a monolith inscribed with inscrutable symbols. Whereupon, the man in the leopard skin produced an enormous diamond from a rawhide pouch tied at his waist and held it aloft. The gem's dazzling brilliance cast a spectrum of prismatic colors in the sunlight.

"The sailors' eyes filled with lustful greed, and as the priest-like man turned away toward the monolith, Veneti struck him down from behind. Without hesitation, his men quickly followed suit, falling upon the outmatched and unprepared entourage of warriors with murderous ferocity, mercilessly slaying them to a man. Their heinous deed done, they set about in a frantic search to plunder the city of riches.

"Finally laden with all they could carry, they again passed through the perils to the mountainside. Upon reaching the river, they commandeered the dugout canoes and paddled with the current, leaving the village behind them. After traveling a considerable distance, they abandoned the canoes and fled into the jungle with the diamond and a cumbersome quantity of treasure.

"The return journey was marked with hardship and disaster. Brutal attrition and treacherous hearts culled the ranks until only two remained – Veneti and one other loyal shipmate. They were but mere shadows of men when they stumbled upon the heartening sight of the 'Corsican'. Veneti still had the precious diamond tucked in his shirt; otherwise, they boarded with but a smidgen of pilfered treasure and a wild story to tell. With more than half the ship's company now dead or missing, they set sail for home.

"Although Veneti tried to keep it secret, news of the diamond quickly spread amongst the crew. Its powerful lure weaved a virulent spell. The crew became increasingly quarrelsome and seditious. Whispers of mutiny brewed to the boiling point; and with the support of his trusty first mate and those still loyal, Veneti quelled the insurrection in a violent melee, killing the ringleaders and clapping the rest in irons. But the lure of the diamond had seduced them all; and one night off the coast of Sicily, the remaining ship's company turned on one another. A deadly brawl erupted, and when it was over, Veneti stood alone over the bodies of his former shipmates.

"Unable to pilot the ship alone, he scuttled the Corsican with the mutineers still shackled in the hold; and taking his charts and log, he rowed to shore in the ship's launch. He clandestinely journeyed back to Venice, where he gave an account of his voyage before the Doge. He pronounced his momentous discovery and professed the undaunted courage of his crew in the face of many hardships. When inquired about the ship and crew, he claimed that the ship was lost in a violent storm with all hands during the return voyage. The vessel being in serious distress, they abandoned her, taking their chances in the sea. Clinging to a piece of wreckage, he was rescued by divine providence when a Sicilian fisherman plucked him from the water.

"Despite misfortune, the Doge heralded the expedition a success, and at his request, Veneti assisted a cartographer in drawing a map to the city. Although absolved, the humiliating loss of his ship and crew left Veneti a broken man.

"He never set to sea again, nor did he divulge the existence of the precious stone he coveted so much. He spent hours gazing into its mesmerizing brilliance; eventually wasting away to become a recluse cared for by his niece, a nun. Though destitute, he refused to part with the stone, for he saw a spellbinding eye within its sparkling facets – an eye that unveiled captivating images to him. At first wonderful things manifested themselves, then bedeviling visions of monstrous things and surreal alien landscapes filled the diamond. In time, the eye haunted his restless dreams, and voices called to him in the night. Gripped by the gem's hypnotic power, he gradually went mad. His niece realized the signs of his growing madness and had him discreetly cloistered away in a monastery, where he lived out his last pitiful days sustained by the charity of the monks."

"So what happened to the diamond?" JB earnestly asked when the Professor had finished.

"That's where the riddle comes in," the Professor said, picking up a sheet of notepaper from the desk and donning his spectacles.

"Well, let's hear it," I impatiently urged.

He cleared his throat and recited the words he had scribed.

Alone this bane to bear forever
Unto the grave I doth take my precious treasure
Condemned to purgatory unto redemption day
To guard the jewel, my penance to pay
Shouldst thou dare seeketh the stone
And covet to possess for thine own
My charts betray the key to find my tomb
Deep within the recesses of the gloom
In hallowed ground I rest
My burial place marked by the unicorn crest
In noble rampant pose
Above the tower and rose
Woe to thee who disturbs my rest eternal
For thy cursed fate shall be infernal
Paying the price for thy greed
Thou shalt sow the devil's seed.

"Sounds like it's buried with him," I said. "I've never stooped to grave robbing, but there's a first time for everything, I suppose. Even if we have the stomach for it, his grave could be anywhere. Without the charts, there's no telling. We might as well be looking for a needle in a haystack."

"As providence would have it, a set of old maps are folded inside the cover," the Professor informed. "I perused them earlier, but did not think them pertinent until now."

"Now we're talking. Let's have a look," I said.

The Professor gingerly unfolded the antique maps, spreading them out atop the coffee table. Stained brown with age, the fragile edges were cracked and split at the creases. Otherwise, the nautical maps were well preserved, rich with elegant calligraphy and artistic illustrations.

"Look, the tower and rose," JB noted, pointing to a coat of arms that dominated the upper left corner of each map. Crowned by a rampant unicorn, a heraldic shield displayed a gold rose on a white field above a black tower on a field of blue.

"Veneti's family crest I would conjecture, based on the Latin text beneath," the professor added.

Somewhere on those charts lay an elucidating key concealed in secrecy, and we set about meticulously searching in earnest. Delving in seemingly endless speculations, our tired minds grew perturbed. While my companions wallowed in the details, I took a short break to clear the clutter from my thoughts, and I returned to tackle the problem with a fresh perspective. Using a broader approach, I soon discovered the answer to be quite evident.

I declared my discovery and explained my reasoning. "The riddle doesn't specify any particular chart. It refers to 'charts' in the plural. There are only two recurring features shared by all the charts: Veneti's coat of arms and the name of the mapmaker. To be a cartographer, one would have to be educated, and at that time the benefit of a formal education was primarily limited to the wealthy and members of the clergy. I'd wager this Vincente Tuscanelli was a clergyman. Does the journal mention anything about him?"

"Come to think of it, I believe so. By George, you may be on to something," the Professor responded, and he went to consult the journal. "Ah, here it is – Vincente Tuscanelli, a friar of the lagoon monastery of Saint Christopher," he read aloud.

"And what was the name of the monastery where Veneti spent his last days?" I further inquired.

"He never disclosed it," he answered.

"That clinches it. Five'll get you ten the monastery of Saint Christopher is the place where he's buried. Let's see, it's hallowed ground, it's nearby in the lagoon, Saint Christopher is the patron saint of travelers, and Veneti spent his last days in a monastery. It all fits. The only remaining question is whether or not it's still there, and that shouldn't be hard to find out."

He stroked his beard, carefully considering my words. "An astute observation, Mr. Blake. I must agree that your correlations make for a sound hypothesis," he concurred.

"Then let's put it to the test," I advocated.

"If we're allowed access, a review of the monastery archives should provide the proof in the pudding," he said, committing himself.

JB jumped on board, and together we determined to seek out the monastery that very day. The clock hands indicated that time had waned into the wee hours, and with dawn short in coming, I retired to rest my bleary eyes for a bit.

It seemed but an instant had passed when a knocking at my door roused me from restful respite. JB stuck his head in to say that he and the Professor were going downstairs for breakfast, and asked that I join them when I was ready. The door gently closed, and I reluctantly crawled out of a warm bed to be greeted by sunlight filtering through the curtains.

I was standing at the bathroom sink in the process of shaving, when I discerned a soft rapping at the door to our suite. I answered the door with a face full of lather to find Sadie at the threshold. Inviting herself inside, she cordially bid me good morning and asked to see JB, all the while projecting her wily charms.

"He's not here," I said, wiping my face with a towel. "He and the Professor went downstairs for breakfast."

She casually walked about the drawing room as if in her own home, her eyes scanning to and fro seeming to verify my words.

"Thank you, Mr. Blake. Please go back to your shaving. I'll let myself out," she sweetly said, heading for the door.

I returned to the bath, and the expectant sound of a closing door assured me that I was alone again. Shortly thereafter, I heard the door to our suite open and close once more. It was too soon to be JB and the Professor returning. In alarm, I stormed into an empty drawing room. The journal was missing from the desktop along with the charts, and the fragrance of Sadie's perfume lingered in the air.

CHAPTER 22

Finally it came to me – the answer to a question that had nagged me ever since meeting Sadie. I had caught a whiff of that enticing scent somewhere before, and now I knew where. That night at my flat when someone put my lights out, the mysterious dame in the dark veil and elegant furs wore the same perfume.

I threw on a shirt and flew out the door in a mad dash, grabbing my coat on the way out. Atop the stairs to the lobby, I stopped dead in my tracks. Sadie was at the front desk using the telephone, and after a brief conversation, she slunk out the front door.

Seizing opportunity, I shadowed her from a covert distance, always keeping her in sight. She maintained a quick and determined pace as she briskly walked this way and that along a maze of narrow winding streets and across bridges. More than once she looked back over her shoulder, but in each instance I ducked out of sight or blended in with the crowd.

After leading me on a lively chase, she entered a coffeehouse at the Piazza San Marco. Weathered gold paint dressed the exterior of the café, and black-lettered signs in relief above the windows denoted the name 'Florian'. A peek through the window revealed a charming establishment decorated with murals and huge mirrors, which made the atmosphere inside seem dreamlike and wonderfully seductive. She exchanged a few brief words with a waiter, who ushered her into one of several small rooms.

Slipping inside, I grabbed an abandoned newspaper from atop an empty table and sat where I could eye her reflection in a mirror. From behind the pages of the open newspaper that veiled my face, I spied the glass to see a host of suspicions confirmed as I watched an intriguing rendezvous unfold in the next room.

She was seated at a table with two men. One was partially blocked from view, his identity a mystery. The other was dressed in stylish threads, slick raven-black hair draped his shoulders, a moustache and tapered goatee garnished his upper lip and chin, and sinister dark eyes befit sharp facial features. The unsettling recollection of those piercing eyes was unmistakable. He struck a stunning likeness to the man portrayed in the portrait hanging in Mallory's library. The resemblance was uncanny. Inaudible words were spoken between them, and she produced the journal, laying it on the table. The sinister man's eyes flashed, and he smiled wickedly with an expression of grim satisfaction. The other man leaned forward, reaching out to take possession, and as he did so, his face came into view. My blood ran cold at the dreaded sight, for it was none other than Mallory. He passed an envelope to her, which she eagerly tucked inside her coat; and then the party broke up.

In leaving, they approached my table. My pulse quickened as I raised the newspaper in an effort to fully conceal my face and hopefully escape their notice. Fortunately lady luck bestowed her grace, for they walked past as if I were paint on the wall. Once outside, they lingered for a few moments of brief conversation, then the two parties separated, each heading in a different direction.

Taking advantage of an opportune chance, I pursued Mallory and his sinister, dark-haired cohort, following them from a distance. Eventually, they led me to the waterfront, where they boarded a waiting launch, which carried them to a three-masted schooner anchored in the expanse of the lagoon. At that point, I surmised that the identity of the sinister, dark-haired man must be Count Francis Borgia. Reconciling to the fact that the journal was now in the hands of our nefarious antagonists was bitter medicine to swallow. But I was confident we had discovered the correct solution, making the journal of little value to us anyway. Sadie had played her hand, and I had the goods on that tawdry trollop at last.

It was almost midday when I returned to our hotel. Entering our suite, I found the Professor in an excited state of agitation.

"Oh thank God, you've returned Mr. Blake. The journal is missing. Do you have it?" he gravely asked with hopeful eyes.

"No, but I know who does," I answered.

"Who then?"

"Mallory," I replied with disdain. "Where's JB?"

"He went downstairs for a cup of coffee."

"Good, because I don't want him to hear what I'm about to tell you."

As I recounted the twisted events that had recently played out and clued him in on the substance I found in JB's wineglass the other night, his mouth opened and a stunned expression gradually suffused his face.

"I'm shocked and dismayed to learn that Sadie of all people is involved," he said in disbelief. "The Doctor should know of this."

"Not yet. That would crush him, and in his present unstable condition it might be too much for him. There's no telling how he'd react. Sadie hasn't a clue that we're on to her, and that's to our advantage," I remonstrated. "No, we must keep this to ourselves for now."

"I see what you mean," he relented. "But won't that place the Doctor in possible peril?"

"Trust me, I won't let that happen," I assured.

"How long do we keep up the charade?"

"At least until we have the diamond. And since Mallory has the journal, there's no time to waste."

"Yes, if he should decipher the key and find the diamond first, all hope of getting the dolls may be lost. We must not allow that to happen."

"There's one other thing, Professor – something that struck me as incredibly uncanny and unreal. The dark-haired man that accompanied Mallory bore a striking resemblance to the portrait of Sir Mortimer hanging in Mallory's library. The match was so identical as to defy coincidence. I know this sounds crazy, but do you suppose it's possible that they might be one and the same?"

"I do indeed," he responded with all rational conviction. "The man you surmise to be Count Borgia could very well be Sir Mortimer in the flesh."

His direct definite response left me pondering on the inconceivable implications of his concordant words. "How is that possible?" I curiously questioned.

He explained. "Within the blasphemous tome is a dark necromantic spell to resurrect the body. It instructs one in how to reduce the mortal clay to its essential salts, then with the proper incantation raise it up again complete in all respects, including the heart and soul of the departed. Such an individual would be classified within the realm of the undead – neither actually living nor dead – never aging and impervious to sickness. Thus, this individual could conceivably live for countless years, acquiring the knowledge of several lifetimes. Imagine the wealth they could amass in that time. Should they meet with a violent end, their salts can again be raised and the body restored to its former living state. Therefore, it is not only possible but rather likely that Count Borgia is Sir Mortimer under another guise, having lived all this time weaving his evil machinations in secret. However, the incantation pronounced in reverse will return the body to the dust from whence it came, and by such means be destroyed. The recipient must be close enough to hear the words being spoken."

"You know what scares me the most, Professor? You're not kidding," I soberly disclosed. "Get your coat," I said, changing gears. "It's time we paid a visit to the monastery of Saint Christopher."

"I've already spoken to the desk clerk as to its whereabouts," he informed. "It's still very much in existence, and situated on a small island in the north part of the lagoon. I took the liberty of having the hotel arrange a private charter."

Downstairs, we hooked up with JB. A motorboat was waiting for us at the landing, and we set out for the monastery with our fingers crossed.

Once beyond the network of canals, the speeding boat skimmed over the gently rippling waters of the expansive lagoon. After rounding a large island completely packed with close-knit buildings, our boatman steered a direct course for a small island on the horizon. As we drew near, the monastery gradually loomed up from the landscape, its defined features taking clear shape in the closing distance. Against a blue backdrop of water and sky, an outer wall encompassed a nestled cluster of brick and stone structures, and a spiring cross stood prominently atop a lofty bell tower.

The boatmen moored at the dock, and my companions and I proceeded up the path to the gate. Beside the gate hung a bell with a slim rope cord dangling from the clapper, and the Professor rang it, announcing our presence. A soft-spoken monk answered the summons, and after a brief conversation with the Professor, he humbly bid us to enter. He ushered us across a courtyard and into a church with a clerestory, through which cascading sunbeams bathed the interior in heavenly radiance, and majestic stained glass dressed the tall slender windows.

"I requested an audience with the Abbot," the Professor said, acknowledging my inquisitive expression.

The Monk led us through a side door into a garden cloister, wherein a silver-haired cleric sat in meditation on a stone bench. He was ascetically garbed in a plain hooded brown robe, a wooden crucifix hung from his neck, and his pensive demeanor exuded a sage countenance. As we approached, he turned his head and gazed up at us with insightful eyes. The monk spoke to him in a reverent manner, presenting us with a gesturing open hand. The Professor stepped forward and addressed the pious silver-haired cleric, whom I presumed to be the Abbot. The Professor's words, although foreign to me, were spoken in a sincere, deferential manner, evoking a favorable response, for the Abbot gave a consenting nod, and the monk who had thus far been our guide directed us to follow him.

He conducted us to a chamber adjoining the sanctuary, in which shelves harboring old books and parchments lined the walls along with closed cabinets. Rising to a tapered arch, niches in the west wall framed stained glass windows that faced the afternoon sun and illuminated the chamber with an iridescent light. The windows depicted a marvel of holy images, each displaying the marks of exquisitely detailed craftsmanship. The monk motioned for us to sit at a long spacious table, and then he retrieved from a locked cabinet a dusty bundle of aged parchment paper tied together with string. He gently placed the bundle in front of the Professor, and with a silent nod he withdrew from the room, locking the door behind him.

The Professor blew away the dust that blanketed the parcel. "These, gentlemen, are the archival records from the period of Paul V, dating back some three centuries. Being a university professor can open many doors – that and telling the Abbot we are prepared to give a substantial donation to the monastery," he clarified, untying the bundle. "Time to polish up your Latin, Doctor. I'll need your assistance if we're to save time."

He divided the stack into three piles and distributed one to each of us. "You can help too, Mr. Blake," he said. "Peruse the text for any indication of Matteo Veneti."

My companions assiduously poured over the handwritten records, while I earnestly sought a name amongst obscure words in which each letter was formed by the rigid strokes of the writer's hand. As the day slipped away, gradually shifting shadows moving with the sinking sun measured the passage of time.

My confidence in our initial conclusion was beginning to waver, when JB suddenly broke the long silence, exclaiming discovery. "I found a reference to Matteo Veneti!" he excitedly proclaimed. "I'm not sure about the translation, Professor. Maybe you should have a look."

The Professor strained to see the writing in the waning remnants of daylight. JB lit the oil lamp on the table and brought it close. My heart beat fast with anticipation as the Professor laboriously perused the Latin text with a stern expression. At one point his eyes lit up, but he said nothing, nor took his eyes from the paper.

"It seems that Matteo Veneti did indeed reside within these walls for a period," he finally informed, looking up at us. "And furthermore, his grave lies within the catacombs beneath the monastery."

"Is there anything about the diamond?" I asked.

"Oh yes," he returned. "The Abbot who wrote these records perceived it to be the embodiment of corruption – an instrument of the devil, and as such, could only work detriment and ruin. To hide it from the outside world, the monks shut it away in Veneti's tomb when they interred him. After which, they all pledged silence unto death, and in time, the memory of the diamond and its place of concealment to be forgotten. However, several pages contain a line of text that was later written in the lower margin. These addendums neither augment the main text nor individually bear any special meaning, yet when pieced together in sequence they comprise a cryptic passage or cipher. One that I believe alludes to the tomb. Allow me a moment to write it down."

He took a folded sheet of hotel stationery from the pocket of his tweed jacket, and as he penned the English translation, an enigmatic message unraveled with each puzzling line.

The archangel Michael guards the path
The number of creation the guide
To the place where angels eternally pray
Virgin at meridian above full moon
Moon revolves to waxing quarter moon
One quarter rotation of the Earth
Heavenly signs realigned prove one worthy
The unjust condemned to a prison of perdition

For a time we pondered over the representation of its symbolic imagery, trying to interpret and understand its meaning.

"I'm having a hard time making heads or tails of it, Professor," I said, looking over his shoulder.

"I must admit certain elements are most confounding and can be construed in many ways," he assented, stroking his beard. "You've been unusually quiet, Doctor. What have you to say?"

Distracted, JB sat in silence, staring in contemplation at the stained glass window behind me. I turned to see the archangel Michael gloriously depicted in a commanding pose. Crowned with a bright halo, he wielded the sword of justice in his right hand, golden wings extended as if in flight, and a gold sash girded the waist of his lily-white robe. Below the resplendent window stood a small altar table, atop which rested three candles in brass candlesticks, and a rug draped the floor beneath.

"By george, the first marker referred to in the cipher, and its propinquity could not be more providential," the Professor remarked upon discovering what had captured JB's attention. "Now we must look for the number of creation," he emphatically urged.

In search of the next clue, JB and I moved the altar table and pulled the rug aside, revealing a trap door set in the floor. "It's not the number of creation, but I think we found the guarded path, Professor," I surmised.

My companions bore the anxious expression of one who has achieved initial success in the ardent pursuit of some momentous goal. Allaying the suspense, I firmly grasped the iron ring and lifted the heavy door. As it yawned open with a groan, a rush of foul stale air brushed our faces; and in the dark opening, hewn stone steps descended into a black foreboding abyss.

"You've got matches, JB. Light the candles," I directed.

"What if someone should come?" he cautioned.

"We'll have to take that risk," the Professor said decidedly.

"You can stay here if you like," I offered.

"No, I'm coming with you," JB resolved, stiffening his composure.

He lit the three candles, one for each of us, and we proceeded into the dark depths of a forbidding realm inhabited by the dead. Recesses in the walls of the confining narrow passageway held the rotting remains of those interred. Seeping moisture gathered into droplets that eventually dripped or trickled into a channeling gutter formed by the slanted wet stones beneath our feet. Slimy mold grew in sweeping patches, and rats scurrying in the shadows mingled a sensation of repugnance amidst the prevailing disquietude.

"This place gives me the creeps," I confessed, as I forged into the uninviting darkness ahead with nothing more than the lambent candlelight to stay the gloom, my companions close behind.

Stretching onward, the morbid tunnel led us to an archway that opened to a circular chamber with a low vaulted ceiling. Barely visible in the dancing glow of the candles, seven other identical archways denoted similar passages that branched out from the rotunda at equidistantly spaced intervals like spokes on a wheel. The numerous paths, each presenting its own possibility, spawned a quandary, and at the Professor's instructions we again sought the number of creation.

In no time at all, the subject of our search became apparent, for etched in the keystone of each arch was a Roman numeral. Our discovery turned out to be as puzzling as it was conspicuous. Contrary to the expected, the numbers were not in sequential order, but were arrayed randomly without any discernible pattern.

"This must be the way," I declared, standing at the threshold of the archway marked with the number seven and peering into the dark opening.

"I'm afraid you're mistaken," the Professor contradicted, standing before a different arch. "The Lord created the heavens and the earth in six days. On the seventh day he rested," he stated categorically, and he held up his candle to illuminate the number six etched in the keystone above his head. "This is the correct path."

His practical reasoning was infallible as usual, and we followed him, pressing forward into the haunted reaches beyond. Like the previous passage, the dead lay motionless on both sides like silent warning sentinels, their lingering spirits demanding penance. At the end of the passage, the walls widened to form a square chamber, and the professor came to an abrupt halt. Evenly spaced bored holes approximately the diameter of a silver dollar lined the ceiling and floor of the entry. Across the chamber, two solemn stone angels knelt in prayer on either side of the entrance to a burial vault in which rested a stone sarcophagus. Vertical wrought iron bars with no apparent means of opening gated the vault's entrance, denying ingress to the vault's interior. On the wall to the right of the barred entrance, a metal disk the size of a ship's wheel was embedded in the stonework, its surface bristling with circling symbols in relief, their shapes indistinct in the faintly lit expanse. The encouraging sight of the praying angels affirmed that the object of our quest was almost within our grasp.

I stepped forward to enter the chamber, but the Professor's perturbed expression imbued in my being a sense of apprehension that stayed me. "What is it?" I asked.

"I don't like the looks of it," he said, examining the surroundings. "There's an insidious devilry lurking here, waiting to ensnare the unwary."

"There's one way to find out," I asserted, and I daringly ventured forth into the chamber.

"Take heed, Mr. Blake," he strongly advised. "For the cipher metaphorically speaks a warning."

My companions tarried behind in the passageway, their nerves teetering on the brink of expectancy as I edged my way toward the vault, each footfall amplified by the forlorn stillness of the grave, and every step tempting some perceived impending fate. Like suspended fragments of time, the agonizing moments seemed to stretch to eternity, and spanning the short distance was like crossing a boundless shadowy sea.

Reaching the barred entrance with no resulting mishap, I breathed a sigh of relief and peered through the bars into the vault's interior. Nowhere was a name displayed to identify the occupant of the tomb; but inscribed on the lid of the sarcophagus was a coat of arms depicting a unicorn crest that crowned a shield decorated with a parapeted tower below a rose. The impregnable gateway had neither hinge nor lock, and the bars were firmly set in the stones both above and below.

"What do you see?" the Professor inquired.

"This is it all right. We found it. Come have a look," I responded definitively.

The impression of danger now allayed, my companions traversed the width of the chamber, and gazing into the vault, they drew the same conclusion with their own eyes. But initial exhilaration evaporated as the discouraging realization of the foiling impediment that stood in our way became fully evident.

"How do we gain entry? That's the question," JB rhetorically said, testing the strength of the bars.

"I believe the answer lies here," the Professor suggested, his attention now drawn to the ornamental disk next to the entrance.

Obliging his request for more light, JB and I brought our candles closer that he might better examine its markings in detail. The metal disk was divided into two concentric rings around a circle. The three sections were delineated by raised borders and separated by an almost imperceptible hairline split that ran the outer circumference of each border. Symbols in relief adorned the surface; in the center was a symbol comprised of a circle cut into quarters by two perpendicular lines; the phases of the moon were represented in the first ring; and the outer ring displayed a band of twelve arcane symbols equidistantly arrayed in a circular pattern.

The Professor nodded his head affirmatively with a lustrous gleam in his eye. "It all makes perfect sense now. This, gentlemen, is a lock – and we happen to have the combination," he said, taking out the paper upon which he had written the cipher. "You see, the outlying symbols denote the signs of the zodiac and no doubt represent the heavens." He pointed to one in particular that resembled a calligraphic 'M' and 'P' combined. "That is the sign for Virgo – the virgin. I'm sure you recognize the phases of the moon, and the one in the center is a symbolization of the Earth."

He looked at the writing on the paper in his hand. "According to the cipher, we simply need to line up the symbols in the proper order," he stated with convincing confidence. "You've got a good pair of strong arms, Mr. Blake. Would you do the honors?"

"Sure, just tell me what to do."

"Let's see, 'virgin at meridian above full moon'," he quoted from the cipher. "Virgo is at four o'clock and the full moon is currently at the twelve o'clock position. The rings should rotate independently. Turn the outer ring clockwise until the sign of the virgin is at twelve o'clock directly above the full moon."

"Why clockwise?" I asked, handing my candle to JB.

"Because the stars pass overhead from east to west."

Using the raised symbols for a grip, I tried to turn the ring, but time had rendered it immobile and it refused to budge. After several attempts met with failure, I exerted every ounce of strength I could muster in a final determined effort. Grimacing and groaning, I strained my muscles to the limit, until finally, the archaic mechanism began to turn, ratcheting round like a gear. When the sign for Virgo reached the highest point and came in line with the full moon, a clunk within the stonework signaled the working of a counterweight; and then suddenly to our dire alarm, a set of bars dropped down in the opening to the passageway behind us, closing with the resounding strike of metal against stone and sealing our only means of escape.

JB panicked. "We're trapped! Doomed – doomed to a prison of perdition just like it says," he despondently exclaimed. "Help! Help us! Somebody help us!" he cried out in despair, his shouts echoing off the stone walls and channeling down the passageway.

Seemingly unshaken, the professor calmly assessed the situation. "Oh yes, quite the predicament," he noted with serious regard, yet nonetheless unconcerned. "Fear not gentlemen. We must not let this setback deter us, for we may, after all, hold the key to extricate ourselves from this incarcerating plight."

The undaunted resilience in the professor's voice possessed a peculiar bolstering quality of assurance that steadied the nerves, and JB's excited emotions relaxed.

"Now we must reposition the phases of the moon so that the waxing quarter moon is aligned with Virgo," he continued, referring to the cipher. "Mr. Blake, turn the inner ring," he instructed. "Counterclockwise this time, for the moon revolves around the Earth in a counterclockwise orbit."

Once again I wrestled with the mechanism, and click, click, click came the sound of cogs engaging as the wheel stubbornly turned round. While our anxious nerves stood on edge, I set the wheel to its new position, and following the Professor's further instructions, turned the center wheel one quarter rotation to the left. Upon completion, the prescribed combination triggered the action of heavy tumblers, succeeded by the motion of creaking gears and chains beyond the wall, at which point the bars gating the entrance to the vault slowly raised with a mournful moan.

Contemplating the gruesome task at hand, we apprehensively entered the long undisturbed tomb and gathered around the sarcophagus. No words were spoken. We simply exchanged nodding glances, then pitting our strength against the heavy overlapping lid, worked together to wrest the cold stone slab from place. It gave way with a harsh scraping growl, and pressing our efforts, we managed to maneuver the cumbersome object such that it rested in a catercornered position. Beneath lay a hollow cavity shrouded in shadow from which spewed forth a stench that fouled the nostrils and churned the stomach.

In the collective light of the candles, the veil of obscurity vanished, and torrents of emotions coursed through me like raging rivers as I gazed with morbid fascination at what lay within the stone coffin. Decay had claimed the flesh of the decomposed body, leaving only bare discolored bones dressed in stale rotting garments; strands of chalky-white hair still clung to the skull, empty sockets stared out from the void, and gaping jaws seemed to scream in silent terror. The ghastly sight repelled the senses, inducing a sickness that shocked the soul; but that is not what made our eyes grow wide – what gripped us and held us spellbound was the magnificent sparkling gem tightly clasped in bony hands near the heart.

"I never envisioned it would be this large. To imagine that such a diamond actually exists," the Professor uttered in awe, staring in astonishment at the dazzling wonder, which was no less than the size of a baseball.

Its shimmering facets gleamed with a prismatic brilliance that thrilled the eye and seduced the heart, fastening my gaze and drawing me with a mesmerizing allure that overpowered all resistance. Captivated, I focused solely on the diamond, and as I stared deep into it, a smoky swirling mist manifested within, growing and filling the precious stone with a billowing haze. As if by puffs of air, the haze began to dissipate, gradually unveiling a blurry image, which became increasingly more defined as the cloudiness cleared.

Distant in the background, a faint audible voice called me by name; when suddenly, the Professor draped his handkerchief over the diamond, interrupting my concentration and breaking the hypnotic spell. "Mr. Blake – Mr. Blake," he repeated, trying to coax my attention. "I warn you," he sternly stressed as I shook off the delirium. "Do not gaze into the diamond, lest you succumb to its corruptive power like the poor wretched soul that lies before you."

While keeping the diamond covered, the Professor pried it from the dead man's covetous grasp. The deceased was loath to give up his treasure, and the brittle fleshless fingers snapped and broke at the joints in the process. In that moment of expectancy, as the Professor plucked the stone loose, the temperature plummeted, and then a sudden chilling gust swept through the tomb accompanied by a reverberating deathly wail from beyond that made my skin crawl and sent an icy shudder down my spine. Two of the candles blew out. JB recoiled in terror, flattening his back against the stone wall of the tomb, his panic-stricken eyes looking to and fro. The Professor froze in place like a statue, gazing down at the corpse as if he half expected it to rise up and reclaim the prize. Stunned and speechless, we existed in a tense state of uncertainty until the dreadful cry died away, leaving us with racing hearts and questioning expressions.

In the ensuing silence, the Professor quickly wrapped the diamond in his handkerchief and tucked it in his coat pocket. We relit the extinguished candles; then mustering what fortitude remained, we shoved the heavy lid shut, sealing the stone coffin and allowing the awakened dead to return to eternal rest. Yet a singular peril remained, for an impassable barrier still barred the way out, holding us prisoner in this dark awful place.

"All right Professor, you're the man with the answers," I said. "How do we get out of here?"

"Heavenly signs realigned," he categorically returned. "One line of the cipher has yet to be tested."

He led us back to the wheeled contraption, where he directed me to reset the signs to their original positions in reverse order, starting with the symbol of the earth in the center. Click, click, click went the mechanism as I again turned the ratcheting wheels, and all the while the nerve-racking tension wound tighter with the rotation of the gears. At the last setting, the sound of sprockets and interconnecting gears in operation reached our ears. The set of bars obstructing the passageway began to rise as the other set of bars simultaneously lowered, resealing the entrance to the vault; and when the mechanical sounds ceased, all was as it was when we first discovered the tomb.

"We're free!" JB rejoiced, and we proceeded back down the passage at a hurried pace.

Upon reaching the circular chamber, we stopped to get our bearings, but all the other passages looked alike, leaving us confused with indecision. In our enthusiasm, we had inadvertently lost our way, and although the passages were numbered, not one of us could agree on which passage led back to the surface.

The candles were nearly spent, and soon we would be groping in the dark. Grasping an idea, I went about searching the stones at my feet, looking for any telltale signs of our previous passing. Luckily, footprints in the muck directed me to the passage from whence they originally emerged, and I followed them into the dark opening.

Urging my companions to join me, I continued on, while allowing them to catch up. Here and there certain features struck a familiar cord, assuring me that this was the right path. We had not traveled far when a dim light glowed in the distance ahead, and we quickened our pace. Soon, we saw the open trap door and the contours of rising steps. I cautiously ascended first to find the room just as we had left it. The oil lamp still burned atop the table, and by all indications, our venture had gone undetected. My companions climbed the steps, and after easing the trap door closed, we replaced the rug and altar table, then returned the candlesticks to their original placement.

JB and I resumed our seats, while the Professor went to the door and knocked. Shortly thereafter, a monk answered the call. Without uttering a word, he carefully reassembled the aged records and put them away. The Professor expressed his gratitude, to which the monk responded with a silent gesture, and we followed the monk into the sanctuary, where he directed us to an offering plate near the altar. JB produced a wad of cash, and without hesitation, put the whole roll in the plate.

Our solemn guide conducted us to the main gate, and as we took leave of the monastery, he smiled and pronounced a blessing upon us. The boatman was waiting, and soon we were under way. In the expanding distance, the monastery faded into the dark horizon, and all around, moonlight danced upon the open waters of the lagoon.

It was New Year's Eve, and upon our return the city was ablaze with light and alive with celebration. At the hotel, the desk clerk imparted welcome news. Inspector Geoffries had arrived in our absence, and was even now waiting for us in his suite. This was good news indeed, for a much-needed ally had come to tip the scales in our favor.

However, our repeated knocks on Geoffries' door roused no response. Light shining beneath the door indicated the lights were on inside the room, and dire thoughts began to cross my mind. The doorknob turned easily in my hand, and when the door swung open, I was confronted by the shocking sight of Geoffries lying prostrate and to all appearances lifeless on the floor in front of a shattered cheval glass.

We rushed to his side. His ashen face was contorted in fear, and his wide eyes reflected a testament to the horror he had witnessed. JB checked his body for signs of life and then looked me square in the eyes. "He's dead."

CHAPTER 23

Those glazed eyes staring sightless up at the ceiling – that unnerving expression – both blended to brew a bitter concoction of unwelcome perturbing sensations that strongly played on the imagination and troubled the mind. With gentle fingers, JB closed the eyelids, giving Geoffries the appearance as it were, of being asleep, albeit in the grip of a nightmare, for nothing could efface the gruesome outlines of his twisted facial features rigidly steeped in an immutable state of terror.

Geoffries' body was arrayed in such a way as to suggest he had recoiled and fallen backwards: the knees slightly bent to one side, the left arm angled at the elbow with the open hand toward the face as if in defense of an attacker, and the right arm outstretched, the hand clenched in a tight fist. Cuts on the knuckles of his fisted hand displayed the only distinguishable marks, and the evidence of their source was just a few feet away. Shards of mirror lay on the floor below the broken cheval glass, which looked like an unfinished puzzle. Cracks splintered outward from a single point of impact, fragmenting my reflection into bits and pieces, some of them missing. For whatever reason, Geoffries had rendered a blow to the glass.

"How long ago, JB?" I inquired.

"Not long at all, I'd say," he matter-of-factly replied.

The Professor's well of words had dried up for the moment, and he stared down in consternation at the inspector's lifeless body.

"What's this? There's something in his hand," JB observed. He peeled back the curled fingers, revealing a crumpled piece of parchment, which resiliently unfolded in the open palm like a shy blossoming flower.

In an instant, I recognized the markings drawn in blood upon its wrinkled surface: the triangle, the strange symbols, and that penetrating evil eye! Except for a few slight differences, it was an almost exact replica of the vile curse so insidiously delivered with our meal at the Plaza Hotel in New York. A dozen disheartening emotions assailed my being, each vying for supremacy, but one transcended them all – insecurity. The disquieting knowledge that our remorseless antagonists were capable of inflicting murder and destruction upon anyone, anytime, anywhere was extremely unsettling. And no one, not even the staunch Inspector Geoffries of Scotland Yard was immune.

"Don't touch it!" the Professor emphatically warned. "Lest its malignant power be unleashed upon us. We were meant to discover it, of that I'm fairly certain."

The door to the hall remained open, and I quickly went to close it. The hallway was empty. Fortunately, we had not attracted any attention.

"We're going to have to notify the hotel management, and have them summon a local doctor. One with the authority to officially pronounce him dead and issue a death certificate," JB recommended, soundly speaking within the scope of his purview.

"We'll need to contact the British Consulate as well," the Professor added. "After all, he is a British subject."

"Yes – but not yet," I decreed, and I took the opportunity to conduct a search of the suite and sift through Geoffries' belongings.

The simple suite held no further clues, and amongst the inspector's few personal items, I came across the culminating sum of a man's life and the marks of his craft: a cherished family photograph, his passport and official identification, a revolver, and an arrest warrant – with Mallory's name filled in; but most importantly was his notebook, which contained copious notes pertaining to the case. I pocketed the notebook; and despite my companions' pleas to the contrary, I plucked the cursed parchment from the inspector's lifeless palm.

"Don't worry, I've got plans for this thing, and they don't include getting nailed," I assured with a scheming expression.

JB still had words to say on the matter, but the Professor must have known what I was thinking, for a spark of realization gleamed in his eyes and his lips curled in a repressed smile.

"It's time we informed the hotel," the Professor said, diverting attention back to the original problem. "I'll take care of it. You two remain here."

While awaiting his return, I used the time to peruse Geoffries' scrawled notes, which revealed a wealth of facts, including a host of incriminating information on one 'Scarlet McCreed', alias Sadie Morrell. JB furiously smoked his pipe and waltzed around the room, incessantly pacing in a whirlwind of anxiety. Submerged in his own thoughts, he seemed oblivious to my presence.

At one point, he abruptly ceased and turned to look at me with sunken eyes. "I think I'm losing my mind," he confided, a grave inflexion of genuine fear in his voice. "I see things – nightmarish things – hallucinations that now haunt my waking hours – and they're occurring with more pressing frequency. I'm not so sure I can hold it together anymore," he unloaded, rubbing his brow and combing back his flaxen bangs with his fingers.

He paused to piece together his thoughts, but before he could say another word, the Professor entered, accompanied by the hotel manager and a rotund man with rosy cheeks, toting a medical bag. The portly Venetian doctor reeked of spirits, and his unsteady balance and slurred speech denoted an advanced state of intoxication. He gave Geoffries a cursory examination and promptly pronounced him dead of cardiac arrest. After filling out a death certificate, he handed it to the manager and staggered out.

The hotel manager expressed polite condolences. "Until the undertaker arrives, you may remain here with the deceased if you like. But I must please ask that you exercise discretion, so as not to alarm the other guests," he said before leaving.

For the sake of everyone, we covered Geoffries with a blanket; and out of courtesy, we decided to wait for the undertaker to at least find out where his body would be taken. A bundle of nerves, JB could not sit still, and soon he was out of his chair, pacing about the room again. The Professor, on the other hand, maintained an air of repose. Although I could not see behind the façade, he had not slept for quite some time, and I wondered how long it would be until his mental faculties began to falter, followed by complete exhaustion and inevitable collapse. I wondered if he suffered from similar waking hallucinations like those that plagued JB. If so, he gave no indication, and his thoughts were a mystery.

The time was now or never. I pulled the Professor aside.

"Read this," I whispered, pointing out a passage in Geoffries' notebook.

He donned his spectacles, and as he read the damaging notes on Sadie, his expression turned to intense interest.

"Erases all doubt, doesn't it?" I remarked.

"It certainly does," he responded.

"It's time to set him straight."

"It's not going to be easy."

"I'll do it – just back me up."

He took a deep breath. "All right," he said decidedly with a quick concordant nod.

The next moment, JB was standing in our midst. "What the devil are you two chattering on about?" he demanded with suspicious eyes.

"I've got bad news to break to you," I grimly stated, choosing the direct approach.

"It's about the journal, isn't it?" he speculated before I could continue. "Funny thing about the journal. It was missing this morning and so were you. Where is it? Let's see it!"

"I haven't got it. Sadie took it," I flatly answered.

He started breathing fast and his eyes blazed with fury. In a physical outrage, he grabbed me by the collar with both hands. "How dare you! Lies! Lies!" he shouted in my face. "You want the diamond for yourself. Yes, that's it – all for yourself. You think you're so clever," he angrily accused in a wild frenzy of paranoia.

Normally, I would have knocked someone's block off for that, but sympathy let it slide by. "You've been led to believe a lie, JB. Sadie's not who she purports to be. In fact, Sadie isn't even her real name. She's an imposter. It's all right here. Read it for yourself," I indignantly returned, shoving the notebook into his chest.

"Listen to him, Doctor. He's telling you the truth," the Professor entreated.

JB snatched the notebook from my hand and sat down in a huff. Frantically, he flipped the pages until his eyes fell upon a familiar name. As his eyes moved down the page his expression went blank, and with each line his head sank lower under the weight of the words. When he had finished, he slowly let the notebook slip from his fingers to fall to the floor, and bowed low, he stared at the pattern on the rug.

Although it pained me to do so, I leveled with him, telling him about the powdery substance in his wine glass the night he was attacked, and how I had followed Sadie to the Café Florian, where she handed over the journal to Mallory and Borgia.

For a time, he issued no response and sat dumbfounded in silence, his head bent, running his trembling fingers through his hair. Eventually, he raised his head, and when he looked up at me, I could see the disgrace mixed with rage in his sorrowful eyes.

I placed a consoling hand on his shoulder. "Don't be hard on yourself. She played us all for a sap," I said.

"Please forgive my outburst. I'm not myself," he said with sincere remorse. Then shifting emotions like the wind, he sprang from his chair. "I want to hear it from her own lips," he sternly declared and started for the door with the resentful determination of a man seeking rectification for an unconscionable wrong.

I barred the way. "Don't go off half-cocked – not like this. Wait here with us for the undertaker. Give yourself some time to cool off and clear your head. Afterwards, we'll all pay her a visit. We're in this together," I said, appealing to his reason.

"Don't be rash, Doctor. I urge you to take his sound advice," the Professor reinforced.

JB's indignation receded, and he subsided into an armchair where he commenced to fall to pieces. No words could I conjure to relieve his emotional pain, and burdened by a sense of helplessness, I watched a man I highly admired sink to the depths of despair. Here was a man dying inside, while another lay cold stone dead upon the floor; and the ugly scene etched its indelible picture upon my mind, filling me with the desire for revenge.

The hour was late when the undertaker finally arrived to take Geoffries away. Seems the inspector was destined to be a resident slab at the local morgue pending his disposition. As for his belongings and the bill, they were left in our charge.

Tending to the next order of business, we marched to Sadie's room, each stride bringing us closer to the moment of reckoning. We were already resolved as to her guilt, and no perjured testimony on her part could alter that. A light shone under the door, indicating occupancy. But was she alone? I knocked.

"Come in, it's open," replied an inviting feminine voice we all recognized.

I opened the door to find Sadie preparing for imminent departure. She was richly decked out in a fur coat and fancy hat, and her bags were packed. She was standing at the vanity, fastidiously powdering her face, her attention focused on the open compact in her hand.

"The bags are by the door," she said as if addressing a bellhop.

Unnoticed, we quietly entered, and the Professor closed the door behind us. At the sound of the latch she looked up from her visage in the small round mirror, and she gasped in shock and surprise upon realizing our unexpected presence.

"Going somewhere, Scarlet?" I inquired.

Her eyes flashed wide upon hearing that name. For a split moment consternation gripped her, and then her gaze shifted to the open purse sitting on the corner of the bed. Anticipating her action, I moved to intercept as she made a mad dash for the purse, and I snatched it from her reaching grasp.

"That's mine. Give it to me," she demanded, clutching at it.

"Sit down toots," I gruffly ordered, pointing to the stool in front of the vanity. "We want a word with you."

Back stepping, she looked at each of our grim faces in turn as we closed in around her. "JB – darling, what's wrong?" she nervously entreated, putting on an expression of innocence.

But her plea only stoked the fuming tempest in his glaring wild eyes, which exuded a madness capable of anything. Shaken, she shrank from his stringent silent stare and sat down on the stool like a cowering helpless kitten.

"Well, well, look what we have here," I remarked, drawing a snub-nosed revolver from her purse. "Is this what you were so anxious to get your hands on?"

I – I keep it for protection," she stammered out.

I chuckled. "Like a viper needs protection," I mockingly joked, slipping the revolver in my coat pocket.

Next I pulled out a passport displaying her photograph, but the profile bore the name Scarlet McCreed, and tucked inside the cover was a train ticket for the midnight express leaving town. Under her protest, I passed her travel documents on to my companions for their own inspection; and then rummaging through the other odds and ends that fill a woman's purse, I came across a small vial of suspicious powder.

"And what, pray tell, might this be?" I rhetorically inquired, holding it up for all to see. "Is this what you put in JB's wine glass the other night?" I implied.

"That's my medicine," she claimed.

I handed the vial to JB. "What do you make of this, Doctor?"

JB examined the powder, subjecting it to the scrutiny of his senses. "No wonder the wine tasted bitter," he assessed upon tasting it.

"We're wise to you, sister," I assured and then rattled off the inspector's rap sheet on her.

All the while, she played the persecuted victim, and even shed a tear when I blatantly accused her of drugging JB's wine. But her face gradually turned to stone as I revealed how I had followed her to the Café Florian and disclosed the details of her meeting with Mallory and his sinister cohort.

Turning on her sweet charm, she appealed to JB, adamantly denying everything, and pulling out all the stops, right down to the waterworks.

He would have none of it. "You lying, contemptible whore!" he rebuked in response.

"Professor, would you be so kind as to get us a glass of water," I requested. "I have a theory I'd like to test."

When the Professor returned from the bath, I dumped the remaining contents of the vial into the glass. It was a sizable dose, and as the powder dissolved, her eyes grew wide with the awareness of my intention.

"Time to take your medicine," I dictated, presenting the glass for her to drink.

"I'll scream," she warned.

"You do and I'll break your pretty little neck," I sternly asserted. "Now drink it!"

"No! No!" she cried, and she forcefully knocked the glass from my hand. It tumbled to the floor, splashing and spilling its contents upon the rug.

Not a shadow of doubt remained as to her guilt and complicity. "The prosecution rests," I concluded. "Time to pronounce sentence – something commensurate with your wicked ways."

Her fearful, questioning eyes followed my every movement as I retrieved the cursed parchment from my pocket. Taking her by the wrist, I deposited it in her palm and closed her fingers around it. Upon my release, she hesitantly opened her hand, and horror seized her the moment she set eyes on the malignant charm. Her very reaction proved that she knew full well the potency of its black magic. At first she was petrified, then suddenly emitting a woeful cry like a banshee, she violently jerked her hand away, discarding the charm as if it was a hot coal.

"Notice how the tinge gets brighter when the end is near. Here's where you exit the scene. Too bad we won't be around to see the end of the play," I tauntingly said. "But if you play ball with us, sister, you might get a reprieve in the bargain."

Broken, defeated and desperate, she was ripe for entertaining any suggestion. "What is it? What do you want?" she implored.

"We want you to deliver a message to your master, Sir Gunston Mallory, and we want you to deliver it now – tonight. Tell him we have the diamond and we're willing to make an exchange for the dolls. We'll be at the bell tower in Saint Mark's Square tomorrow morning at nine. If he wants it, he better be there, and if he tries anything in the meantime, he'll never find it. Tell him that," I resolutely stated. "Oh, and while you're there, maybe his African magician can do something to rid you of your plight – and you know darn well who I'm talking about."

She stewed for a minute, gritting her teeth and intermittently looking down at the insidious charm on the floor. "Seems I have little choice," she said resignedly. "All right, I'll give him your message."

I pocketed her passport. "You'll get this when you return with the answer."

On her way out, I drew her attention to the empty space on the floor where the charm had been. "Time is ticking. I'd hurry if I were you," I advised.

She reluctantly searched her pockets, and her gasp spoke volumes when she found the thing upon her person.

Her face scrunched up in an assaulting expression of defiance. "I don't think you realize who you're dealing with. You're playing with fire, and when you play with fire, you get burned," she reproved with disdain, and she stormed out.

Untrustworthy and unpredictable, she was too wily to be left to her own devices, and thus for several reasons that merited my companions' endorsement, I chose to follow.

Avoiding the dark and solitary byways, she stuck to the more populated streets with lighted establishments. Then after crossing an arched bridge that spanned the Grand Canal, she entered the residential district of Dorsoduro, where she navigated the streets as if intimately familiar with the way. Her quick pace came to an abrupt stop in front of a palatial house. Hesitation seized her for a moment or two, and then she went to the door and knocked. The door opened, and a man appeared in the doorway, his dark outline silhouetted against the dimly lit interior. He solemnly ushered her in, and she disappeared behind the closing door.

Nary a glimpse of light escaped the closed shutters, and I was left to surmise what may be taking place within those walls. Cloaking myself in the shadows, I watched and waited in the cold night while a train of questions circulated in my thoughts. Whose house was it? Were Mallory and Borgia inside? Was she conveying our message, or had she slipped out the back door? Was there a back door? I had little choice but to wait it out.

About a quarter of an hour later, the front door opened and she reemerged. For a few moments she lingered on the threshold, speaking to a man in the doorway. His features were a vague mystery, but I recognized the unmistakable voice. It was that of Sir Gunston Mallory, and although his actual words were indiscernible to my ears, they were emphatic and direct. He curtly shut the door in her face, and she turned on her heels. Preoccupied and looking flustered, she whisked past me unaware as she walked down the other side of the narrow street at a rapid gait.

Straight back to the hotel she went, and upstairs to her suite where I caught up with her.

Poised to knock at the door, she suddenly turned to face me as I approached from her blindside. "Do you make a habit of surprising women?" she scornfully sniped.

"Only wily ones," I retorted. "Shall we go in? I'm sure my companions are anxious to hear what you have to say. I know I am."

Pretentiously displaying the propriety of a gentleman, I opened the door and motioned for her to enter. Once inside, she wasted no time getting to the point, and did not mince words in relaying Mallory's response.

"If you really have the diamond, you're to take it to this address in Dorsoduro tonight at one o'clock – and don't be late," she said, handing me a folded piece of paper, which contained an address as well as an accompanying unsigned note written in Mallory's handwriting.

Mr. Blake,

You and your colleagues are to call upon the above address promptly at one o'clock, and bring the item for trade.

Should you fail to arrive at the appointed hour, Doctor Hawkins and Professor Hanson shall suffer a most agonizing demise. As a measure of persuasion, an effective demonstration will occur at the stroke of midnight.

To assuage my companions' hungry impatience, I read the note aloud before passing it on.

The Professor looked at his newly purchased pocket watch. "Three minutes 'til midnight," he gravely informed.

I wheeled to face Sadie. "You know what's going to happen. What is it? What's the demonstration?" I demanded in no uncertain terms.

She cowered before my threatening stance. "I don't know. I really don't know," she proclaimed. "He doesn't tell me everything. I swear I don't know."

For once I considered that she might be telling the truth.

"I did what you asked. Now give me my passport and let me go," she implored.

"Oh no sister, you're sticking around for the demonstration," I insisted.

As midnight drew nigh, the paralyzing suspense became unbearable, and my companions' apprehension evolved to near panic. Finally, resounding church bells rang throughout the old city, tolling the hour and marking the conclusion of those timeless minutes. When the last toll had died away, we looked at each other expectantly. Initially nothing happened, and then hell unleashed its torment. Suddenly, the Professor cried out in anguish. Clutching his wrenching right hand, he grimaced and groaned in pain. JB looked extremely perturbed, and although he was looking directly at me, his eyes did not register my presence.

"I can't see you. I can't see. I – I can't see anything," he exclaimed in distress, rubbing his eyes and trying to focus.

The Professor ran into the bath, turned on the spigot, and stuck his pain-stricken hand under the flow of cold water. JB groped about with his arms outstretched, bumping into the furniture.

I seized Sadie by the throat. "Make it stop. Make it stop!" I petulantly barked, constricting my choking grasp.

"I can't," she hoarsely gasped.

Heeding JB's pitiful calls for aid, I released her, and she fell to her knees, coughing and gagging. Then taking JB by the arm, I guided him to an armchair and helped him into it. The Professor appeared in the doorway to the bath, still holding his misshapen hand and repressing the impulse to cry out.

Leaning against the frame, he spoke through clinched teeth. "My hand is on fire, and nothing will extinguish it. I earnestly urge that we accept their terms."

Grim circumstances had turned the tables, and all options vanished as I considered the miserable afflictions cast upon my companions. In the face of a dire dilemma, I felt the pressure to concede squeezing me like a vise. "All right, we'll play it their way," I relented.

Strangely, no sooner had the words left my lips than the Professor's malady ceased as instantaneously as it had begun. "The pain is gone," he remarked in astonished relief.

"Can you see anything, JB?" I immediately inquired, waving a hand in front of his face.

His eyes remained fixed. "Not a darn thing. I'm blind as a bat," he despondently informed.

"If the Doctor's eyesight does not recover, his severe handicap will most certainly hamper our progress. To allow for sufficient time, I strongly suggest we start for Dorsoduro without delay," the Professor advised, looking at his watch.

"The Professor is right," JB affirmed. "I'll only be a burden. Maybe it would be better if you left me behind. Just take me to our suite."

"No – you're coming along," I said. "The note says all of us, so the matter is already settled. One question remains though. What to do about the dame?"

"Let her go. She can't hurt us anymore," the Professor said, advocating mercy.

"You're right, she's not worth it," I concurred.

The Professor assisted JB with his coat. On the way out, I tossed Sadie's passport onto the bed and then closed the door behind us, leaving her to whatever fate may design.

Still robbed of his sight, JB cleaved to me, absolutely dependent on another for direction. For him, the journey through the tangled streets was fraught with pitfalls and lurking obstructions. For us, the old city had denied its charm, and an irrepressible sense of impending dread welled up inside me, growing stronger as we neared our destination.

We reached the palatial address with little time to spare, and soon found ourselves standing at the same door Sadie had knocked on. Albeit with warranted reservation, I struck the heavy door with the brass knocker. Almost immediately, the door opened, and a stone-faced butler stood in the doorway.

"You're expected," he said in a Balkan accent, and stepping aside, he motioned for us to enter.

The foyer seemed overly expansive in the dim light of the candelabra in his hand. As we crossed the threshold, I could not help but think we were entering the lions' den, and the sound of the closing door was like a trap snapping shut. Without uttering a word, the butler proceeded with a hobble up a flight of stairs and to a pair of doors off the landing. He opened the doors and silently gestured for us to go in.

We passed into a spacious rectangular room lit solely by the flames of a crackling fire. Fluttering waves of firelight and shadow swept over the diamond-checkered pattern on the marble tiled floor and rippled up the lengthy drawn curtains to dance on the tall ceiling above. Half-cloaked in obscurity, Mallory casually stood to one side of an imposing fireplace at the other end of the room. Atop the mantel rested two reed dolls fitted to resemble my companions. One had a scorched appendage, and the other had a blindfold tied around the head. Except for two wing chairs arrayed before and facing the fireplace, the expansive room was devoid of furniture. An unidentifiable man occupied one of the chairs, his resting arm being the only visible part of him. The butler remained behind on the landing, and one by one he closed the pair of doors.

"Good morning gentlemen," Mallory greeted with a sardonic flair. "I did not expect for us to meet again so soon, nor at such a late hour. Come gentlemen, come closer into the light."

Warily, we slowly advanced across the length of the room. Inklings of deceit tingled my nerves with each step forward and propelled my senses to the pinnacle of alertness.

As we drew near, the unseen seated man raised his hand. "That will be quite far enough," he dictated. "So we meet at last. Mr. Blake, you have proved to be a most resourceful man, and as such, I would warrant you are carrying a pistol. I must insist that you remove it –

slowly of course, and slide it across the floor in this direction. And I advise you not to take any foolish action. The welfare of your colleagues hangs in the balance."

Our adversaries were not playing with an ordinary deck, and one could only imagine what cards were hidden up their sleeves. Reluctantly I complied, easing out my Luger and setting it on the floor. I gave it a shove, and it skated across the tiles, coming to a stop by the empty chair.

"Now that we have that settled, shall we get to the business before us?" the faceless voice proposed, and then the mystery man rose from the chair, revealing himself.

When he stepped around the chair to face us, the Professor's expression was one of sheer astonishment, for the man's build, raven-black hair and sinister features were identical to the portrait of Sir Mortimer Mallory. Cold and stolid, he recited our names, his lustrous eyes shifting to each of us in turn as he spoke them, and he mockingly referred to JB as "the blind Doctor Hawkins".

"I am Count Francis Borgia, and this is my home," he said, introducing himself without expressing further amenities.

Mallory came forward to join Borgia. Casually, he picked up the Luger, but did not brandish it. Rather, he exhibited an unthreatening posture, and held it loosely, letting it dangle at his side.

"Fear not, gentlemen. We have every intention of conducting this exchange without undue hostility," Borgia said with calm reserve.

Despite his assurance, the air was thick with tension. "All right then, let's get this over with," I pressed.

"Show us the diamond. If it is genuine, we will deliver up the dolls," Borgia bargained.

"It's genuine, make no mistake concerning that," the Professor certified.

From deep in his pocket he pulled forth the priceless treasure wrapped in a handkerchief and peeled away the cloth. Unveiled, the magnificent gem shimmered in the firelight with dazzling brilliance, reflecting and casting iridescence upon everything.

The eyes of our adversaries flashed with covetous desire. In the next instant, their countenance turned grim. Mallory raised the pistol and leveled it at point blank range straight at me, his finger now firmly wrapped around the trigger and murder in his eyes.

Borgia grinned wickedly. “Kill them, Gunston.”

CHAPTER 24

Mallory pulled the trigger, but the expected report never came. Instead, an empty click sounded, followed by silence as he pulled the trigger of an unloaded pistol again and again in mad frustration.

The Professor fixed his forceful gaze on Borgia. "Sir Mortimer!" he addressed in a stern forbidding tone.

Impulsively, Borgia met his gaze with an immediate expression of recognition, involuntarily giving himself away. The Professor began to chant. Slow and methodical, he demonstratively spoke in phrases comprised of strange inscrutable words, accentuating each syllable in order to achieve the precise pronunciation. Borgia's eyes flared wide with incredulous shock. Stricken by a sudden onset of inertia, he was powerless to act.

"No! Nooo! Stop him!" Borgia cried in desperation.

His echoing cries grew faint, ultimately to fade away in the far recesses and dark corners of the room. Mallory discarded the Luger; and even as he raced against time toward the fireplace and the dolls, it was already too late, for it all happened in the blink of an eye. Utterly unreal was the sight that seized my gaze, one that shattered my preconceived perception of the world and held me in the grip of bewildering astonishment. Borgia's flesh turned a milky pallor and took on a crusty texture, his hair became brittle and fell away, then the entire fabric of his altering physical body transformed into a compound of salts, which broke apart and crumbled into a reduced pile mixed amongst the bundle of collapsed clothing on the floor.

Mallory snatched the dolls from atop the mantel and vehemently pitched them into the burning hearth. Screaming, JB crumpled to the hard floor, writhing in a fit of sheer agony. Racked with excruciating pain, the Professor grimaced and groaned loudly, then crying out a long wail of anguish, he dropped to his knees, his body contorting like a crippled wretch. The diamond fell from his abandoning grasp, tumbling to the floor and skipping across the tiles. In that dire moment, even as their unbearable shrieks and wails assailed my ears like a rhapsody of madness, and the flames lapped over the dolls, the sparkling allure of the diamond just a short distance away was almost irresistible; but in comparison to the lives of my companions, it was insignificant.

I sprang to action with but a single aim driving me – to save the dolls. Mallory grabbed the fireplace poker, and moving to intervene, he raised it to strike. But I struck first, dealing him a fisted blow to the jaw. He reeled, losing his balance, and the poker swished through the empty air between us, barely missing my skull. Dazed, he staggered backward into the enveloping shadows; and grasping those brief fleeting moments before he could recover, I reached into the burning hearth with reckless disregard. Quick as lightning, I plucked the smoking dolls from the consuming flames; and in the next instant, I was down on my knees, frantically patting them with my hat to smother the lingering flames that still clung to their flammable makeup.

Anticipating an imminent attack, I glanced over my shoulder to see no assailant. Immediately, my eyes sought the diamond, but it was no longer there. Then as the screams subsided, the clapping of running footfalls captured my attention. Mallory's dimly lit figure was dashing toward a pair of crossed rapiers hanging ornamentally on the wall near the fireplace.

I rushed to intercept him; but he was already close, and I was too late. He seized one of the rapiers, and wielding it with the expertise of a master swordsman, he sliced the air to ribbons within an inch of my face, the motion of the blade so quick as to escape the eye. Now poised to run me through, he smiled maliciously, and when his eyes flashed, I knew it was coming. He lunged with murderous intent. I sidestepped, narrowly dodging the cutting blade; and taking evasive action, I retreated behind an interposing wing chair.

Instead of pursuing, he stepped in front of the fireplace and stood over the dolls. Firelight danced on the fabric of his dark suit and glinted down the length of the shining blade he brandished. Gleefully, he kicked the Professor's doll into the fire, and again the Professor's pitiful cries resonated throughout the room.

"Checkmate, Mr. Blake. I have the diamond, and now it is finished for you and your meddlesome colleagues," he stated with arrogant confidence, and he remorselessly kicked JB's doll back into the fiery furnace as well.

"Not yet, it isn't," I retorted, drawing Sadie's snub-nose revolver from my coat pocket.

At the sight of the revolver in my hand, Mallory furiously hurled the sword at me before I could take aim. The speeding deadly projectile sailed through the air toward me with uncanny accuracy. In the nick of time, I ducked just as the point struck the crown of the chair with a thud and lodged in the leather upholstery.

Every fiber of my being shifted into high gear. My nerves pulsed. My blood raced. I popped up, fully prepared to exact vengeance, but the contemptible object of my vindictive rage had vanished into thin air. Quickly, I looked to and fro, but he was nowhere to be seen. Could it be some devilish trick?

With no time to deliberate, once again I raced to rescue the dolls from the fire and extinguish the searing flames that inflicted such terrible pain and suffering upon my companions, singeing my hands in the process. That accomplished, I removed the blindfold from JB's doll, then picked up both dolls and rushed to guard over my companions, who were now recuperating from their harrowing ordeal. I helped them to their feet, while keeping a keen eye peeled for any sign of Mallory. Soon, it became apparent that he was no longer in the room, and I deduced that he probably had escaped by means of some secret portal.

"I can see!" JB rejoiced.

The Professor expressed exhilarated relief upon seeing the dolls in one piece and finding his treasured old pocket watch still in working order. "Where's Sir Gunston?" he inquired, anxiously looking about.

"I don't know, and I don't like it," I replied. "I took my eyes off him for just a few seconds, and when I looked again, he was gone."

"And what of the diamond?" he asked.

"That reprehensible fiend has it, and we had better get out of here post-haste before he or someone else shows up bent on our destruction," I said, retrieving my empty Luger.

"Just one more thing to do," he said; and bending over Borgia's remains, he scooped up a handful of salts and deposited it in his pocket.

"Is that Count Borgia?" JB asked.

"What remains of him," the Professor responded. "I'll explain it all to you later."

I reiterated our urgent need to make a fast getaway; and without hesitation, my companions started for the pair of doors that led to the landing, each dearly holding onto their respective likenesses.

"Not that way. They'll be waiting for us. The window – that's the ticket," I directed, pointing to the nearest set of drawn curtains.

I rushed over and threw wide the curtains. A tall arched window rising up from the floor opened to a balustrade. JB went first. Clasping his hands, I lowered him down to where he made the easy drop to the street below. The Professor tossed him the dolls and then went next. I was preparing to make the descent when the door handle began to turn, and with time running out, I jumped the precarious distance to the hard pavement, luckily landing without serious mishap.

Making all haste, we retreated into the night, and did not stop until we reached the arched footbridge that spanned the Grand Canal. There atop the bridge, the Professor emptied the morbid contents of his pocket into the dark waters. "May you rot in the eternal fires of hell, Sir Mortimer," he denounced as the salts poured forth from his funneled hand like the sands of an hourglass. Then he turned his pocket inside out and shook off the remnants.

Once back at our suite, my companions collapsed on their beds from sheer exhaustion, and for the first time in many nights they slept peacefully in an unbroken restful slumber. Even the Professor's snoring was a welcome sound. I, on the other hand, remained awake and vigilant for a time, finally dozing off as the breaking light of dawn repelled the dark shades of night and heralded the first day of a new year.

In the early afternoon, I awoke to find my companions refreshed. During lunch the Professor dominated the discussion, imparting his plan to dispel the black magic of the dolls once and for all. It involved a counter-spell derived from the pages of the blasphemous tome. He had made all the necessary preparations, except one: the ritual must take place on hallowed ground. He suggested using the ruins of an old stone church he had seen from the window of the train en route to Venice. The ruins stood atop a hill about a half-mile from the outskirts of a village on the mainland not far from here. The village had a train depot, affording us easy transport by rail, and the ruins would provide a suitable consecrated place to perform the time-consuming task with little probability of being detected.

He emphatically urged that we address this grave matter without delay; and after lunch, we packed the dolls and then caught the next train to the mainland. Being a holiday, the trains were not running on a routine schedule, and our wait at the station was a long one. The Professor carried a satchel over his shoulder, the contents of which clinked and clanked at times as he walked along. He kept it close at his side and never vouchsafed any indication as to what it contained. On the train, he sat in quiet reserve, his mind engaged in serious contemplation. Sometimes, he would momentarily look at me as if silently evaluating me and then reticently look out the window.

After a time, he pointed out the neglected ruins of a stone church in the passing scenery. Soon, the train crawled to a stop, and we debarked onto the platform of a nondescript little depot that linked a vagabond cluster of pastel structures with the outside world. The sun was dipping below the shadowy hills, relinquishing the sky to the gathering twilight, its last defiant rays casting their magical splendor upon the tiled rooftops, and everywhere in the crisp, sparkling air was the rigid spell of winter.

We procured accommodations at a quaint, modest inn, and shared an evening meal in the inglenook by a warming fire. The landlady treated us with utmost hospitality, and the locals, although curious, exhibited a friendly demeanor. We retired to our rooms shortly after supper with the intention of arising in the early morning hours and stealing away to the ruins when all were asleep in their beds.

Upstairs in the seclusion of the Professor's room, he imparted to me that which weighed so heavily on his mind. He was relying on me to perform the ritual, for he and JB would be under the hallucinating influence of the lotus extract, and all was to be entrusted to me. Their fate was entirely in my hands. This burden was something far beyond the scope of my purview, and although I expressed my reservation and doubt, he insisted it was the only way. Thus for the next few hours, he versed me on everything entailed and had me rehearse the prescribed incantations and procedures several times; but each time I failed, always making some mistake in the reciting of the alien words or in the performance of the unwholesome, bizarre rites. Despite my frustrating failures and shortcomings, he never lost patience, consistently exhorting and encouraging me in my efforts until we were both too exhausted to continue.

Sleep came to me sparingly in restless periods that were all too brief. My stomach churned with nervous jitters like a schoolboy dreading an exam, and as I mulled over my role in the upcoming incredible affair, it all seemed more like a dream than reality.

Too soon came the time when the Professor awakened us in the dead of night. Like thieves, we slipped away into the cold gloom to perform our secret deed. Furtively, we crept along the empty streets, three strangers passing unnoticed in the silent shadows, and then made our way up the moonlit path to the standing ruins.

Alone on the barren windswept hilltop stood the derelict shell of what was once a place of worship. Four remaining walls enclosed a roofless sanctum. Moonlight whitewashed the weathered gray stones eroded by time, and the dark empty apertures observed our approach like lonely eyes seeking solace. Inside, the church had long since been looted of its eminent trappings. The windows, pews and beams were gone, leaving only tumbled fallen blocks and an engraved stone altar overrun with creeping brambles and vines under a canopy of stars.

The Professor lit the lantern he had brought and turned the flame down low. "This will have to do," he solemnly said, standing before the dimly illuminated altar.

He retrieved the blasphemous tome from the satchel, laid it upon the altar and opened it to a page marked by a purple ribbon, then extracted three candlesticks and a chalice. He placed the chalice next to the book and arranged the candlesticks in a triangular pattern atop the vine-covered, hallowed stone. After the dolls were made ready and the candles lit, he poured water from a canteen into two tin cups; then producing the vial he had pilfered from Mallory's laboratory, he added the prescribed dosage of lotus extract.

JB took the cup passed to him willingly in the quiet, hopeful belief that his torment would soon be over.

Before drinking the potent drug, the Professor spoke a few last words to me. "Remember, the virtue of the magic lies primarily in the formula, which has been handed down from immemorial antiquity, hence, the insistence upon the correct recital of it, lest variation in the text render the magic of no avail. Any slip, any omission, any alteration of wording will deprive the magic of its efficiency. And do not forget the importance of the rites, the primary function of which is to convey the spell to the object or person which it is desired to affect. The rite is thus the vehicle of the spell and its equivalent, the translation of the word into action. I will be first. You know when to begin."

CHAPTER 25

JB lay unconscious upon the altar, all traces of his scar now completely gone; and as I spoke the final words to conclude the ritual, a cascading beam of morning sunlight poured through the tall empty window frame in the eastern wall, bathing the altar in golden rays of glorious radiance that carried the welcome promise of restoration. It was Sunday, and its dawning shone with spotless purity yet untouched by the corruption of the world.

Awakened by the bright light, JB sat up, and I wrapped his overcoat around his shoulders to shield him against the cold. Initially somewhat befuddled, he took a few moments to reorient himself; then upon discovering that he no longer bore the hideous scar on his chest, he instinctively checked for signs of a heartbeat. A broad smile lit up his face, and he hopped down from the altar.

"I'm delivered. You did it! I'm free!" he exclaimed with unrestrained elation, firmly shaking my hand and embracing me like a long lost friend.

Soon, the Professor too arose in good spirits: for by all indications the fantastic undertaking had resulted in success. "Well done, Mr. Blake," he said, bestowing congratulations and heartily shaking my hand as well.

The curse now lifted, the dolls destroyed, we knelt down and the Professor led us in a prayer of thanksgiving. A quiet comforting stillness pervaded the sanctuary; and with a renewed sense of peace we returned to the inn for a hearty breakfast. For the moment, we reveled in the gratification of accomplishment; but on the train back to Venice, the haunting awareness of unfinished business redirected our thoughts to the unresolved matter of what to do about Mallory, and of course there was the diamond to consider.

In the confines of our hotel suite, we deliberated the question openly. All agreed that Mallory deserved to be punished for his heinous crimes. However, without Inspector Geoffries' corroborating witness, no one would believe the truth, and thus we resolved to take it upon ourselves to duly pursue justice and reclaim the tablet. But as for the diamond, our motives differed. To me it represented wealth. My share alone would make me rich beyond my wildest dreams. The Professor's perspective remained purely objective and altruistic. To him, it was imperative that Mallory be deprived of the tools by which he planned to achieve his machinations, and the diamond was simply one such tool. He adamantly stressed that if allowed to succeed, Mallory would unleash an irreversible series of horrific events that would spell catastrophe and doom for the human race. JB was of like mind and noble sentiment. In his view, the welfare of humanity was exceedingly more paramount than any material gain, and he reiterated the Professor's assertion regarding the corruptive power of the diamond. Either way, I was bound and determined not to let that English popinjay make off with the prize.

In order to determine a course of action, we speculated what Mallory might do next or where he might go. We were fairly certain he would not return to England where he risked arrest; but the world is a big place, and a man of his means could hide just about anywhere. The Professor soundly conjectured that Mallory would seek refuge in the hinterlands of Africa amongst the Matoomba tribe, and he convincingly expressed the logical reasons supporting his deduction. Foremost, it was sure to be Mallory's ultimate destination sometime between now and the upcoming summer solstice; and once far beyond the jurisdiction of British law, he could bide his time, secure in the protection of the savage Matoomba. Also, Borgia's yacht granted a convenient and private mode of travel.

I recommended that we keep him under surveillance at least for now, discover what we could, and seize the first viable opportunity to act before he departed Venice. Persuaded by prudent reasoning, they agreed, and we decided to start that very afternoon. JB would watch the house in Dorsoduro, while I kept an eye on the yacht. Meanwhile, the Professor would pay the necessary call on the British consulate to notify them of Inspector Geoffries' death, and then get a good rest in preparation for his turn at stakeout duty. We departed our separate ways with the intention of meeting back at the hotel for supper to compare notes.

At the waterfront, I perched on a bench from which I gazed out at the shimmering waters of the lagoon. In the distance, the yacht 'Anaconda' lay at anchor with furled sails, her tall masts towering skyward. The world moved around me as I kept my attention focused on the tall ship, and after a while even time passed unnoticed.

Strangers shared the bench. They came and went in anonymity, until a peculiar man sat down. He immediately sparked my curiosity, for he was an odd sort, seemingly out of place. His overcoat denoted a man of class and taste, and his black oxford shoes were polished to mirror perfection. Deep wrinkles creased his rugged facial features weathered by time, and a woolen tweed cap covered a crop of neatly trimmed silver hair.

"Good afternoon," he cordially said, sporting an English accent.

I returned in kind.

"She's a grand vessel, the three-masted schooner you've been admiring. Sleek she is. I'd wager she's capable of eleven or twelve knots in a fresh breeze," he continued, striking up a conversation.

"I suppose so," I replied.

He smiled. "Allow me to introduce myself, Commander Harding, Her Majesty's Navy, retired."

His air of dignity and pleasant demeanor exuded an honorable charm. Again, I returned his outgoing gesture, giving him my name.

"Pleased to meet you, young man. Would you care to have a closer look with these?" he asked, offering me a pair of binoculars.

I accepted his kind offer and peered through the glasses, adjusting the magnification until the structural details of the schooner became well defined, such that even her name was readable. Fine-tuning the focus, I spied the unmistakable figure of Mallory standing on deck near the stern. He raised a telescope to his eye and began to scan the landward view. Inevitably, his searching eye looked in my direction, then to my relief, slowly passed on. It seemed I had avoided detection, when suddenly he reversed motion and trained the telescope directly on me. He leaned forward as if to verify his senses with a closer look. Our fixed gazes locked upon one another. Startled, he took a step backwards, lowering the telescope. He turned and spoke urgently to a man wearing an officer's cap, who then rang the ship's bell and shouted orders down the ladder way. Soon, the ship's crew was on deck, hastily preparing to set sail.

"So she sails on the evening tide," the Commander remarked. "Wonder where she's bound?"

"Cameroon, and it'll be the devil to catch her if she gets a head start," I indiscreetly said, revealing more than I wanted.

"You mean to catch her then?"

"If I had wings, maybe."

"It seems your interest in that vessel is more than mere fancy."

"You could say that," I stolidly said, and then I made a blind inquiry. "Would you know where I could charter a fast vessel?"

"I just might. Let us discuss it over tea," he unexpectedly replied with a kindhearted smile, and he stood up, inviting me to accompany him.

It was but a short walk when he gestured to a rowboat moored at the water's edge and directed me to climb in. "Watch your step," he said as he untied the mooring line and climbed in after me.

Taking hold of the oars, he pushed off, and then he began to row out into the lagoon. He was a fit man for his age, for he rowed at a good steady pace.

"Mr. Singh makes an exceptional pot of tea. Met the fellow in Bombay," he said whimsically.

Even though it all seemed a bit queer, I sat tight and humored the man. Eventually, my curiosity was appeased as our apparent destination loomed ahead – an impressive sailing vessel of similar type and size as the 'Anaconda'. He eased the rowboat up alongside, and we ascended a temporary set of boarding steps to the deck above.

"Welcome aboard the 'Traveler', young man, my pride and joy," he proudly proclaimed with an almost youthful enthusiasm.

I was amazed at the pristine condition of the vessel. It bore all the marks of sedulous care. The woodwork and brass were polished, the decks spotless, and everything trim.

"I like to keep things ship shape and Bristol fashion," he boasted.

A breeze swept over the deserted deck and whistled through the hollow rigging. "I granted the crew liberty for the day," he informed. "But Mr. Singh is about, probably somewhere below deck. Follow me, if you please."

He led me down a narrow companionway to the deck below and cordially conducted me to a spacious cabin with all the sumptuous trappings of class and comfort. Military honors and medals were framed and prominently displayed on the wall above a shelf bearing trophies, an inlaid cabinet sported a collection of guns, and the stuffed head of a roaring tiger was mounted above the door.

"Mr. Singh," he summoned through the open cabin door, and he bid me to sit at a dark-wood table in the corner. "Mr. Singh!" he called out again. "Confound that fellow, where is he?"

Shortly, a swarthy man wearing a white coat and turban appeared in the doorway.

"Ah, there you are. My guest and I will be having tea, Mr. Singh," the Commander fondly requested.

Mr. Singh bowed his head. "Yes Sahib," he deferentially said – and withdrew.

"Remarkable fellow, don't know what I'd do without him," the Commander commented.

In his next breath, my gracious host offered me a spot of gin, and after pouring two small glasses, he sat down at the table. "To your very good health, young man," he toasted, then emptied his glass and poured himself another.

It took more than one swallow to consume the strong drink, and when I had, he refilled my glass, adding a measure more this time. I remarked with inquisitive interest as to his various accolades, to which he told me the stories behind them and then regaled me with fascinating tales of his career at sea in the Royal Navy, which included an account of his harrowing experience during the battle of Jutland. "Nip and tuck it was, and Gerry firing shells that fell so perilously close the spray washed the decks," he claimed. His well-told adventures captured my attention, and I barely noticed when Mr. Singh returned with a tea set and a plate of scones.

"So tell me, young man, why the keen attraction to that schooner you were observing?" he casually inquired, reclining back and sipping his tea.

His curiosity seemed genuine, and I felt there was nothing to lose by telling him the truth. "I'm a detective from Boston, and I'm pursuing a fugitive from both American and English justice. The man is a criminal who will stop at nothing. He's even responsible for the murder of an inspector of Scotland Yard – and he and his accomplice are aboard that ship."

"Murder is it?" the Commander remarked. "And an inspector no less. Why not just arrest the man?"

"I wish it was that simple. He's one difficult customer and sly as a fox."

He reflected on my words with a contemplative expression. "A fugitive from English justice you say?"

"I have the warrant for his arrest right here. It's issued by your authorities in London," I said, presenting it for his inspection.

The commander read the document, intelligently scrutinizing it for authenticity. "It seems the matter is clear then. Well, by Jove, we can't just let the villain get away, now can we?" he excitedly said. "Ah, a noteworthy challenge, and I believe the 'Traveler' will manage quite nicely," he continued with a gleeful smile, rubbing his chin. "I'm delighted to assist you in any way, detective. Consider the 'Traveler' at your disposal. We'll beat the bloody rascals to Cameroon, and you can catch your bird."

It seemed a chance encounter had laid opportunity in my lap, and I accepted his offer without hesitation. Pleased, he beamed with eager enthusiasm, speaking of the upcoming voyage as if it was some race with a trophy to win.

"I'm traveling with two companions who also have a stake in the matter – a Harvard professor and a doctor. Can you accommodate them as well?" I asked at the risk of imposing.

"Most assuredly," he responded with agreeable certainty. "Suitable quarters can be arranged for three passengers. You might find the cabins a tad cramped and uninspiring, but they're comfortable enough. I'll have Mr. Singh prepare them. I welcome the company and fresh faces, detective, and the opportunity to introduce some excitement to what otherwise has been a mundane routine as of late."

After tea and a diversion to more casual conversation, he conducted me topside, where he firmly shook my hand, cementing his hospitable offer. In the distance, the 'Anaconda' was under way, and heading into the twilight toward the open waters of the Adriatic.

He saw the apprehension displayed in my expression as I gazed at the departing vessel. "Don't worry, detective," he confidently assured. "The 'Traveler' is fully capable of surpassing any lead. And we have a significant advantage – she doesn't know she's being pursued."

"Don't underestimate him," I forewarned. "He's crafty, and has an uncanny knack of being aware of the impossible."

He pointed out that he presently lacked a crew and urged patience on my part. We then boarded the rowboat, and he ferried me back to shore. I offered to row, but he declined, remarking how the robust exercise was good for one's vitality.

"Get your gear, and report back here with your companions by 0900 tomorrow morning," he instructed when I had disembarked.

"Tomorrow morning?" I questioned impatiently.

"That will allow sufficient time to plot a course and stock up on proper provisions. Furthermore, I have no doubt the crew will be full of wine upon their return. Until tomorrow, detective – don't worry, we'll catch your bird," he said as he rowed away.

At supper, I relayed the news of Mallory's departure to my companions and then dispelled their resultant despondency with all the news of my fortuitous encounter with Commander Harding. I recounted the afternoon's events in detail, noting the peculiar but gracious nature of our new found benefactor, and described his sailing vessel, assuring them of the Traveler's capability to overtake our adversary.

Next morning after an early breakfast, we checked out and hired a gondolier to take us to the spot where the Commander had dropped me off. Two crewmen from the 'Traveler' dressed in sharp blue and white uniforms were there to greet us. They transferred our belongings to a waiting ship's longboat and rowed us out to the splendid sailing vessel anchored in the lagoon. The Commander welcomed us aboard, and after proper introductions, he showed us to our cabins, which were as quaint as they were confining.

The Commander wasted no time in getting under way; and when we had settled in, we went up on deck to find him at the helm and the crew working with the harmonious precision of a well-oiled machine. A man introduced to us as Mr. Hightower was shouting orders. A brisk breeze filled the sails, and the vessel was already making good headway on a heading of south-southeast.

For two uneventful days we sailed, during which my companions spent considerable hours relishing in the respite of sleep. At the Commander's sumptuous table we listened to his entertaining stories, while dining on delicious fares prepared by Mr. Singh. The serene sea voyage granted me time to reflect. Many times my thoughts lamentingly returned to Boston. At other times they were consumed with the haunting allure of the diamond, something that kept my vigilant eyes searching the horizon for any sign of the 'Anaconda'.

On the third morning, the rising sun cast an ominous red hue across the sky. A crewman on watch loudly announced the sighting of another vessel. "Ship off the port bow," he shouted out.

Mr. Hightower was at the helm, the Commander leaning on the aft railing nearby. "Steady as she goes, Mr. Hightower," the Commander ordered, and he proceeded to the bow.

I hastily joined him and stood anxiously at his side while he peered through binoculars at a looming speck on the horizon.

"Three degrees to port, Mr. Hightower," he called back.

Mr. Hightower turned the wheel. The deck tilted, the swelling sails stretched, and the strained rigging creaked as the ship picked up speed, slicing the rippling blue surface as if riding on a cloud. Slowly the gap closed, and the emerging outline of a tall ship became clearly distinguishable.

"There's your schooner, detective," the Commander said, handing me the binoculars. "It's her, all right. She's flying the flag of Venice. The same colors she was flying when she left port."

Within the highly magnified scope of the binoculars, I descried Mallory at the railing intently gazing at our approaching vessel through a spyglass. Apparently, he discerned me as well. The African man was on deck, and at a word from Mallory, he lifted his face and arms to the heavens. Moving his upraised arms in a swaying motion, he appeared to chant.

Shortly, the skies darkened as a rolling canopy of black sullen clouds gathered, blotting out the sun. Instantly, the wind increased to a furious pitch, and the once relatively calm sea grew angry, erupting in towering swells that thrashed against our intrepid vessel. The ship rocked from the force of crashing waves that now relentlessly pounded the hull and swept over the deck. Roaring gusts ripped the fabric of the sails to tatters, rigging snapped, and a swinging boom, which had broken loose, hurled a hapless crewman overboard headlong into the tumultuous sea.

All at once, everything was chaos. The Commander shouted something to me, but no earthly voice could penetrate the tempestuous roar that deafened my ears. The deck rolled wildly on huge cresting waves that threatened to capsize the vessel, and it was all I could do to keep a handhold. A crewman emerged from below deck and made the arduous endeavor to reach the Commander's side. Cupping his hand over his mouth, he yelled into the Commander's ear. The Commander's expression exploded in alarm.

Resorting to hand signals, the Commander enlisted the aid of several crewmen and myself in readying the ship's longboat. JB and the Professor appeared on deck. JB was tightly holding the blasphemous tome under one arm and steadying himself with the other. The Professor was clutching a life preserver, and his distressed state reminded me of a conversation we once shared in which he told me he could not swim. Without warning, a monstrous wave engulfed the deck in a mighty torrent. I held on for dear life as the rushing water buried me; and when I had shaken off the daze, the Professor and Mr. Hightower no longer remained. They had been swept away. With no one manning the helm, the ship now floundered aimlessly.

At the Commander's direction, JB and I climbed into the ship's longboat, our eyes and voices desperately searching for any sign of the Professor. Mr. Singh was about to climb on board, and two crewmen were poised to lower the boat, when an enveloping wave crashed over the deck. The pulleys broke from their mountings, and the small craft plunged into the heaving turbulence.

Somewhat swamped, but afloat, the tender was swiftly carried away by the raging sea; and despite all exhausting efforts to the contrary, the distance between the small craft and the ship continually widened until the volatile waves, which tossed us about like a toy, blinded us to all but the blackened sky and the treacherous turmoil around us. Then upon being lifted up on a rising swell, we briefly sighted the hapless vessel. Amidst the pandemonium on her deck, the Commander and a crewman were at the helm, vainly struggling with the wheel when another massive wave struck. The masts snapped as if they were toothpicks, and the reeling ship listed precariously. She disappeared from view as our small craft descended into a deep trough between two waves, and when we rose up again, she had vanished.

Trying to shout above the screaming wind, JB and I frantically called out for the Professor; and after a time, despondency gave way to despair.

CHAPTER 26

Under the constant harrowing prospect that the agitated sea would sink our insignificant craft at any moment, we weathered the storm for some time until the sun's rays pierced a rift in the clouds and the waters calmed. Cold, wet and exhausted, we succumbed to sleep, leaving the boat to wander adrift on the vast desolate expanse.

When I awakened, it was twilight and night was fast approaching. As my clouded eyes adjusted, I caught sight of a dark funneling shape on the near horizon, a rising shadow silhouetted against the deepening blue. Was I dreaming? Was it some phantom vortex designed for our destruction? No, it was surely a plume of smoke drawing nearer, and the source became apparent, as the outline of a steamer loomed larger. Immediately, I roused JB, apprising him of the approaching ship; and driven by the potential for rescue, we frantically searched for any viable means of hailing it. Fortunately, the Commander had prudent foresight, for stowed in the bow was a survival kit containing first aid supplies, fresh water, and more importantly, several signal flares.

I ignited one of the flares, and it burst with an intense flame of phosphorescent red. Holding the bright torch aloft, I slowly waved it back and forth to hopefully increase our chance of being spotted. The beacon must have drawn attention, for the steamer abruptly changed course and headed in our direction, its running lights now turned on, shining and twinkling in the creeping gloom like luminary bodies sent from heaven to bestow deliverance from the depths of tragedy. The thumping drone of the steamer's engines grew louder and louder until the pulsing rhythm drowned out all other audible impressions. Then, when the sizeable vessel, which dwarfed our minuscule craft, was almost upon us, the engines ceased, and the steamer slowed to a stop a short distance away. With JB now holding up the flare, I rowed like the devil to reach the steamer. A man at the railing with a lantern called out in a foreign tongue, and as we drew close, a Jacob's ladder was lowered over the side of the hull. Weathered, rust-stained letters painted on the bow spelled the name 'Jade Duchess'.

I grabbed the tome, JB went first, and we clambered up the ladder while a number of shadowy faces peered down at us. When we reached the top, two sets of strong hands hoisted us each in turn over the railing and roughly placed our feet upon the deck. Around us stood a motley gang of ruffians drawn from the dregs of disparate races, cultures and nationalities, all of them examining us with ruthless eyes that glared with almost sinister intent.

"Look what the sea coughed up. They've got a book, must be a couple of schoolmarms," said a dark-skinned one, and they all chuckled.

"I say we throw 'em back," said another.

"No, I say we make 'em stoke coal," said a longhaired, ugly soot-faced man sporting a gold earring.

"Gangway!" came a commanding voice from behind them, and they parted for a tall, stalwart Caucasian figure wearing a worn leather jacket and a dirty white officer's cap with a black visor. A well-trimmed flaxen beard accented his Spartan facial features and his eyes glistened with keen wit. Beside him was a burly, bald-headed middle-eastern brute with a nasty curved dirk tucked in his wide belt.

"There'll be none of that. Now get back to your duties, you pack of despicable derelicts, all of you, or I'll have your livers for dinner and throw the rest to the sharks!" the man in the white cap barked in a fearless, intimidating voice. "Time is money."

"What about the dinghy?" asked one, cowering.

"Cast it off," came the authoritative reply. "And the rest of you disperse. Now be off with you!"

There we stood, JB and I, thoroughly drenched and shivering from the cold, not knowing if we had been rescued or had exchanged misfortune for adversity.

"I apologize for your less than cordial reception. I'm Captain Butch Harmon," the man in the white cap said, his speech articulate and his accent clearly American.

The brute merely grunted.

"This is Ahmed. He's mute. The Turks cut out his tongue," Captain Harmon informed about the giant of a man. "Come with me, and I'll see to your comfort." He turned to the Brute. "Have the Spaniard crank the engines. Resume course and speed. We've a schedule to keep."

The Brute nodded in compliance, and following orders, he ascended the companion ladder to the bridge.

"You're not the only stranded fish we plucked from the sea today," Captain Harmon conveyed as he conducted us to the galley.

His inadvertent words sparked a glimmer of hope, and when we entered the galley, our faces lit up with elation, for seated at a table was none other than Professor Hanson wrapped in a dry wool blanket and sipping hot coffee. At the moment nothing else mattered, and together again, we rejoiced in the miraculous reunion that providence had seen fit to orchestrate.

"I assume these are your lost companions," Captain Harmon remarked to the Professor.

"Yes, Captain," the Professor affirmed, parading a wide smile. "Allow me to introduce my good friends, Doctor JB Hawkins and Mr. Conrad Blake."

Captain Harmon then had us provided with blankets, hot soup and coffee, and whiskey to take the chill off. "I'll see that you get some dry clothes," he assured. "Also, the passenger berths are unoccupied at present. You can make use of them for the time being."

"Did you find any other survivors?" JB asked the Captain.

"No, you're it, although we did spot some wreckage near to where we picked up Professor Hanson," he replied.

"What is your next port of call, Captain?" the Professor inquired.

"Trieste, and that's where we'll put you ashore."

"Sir, it is imperative that we get to Cameroon with all haste. Would you transport us there? We can pay for our passage."

"Out of the question. After Trieste, we sail to Cyprus, and I stand to make a handsome profit on the trip."

"We'll pay you five thousand dollars," JB vehemently interjected, naming a more than exorbitant sum.

The Captain's eyes grew wide, and his face froze in a stunned expression. "That's a tidy sum. Considering your current circumstances, I'd like to see as how you produce that kind of money."

"I have a letter of credit in that amount. And if you take us to Cameroon, I shall endorse it over to you when we arrive."

"Let's see it," Captain Harmon skeptically requested, cocking back his cap.

JB produced an envelope wrapped in wax paper to keep it dry, opened it, and presented the folded contents to the Captain.

"Drawn on the Bank of Boston, eh," Captain Harmon remarked as he read the financial document. "Right now I'm a little tight for cash, and this won't pay a cash-starved crew that demands immediate gratification or buy coal for the journey," he said, handing it back.

JB pulled out a wad of wet bills and peeled off several hundred dollars, "Will this suffice to get us there? And when we arrive, the letter of credit shall be yours."

"This'll do for starters," Captain Harmon said, pocketing the money. "Gentlemen, you just bought yourselves passage to Cameroon."

Presently, no one else occupied the galley except the cook. "Breath a premature word of this and it'll be your last, Frenchy," Captain Harmon said to him in a tone that left no discretion as to the reality of the threat.

"Oui, mon Capitaine," came an obedient reply.

The Captain returned his attention to us. "Nevertheless, we sail to Trieste first," he dictated. "We've a cargo to unload and the coal stores need to be replenished. After that I'll transport you to Cameroon as fast as the engines and weather will permit.

It was the only deal in town, and considering our predicament, we agreed and graciously thanked him for rescuing us.

He left us to see about some dry clothes and later returned to conduct us to our berths. Upon each of our bunks lay a change of clothes that were better suited for a man of menial task, and the fit was almost comical.

Captain Harmon had the engines running at full speed the next day, and on the following day, the steamer lay at rest in the port of Trieste. During the short stay, we invested the time to procure clothing. One proper fitting set made for a woefully insufficient wardrobe. The aftermath of the crew's decadence while in port somewhat delayed our urgent departure, but once the 'Duchess' was under way, fair skies greeted us and the empty hold augmented our speed. We stopped in Algiers long enough to top off the coal stores, and then the ship's course took us through the Strait of Gibraltar into the Atlantic and south along the west coast of Africa.

As the passing days grew warmer, the ceaseless rapid drone of the engines began to wear on the nerves; and in inclement weather, the rust bucket pitched and rolled, inducing a queasy uneasiness that usually confined me to my bunk. Captain Harmon often invited us to dine in his cabin. He had an American heritage, having grown up in Baltimore where he signed onto his first ship at an early age. An avid reader, he took pride in showing off his collection of books, which consisted of numerous classic volumes and learned texts on various subjects, and boasted that he was self-educated, adept in literature and mathematics. He relished the intellectual conversation we provided, and he proved to be quite knowledgeable, especially in his discourse with the Professor. They spent hours engaged in games of chess. According to the Professor, Captain Harmon was a surprisingly challenging opponent who demonstrated exceptional mastery of the game.

The Captain was an enigma. One side of his personality wore a rough exterior – brute, confident and authoritative, keeping the motley crew of ruffians in line through sheer intimidation and fear. Versed in several languages, he routinely barked at them in their own native tongues. However, his private self was quite different in contrast; that part was a tame man of reason who craved knowledge and ardently strove to expand the mind through intellectual pursuits. "Knowledge itself is power," he frequently proclaimed, quoting Francis Bacon. The parts added together produced a man who was shrewd, calculating and cunning.

Although we had fair roam of the ship, we were never alone. A prying ear or a watchful eye hiding behind a pretense of indifference was always conspicuously near. On one occasion, I returned to my berth to find my passport out of place. On another occasion, the three of us were gathered in my berth speaking indiscreetly. I felt a draft and discovered a slightly open porthole behind the drawn curtain. Thus far, we had not divulged our true purpose, and the alarming prospect that someone out on deck might have been eavesdropping sent a shudder of anxiety through our speculative thoughts.

After that, we kept a tight lip and our passports close. All seemed as if our secret was safe, and we bided our time trying to fill the empty boredom. But on the last leg of the journey, our fear of exposure confronted us head on. We were dining with the Captain in his cabin as we often did. In the middle of the meal, he casually reclined back in his chair, one side of his mouth curled up in a sly grin and a keen glint in his eyes. No questions had been the understanding, yet he boldly broached that topic we had done our best to elude. He began testing the waters with subtle inquiries, to which we responded with evasive answers; then he struck with direct probing questions that had us struggling to concoct one fabrication or half-truth to cover another. When his game of wits had us cornered, he played his cards.

"You're prevaricating, and Doctor Hawkins makes a bad liar," he stated, seemingly amused. "Don't look so shocked, Doctor. I'm no fool! Your venture is no mere excursion. Otherwise, why would anybody pay five grand to hurriedly reach a destination that has absolutely no appeal? And you have to admit, the three of you do make a curious combination."

He leaned forward, studying our expressions.

"You're treasure hunters – plain and simple," he asserted. "Correct me if I'm wrong. You desperately need to get to Douala, Cameroon in time to intercept some rival, an Englishman named Mallory; because he currently possesses something you're itching to get your hands on – a rare diamond! Worth a king's ransom, I would venture. There's also the matter of an artifact he swindled from you. And one can't ignore the palpable evidence, such as that relic of a book you saw fit to save."

"Nothing more than wild speculation, I assure you," the Professor indignantly returned.

"I think not."

"So what?" I interjected. "What does it matter who or what we are? Our business is our own."

"It doesn't matter one bit as far as I'm concerned," Captain Harmon said, reclining back in his chair. "I just wanted to root you out, so I could propose an addendum to our deal."

"And what might that be?" I asked, coming directly to the point.

"There's only two ways out of Douala: the jungle or the sea," Captain Harmon expressed. "Assuming you find this Englishman, your handiwork, whatever that might entail, may draw the attention of the French authorities. You don't want to risk a stint in a French penal colony. It's a living hell, and the survival rate is abysmal. The 'Duchess' can provide a ready means of escape should you need to make a fast getaway. I can see to it that she's available for your immediate departure and conveyance to the destination of your choosing."

He paused, waiting for a response.

"What's in it for you?" I asked.

"The price for this ace card is simply an equal share of the treasure. That, of course, hinges upon your success – something I'm banking on."

Speechless, the three of us exchanged glances while the Captain's scrutinizing eyes searched our faces.

It was the Professor who took the initiative. "At present, I'm afraid we are unable to grant you the satisfaction of a definitive answer. However, in the time remaining, we will duly consider your interesting proposition, and advise you of our decision at the conclusion of our original arrangement," he categorically stated.

Captain Harmon swilled his wine. "Fair enough," he conceded. "Weather permitting, we should arrive at Douala in approximately forty hours," he informed, and then he changed the subject entirely.

In the morning, the Professor asked JB and I into his berth. Speaking in a hushed whisper, he strongly advised not to accept the Captain's proposition, and he reminded us of the tale of Matteo Veneti, stressing the parallel and emphasizing how covetous desire had spelled ruin for both ship and crew.

"Captain Harmon's knowledge of the diamond is too dangerous," he declared. "Should by divine providence we succeed in our endeavor, it would be extremely unwise to bring the thing aboard this ship. Its allure is too great, and its corruptive power would inevitably breed violence. Our lives would be in danger every minute."

"It does smell of a trap," I said. "What's to keep us from being robbed and thrown overboard once we're at sea? Or more likely, it would be our murdered corpses that get tossed in the drink. I agree, let's roll the dice and take our chances without his involvement."

JB was in full concordance. "Personally, I find the man's integrity to be highly suspect, and the sooner we disassociate from this band of unscrupulous pirates the better," he assessed.

Growing anticipation pricked our nerves as the remaining hours ticked away. That evening we endured one more dinner with the Captain; and after a sleepless night, I gazed out my porthole at a green coastline.

By midday we were steaming into a crystal blue harbor resting in the overshadowing presence of a tall majestic mountain with soaring ridges that climbed to lofty heights where the peak became lost in a ring of clouds. A sprawling mass of shanties crowded the shoreline and crept up an inland rise, fishing boats lined the sandy beaches, and larger vessels lay quietly at anchor in the shelter of the harbor. My searching eyes sought one in particular, and initially I was somewhat relieved to discover it missing; that is until I descried three tall masts jutting upward from behind a derelict wreck in the foreground. As we slowly steamed past the hulk and the view became unobstructed, the full form of the sailing vessel emerged; and my thoughts started to swim in a pool of mixed emotions when I recognized the unmistakable features of the 'Anaconda'.

CHAPTER 27

On one hand, Mallory had won the race; but on the other hand, the Professor had been correct in his reasoning, and with luck, maybe our quarry was still close at hand. JB endorsed the letter of credit, thus concluding our arrangement with the Captain, and we tactfully informed him of our decision to part ways.

Brandishing a conniving smile, Captain Harmon pocketed the financial document. "It's been a pleasure, gentlemen. Fastest five grand I ever made. I'll miss our chess games, Professor. It's hard to find an opponent of your caliber," he said. "Anyhow, we'll be moored here for a couple of days should you change your mind."

When we set foot upon the dock, we found ourselves far from home on the threshold of the African continent, a vast and foreign land with whole unexplored regions that fiercely guarded their hidden secrets from the world. A brilliant sun adorned the day and bathed us in a warmth that compared to a summer's day in Boston. In my notes from that first night were a name and address: Jake 'Brandy' Brandon, Hotel L'Afrique, Douala, Cameroon; and with the hotel as our predetermined destination in mind, we entered the town, hoping among other things to hit on a cold lead.

Speaking French, the Professor asked directions from a barefoot local wearing a Dashiki, and we made our way along unpaved streets under the eyes of curious onlookers. Narrow alleys haphazardly branched off here and there, each disappearing in a squalid maze of ramshackle hovels and huts, and an offensive stench drifted up from a shallow ditch that served as a gutter. A bustling open-air market had exotic fruits and strange viands on display; vendors marketed wares of all description, and half-naked small children played about the sullied skirts of women who balanced burdens on their heads.

Dominating a square in the European sector stood the Hotel L'Afrique. A covered veranda adorned with gazebos stretched around the two-story structure, and atop the roof, the French flag hung listlessly on a flagpole. Inside, the lobby flowed out to the veranda through tall empty apertures with open shutters; white wicker chairs and tables were arranged in settings bordered by decorative potted plants; and electric ceiling fans circulated the stagnant air. Neither our hope nor fear of a chance encounter with Mallory was realized, and nowhere was his visage present amongst the occupants of the lobby. We checked in with the desk clerk, who spoke rudimentary English with a thick French accent, and settled into rooms that overlooked an enclosed courtyard in which a flourishing tropical garden teemed with magical colors beyond imagination.

Downstairs, we began our inquiries with the desk clerk. Mallory's name was unfamiliar to him, but he immediately recognized the name Jake Brandon; and much to our thrill and surprise, he informed us that 'Brandy' was in the hotel bar at that very moment.

Three patrons occupied the establishment. At the bar, a smartly dressed Legionnaire, sporting a well-groomed moustache, was conversing in French with a man wearing a white suit and Panama hat. At a table, a man clad in khakis was slumped in a chair, his dirty boots propped up on the table and a sweat-stained slouch hat cocked down over his face. The Legionnaire took immediate notice of us when we entered, and his eyes followed us as we approached the bar.

The bartender was slow to address us, another victim of the lethargy that seemed to afflict everyone in the town. In response to the Professor's question, he pointed to the man in khakis. Seemingly dead to the world, the dormant figure remained motionless as we stepped up to his table. The Professor questioningly addressed him in French, but the statue never stirred. "Monsieur? Monsieur Brandon?" the Professor continued, raising his voice a notch. Coming to life, the subject of our prodding slowly lifted his head, tilted up his hat and glared at us from under the brim. An unruly scruff carpeted his square jaw and halfway hid a nasty scar that extended down his nose and across his cheek.

"That's my name – and you can dispense with the French," he said with a touch of annoyance in his voice.

Relieved that he preferred English, I politely introduced my companions and myself in a conciliatory manner. "May we have just a word with you?" I asked.

"Buy me a drink," he stipulated.

"Name your poison, and we'll join you," I replied.

He removed his feet from the table and sat up in his chair. "In that case, have a seat," he said, and he called out an order for four double ryes straight up.

As we sat down, I wondered about this man, and for some reason, I could not picture him fitting in anywhere else.

"Let me guess. You want to go on safari," he presumed. "Well, if your intention is to kill for sport or profit, I'll have no part of it."

"We're not interested in a hunting expedition. We thought you might help us by answering some questions."

"What sort of questions?"

I retrieved the photograph showing the members of the Bradford expedition from my pocket and placed it in front of him. "Do you recognize this man?" I asked, pointing to the image of Harold Drayfus.

The moment he cast his eyes on the photograph his expression went completely blank, and wide-eyed, he stared down at it as if an unwelcome memory had abruptly been awakened.

"Oh yes, I know him all right," he soberly stated. "I ought to, I've been to hell and back with him. He's an American anthropologist named Harold Drayfus, but I guess you probably already know that. As for the others, I know them too, or knew them, should I say. They're dead – all except Drayfus, and you won't find him here. He left months ago."

"How do you know they're dead?" I queried.

"Because I witnessed it all," he shot back; then he swallowed his drink in two quick gulps and ordered another on our tab.

"Then you were with them when they died?"

"Killed – or murdered is more like it."

"How is it that you and Drayfus survived?"

"That's a long grueling story. One I'd rather forget."

"Look, we're friends of Harold Drayfus," JB communicated. "And we're trying to find out what happened while he was in Africa. You're the one man who can tell us. Is there anything that can persuade you?"

"If you're friends of his, why don't you ask him yourselves?"

"We can't. He's dead." I informed.

After breathing a lamenting sigh, he assented to tell the 'damnable' tale, and requested the whole bottle, saying he would need it. He downed his second drink, and when the bottle came, he poured himself another. For a brief while, he collected his thoughts; then in a solemn voice, he provided the remaining pieces to an unfinished puzzle.

"It's been nearly a year and a half since that fateful day when they engaged me to be their guide. Oh, their intentions were high-minded enough, and they were most insistent on following the footsteps of two lost colleagues. Everything started off without a hitch. We traveled upriver by launch, safely reaching Baneard Station with ample supplies and ardent spirits. A Lutheran doctor runs a hospital and mission there. The natives are friendly, and we were able to take on bearers for the overland journey.

"Shady and faded word of their lost colleagues compelled us to journey eastward into the interior. The days passed without incident, and each evening, Dr. Gibbons and Sir Charles painstakingly documented and cataloged samples of plants they had collected, along with wildlife they had observed that day. Many times our progress was halted so that Dr. Gibbons could sketch a drawing of some observation. He was a good artist and his depictions were strikingly detailed. Your American friend was eager to learn the customs of the peoples we encountered. He wrote copious notes and asked me a never-ending fountain of questions. I took a liking to his good nature, and we struck up a friendship. Bradford was a pompous ass, who regarded the indigenous peoples as uncivilized savages, lacking in Christian virtues.

"Anyway, information derived from friendly tribes and promising rumors of a party of whites, pressed us onward toward the mountains and the inaccessible reaches beyond. At times, the dense vegetation slowed our going to a sluggish pace. The oppressive heat and stifling humidity exacted a heavy toll on all, and rest periods became more frequent and longer. Lord Robert possessed an indomitable spirit. When the going got overly demanding, he was always assisting and exhorting the others to forge ahead, and making light of the difficulties.

"The mountains presented a formidable obstacle, but I know of a pass – a series of caverns carved out long ago by a subterranean river. Our superstitious bearers refused to enter the dark narrow entrance, fearful of the mountain spirit that dwelled within. It took considerable coaxing to avert a mass desertion and get them moving. Poor fellows, they were spooked the whole way, and Lord Robert had to take up the rear to prevent any from bolting. After navigating the sometimes treacherous path by lamp and torch, we emerged into the sunlight and stepped out onto an outcrop overlooking a plush, green valley. Far in the distance flowed the mighty river Sanga, and the jagged peaks of the Three Sisters stood tall against the Eastern sky.

"That night, a refreshing breeze blew as we camped on the slope, and it was good to see the stars again. At daybreak, we broke camp and descended into the unknown wilderness of an uncharted region. Driven by hope and determination, we were oblivious to the lurking danger that lay ahead."

He gazed into his glass for a few moments, then swigged his drink, wiped his lips with his sleeve, and poured another.

"As we ventured deeper into the recesses of the valley, things began to go amiss. First a strange phenomenon occurred. Every compass went haywire, and not one of us could make sense of it. Then I discovered a single curious observer hiding in the brush. He was with us for a while, content to keep his distance, and then mysteriously vanished into the jungle.

"Not long thereafter, drums started to sound – and that's when things got hairy. I didn't recognize the repeating sequence, but I knew it heralded no good. Terror-stricken, the bearers stopped dead in their tracks, and completely unnerved, dropped their loads and deserted on the spot, running away like frightened sheep.

"Bradford grumbled over the loss of the bearers, and precious time was lost in the panic of indecision. By the time the essential supplies were divided amongst us, it was too late to follow suit. A host of hostile warriors were encroaching on all sides. Hopelessly outnumbered, we took cover, readied our weapons, and mustered our nerve for the inevitable assault. By all rights we were dead men!

"Unexpectedly, they didn't immediately attack. Instead they made us sweat, and the prolonged suspense was unbearable. Every sporadic rustle in the brush, every glimpse of movement gave strength to the gripping fear, until time stretched to the point where we welcomed the storm and wondered why they just didn't rush us and get it over with.

"Suddenly, as if out of nowhere, a lone warrior adorned in a headdress of lion's mane deliberately emerged from concealment and boldly stood in the open. White paint masked his dark face in the gruesome image of a human skull, and his stark, powerful frame towered well over six feet. His nearness and size made him an easy target; but he took no aggressive action, which caused me to think he might want to parley, and I stayed Lord Robert as he raised his rifle to fire.

"Silently, the skull-faced warrior stretched out his arm, pointing his spear in the direction of the river. There was little doubt as to the meaning of his unspoken communication; but in that moment of uncertainty, reluctance seized us, and Bradford, ever the arrogant blowhard, adamantly argued that it was a trick, contending that the bloody rascal be shot straight off. The darn fool would have done it too if I hadn't stood in the way.

"Again and more sternly, the fearsome figure made the directing gesture. This time it wasn't a request. It was a demand; and considering the alternative, I implored the others to concede to reason on the offhand chance our lives might be spared. Bradford sputtered and spewed, but under the threat of abandonment, he was quick to catch up as the rest of us followed the warrior's lead to whatever destiny awaited.

"Scores of devils became visible and kept pace on either side, providing an escort that hemmed us in and prevented any escape. Some came so uncomfortably close you could see the whites of their savage eyes. They intimidated us with taunts and antagonizing gestures, but I showed no fear and encouraged the others to do the same.

"Eventually, the jungle receded, and we came to the edge of an expansive glade. The hot afternoon sun beat down on us as we stepped into the open. In the clear distance, nestled along the river, was a sprawling metropolis of thatched huts enclosed by a wooden palisade. Drums beat, horns trumpeted, and the gates opened as we approached. The jubilant warriors danced and beat their spears against their shields in a disconcerting, harmonious rhythm as they paraded us down an avenue before the gawking eyes and jeers of the gathered populace; and when the gates closed behind us, I began to abandon hope, feeling as if we were sheep being led to slaughter.

"We were presented to a large bulbous-bellied man garbed in regal trappings of lion's hide and seated in a raised thrownlike chair under the cooling shade of the shadow cast by the great round hut behind him. To his right stood a youthful man of stature. A leopard's hide draped his shoulders and crowned his head; in the crook of his arm he cradled an ivory scepter ornamented with a leopard's paw; and around his neck hung a necklace made from the teeth of a great cat. Their dialect was not dissimilar to other tribes in the region, and I was able to pick up a few key words. Based on my interpretation and the angry tone and gestures of the warrior presenting us, our fate looked rather bleak indeed.

"The kingly fat man brushed the warrior aside with a motion of his hand and then sternly gazed at us as if he was deciding what judgment to pronounce. The others were getting restless, and Lord Robert asked for my assessment of the situation. At that moment, the leopard clad man, who had thus far remained stoically silent, stepped forward, and much to our surprise, spoke in oxford English. He stated that we were unwelcome trespassers on Matoomba land, and as such would be tried by tribal law. It was, as I had feared. We had fallen into the hands of the legendary Matoomba – a tribe of ruthless cannibals.

"Then, something entirely unexpected happened that saved our skins, at least for the time being. A white man in shirt and trousers emerged from the crowd and approached the king. Several members of the expedition recognized him, and when Bradford called him by name, I realized he was one of the very men we had been searching for all that time. Speaking their language fluently, he appeared to be interceding on our behalf. Whatever he said worked, for the king acquiesced with a nod. Then our intercessor addressed us, telling us that if we wished to live, we should immediately surrender our arms as a token of good will and bow low before King Paga. Well, that seemed to appease the fat king, and sentence was suspended. Hearty handshakes ensued, and I was introduced to the most guileful man I ever met – Gunston Mallory.

"He cordially introduced us to King Paga, who spoke a little English himself, and to the man clad in leopard hide, a man he called Manbootu, a witchdoctor of high status. When his elder brother, Sir Jonathon, and his nephew, Edward, appeared on the scene, gratified spirits held the day, for the search was finally over, and a long arduous journey had come to a celebrated end. Sir Jonathon was an amiable man worthy of his title, and young Edward was a strapping lad with a bright smile and courteous disposition. However, he could not resist the beckoning call from a group of other boys his age, and soon, with the permission of his father, he was off to play.

"A curious crowd followed close behind as Gunston and Jonathon conducted us to a large sturdy hut, which was to be our lodgings, and we were afforded with all the amenities of welcome guests. Gunston curtly cut short the barrage of questions, assuring that all would be answered in good time, and strongly suggested we stay put until he returned. After he and his reticent brother departed, the speculations flew, and the warriors guarding the entrance made me feel more like a prisoner than a guest.

"That night our presence was required in the great hut, where we dined on uncertain fare amidst an uneasy atmosphere presided over by the gluttonous king. All the tribal bigwigs were there, along with the Mallory brothers and Manbootu, the witchdoctor, whose piercing eyes seemed to read your very soul. It was some powwow all right – with us as the main topic.

"While Gunston eagerly played the role of interpreter, Jonathon said nary a word. He seemed tense, and kept rubbing his hands on his knees. When it was time for us to return to our lodgings, he turned to Dr. Gibbons seated next to him, and with a handshake, secretly slipped him a note. On the paper were scribbled two words – 'help me'.

"That's when the undercurrent of fear evolved into a real sense of danger, and I kept one eye open that night. Come morning, Gunston dropped by to see how we were getting along. Jonathon accompanied him, and in their wake several native girls came bearing bowls of food. Their visit was cordial but brief, and once again urgent inquiries went unanswered. Jonathon stuck primarily to the proper exchange of amenities, choosing his words carefully as if keeping up appearances. Gunston insisted that we remain in our hut for our own safety and promised to return in the afternoon. As they departed, Jonathon lagged behind, and when the others had gone ahead, he turned in the entranceway to face us. Barely able to contain himself, he said our presence was a godsend and entreated us to take him and his son far away, for his brother's obsessions had turned to madness, and he was planning something terrible. Then he clammed up, and heeding his brother's call, he left us perplexed and pondering.

"Gunston returned that afternoon alone, only to be assailed by a torrent of pressing demands for a complete account. He was congenial and bubbling with enthusiasm as he imparted the news his colleagues had long awaited to hear. He fervently informed of his recent experiences and findings, how he had been abiding with the Matoomba people for some time, studying and learning all the aspects of their rich culture. He had even been inducted into the tribe, and had since achieved a position of high status. He was extremely genuine, and while he exhibited prideful zeal, nothing in his manner supported the suspicions bred by Jonathon's portrayal.

"Over the next few days, our movements were much less restricted, and the atmosphere more relaxed. Yet one thing persistently perturbed me. Not one of us was able to speak with Jonathon alone. He was always conspicuously absent or in the company of Gunston.

"Then one day, Gunston confided to his three Royal Society colleagues about a momentous discovery he had made, and took them up into the mountains on the other side of the river. There, he showed them the site of ancient ruins and an inscrutable tablet of great antiquity; and when they returned, blank eyes stared out from the ashen faces of Bradford, Gibbons, and Sir Charles as if they had experienced some traumatic shock. Dr. Gibbons had to be guided and assisted, and for several hours he lay in a wide-eyed, unresponsive state, muttering and murmuring to himself. What exactly happened up there they would not say, but they were convinced that Gunston was indeed mad, and delving into things beyond the laws and boundaries of acceptable science. Together they decided to persuade Gunston to return to England and seek treatment.

"When next Gunston came around, he got a reception he didn't expect. They argued and tempers flared. It ended with Gunston calling them narrow-minded buffoons and storming out. After that we were confined to our hut again. The next day, Gunston gave them a chance to change their minds, but the lines had been drawn. He said that they should never have come, and since they chose to oppose him, they would pay the price for their insolent interference.

"He gave an order in Matoomba over his shoulder, and a group of fierce warriors entered the hut. Amidst a hail of protests, which Gunston coldly ignored, our wrists were bound. We were rowed across the river by canoe, and then he and the witchdoctor led the way as we were forced to climb a steep narrow path that meandered up the rugged mountainside. Those who stumbled or delayed were prodded with the point of a spear to get them moving. The arduous climb up that dangerous slope ended atop a ledge dominated by a giant projecting rock formation that resembled the visage of a roaring lion. Perfectly arrayed stalactites formed a row of teeth, and within the gaping jaws was the dark mouth of a cave.

"Torches were lit, and we proceeded through the opening into a mammoth cavern. Centrally located on the floor of the cavern lay a large stone disk engraved with etched drawings and symbols. Several warriors moved the disk aside with surprisingly relative ease, uncovering a pit from which spewed forth maddening moans of agony amidst a hideous cacophony of indiscernible screams and cries. Gunston said that the natives called it 'the pit of screaming souls', and told Bradford he was to be the first. Bradford struggled with his heathen captors as they forced him toward the edge of the pit. Fortunately for me, I did not see what awful peril that pit contained, but its unsettling impact was clearly evident in the look of abject horror on Bradford's face right before they pushed him in, and then one more scream joined the cacophony. Next went Sir Charles Kettering, who displayed dignity and showed no emotion until he looked into the pit, and when he did, he uttered an exclamation induced by sheer terror. Then came Dr. Gibbon's turn. He earnestly appealed for mercy, but to no avail, and he too was pushed into the pit. Then the disk was replaced, covering the pit and silencing the screams; and that's the last I saw of Bradford, Kettering and Gibbons.

"Gunston had a different fate in store for the rest of us, and we were taken back to the village to be tied to posts outside the great hut. That evening, Drayfus and I watched while they roasted Lord Robert alive, delighting in his horrid screams, and then feasted on his cooked flesh. The sickening sight only intensified the awful reality of knowing we were on the next day's menu. Seated beside the king, Gunston gloried in his hierarchic position; however, Jonathon was absent from the celebrations that lasted well into the night.

"When all fell quiet and the village was asleep, a crouching figure emerged from the shadows and moved swiftly towards us. Upon reaching us, the bent figure stood erect, and I saw the face of Jonathon Mallory illuminated in the moonlight. He quickly set us free, then handed us each a revolver and compass, and motioned for us to follow him. Silently we crept as he led us to the gate where two guards slept unawares. Drayfus and I slipped outside, but Jonathon, for some reason, remained behind. I asked in a whisper if he was coming with us, to which he somberly shook his head no and closed the gate. So under the cover of darkness, we darted for the dense jungle and possible escape, unable to even express our gratitude.

"Despite our evasive efforts to thwart pursuers, we didn't make it far before being hunted down and recaptured. Somehow they found out who helped us, 'cause they dragged Jonathon into the central clearing and tied him to a post. The whole village was there to witness the abominable proceedings, along with Gunston, who sanctioned it all.

Being bound and most unwilling observers, we were powerless to help Jonathon. In a gruesome ritual, they sacrificed his son before his very eyes, and the atrocities they committed upon Jonathon were unspeakable.

"We were then interned in a hut to await our own ghastly demise; but we had no intention of sticking around for dinner, and working together, we immediately set about trying to free ourselves from the bonds that restrained our wrists and ankles. Our joint efforts eventually paid off without alerting the guards outside the entrance.

"While we cooked up a daring plan of escape, providence intervened and came to our rescue, presenting an uncanny but timely opportunity. It started with a rumble. Then the ground began to violently quake and tremble. The hut creaked and swayed, threatening to collapse at any moment. Outside, cries of panic resounded everywhere and the guards had deserted their post. With nothing to lose, we seized the moment and made a mad dash for the river. In the fright and confusion, no one made any serious attempt to stop us; and upon reaching the river, we dove headlong into the waters and started to swim downstream with the current, ignoring the ever present danger of lurking crocodiles.

"When we had attained a reasonably safe distance, we made for the west bank of the river and began the grueling journey to the coast. Sure to be hunted by the Matoomba, we kept on the move, and by the time we located the mountain pass that would take us out of the valley, we were utterly exhausted; but with certain danger at our heels, we pressed on into the dark underground with the aid of makeshift torches. Sheer will to survive drove us relentlessly onward; and after emerging on the other side, we subsisted on whatever nature provided, while combating the dangers of the jungle. Finally arriving at the haven of Baneard Station, we stumbled out of the brush, haggard and emaciated. Days later, my friend Dutch showed up in his launch right on schedule to deliver supplies, news and mail, enabling us to hitch a ride back to Douala.

"In his indignation, Gunston had told his colleagues that he would indeed return to England soon enough, but on his own time and for his own purposes. Banking on those words, we knew that sooner or later he'd have to show up in Douala. He did. But in spite of our vigilance, he slipped through our fingers and shipped out on a three-masted Schooner. Drayfus left shortly thereafter in pursuit, and that's the last I saw of him."

A drawn expression on his face, Jake Brandon refilled his empty glass and reclined back in his chair, drink in hand.

I addressed him as Mr. Brandon, and he cut me short. "Call me Brandy, everybody else does," he casually insisted.

"Ok, Brandy, we have news for you. Gunston Mallory is back," I flatly informed him.

His face lit up. "Here? Here in Douala?"

"We followed him here," I replied. "He couldn't have arrived too far ahead of us. So chances are he's still around, probably on his boat. We only just arrived ourselves, and haven't had time to track him down. You obviously must know this port. Would you help us ferret him out?"

"Sure, I'd love to get my hands on the bastard."

Just then, a burly black-skinned native wearing only a pair of tattered trousers came rushing up to the table in an excited state. "Boss! Boss!" he echoed loudly, addressing Brandy, and then he rattled off something in his native tongue, Bantu.

"Later," Brandy responded.

"But boss!" the man protested.

"Later, I said," Brandy forcefully reiterated. "Right now I have a job for you." He relayed some instructions in Bantu and then placed a coin in the man's hand.

"Right away, boss," the man compliantly said, and he hurried off.

"That's Ben," Brandy related. "He's my right hand man – and a good one too. He was born here. After the death of his parents when he was young, he became an orphan living by his wits on the streets 'til a missionary took him in. He knows just about everyone and every shanty. I put him on the hunt, and if Gunston Mallory is anywhere in the vicinity, we'll soon know. It won't be hard. A white Englishman stands out like a bright moon on a clear night. Meet me back here at sundown. By then I'll know something. In the meantime, I have a pressing matter to attend to. Until then, I bid you adieu." With that, he polished off the last remnants from the bottle and left.

At nightfall we returned to the bar to find Brandy seated at the same table, drinking his fill. He displayed the signs of both intoxication and disappointment, and his first words were not encouraging.

"Seems our man boarded the train to Widimenge yesterday. Widimenge is the end of the line, where the last influences of western civilization intrude into the interior. By now he's already there, and I've got an easy bet on where he's ultimately headed."

"That's exactly why he must be stopped," the Professor strongly stated. "There's still time. With your skill and experience as a guide, we stand a good chance of catching him if we act quickly."

"Hold it right there," Brandy interposed. "In the first place, what do you mean we? And in the second place, if you think for one minute that I'd set foot in that devil-infested valley again, you're out of your mind."

"Should we catch him in time, you won't have to," the Professor assessed. "If it's a question of money, you'll be paid handsomely."

"Do you understand the time and hardship involved in such an undertaking? Not to mention the hazards. I'd like nothing better than to get my hands on the man, but I have other plans. I'm going back to British Columbia. It's been far too long since I've seen my native land. Besides, the cute doll over there already made inquiries," Brandy said, casually pointing toward the bar. "And from where I'm sitting, she's got a lot more charms than you."

CHAPTER 28

All eyes looked in the direction Brandy was pointing. At the bar stood a slender young woman. How long she had been there I could not say. She was wearing Khaki riding pants tucked in tall brown leather boots and an olive green shirt; and her long brown hair was pulled back and woven in a single braid, revealing all the pleasant features of her pretty face. JB's initial curiosity burst into an expression of surprise and recognition, and she, upon second glance, froze with astonishment before a spreading smile produced dimples on her cheeks. JB bounded to his feet.

"I don't believe it! JB – JB Hawkins!" she excitedly exclaimed; and then she rushed to him, threw her arms around him in a friendly embrace, and kissed him on the cheek.

"What are you doing here?" he asked in the reproving tone of a protector.

"I came here looking for Harold. It's been so long since we received any word," she replied. "Oh please, tell me you know where he is."

JB was silent.

She discerned the reticence in his eyes and all remnants of her smile flew away. "You do know, don't you? Please tell me, JB. Where's my brother? What's happened to him?"

"I have something terrible to tell you, Kitty. Your brother is dead," he answered with mournful reluctance.

Tears welled up in her eyes and trickled down her innocent cheeks. "Oh, dear God, no," she uttered through quivering lips.

"I'm afraid it's true," JB sadly confirmed.

Her tears now came in streams. She buried her face in JB's shoulder and wept uncontrollably. JB held her in his arms and tenderly consoled her until her sobs subsided.

She looked up at him with grieving eyes. "How?" she pleaded.

"Murdered."

His response left her puzzled. "Murdered? When?" she asked, wiping away her tears.

"Last December."

"Why would anybody want to kill Harold?"

"He was silenced because he knew a dangerous secret. I'm here with two friends, and we're after the virulent fiend who orchestrated your brother's death."

JB took that moment to cordially introduce Kitty Drayfus. She recognized the Professor by name. Her brother had spoken of him often, always holding him in high esteem. She expressed herself with grace and dignity, and I could not help but admire her courage and resolve. Gladly accepting our company, she joined us at JB's invitation.

She immediately addressed Brandy. "I heard what you said to these gentlemen, and I implore you to reconsider and help them find my brother's murderer. I appeal to your sense of honor and justice – if you have any. Or are you a coward?"

"Listen here, missy. I'm no coward," Brandy indignantly returned.

"Then help them," she pressed.

"It's not a question of bravery – or money. Like I said, I have other plans."

"Can't you postpone them?"

While Brandy searched for a reply, I interjected. "There's something you don't know," I said. I rapidly scanned the room, and seeing that no one appeared to be interested in our conversation, I continued in a lower volume. "Knowledge so enticing, that at the very least, it may give you sufficient cause to abandon your plans."

"I'm listening," he said, leaning forward, seemingly intrigued.

"Mallory is in possession of a diamond," I directly imparted. "Not just any diamond, a gem of such amazing size and magnificent splendor, that the very sight of it inspires wonder and awe. Imagine being rich beyond your wildest dreams. We get him, we get the diamond."

"I can assure you that he is on the level," the Professor solidly confirmed.

Brandy rubbed his chin. "Now there's food for thought," he said. "Just how big of a diamond are we talking about?"

"Approximately 2.8 inches in diameter," the Professor answered.

Brandy's stunned expression was met by three affirming nods. "Holy mother of…!" he remarked, and during the long silent pause that ensued, he deliberated the implications of our claim.

"No wonder you're so hell-bent on catching the man," Brandy stated. "Ok – count me in. I'm not one to pass up the chance of a lifetime. But there are several things we gotta get straight up front. First, you foot the bill for the necessary equipment and supplies. Second, I need three hundred francs. I've some debts to settle. And lastly, this isn't gonna be some stroll in the park. We'll be traversing inhospitable terrain under harsh conditions. That leaves the girl out."

Kitty fumed, and her face developed an ugly scowl. "I'll have you know, I can endure hardship with the best of them, and I can outride and outshoot any of you," she adamantly declared.

"Missy, you've no idea what you'd be getting your pretty little self in for," Brandy impassively returned.

"He's right, Kitty. It's for the best," JB calmly told her.

Still, she stubbornly argued the point, but Brandy would not budge an inch.

"We'll have to wait for the train to make the return trip from Widimenge," Brandy said, continuing with the matter at hand. "And it won't be ready to depart again until the day after tomorrow. That'll give us time to procure what supplies we can, and store them overnight at the depot. The rest we can pick up in Widimenge. And I strongly suggest you outfit yourselves with proper attire. I'll meet you in the hotel lobby tomorrow morning around nine. As for the money, it can wait 'til then."

He firmly shook our hands to seal the pact. The diamond card had been played, and the allure of the colossal gem had captivated another victim. It was a dangerous card to play, one that could portend disaster, but even the Professor privately admitted later that evening that it was an acceptable risk worth taking.

As arranged, Brandy was waiting in the lobby the next morning, and we embarked on the key task of procuring essentials for the journey. Throughout the day, Brandy took us here and there, supervising the acquisition of the things that we would require. At one shop, a rack behind the counter displayed several rifles. Brandy inquired about the Remington that used to occupy a now empty slot, and the storekeeper informed that it had been sold earlier that same day. By the time the day's affairs were settled, JB's money was nearly tapped out and a bulk of parcels sat on the platform at the depot. To deter any thieves, Brandy called in a favor from Major Leblanc of the foreign legion, the colonial authority, who obliged to post a guard over the goods.

Early the following day, my companions and I arrived at the depot to find Ben and a couple of laborers loading the supplies onto a flatcar, which also provided austere accommodations for those passengers that could afford nothing more.

"Boss not here, but he come soon," Ben spouted in broken English.

Anxiously, we waited on the platform, keeping our eyes peeled for an unmistakable figure. Then, with time running out, and the train scheduled to depart, Brandy decided to show. He strolled up with an easy strut, a haversack slung over one shoulder, a cartridge belt slung over the other, and toting a double-barreled gun. A sharp whistle blast announced the train's imminent departure. Ben hopped on the flatcar, and we hurried to board the passenger car, getting aboard just as the wheels began to roll forward with a grinding squeak.

As we made our way down the aisle, a striking face stood out from the others. Kitty Drayfus sat by a window, a haversack and Remington rifle beside her on the long seat. She acknowledged our approach with an unruffled expression of bold determination.

"Good morning, gentlemen," she smartly greeted.

"Missy, I thought I made it clear that you were not to come on this expedition," Brandy snarled.

"Yes, I let you express your point, but I'm here now, and the train is moving. So you see, you have little choice," she defiantly stated.

Brandy unwillingly resigned himself to the reality of the situation. "All right, have it your way," he sourly conceded. "But don't expect any special treatment. And let me remind you, the untamed wilds of Africa are not the backwoods of New England."

He chose a seat on the other side of the aisle, and after shedding his gear, he settled back and pulled the brim of his hat down over his face. JB and the Professor sat in the company of the girl, and preferring to stick close to my companions, I joined them.

"No wonder you said your goodbyes at breakfast instead of seeing us off at the depot," JB said to her.

"Please try to understand. This is something I have to do. He was my only brother, and I loved him dearly," she said.

"I assure you Miss Drayfus, no one here doubts your noble intentions," the Professor said with a comforting sense of understanding that melted her defenses and put her at ease.

In the ensuing relaxed atmosphere, a conversation spawned in which I found myself a passive listener, learning more about the notable character of a man I never met. They whiled away the hours recounting memories of Kitty's brother. JB told numerous tales of their days at Harvard. Some were solemn and personal, while others were amusing and pitched with such humor they excited us to laughter. The Professor spoke of a man of high promise, and Kitty related stories gleaned from their youth. It was an impromptu funeral, and each one of them was giving their own special eulogy.

Slow and steady, the locomotive pulled the heavy train along tracks that crossed over trestlework bridges, rambled through deep forests, crept around tight bends, and followed the course of an indomitable river, before crawling to a stop at a vagabond riverside settlement in the middle of nowhere.

Long shadows signaled the closing day when we debarked. Brandy, who so far had been close-lipped about the details of our route, now disclosed the next leg of our journey. He had wired ahead to secure our mode of transportation, and pointed to a broken-down steam engine launch docked at the riverbank. We were to travel by boat up the Nyong River to Baneard Station.

Ben stayed with the supplies, while Brandy led us to the boat. The name displayed on the bow, 'La Vierge Capricieux', was barely discernible, and the entire vessel was in dire need of a good coat of paint. A scrawny little man in oil stained overalls was tinkering with the engine under the shade of a canvas canopy. The wrench slipped in his hand, and in a fit of frustration, he spouted off a string of curse words.

Suddenly, he took notice of us, and a smile lit up his grease-smeared face. "Brandy my friend, so good to see you," he cheerfully acknowledged, wiping his hands on an oily rag.

"It's good to see you too, you shiftless rascal," Brandy amiably returned. "Wrestling with the old girl I see."

"She's been giving me trouble lately, telling me it's time to replace some worn parts."

"Will she be ready by first light?"

"She'll be ready all right, even if I have to kick her in the can."

Brandy then introduced his friend and associate, Dutch. "Best pilot on the river," he acclaimed.

"On the river, I'm a free man, answerable to no one," Dutch said. "I've seen spectacular wonders that very few white men have ever seen, wonders that thrill the soul and humble the heart. But like the rose has thorns that prick, nature can be cruel and unforgiving as she can be beautiful, eh?"

"When you're finished here, come by the Yellow Bird for a couple of snorts," Brandy said.

"And perhaps a few hands," Dutch eagerly suggested.

We left him to resume his repairs and went to secure lodgings for the night at the only place available, a run-down hotel named the Yellow Bird. That night, Brandy and Dutch tied one on in the hotel bar, gambling at cards and drinking till all hours.

At sunrise, our guide and pilot gathered their dulled senses; the supplies were loaded on board, the boiler was stoked, and we embarked on a journey that would take us into the remote reaches of a far away land. The launch slowly chugged along against the current, its stack puffing a constant trail of smoke. As the day progressed, I began to realize the extent of our isolation, and I was bewildered by the splendor and wonder of the abundant vegetation and wildlife. The river was not without its obstacles and danger. On one occasion, Dutch steered clear of a herd of hippopotamuses bathing in the cool water. One, a bull, raised his big ugly head above the surface, opened wide his massive jaws, and angrily groaned at us, while the peering eyes of crocodiles lurking at the water's edge watchfully observed our passage.

Afternoon slipped into evening. Dutch brought the launch to a halt by the riverbank; and while the last remnants of sunlight still remained, we set up camp for the night. Brandy cooked up a meal from the provisions, and we ate the filling fare around a comforting campfire. When it came time to retire, Brandy and Ben bedded down by the fire and took turns standing watch throughout the night, while the rest of us slept peacefully in the shelter of canvas tents.

Daylight came all too soon, and after a rushed breakfast, we were underway again. Around midday, a disturbing sight interrupted the monotony and ruffled our nerves. On the north bank, a stranded boat was snagged on a tangled mass of exposed mangrove roots. Dutch slowed the engine and steered toward the bank for a closer look. The derelict craft was empty and deserted with no visible clue as to why the craft was abandoned, nothing, not even the slightest trace to indicate what could have happened. The unsettling encounter cast a mournful shadow of dread on our party, and we were left to ponder the mystery as we proceeded on our journey.

The incident left Dutch riddled with apprehension, and although he tried, he was unable to hide the unknown fear that gripped him. He kept looking to the shore, as if some lurking peril lay concealed amongst the trees and plush ferns. Brandy avoided all eye contact and stared at nothing in particular. Ben too seemed distant and strangely troubled.

After a while, Ben turned to Brandy and ventured to pose a question. "Wambusi maybe?"

"Maybe," Brandy concurred.

"This not so good, boss. Wambusi bad – very bad."

Kitty inquisitively broke in. "Excuse me, but what on God's green earth is a Wambusi?"

"The question is who, not what," Brandy retorted. "For your information, the Wambusi are a hostile primitive tribe of vicious headhunters with a myriad of recipes for cooking human flesh. Fall foul of them, and you'll end up with your shrunken head hanging in a Wambusi hut. And your pretty little white head would be a prized trophy."

Kitty put a hand to her throat. Her face scrunched up in fearful disgust, and she swallowed her spit.

Just then, the engine started to emit a peculiar thumping sound coupled with an erratic banging. Dutch turned the tiller over to Brandy and rushed to read the gauges. He thumped his finger on the glass to exclude the possibility of a needle malfunction; and disconcerted, he grabbed a rag, which he used to frantically work a hot valve, allowing a violent emission of scolding steam to escape.

"We've got trouble," he declared, and he directed Brandy to steer for the near shore.

"Is it bad?" Brandy asked.

"If it's what I think it is," Dutch replied.

He shut down the engine, and the eerie echoing sounds of the jungle now predominated as the launch coasted up to the bank. Dutch sought to determine the cause of the engine trouble, while the rest of us anxiously waited on the shore. When he discovered the problem, he related mixed news. It was not as bad as he thought, but the repairs would take considerable time, several hours in fact.

Stranded, all we could do was linger in distress for the time being. The foreboding jungle encroached on three sides, and no one dared venture far from the perceived safety and refuge of the launch. Sunlight sifting through the jungle canopy speckled the blending shades of green with patches of gold, creating a dancing array that played on the imagination; and the ever-present threat of hostile natives kept us on edge, a tension that grew with the passage of time and tricked our minds into conjuring all sorts of menacing illusions. Brandy was constantly on vigilant alert, his wary ears listening for any sign of danger and his keen eyes searching the murky shadows amidst the dense undergrowth.

Finally, completion of the repairs brought a welcome sigh of relief. Dutch began stoking the boiler, and we considered ourselves on the verge of being delivered from a misfortunate situation, when Brandy suddenly cried out in alarm. Before I knew what hit me, a spear hurled by an unseen assailant struck me in the chest. Knocked off balance, I fell and collided with the ground amongst a batch of ferns, which obscured my sight. Pain seared my chest, and the ability to breathe escaped me. In a distant daze, I remotely heard the loud report of Brandy's elephant gun, followed by the crack of a rifle.

CHAPTER 29

Facing the prospect of death, I desperately sought to determine the severity of my wound; but to my utter astonishment, where I anticipated to find a copious flow of fresh blood, the fabric of my shirt was inexplicably bone dry. By some strange miracle, I was relatively unharmed, except for perhaps bruised ribs, and as I groped for an explanation, the source of the miracle readily became apparent. The badly dented whisky flask in my breast pocket told the story. By sheer luck, it had absorbed the brunt of the impact, saving me from being mortally impaled. A flask of booze, of all things, had spared me from death.

Immediately, I sprang to my feet. Violent pandemonium swirled all around me. At the sight of a dead man risen, several fiercely adorned warriors stopped dead in their tracks, and completely flabbergasted, gaped at me with wide bulging eyes full of fear. Like a contagious affliction, the paralyzing psychosis soon seized them all; and the melee came to a halt as even my companions stared in amazement and disbelief at my resurrection. Grasping a notion, I shouted insanely and wildly flailed my arms. As if they had seen a ghost, the superstitious natives turned tail and ran back into the jungle, shrieking and wailing. We boarded the launch in great haste, and Dutch made every effort to get us away with all speed.

Freed from a perilous plight, we counted our blessings. Fortunately, no one in our party had suffered serious injury during the brief scuffle; and everyone was curious to know the reason why I was still alive, for the spear should have pierced my heart. When I showed them the instrument of my preservation, the very irony induced smiles and laughter. Being a symbol of good fortune, the flask was jokingly proclaimed a revered relic and passed around in celebration.

That night we camped on the opposite shore. No fire comforted us, supper consisted of cold rations, and the lingering threat of another attack made sleep nearly impossible. Darkness lasted all too long, and at the break of dawn we set out again, eager to gain distance.

As the day wore on, I noticed a remarkable change in Brandy's attitude toward Kitty. He no longer resented her presence, and his once condescending tone had been replaced by cordiality and respect.

Somewhat perplexed, I inquired of the Professor as to what had sparked this strange transformation.

He obligingly replied. "That's right, you were incapacitated at the time, or so we thought. Suffice it to say, in an act of extreme courage, she saved his life back there. She's a young lady full of surprises."

Late in the afternoon, the welcome sight of our destination loomed ahead. Nestled in a clearing was the missionary outpost of Baneard Station. An elongated thatched building stood in the company of a mud brick church and a wooden house with a wide veranda, and nearby, a collection of huts lounged by the riverside. A middle-aged white man stood on a dock that jutted out into the waters, and he heralded our approach with a friendly wave.

"That's Doctor Otto Schwartz," Brandy informed. "The natives call him the white magician. The sick and injured travel for miles to seek his healing powers."

Doctor Schwartz was soon joined by a small gathering of natives, who greeted our arrival with enthusiastic curiosity. Speaking with a German accent, he gave us a hearty welcome, and he was delighted to hear that Dutch had brought much needed medical supplies. Happy to see Brandy again, and pleased at our company, he invited us to take refreshment at his house, and soon we were seated around a table in the shade of the covered veranda. Almost immediately, Brandy raised the subject of Gunston Mallory, inquiring if the Englishman had passed this way.

"Yes, he was here," Dr. Schwartz responded with contempt. "That madman terrorized us all at gunpoint, and his cohort was the devil incarnate. They pressed several able-bodied men from the village into servitude as bearers, took what they wanted, and headed east toward the mountain range."

"When did this happen?" Brandy asked.

"Two days ago. If you seek to find this Englishman, you must not delay. Obviously, you will need bearers for the journey. Considering recent events, you may find that difficult. I will speak to the village elders on your behalf."

"We'd be much obliged," Brandy said. "We have some splendid goods in payment. We want to get an early start come morning. When can you and I speak with them?"

"No time like the present. Shall we go now?"

Brandy and Dr. Schwartz then started across the clearing toward the gathering of huts. Some time later they returned, having achieved positive results, and final preparations were made for the morning's departure.

That evening we dined on the veranda with Dr. Schwartz, who was glad to have the company of a younger practitioner. He queried JB at length concerning the newest developments in medical science, and their intellectual discussion on the subject dominated the conversation. Even so, Kitty's attractive appearance was not lost to our gracious host's attention. It had been a long time since he had the opportunity to talk with a young lady of western persuasion. Something about the place made time stand still, and it was late when Brandy advised us to get a good night's sleep, for an arduous trek lay ahead.

Early the following morning, Dr. Schwartz bid us farewell with a blessing of Godspeed, the bearers picked up their loads, and Dutch waved a last goodbye as our party disappeared into a dense primeval forest. Enormous trees grew to towering heights of two hundred feet or more, where a vast canopy of leaves and limbs screened the sun's rays. Orchids and Arums covered their broad trunks; and an immensely thick assortment of tall leafy plants flourished in the scattered sunlight and shade on the forest floor.

Hour after hour, we doggedly trudged onward with little afforded rest. In all directions a deceiving sameness distorted one's sense of bearing, and the compass was frequently called into requisition. Sometimes, Brandy and Ben had to use machetes to cut a path through the impenetrable foliage. Danger lurked everywhere, for the region was infested with venomous snakes and wild beasts of prey roamed the forest. Mosquitoes constantly harassed us. The stagnant air was suffocating, and despite the shade of the forest canopy, the stifling humidity and oppressive heat caused one to sweat profusely. Every stitch of clothing became miserably soaked and clung to the skin like sticky paste. The Professor regularly removed his pith helmet to wipe the dripping perspiration from his brow and neck. He was not the only one coping with the strain of hardship. I too felt the taxing drain, as did the others; except for Brandy and Ben, they on the other hand, were apparently acclimated and immune to the grueling climate and harsh conditions.

Sunset brought respite, and supper was devoured with such ravenous intensity that all vestiges of urbanity were tossed to the wind; even JB shoveled the fare on his tin plate into his mouth with no other consideration than to feed his hunger. After every allotted portion was consumed, exhaustion from the day's toil swiftly crept up with a subtle, irresistible force. The Professor fell fast asleep seated with his back against a tree, his empty plate and utensils still resting in his lap; and I have to admit, that upon reaching the confines of my tent, I succumbed to the most delicious sleep imaginable.

One day dragged into another on a quest that drove the body to the extreme limits of endurance. On the surface was the virtue of a valiant crusade, resolute and determined; yet all the while, underneath, in those remoter regions of consciousness, where secret emotions are kindled and fueled, the inexorable allure of the diamond burned like an inextinguishable flame.

At times, Brandy picked up hints of our quarry's trail. He was on friendly terms with those native tribes we encountered, and communicated in their inscrutable languages with impressive proficiency. Word from them and telltale signs along the way revealed evidence of Mallory's passing; and each successive discovery brought the promising realization that we had closed another measure of the gap. The discovery of a recently abandoned campsite indicated that our quarry was indeed close at hand, but a long torrential afternoon rain did much to wash away the distinguishable traces of the path forged by his party.

Then the awe-inspiring mountains rose before us. Steep rocky slopes and torn ridges, unyielding in defiant challenge, soared to angry, perilous summits that thundered their dark terror in the sky.

By now the trail was hot, and we picked up the pace, hoping to catch Mallory before he reached the mountain pass. It was Kitty who sighted him first, and Brandy confirmed it with his binoculars. Mallory's party was ascending the hazardous slope toward the entrance to the caverns. Moving amongst the rugged terrain in the early morning light, they appeared now and then for brief intervals only to vanish into the landscape again. The extreme range made any shot difficult, if not impossible, and so the chase was on. Brandy ordered Ben to take charge of the bearers, and we raced to reach the slope and close the distance, leaving the short-legged Professor and the bearers to keep up as best they could.

Taking desperate chances in our haste, we clambered up the escarpment, expending every ounce of strength, every measure of stamina to maintain the strenuous rate of climb, while betting against the risk of being spotted from above. That risk became a real threat, and in an instant, events took a dangerous turn when a bullet struck a boulder close to Brandy and the crack of a rifle echoed down the mountainside. Everybody scrambled for the nearest cover. Brandy dared to peer through his binoculars, and almost had his head shot off by a solitary round that grazed his ear. Expletives shot from his mouth as he ducked down and pressed a hand to his ear.

"Nearest I can figure, there's just one, but whoever the s.o.b. is, he means business," our guide assessed.

Motionless we remained, afraid that any abrupt movement, any attempt to hazard exposure, might draw the sniper's fire, and after a period of nerve-racking tension, the sniper called out.

"Is that you, Brandy?"

An expression of unwelcome recognition seized our guide. "Yea Rimshaw, it's me. I see you're still catering to the wrong sort," he shouted back.

"Man's got to make a living," came the response. "I'm not saddled with a high-minded conscience like you."

"No argument there. So why shoot at me?"

"Can't afford to have you doggin' our steps. Those first two shots, they were just a deterrent. Next time I won't waste ammunition. Do yourself a favor, turn around and go back."

Further up the mountainside, several pistol shots rang out. Distressing cries of panic erupted – then two more shots – then dead silence, even the still air refused to whisper a breeze. Disconcerting speculations ran amok amidst the confusing fear as we frantically sought to devise a swift plan of action; but before any daring scheme could be executed, another new and unexpected development entered our harrowing circumstance – from a different direction, near and behind, the startling report of a rifle abruptly broke the uneasy hush.

Rimshaw emitted a woeful groan followed by the clink and clack of his rifle tumbling on the rocks; and while we pondered the mystery of what had just occurred, the distinct sounds of someone approaching elevated the nerves to the pinnacle of apprehensive anticipation, shortly to be deflated by sheer relief when Ben came crouching into our midst, a beaming white smile contrasting his black-skinned face and a scope-equipped rifle in his hand. With a proud heart, he verified that it was his feat of marksmanship that felled Rimshaw, an act which earned him praise from our guide.

During the lull that followed, Brandy again peered through his binoculars, but spotted no threat; and after instructing us to stay put, he boldly ventured up the slope while Kitty kept him covered. When he safely reached Rimshaw's position, he signaled for us to come up, and we climbed the rugged incline to find him stooped over Rimshaw, who was still alive and bleeding profusely from a chest wound. Ever the humanitarian, JB immediately examined the man's wound; and after determining the wound to be mortal, he regretfully stated that the man's condition was hopeless and there was nothing he could do.

Rimshaw grabbed Brandy by the shirt. "Don't leave me to the vultures," he pleaded, sputtering and coughing blood.

He then asked for a drink of water, and Brandy gently lifted Rimshaw's head and put a canteen to his lips. "Looks like your associates deserted you, old man," Brandy said.

"Damn traitorous bastards. Get 'em for me, will ya?" Rimshaw petitioned, his voice growing faint.

"You bet," Brandy assured him, and then Rimshaw breathed his last.

Lost time and frustration unlocked the callous and calculating side of our trusted guide. He seemed unmoved by the lifeless body of Rimshaw as he ordered Ben to hastily fetch the rest of our party and have the bearers bring up our gear. Taking charge, he enlisted me to accompany him, and we hurried the remaining distance to the cavern entrance, leaving Kitty and JB to wait for the others.

Nothing could have prepared me for the shock of the grisly scene we discovered. Before retreating into the heart of the mountain, our adversary had left behind more than abandoned equipment and supplies. Mallory had shot his own bearers in cold blood, two in the back as they tried to escape; and at that moment, as the sickening impact rushed upon the soul, evidence of a deadly peril instantly struck us dumbfounded. First we smelled it – the acrid stench of burning sulfur. Then we heard the audible impression of it – a distinct fizzle. Then we saw it – a sparkling fuse connected to a bundle of dynamite that had been placed just inside the dark crevice, and the fuse was nearly spent.

CHAPTER 30

Every reflex sounded alarm, yet in that charged split-second that defines destiny, when one does not necessarily act upon instinct, the fever of the diamond obscured all reason and dominated decisive thought. My heart racing furiously, I dashed foolhardily to the explosive bundle and snatched it up in almost a single motion, and with only seconds to spare, hurled it in the direction deemed safest. It sailed through the air, the fuse sputtering and trailing sparks, and then arched into a tumbling descent of several hundred feet down the steep falling slope, where it exploded in midair with a force that rocked the mountainside. Every bird within a mile took to flight, filling the air with avian cries of distress amidst the ebbing boom.

"That was close – too close," Brandy remarked, removing his hat and wiping his brow with his sleeve.

Hails and calls of concern resounded from below, and by the time Brandy shouted back in reply, several members of our party were already making the ascent. The first to reach our position was Kitty and JB. The sight of the slain bearers appalled both of them. Kitty turned away and became violently ill, while JB made a vain attempt to discover if any still clung to life. Shortly, the Professor arrived on the scene. Huffing and puffing, he leaned against a rock to catch his breath.

"Oh my Lord," he exclaimed in horror, his voice subdued. "What happened here? What was that tremendous explosion?"

"Gunston Mallory shot these poor innocent souls, probably because they refused to enter the caverns, and then he rigged a bundle of dynamite to blow the entrance and obliterate all traces of his dirty work," Brandy answered. "Conrad here saved the day by tossing the lit dynamite down the mountain."

Time was the enemy. Anxious and agitated, Brandy shouted down to Ben to speed things up, but the difficult climb retarded the laden bearers to a sluggish pace. Impatient, he paced to and fro, and kept peering into the dark crevice. When the bearers finally arrived, they dumped their loads, and grief-stricken, flung themselves upon the strewn bodies of their friends and loved ones with wails of sorrow. Wading into the sea of grief, Brandy briefly consoled the bereaved natives and swore to avenge their loss. He then acted swiftly to hand out the lanterns and allot the bare essentials. The remaining supplies would have to be left behind, along with the bearers, who were in no mental shape to continue.

Brandy led the way as one by one we slipped into the dark narrow opening, and in single file, we followed the tight passage for some distance to emerge into a vast subterranean cavern. Solid rock walls, rich with moisture, glistened in the lamplight; and colossal columns formed by the union of stalagmites and stalactites rose to a cathedral ceiling, where amplified voices and distorted sounds echoed in the shifting shadows as if the spirit of the mountain was mocking us in rebuke.

Moving rapidly, we pursued our foe through a confusing maze of tunnels and caverns in which one could easily become lost. Hazards lurked in the deep underworld. Pitfalls waited to snare the unwary, and at one point the path traversed a precariously narrow ledge that overlooked an unknown abyss. For hours we relentlessly kept up the chase, and then Brandy suddenly called a halt.

"Can you hear it?" he whispered.

Our nerves thrilled with anticipation as we listened to hear the faint impression of footfalls in the distance ahead, and with renewed vigor, we quickened our pace. Soon, the bouncing illumination of lamplight down the passage signaled that our foe was yet at hand. Brandy drew his revolver and fired wildly on the run. In response, Mallory smashed an oil lantern, which erupted in a conflagration that filled the passage in front of us, obstructing our progress and veiling our opponent's flight. Precious moments evaporated until the flames, which burned with an unnatural intensity, subsided enough for us to pass. Once across the pool of dying flames, we bolted into the silent darkness beyond, and after a few twists and bends, the passage opened to a cave where fading daylight flowed through a sunlit aperture.

Outside in the open air, we shed the gloom of confined spaces. Below lay a lush valley that channeled the course of a mighty river, and on the far side, three tall peaks shaped the eastern horizon just as Brandy had described. A sudden sense of foreboding caused us to briefly hesitate, but the sun was waning, and the window of opportunity was closing with the day; and so we plunged headlong into the valley in a mad race to catch Mallory before he could link up with his deadly allies.

We plowed through dense jungle thick with undergrowth in a hot pursuit that dragged us deeper into a hostile land, until at last the jungle halted at the edge of an expansive clearing that stretched to the river. Mallory and Manbootu were dashing across the open expanse toward a palisaded village at the river's edge. The darkening shades of nightfall dulled the melding colors and distorted the perception of distance, such that their faint figures blended into the seemingly two-dimensional background.

A horn sounded from the village gate.

The Professor emphatically cried, "End this madness. Kill him. Shoot now before it's too late!"

Kitty cocked the bolt of her rifle, took steady aim, and fired.

Suddenly, the air was alive with a flurry of small pointed projectiles. Prick, prick, came the stings. Kitty slumped, dropping her rifle, and then collapsed. All around me, my companions fell feint, as I too succumbed to some overpowering soporific influence; and when we awoke, the nightmare began.

* * *

Dancing torchlight and a haunting face swirled in a blurry haze; and as the visual impressions gradually sharpened, the grim visage of Gunston Mallory stood out against a turbulent setting. Above, shadows fluttered on the ceiling of a cavern lit by the flames of many torches, and behind him, a host of tribal warriors advocated our demise with angry gestures and harsh inscrutable words. With but a swift sign from Mallory, we were roughly lifted to our feet and rousted to full awareness.

Mallory first projected his hostile gaze upon me. "You, Mr. Blake, have been an irritating thorn in my side long enough. Mark my words – you will regret having meddled in my affairs," he scornfully rebuked.

His ugly countenance shifted, and his lips curled in a sardonic grin as he turned his attention to Brandy. "Welcome back, Mr. Brandon. Your choice to return here will prove to be a foolish one." He grasped Kitty by the chin, forcing her to look into his lustrous eyes. "What have we here," he whimsically remarked. "Such a pretty flower. I have just the use for you." Then, disregarding her like yesterday's news, he addressed the Professor. "Again I find you under my heel, and yet again I find you in possession of my property. I am surprised that a man of your stature and learning would stoop to the level of a common thief.

I now understand how you acquired the arcane knowledge that enabled you to destroy my forebear. However, despite his ignominious demise at your hands, you have ultimately failed, for I now possess all the tools and means necessary to achieve the fulfillment of a grand design. Soon the stars will be in perfect alignment, and it shall be my great pleasure to have you bear witness to a power that will shake the very foundations of the world and bring new order to the cosmos."

He paused while his shrewd eyes read our fearful expressions, and one could only imagine what nefarious thoughts were brewing in his mind.

At last, his attention gravitated to JB. "As for you, Doctor, your skills as a physician are about to be severely tested. Manbootu lies close to death with a bullet wound, and you are going to remedy his plight. Let me remind you of your precious Hippocratic Oath, Doctor. However, should that prove to be insufficient incentive, I have provided for an additional measure of persuasion." Never diverting his eyes from JB, he mockingly addressed our guide. "Mr. Brandon, I'm sure you recognize this place."

"Can't say that I do," Brandy replied, displaying a façade of nonchalance; but the fear in his eyes spoke differently, and the beads of cold sweat trickling from his brow denoted the nervous anticipation of some nameless and unspeakable horror.

"Then allow me to refresh your memory," Mallory persisted with sinister glee.

His face hardened in a stern expression of subdued rage. He barked a command, and the gathering of warriors behind him parted to reveal an ebony stone disk of broad dimension resting on the cavern floor. By all appearances, it had been fashioned in the same manner as the tablet, and the engraved markings on its glossy surface were strikingly similar as well. Several strong bodies were employed in moving the thing. Slowly, but without difficulty, the circular mass slid to one side, uncovering a round pit from which emanated a luminous glow that filled the cavern with an eerie illumination. Discordant voices, wailing and crying in torment, issued forth from the bowels of the pit and assailed one's ear with maddening impressions of woe and despair.

Mallory bellowed a few words in the native gibberish, and although our guide alone fully comprehended the implication of those words, we all understood the meaning in Mallory's stern gesture.

Brandy's face turned pale, and it appeared that our long journey had come to a bitter end as we were seized and forcibly crated to the edge of the pit.

CHAPTER 31

Mallory stood on the other side of the pit, his fiendish gloating expression accentuated in the effluent glow. "Behold the pit of screaming souls. Look upon the throes of perpetual agony and misery," he decreed.

"Oh, dear heaven," the Professor uttered in incredulous shock, and he averted his eyes, shutting them tight.

What I saw ripped the fabric of reality and assaulted the innermost bastions of reason and sanity. Our intrepid guide melted. JB gasped and cringed. Kitty screamed and fainted. Ben's eyes grew wide as saucers, his gaping mouth emitted no sound, and the big man shuddered.

Aghast, I stared in astonishment at the horrific maelstrom that stirred in the hellhole. An agglomeration of distorted faces attached to deformed bodies writhed in a fibrous mucus, which ebbed and flowed with the clambering of misshapen forms striving to break through the membranous surface; and amidst feeble disunited efforts, wide mouths expelled hideous pitiful cries and crazed eyes pleaded respite from ceaseless affliction.

"This perdition shall be your collective fate should the Doctor fail!" Mallory dictated.

A sudden rush of relief was unleashed when his next command prompted our captors to pull us back from the edge of doom. The great disk eclipsed the glow as it was pushed back into place, and the awful screams died away with the covering of the pit. Swept away by the angry throng, we passed through the mouth of the cavern and out into the night. The entrance had been shaped by the sheer forces of nature into the visage of an immense roaring lion that watched over the serene valley from high above. Moonlight shone with wings of ghostly radiance and shimmered like silver on the oily surface of the river, and the quaintness of the village nestled in shadow below concealed in pretense the savage hospitality that no doubt awaited us.

We were then taken along a precariously steep and rugged narrow path that wound in a crooked course down the mountainside. A flotilla of canoes waited at the river's edge to carry us across the dark waters to the village; and once we had debarked on the opposite bank,

Mallory had JB and Kitty whisked away in one direction, while the rest of us were taken to a hut and confined there under heavy guard.

The lingering shock of what we had recently witnessed and experienced left us enveloped in a brooding malaise, and for a while, everyone kept to his own thoughts. Our destiny hung on the whims of a madman who now held all the cards, and the frightening realization of our dire situation produced a disheartening sense of hopelessness that subdued our spirits. Eventually, the Professor spoke up to express that which weighed foremost upon our minds.

"I have the utmost confidence in the good Doctor's skill. However, I fear even his success may not avail us, and I am gravely concerned for the welfare of Miss Drayfus," he somberly said.

"Even if the witchdoctor pulls through, it'll only buy some time," Brandy added. "When your Doctor friend is no longer needed, it'll be the end for all of us. I've seen first hand what these crazed savages are capable of, and I can assure you that our deaths will not be pleasant ones. I for one plan to get out of here first chance I get."

"I'm with you on that, boss," Ben eagerly piped in.

"Escape is irrelevant unless that maniac has been stopped. Too much is at stake," the Professor gravely stated.

It was then that a strange and peculiar figure entered the hut, and all discussion took a back seat as we pondered what to make of the surprising visitor. The sun had long since browned the pigment of his Caucasian skin. Tattered trousers were secured to his thin frame by a rope belt, a worn khaki cotton shirt frayed at the elbows and cuffs draped his torso, and a crop of long flaxen hair dangled about his shoulders. The most puzzling aspect of his appearance was the fiendish wooden mask he wore, a mask that completely hid his face and veiled his features in mystery. Forlorn blue eyes peered through two eyeholes, and openings at the nostrils and mouth allowed him to breathe and speak.

He set his eyes on Brandy. "Brandy, it is I, Jonathon, Jonathon Mallory," he revealed.

Brandy reacted as if he had seen a ghost. Then shock turned to exhilaration, and he reached out to earnestly shake the man's hand. "I figured you for dead," he said.

"It would have been better if they had killed me, but my brother decreed a worse sentence," the masked figure dolefully communicated.

"That is why I must wear this mask. Not only is it a mark of ridicule, it is taboo to look upon my true face. Shunned, ostracized, and confined to the village compound, I live a lonely existence as a prisoner of these people."

Brandy then introduced us to a man purported dead by all accounts. Despite the trials of betrayal, unwarranted suffering, and loss of identity, he still retained a soft-spoken, cordial manner and an evenness of temper that reflected the best of his social class.

"My time is short," he said. "The two other members of your party are with my brother in the hut of the Shamba, Manbootu. For your sake, I pray he lives. I will do what I can to help you, but my liberties are extremely limited. As it is, I have endangered myself by coming here."

"Escape with us," Brandy urged.

"Alas, my destiny lies here. I cannot leave this place," he regretfully replied.

"Why?" I inquired.

"Allow me to show you, that you may better understand."

He removed the mask to reveal a gruesome sight that transcended the unimaginable – a face so grotesquely disfigured, so maimed and marred, as to be hardly recognizable as human, and the awful repugnance of it compelled me to avert my eyes.

"Forgive me," he said, replacing the mask. "You see now why I cannot return to the world I once knew. To be a self-imposed recluse living in seclusion is a life no better than my current existence."

He edged toward the entrance.

"I must leave you for now. Whatever your reason, you were fools to journey here, for one thing is certain, my brother will never allow you to leave here alive," he concluded, and he exited, vanishing from our sight.

Several hours passed while we anxiously waited for any further news or development, until eventually sleep overcame us like an unstoppable incoming tide. I awoke to the light of day stealing through the porous thatch. Brandy was already up, and before I could reclaim my senses from the dullness of slumber, he drew near and knelt down on one knee beside me.

"Listen Blake, I have a plan," he disclosed in a suppressed volume. "First chance we get, we take Gunston hostage and make him our ticket out of here – all of us. And I got the tool to do the job." He produced a knife from his boot, and as he revealed his secret stash, his eyes gleamed with hopeful resolution. "Are you with me?"

At that moment, the flap covering the entrance flew open. The knife disappeared in the blink of an eye, and Brandy sprang to his feet. Mallory burst in with an entourage of warriors, and soon we were all on our feet.

Brandy and Ben were immediately seized.

'Where's Kitty?" Brandy demanded, struggling to break free of his captors. "What have you done with her? If you lay a hand on her, I'll kill you! I swear I'll kill you!"

"A futile display of chivalry," Mallory scoffed, and he had them taken away.

Several sizable brutes surrounded me, and I knew they did not want to play ring around the Rosie. Two of them held me fast while the other ruffians pummeled and beat me. Mallory wore a cruel grin that widened with each blow. When the ruthless beating was over, they released me, and I collapsed in a heap. For a time imperceptible I languished in a senseless blur, and then the dimming light slipped into blackness.

In what seemed a dream, I heard JB's voice, faint and somewhere beyond reach. Then as his seeking voice grew stronger and more distinct, light penetrated the darkness and his face emerged from a fog of obscurity. Conscious awareness suddenly struck me along with a torrent of pain that surged from every inch of my body.

"Lay still for now," JB advised. "The Professor told me of the sound thrashing you received. Fortunately, your injuries are not too serious, and given time, you'll mend. But for now, you're in no shape to be up and about."

"What about Manbootu?" I asked.

"Too early to tell. I did what I could. Now it's wait and see," he replied.

Only JB and the Professor were in the hut with me, and I inquired about the others.

"The best we can suppose is that they are being held in separate quarters," the Professor answered.

In the days that followed, we were strictly confined to our hut and closely watched. Jonathon failed to return, and the whereabouts and condition of the other members of our party remained a mystery. Manbootu took a turn for the worse, and JB had to debried the wound. For a while it was nip and tuck, while an ominous dark cloud hung over us. Fortunately, Manbootu improved, a development that brought great relief to our stressed doctor, whose unsettled nerves were on the verge of cracking. One day the natives celebrated in grand fashion, a party we were not invited to. From the confines of the hut that served as our prison, we listened to the wild revelry: the beating drums, the harmonious singing and chanting, and scores of warriors pounding their shields in rhythmic unison. Late in the afternoon, the delirious festivities abruptly ceased, and an eerie lull settled over the village. Then came the bloodcurdling screams – screams of two men in the throes of indescribable pain and agony, and we thought the worst for Brandy and Ben. After the distressing pitch of those cries ended, a chorus of whoops and hollers erupted, and the celebration was on again.

CHAPTER 32

Days passed into weeks, and weeks into months. Of Kitty, we learned nothing. Manbootu fully recovered, and so we escaped the horror of the pit. In desperation, we contrived daring plans, all of which came to naught. Then that fateful night arrived – the summer solstice.

Twilight was fast approaching, and the entire village was bustling with excitement and activity. All day an electric air of anticipation had been brewing, and now forces were moving to a climax. Something was about to happen, something important, something dreadful. All the revelations the Professor had imparted to me now gathered at the frontiers of my mind, pounding at the doors of my thoughts and threatening to rush in like an unbidden tide. In tacit expectation of the inconceivable, we all sat on pins and needles, helplessly it seemed, waiting for events to unfold.

Elaborately adorned warriors, their faces painted like death itself, came for us at the encroachment of night, bound our hands, and forcibly conducted us to the riverbank. A foreshadowing hush draped everything. Everywhere empty lodges stood like silent tombs, and we passed no one en route to the river. Other than our keepers, not a single denizen was in sight. The vast metropolis had turned into a ghost town. The air was uncannily still, warm, and perfumed with night smells. Not a wrinkle disturbed the placid surface of the water. All the million candles of the heavens were alight, and in the eastern sky, a single bright star blazed with a brilliance greater than all the others combined.

Nothing stirred. The only movement was the gliding motion of the canoes and the lapping of the oars that now propelled us to the eastern bank. Prodded by spears, we made the precipitous ascent to the lofty ledge and the huge black mouth of the roaring lion. Torches were lit, and into the dark hole we went. A thousand shadows fled on black wings and the cathedral-like cavern within unfolded. Visible in the torchlight was the prodigious disk that covered that awful cesspool of horror. The prospect of being cast into it made my heart race and sent shudders of panic through every nerve; but as they pressed us onward, it became apparent that they had another intention in mind.

We passed into a branching tunnel that led to a great vertical rift in the solid rock. Sheer parallel cliffs drew a jagged outline against the starlit sky and noxious gases floated up from abysmal depths that burned with a slender orange glow. A natural causeway spanned the hollow distance to where the tunnel continued on the far side. The dizzying height made for a precarious crossing; my muscles stiffened, my breathing diminished to short breaths, and every step was fraught with the fear of losing one's footing. Stern shoves from behind only accentuated the danger, and upon reaching the other side, I nearly collapsed from the sudden release of tension.

Down the subterranean passage the procession marched, like three condemned men being taken for their last walk. The black and inscrutable emptiness ahead hid its secrets well until the retreating darkness unveiled an arched portal forged in long past ages. Inscribed into the face of each perfectly set supporting stone was a single enigmatic rune, and etched into the mighty keystone was an all too recognizable symbol, a symbol that signified dread – the menacing eye.

Beyond the portal stretched a lofty, spacious corridor constructed of smooth stone blocks varying in size from massive to small, each precisely cut and masterfully fitted in an awe-inspiring display of craftsmanship. A solemness fell over our native guards, and we proceeded in silence. They moved like phantoms, almost noiseless, their bare feet treading softly on the stone floor. Something about the place, shrouded in ancient mystery, gave me the unsettling sense that we were interlopers in a forbidden domain undisturbed for centuries. Murmurs, faint and indiscernible at first, acted upon my imagination. Shadow called to shadow as they grew and gathered power. Now unable to be ignored, inhuman disembodied voices, seeming to emanate from the very stones themselves, spoke in ghostly whispers, telling me things, maddening things, things not of this world. Beguiling delusions sowed seeds of doubt and confusion in my mind that sprouted and spread like a choking vine, creeping into the recesses of rational truth, and eroding the foundations of my most sacredly held beliefs until they collapsed like a house of cards. My companions too were tormented by the unreal phenomenon. "No, no," JB uttered, as if trying to ward off some internal monster. The Professor, although affected, remained silently resolute and retained a defiant expression of refusal.

When I had about reached the end of my tether, the awful voices faded, and we emerged from the corridor to behold a bewildering sight. Steep soaring ridges greeted the night sky and encircled a plateau whereon stood vast megalithic ruins that had traveled far, far down the river of time. Colossal rock-hewn blocks of glossy black piled themselves at oblique angles to erect cyclopean edifices that rose to heaven and moved in shadowy procession along endless and stupendous avenues. The massive structures, abiding for eons, had long since been abandoned by their builders who left behind only the lonely monuments of their craft.

Continuing on, we tread the length of a broad avenue that stretched to a grand rectangular plaza at the heart of the primordial metropolis. At the plaza entrance, an ebony obelisk inscribed with hieroglyphic runes towered skyward, and at the other end stood a monumental structure of pyramidic design. On the side facing the plaza, wide over-sized steps, bordered by sculpted ghoulish figures, ascended to an extensive level plane, from which came the distant sound of beating drums. A single row of torchbearers lined the steps in upward procession. In the heavens above, the blazing star projected a traveling beam of light that concentrated its energy on the plane atop the pyramid, bathing it in a white luminescence. The incredulous picture was like something out of a dream – absolutely surreal.

"I've seen this place before," the Professor divulged, his eyes filled with curious recollection – "in a portentous vision I suffered during that terrifying ordeal at Blytemoor Manor. Prepare yourselves, gentlemen, for tonight you may face the unimaginable."

To the pyramid we marched, and up the steps we climbed, the torchbearers falling in behind our retinue of guards as we passed. The growing rapid beat of the drums was now joined by the wild fervor of a thousand voices tuned to the same intonation. In that moment, all around me faded in a fog and a flood of images flashed in my mind. I saw the faces of those I knew and those I cherished. I thought of home so far away, of Cindy and Mrs. Coggins, and what I would not give to be at Mahoney's right now working on a manhattan. But as we crested the last step, the reality of the situation hit me with sobering impact.

Basking in the unearthly light, countless bodies danced and flailed in a sea of jubilant frenzy that undulated with the driving drumbeat, their raised voices chanting in song. One of our retinue blew a horn, and the tumultuous mass parted to open an aisle that led to the core of the proceedings. At the far end stood Gunston Mallory garbed in a hooded vestment that bore the symbol of the eye, and a mystical medallion dangled from an ornate necklace that loosely draped his neck and shoulders. A sinister grin on his lips, he beckoned with a courtly motion of his hand.

He had us conducted to a place right up front with an uncomfortably near and unobstructed view of all that was about to unfold. Close by, a hexagonal pit of immense proportions rumbled and groaned. By the pit, Kitty lay motionless and unrestrained upon a sacrificial stone, her glazed eyes fixed in the blank stare of a hypnotic trance. A sheathed dagger rested on the stone beside her, waiting for its ritualistic purpose to be fulfilled; and there to enact the deed, stood the imposing figure of Manbootu fully adorned in leopard skin regalia. Aligned with the stone and pit, a narrow-sided monolith, fashioned in wonder like the tablet, rose to the stunted height of a man. Runes in vertical sequences marked the glass-like surface, which glistened with a strange fantastic luster in the white light; and adjacent to the monolith, the fat-bellied chief cradled in his arms the very arcane artifact that had brought us to this inauspicious juncture.

Mallory raised his arms. The clatter of drums ceased, and a wave of hush swept over the assembly.

He strutted up to the Professor, who was next to me, and looked at him with cold eyes. "Now, my dear Professor, you shall see what rises in the east!" he demonstratively stated.

Resolved to silence, the Professor gave no protest, no remonstration, but his eyes shouted volumes.

"What? No last words?" Mallory smugly remarked.

Receiving no satisfaction, he turned on his heels, and the bizarre ritual commenced. He took the tablet, presented to him by the chief, and placed it atop the monolith in regal fashion, as if he was crowning a king. It fit atop the monolith like the remaining piece of a puzzle; its sides matched in every horizontal dimension, and the runes upon them completed the sequences on the monolith like missing notes on a scale. He then produced the diamond from a pouch that hung from a decorative belt girding his waist. He held it aloft, and the magnificent gem sparkled with prismatic effulgence that shot forth rays of magical colors in all directions.

"Zaku-tog! Zaku-tog!" the assembly ardently resounded.

Mallory again brought the passion of the crowd under control. Methodically, he chanted strange esoteric phrases; and when he had finished, he placed the diamond in a socket on the face of the monolith.

The runes burned a phosphorescent green. The pit thunderously groaned, and a crimson glow emanated from deep within the bowels of the cavity. A miasmatic mist billowed forth and spilled over the rim, spreading a thick mantle of swirling vapor that soon engulfed us to the ankles. Spellbound by the overwhelming spectacle, I dipped into my well of fortitude, but came up empty, and a growing apprehension gripped me in a suffocating embrace.

Slowly, Mallory circled the monolith, reading aloud the mysterious writing; and explosive anticipation waited for a spark as Manbootu took up the blade, and raising it high, prepared to strike. In the midst of it all, my ears received the impression of another voice, soft, yet full of strength and character. It was the Professor reciting psalm 23.

All was perceived lost, when the loud report of a high-caliber gun suddenly seized the attention of all, and the proceedings came to an abrupt halt. Down the aisle that parted the masses, at the head of the steps stood two men. One was Brandy, wisps of smoke drifting from the barrel of his elephant gun, and the other was Jonathon Mallory, his gruesome face unmasked. The crowd shunned away, shielding their eyes and shrinking from his presence as he boldly advanced toward the monolith – and his brother. Gunston placed a hand in front of his face, and remarkably, even Manbootu dared not look at the approaching phantom. Shouting vile threats, Gunston Mallory commanded his brother to go back, but Jonathon paid no heed, and Gunston recoiled before a lean frame that loomed larger with every stride.

Jonathon's first act was to cut the Professor's bonds. Instructing him to free his comrades and not to interfere, he put the knife in the Professor's hand, and then, unarmed, he confronted his younger brother. "I'm putting a stop to all of this!" he sternly proclaimed, his eyes ablaze with reproof.

With premeditated intent, he headed straight for the monolith, and Gunston extended an arm in an attempt to bar him. "It is taboo to look upon my face, brother. It is your own decree, so you well know the penalty," Jonathon stated, brushing Gunston aside.

"No, you fool! You'll ruin everything!" Gunston cried as Jonathon reached out to seize the diamond; and defying his own decree, Gunston pounced on his brother with raging madness.

Jonathon plucked the covetous gem from the black stone. The glowing runes dimmed to lackluster carvings, and the pit belched a cloud of putrid steam accompanied by an angry roar. In the next instant, the two brothers were locked in a grappling embrace. Both will and muscle collided in a desperate struggle for the diamond. Time stopped and the world stood still while the two men danced a violent waltz that took them precariously close to the pit. Jonathon maneuvered the contest ever nearer and nearer to the edge until both teetered on the brink, each now clutching the diamond and trying to wrest it from the other's grasp. Back and forth they fought on the threshold of doom, two wavering figures amidst a hazy shroud of swirling vapor. Gunston's earnest demands met with defiant resistance. Destiny balanced on a tight rope as Jonathon's heels touched the edge, his back to the pit. Gunston latched a hand around his brother's throat in a lethal grip. Jonathon released the diamond. He reached out with both hands, tightly grasped the collar of Gunston's vestments, and leaned back with all his weight.

"No, Jonathon! No!" Gunston pleaded in vain, and together with the precious gem they plummeted into Hades.

Gunston, Jonathon, the diamond – all three were gone in a fleeting instant. Waves of fierce rumbles quickly evolved into violent tremors that rocked the stones beneath our feet. Manbootu staggered about in a paralyzing fit of perplexity and indecision, while an infectious panic spread like wildfire through the assembly. In a flash, I rushed to the sacrificial stone. Overlooked in a sea of pandemonium, I swooped Kitty up in my arms and draped her over my shoulder. The next moment, my companions and I were racing to reach Brandy and the steps before the shrinking way through the crowd dissolved altogether in the confusion. The Professor's short legs never moved so fast, and we met up with our guide barely in time to bound down the shaking steps, closely pursued by a panic-stricken and angry mob.

Hell unleashed its fury as we fled down the length of the grand plaza. Splintering cracks split the earth and swelled to dangerous rifts that threatened to swallow anyone at any given moment. The towering obelisk toppled and crashed with a deafening boom. Behind us, wails of distress filled the air, and ahead, the broad avenue stretched endlessly. Run – and run we did, while Babylon fell all around us. Along the avenue, gigantic structures that had stood for eons swayed in turbulent waves. One by one they crumbled into cascading fragments, and huge falling blocks tumbled like dice.

Imminent catastrophe dangled on a thin thread of sheer luck, while the sight of the corridor still intact kept hope alive. Brandy grabbed a burning torch from a sconce at the entrance, and into the perilous passage we flew. The mountain shook with vengeful wrath, and fissures channeled along the seams of the stones, which began to give way under the pressure of mighty forces.

Finally, we reached the causeway that spanned the deep chasm, and made a mad dash to the other side, making the crossing just before the causeway broke apart and collapsed at our heels. Dozens of hapless Matoomba plunged to their deaths as those at the rear of the stampede pressed forward. Onward we raced in a marathon for survival. In the enormous cavern that housed the awful pit of screaming souls, stalactites fell like giant spikes and shards of rock rained down from the ceiling. Miraculously unscathed, we shot through the mouth of the cave as if the mountain had disgorged us, and recklessly scrambled headlong down the harrowing path to the river.

My eyes thrilled to the welcome sight of Ben waiting at the river's edge. Three canoes, loaded with our confiscated weapons and gear, were ready to go. In great haste, we launched the canoes, and we rowed for our lives as the mountain exploded in a cataclysmic fiery upheaval.

EPILOGUE

It was good to be home in Boston where I belonged. Shortly after our return, I paid a visit to Lt. Briggs. He accepted my plausible explanation, relieved to finally close an obscure case that had grown cold. Cindy paid the bills until the money ran out, and I found a stack of past due notices waiting on my desk. Mrs. Coggins, ever the optimist, kept my rooms as if I had left yesterday. I introduced the Professor to her, and after a taste of her cooking, he has been a frequent visitor ever since. They sit for hours in the parlor, enjoying each other's company and listening to the radio. It is nice to see that two lonely people can find happiness in this crazy, mixed up world. Even after a restful ocean voyage, JB still teetered on the brink of a nervous breakdown. Soon after our return, he took a sabbatical and escaped to the countryside to convalesce so to speak. He writes often, and his most recent letter mirrors many of those traits that comprise his former self. Brandy traveled back to his beloved British Columbia, and Kitty tried to go on with her life. But once the darkness has touched you, after you have looked into the abyss and seen the gates of hell, when your perception of reality is forever changed, how do you go on with your life? As for me, I think I will have Joe make me another manhattan.

About the Author

A.J. George is a CPA residing in the Commonwealth of Virginia. An avid historian and researcher, he enjoys reading and has a penchant for the Edwardian authors. When not reading or researching he can be found writing tales blended in the pages of the past or devoting his time as an officer in a writers club.

Made in the USA
Middletown, DE
30 September 2019